Morticai stood in a ⟨...⟩ e
large golden idol to ⟨...⟩
ings, and the gold ca⟨...⟩
wrapped around the ⟨...⟩
that held the Arluth⟨...⟩ to draw a
ragged breath. . . . The ⟨...⟩ had moved on both sides of him
now, and though Morticai knew he could not hope to escape, he
could not help but struggle as they pulled him toward the
blood-covered platform and the chains that hung down to it.

Other TSR® Books

Dragons Can Only Rust
Chrys Cymri

Winged Magic
Mary H. Herbert

Mus of Kerbridge
Paul Kidd

F.R.E.E.Fall
Mel Odom

Dragon Reforged
Chrys Cymri

Runes of Autumn
Larry and Robert Elmore

Trail of Darkness

Darlene D. Bolesny

TRAIL OF DARKNESS

©1996 Darlene Bolesny
Cover Art ©1996 TSR, Inc.
All Rights Reserved.

Random House and its affiliate companies have worldwide distribution rights in the book trade for English language products of TSR, Inc.

Distributed to the book and hobby trade in the United Kingdom by TSR Ltd.

Distributed to the toy and hobby trade by regional distributors.

Cover art by Ciruelo Cabral. ©1996 TSR, Inc. All rights reserved.

First Printing: September 1996
Printed in the United States of America.
Library of Congress Catalog Card Number: 95-62251

9 8 7 6 5 4 3 2 1

8257XXX1501

ISBN: 0-7869-0517-4

TSR, Inc.
201 Sheridan Springs Rd.
Lake Geneva WI 53147
U.S.A.

TSR Ltd.
120 Church End, Cherry Hinton
Cambridge CB1 3LB
United Kingdom

This dedication is a
Formal and Public thanks to
ROBERT L. ASPRIN
everything in a friend and mentor
that a young writer could ask for,
and more!

Further, special thanks are to be given to: the Bell Helicopter International employees who lived in Isfahan, Iran; Jim Nichols and the firefighting rookies of that hot summer of 1978; all the brave firefighters in Denton, Texas, who blessed (and cursed) my five years there as a firefighter; Thomas K. Martin and the original weekend warriors (Darron Shaffer, Bryan Yates, John Green and Steve Pagel); Jonathan Martin; Dr. Bill Christmas (for putting me back together after my real-life adventures!); the Four-armed Dealer; all the special, special fans in Dallas, Texas, and House Pegasus; all the friends and members of the N.O. Quarter Sword Club ("No Quarter Asked—No Quarter Given!"); the past and present members of the Agents of Chaos 8-ball team and the Racking Krewe 9-ball team; and last, but certainly not forgotten, special thanks to Gordon R. Dickson. You taught him well, sir. I shall endeavor to carry on the tradition. . . .

Historical Note

Humans and corryn have coexisted on Duanor for centuries. The corryn are tall and slender, with upswept ears and eyes like gems; unsurpassed in grace, they frequently live past 500 years. But their women are often barren—their burden, it is said, for their beauty and long life. Humans, shorter than the corryn, are heartier, and have no difficulty bearing children. But their lifespan averages only 125 years, their payment for the many children they have.

Before the Great Darkness, the people of Duanor lived in small villages and towns scattered across the land. Then the foul god Droka vied with Almighty Aluntas for control of the domain. The servants of Aluntas—lesser gods known as the Levani—fought with Aluntas against Droka. Most humans and corryn supported their god, but some supported Droka—and war between the Faith and the Droken erupted.

Droka was driven away, and many of the Droken were killed or banished; those who remained hid their beliefs. But Droka brought a Great Darkness to the land, and extreme cold caused many to perish.

The Levani warned the humans and corryn that the Darkness would return for one season every year. Kings built great walled Cities in which they could gather the people for warmth and protection every year during the Dark Season.
Brisk trade developed between the kingdoms, but bandits became commonplace, and the kingdoms formed military groups, such as the Northmarch, to patrol the highways and territories between the Great Cities and to keep caravans and travelers safe from harm.

Centuries have passed since the first Great Darkness. The Faith is strong; yet still are the Droken feared. Hooded and masked to hide their true identities, they meet secretly. Those who discover them know that at any time Droken may burn their homes and kill their children.

Index of Characters

Jendall, Lord—human; close aide of King Almgren; also, Heather's current paramour.

Kinsey, Geradon—human; aide to Inquisitor Rylan Glaedwin.

Kithryl—corryn; co-owner, with her husband, Breslen, of the Cobblesend Pub in Watchaven.

Luthekar, Prince—corryn/god; one of two princes of Cuthaun; son of a corryn woman and Droka.

Luvena, Madam—human; Watchaven hedge wizard.

McFerrin, Kirwin—human; Commander of the Northmarch at Watchaven.

Moranekor—Morticai's true name.

Mortern, Prince—human/god; one of the two princes of Cuthaun; son of a human woman and Droka.

Morticai—corryn; Northmarcher; ex-street urchin (of Watchaven); true name, Moranekor of Lorredre; urchin name, Dyluth.

Nelerek—corryn; Morticai's Arluthian advocate; true name, Perlagus Myrgalon of Watchaven.

Paxton—human; owner of the Dappled Stallion Inn in Watchaven.

Perlagus—corryn; Nelerek's true name.

Quinson, Lord—human; Watchaven nobleman who runs afoul of the Droken.

Riamel, King—corryn; king of Dynolva.

Richard—human; born in Briarwood, Richard is a knight of the Faith in the service of Inquisitor Rylan Glaedwin.

Scatla—human; Arluthian friend of Morticai's.

Seabrook, Lord—human; supreme commander of the Northmarch.

Tagger—human; one of Morticai's many street urchin friends.

Trahern, Captain—human; a captain in Watchaven's City Watch and one-time drinking friend of Morticai and Coryden.

Udall—human; Northmarcher; Droken.

Valdir, Lord—human lord in Watchaven; another noble whom Morticai suspects of belonging to the Droken.

CHAPTER ONE

At least I found something! Morticai tucked the papers into his pack and took one last glance around the moonlit study. Traditionalist paintings adorned the richly paneled walls. The expensive furniture was cluttered with books and maps. A hawking hood, leash, and jess lay scattered across the desk. Everything was where it had been before he entered.

He moved to the narrow window where, as always, the night view of Watchaven gave him pause. He allowed himself a moment to savor it before glancing to the ground, twenty-five feet below. The still courtyard was cloaked in deep shadows from the interplay of the two moons.

Muffled sounds from the servants' party could still be heard coming from the manor house, but they had changed from bawdy tavern songs to quiet murmurings. It was a good sign that the servants had discovered their drinking limits.

Ah, Lord Aldwin. If you only knew how your faithful servants celebrated your travels.

Lowering his rope, Morticai began his descent. Within moments, he lightly touched down.

"Hey!" The shout erupted from the dark recesses of the coach house.

Morticai spun, his right arm still entwined in the ropes, a throwing knife in his left hand. He saw the blow coming, too late—the wracking clout landed solidly on his right shoulder—but his knife flew sure, making certain the swift opponent would land no more. He drew his fighting dagger and held it ready in his left hand.

The night air was ripped with shrieks; Morticai ignored the naked women who fled from the coach house, clutching their maid's uniforms in front of them.

The well-muscled human who held Morticai's attention crouched low, ignoring his fallen friend with the dagger in his throat. Morticai remembered having seen the huge arms before.

Wonderful. Of all the people to interrupt, I have to pick Aldwin's blacksmith.

They couldn't have been more mismatched. Morticai was full corryn but was short for his race, standing only as tall as the average human. Nonetheless, his slight build, gently upswept ears and boyish face were undeniably corryn. The blacksmith easily outweighed him by a hundred pounds.

The blacksmith held a dagger in his right hand; grinning wickedly, he beckoned Morticai to come closer with his left. Remaining on guard, Morticai gritted his teeth against the pain in his shoulder and smiled back.

The man's grin faded. He charged, lunging with his blade toward Morticai's midsection. Morticai jumped to the left, grabbing the man's knife arm and pulling him headfirst into the wall. The hit was solid; Morticai allowed himself to keep spinning—the courtyard wall wouldn't be far. His timing couldn't have been worse.

He was hit full speed, the tackle driving him back and down, his head and upper back slamming against the tower's wall.

No! Morticai's senses reeled as he fought to remain conscious.

The dagger slipped from his fingers to land silently among the crushed flowers. He could smell wine, heavy on his new assailant's breath.

The buzzing began to subside. This human was more drunk than the others had been; he wasn't beating Morticai, wasn't throttling him. The drunk seemed content to hold him, pinned with his crushing weight. Perhaps he wanted him alive. . . .

The fear of capture filled Morticai's mind. He had grown up an orphan in the streets of this human city—the instinct to run was one of survival. His knee came up, driven by the terror that enveloped him.

The man howled in agony and rolled away. Morticai dashed for the gate, abandoning his rope and daggers. As he swung over it, he lost his balance and fell to the cobbled street, his low-slung pack taking most of the impact. Waves of dizziness washed over him, and again, he fought unconsciousness. But others were running into the courtyard now, their cries of alarm spurring Morticai onward.

Morticai gained his feet and ran as he hadn't run in years—as though the Watch were after him, or the slavers, or the Droken. When he stopped, he was far from Aldwin's tower, deep within the tangle of narrow alleys that lay behind the Bazaar. He looked behind him, but there appeared to be no pursuit. Walking slowly, he tried to slacken the racing of his heart; then, unsuccessful, he leaned against a wall, panting and shaky.

A ragged peddler smoothly crossed the alley and passed him with a cautious glance. A little farther away, a drunk moaned in his sleep. Rats skittered a few feet away, hunting for their evening meal. Nauseated and dizzy, Morticai sank into a sitting position. He wasn't certain how badly he was hurt, but he knew it was worse than he'd first thought.

Gods, you've done it now. Perhaps if he closed his eyes, for just a moment, until his head stopped spinning . . .

* * * * *

He awoke with a start, his left hand flying to the token of

Glawres that hung around his neck. It must have slipped from beneath his shirt when he fell. The alley was deserted, the shadows from the moons showing that much of the night had passed. His head pounded, and his shoulder throbbed, but it was not his physical condition, or even the earlier events of the night, that caused him to shake.

There were demons, called jevano, that preyed in the darkness. It was whispered that they were made by the Droken to prey upon the enemies of their evil god, Droka. Jevano could take corryn or human form, male or female, in order to hunt their prey. They sapped the souls of those upon whom they fed, claiming the soul; then it was said that they could assume the form of the victim.

As a child, Morticai had sat frozen with fear as the older children told such tales. Later he would chide himself for allowing them to frighten him. Then came a night when he had huddled in a barrel, listening to the cries of a friend who had been sleeping in a doorway a few feet away. Morticai had peeked over the edge of the barrel to see his first jevano and the death of his friend. The jevano had never even known he was there.

Whether or not a jevano had passed him on this night Morticai did not know, but he thanked his patron Levani, Glawres, that the god's token had fallen outside his shirt. Perhaps it had protected him.

Inhaling sharply, he forced himself to start moving. He knew there would be trouble when he reached his barracks at Northgate. Already Morticai suspected that he'd be unable to make his patrol. He gained his feet and leaned heavily against a wall, waiting for his head to stop spinning.

He began moving, with one hand on the wall to steady himself. His better clothes were stashed a few miles away.

CHAPTER TWO

Lord Aldwin pulled his cloak to him as the light mist threatened to turn to drizzle. The human nobleman glanced at the overcast night sky and scowled. *This cursed weather has followed me all the way from Watchaven.*

His corryn guide stopped before a wooden door.

"Here we are!" the guide whispered. He glanced up and down the short alley before unlocking it. "We control every property attached to this one. This gives us a level of safety we've never had in Dynolva before."

Aldwin checked his natural instinct to squint into the blackness beyond the doorway. His guide took a step inside, returned with a lantern, and then struggled to light it.

Lord Aldwin grimaced. *I shall be soaked before we continue!*

Once lit, the lantern revealed a long hallway, barely wide enough to accommodate them one at a time. As they walked the long hall, Aldwin's guide babbled as though he were bragging about Dynolva's most recently constructed monument.

"Now, the walls of this hallway are actually the walls of the two properties that you noticed adjoining this one. The property records filed with the city's leasehold department do not show this hall at all. Instead, the plans show the door I just opened for you as nothing more than a second door into the servants' quarters of the building on the right."

Aldwin's interest increased.

"They do not perform property inspections?" he asked.

"Not in this portion of the city," his guide replied. "Too much money and influence here. We corryn do not take lightly to having our dinner parties interrupted for such frivolous activities as having our bedrooms counted," he finished with a laugh.

Aldwin scowled at the inference that humans were weak for allowing such activities, but they had now entered a small, open courtyard and any comment he might have made was wisely kept to himself. Although the courtyard was deserted, Aldwin knew that the chances were high they were being spied upon.

His guide stopped before a second door, which, once unlocked, led into a small room containing a number of curtained booths. Nodding silently, the guide held back a curtain for Aldwin. The nod signaled the end of the idle chatter—now they were on hallowed ground.

Aldwin removed his cloak and withdrew his Droken robe from the hidden pouch sewn into the cloak's back inside panel. He pulled the silk robe over his clothes and adjusted the masked hood. His guide was waiting for him when he reentered the small room.

"Shall we?" the robed and masked guide asked softly.

Aldwin nodded and was led through another door and into the temple. It was smaller than the temple in Watchaven, but Aldwin had heard that the Droken in Dynolva had been repeatedly forced to move. He also noted that the security precautions he had seen were appalling.

It was apparent from the austerity of this temple that they had lost much in the recent raids. The room was laid out in the traditional octagonal design, but the stone walls were completely bare, the candelabra were of iron, and the altar, in the middle, was a hideous wooden affair. Aldwin smiled smugly behind his silk mask. *The common populace in Watchaven must allow their bedrooms to be counted, but at least we have a decent temple.*

The temple was already half-filled. The varying heights of the congregation told Aldwin that about one fourth of the attendees were children. They were as silent as their parents, but this came as no surprise. Droken children were always perfectly behaved.

A door on the opposite side of the temple opened and the red-robed high priest led in the procession. The soft drumbeat and scent of incense stirred deep memories in Aldwin. They had quit using drums in the service in Watchaven in favor of a chant when he was a child. The procession arrayed itself around the raised dais that held the altar. As the high priest stepped onto the dais, the drumbeat suddenly stopped.

"Tonight we come into the presence of our most hallowed Master, Droka," the priest began. Aldwin sighed. He should have known that here, in the corryn city of Dynolva, the service would be conducted in corryn.

"We come with hearts laden with sadness," the priest continued, "for there is one here among us who has sought to leave the love of our Master."

A soft gasp escaped the crowd of worshipers.

"Yea, it is so," continued the priest. "But there is gladness, as well, for this one comes now to us penitent—and choosing life over death."

A robed Droken was brought onto the dais, his hands tied behind his back.

"This is the offender!" the priest proclaimed, pulling the offender's mask and hood back.

The murmuring among the congregation told Aldwin that few, if any, of the worshippers recognized the human. It was common to send such an offender to a sister-congregation for sentencing or penance. It was the offender's identity, however, that had brought Lord Aldwin to Dynolva.

"This is Lord Quinson of Watchaven," the high priest proclaimed.

Aldwin noted that Quinson closed his eyes and visibly swallowed at the high priest's utterance of his name.

Fool. He should have known that once admitted, no one leaves the Gathering.

Quinson's hands were untied. After a moment's pause, he knelt before the priest.

"Lord Quinson, what is thy sin?"

"I-I sought . . ." he gulped a deep breath, audible to the entire congregation. "I sought to forsake our Master," he finished with a sob.

Fool! Aldwin thought again.

"And dost thou repent?" asked the high priest.

"Y-yes," Quinson replied.

"And dost thou choose life?"

"Yes!"

"Are there any here among us," the high priest continued, gesturing broadly to the congregation, "who can vouch for this proclamation of faithfulness?"

"Yea, I shall," Lord Aldwin replied, raising his hand.

"And art thou in a position to report to our loyal Gathering, should Lord Quinson again betray Droka?"

Lord Quinson looked nervously at Aldwin, obviously wondering who it was behind the mask who could claim to report on him. Quinson also had to know now that at least one other member of Watchaven's nobility was Droken, for only a nobleman could possibly vouch for his future actions.

"Absolutely," Aldwin replied calmly.

Quinson averted his eyes and lowered his head in submission.

The priest nodded and turned back to Lord Quinson. "And dost thou know the penance for thy sin?"

Quinson's head jerked up, and as he studied the high priest's unmoving form, his face filled with fear. Finally, Quinson broke down, and it took him several attempts before his proclaimed "yes" was understandable.

Disgusting! To act such a way in front of the peasantry!

The high priest gestured, and a human boy, about ten, was brought to the dais. The boy was tied, blindfolded, and gagged. Aldwin had met Quinson's son only once before. *He's grown like a weed.*

The boy was placed on the altar. Quinson was now shaking from head to toe; Aldwin wondered if he would begin convulsing. He had seen it happen before. That incident had resulted in both the child and the penitent being sacrificed.

But the high priest began the first litany, and, as the congregation joined in, Quinson's shaking began to slow. The priest went straight from the first litany into the sacrificial chant, and although all the color had drained from Quinson, he did not faint or try to flee. At last, Quinson began to sway ever so slightly with the chanting and began to mumble the chant himself. It was apparently the signal the high priest had been waiting for.

The sacrificial dagger was brought forward. It was placed in Quinson's open hand, but Quinson did not close his hand around it. Instead, he stared at it blankly.

Father of Darkness! Aldwin thought. *Why can't he take this as befits the nobility! It is noblemen like Quinson who make the peasantry look at us with disgust!*

The high priest closed Quinson's hand around the dagger and turned him to face the altar. He said some words of encouragement to Quinson, which Aldwin could not hear. The chant continued, and, as the priest rejoined it, he began to increase the pace. Finally, Quinson squeezed his eyes shut and, raising the dagger high, let out a cry and plunged it downward; the muffled cry of the child was barely audible over the chanting worshippers.

Now that the sacrifice had been made, all that remained to be done was the dissection of the child, and communion. . . .

* * * * *

The northern gate to the city of Watchaven had been given to the Northmarch long ago. Over the years, the gate had been fortified and enlarged, and now the original gate was engulfed by the fortified structure that had become Northgate, headquarters for the Northmarch in Watchaven. At the top of the eastern side of the fortress, beyond the attic rooms filled with extra armor and weapons, lay Morticai's room. A clutter of trunks, old furniture, and knife targets filled the bulk of the spacious room, and yet well-defined paths crisscrossed from doorway to window and fireplace to fireplace. Captain Coryden had always found it an easy room to pace in.

Coryden's very name meant half-corryn, and his features were as mixed as his heritage—his deep amber eyes and upswept ears and brows bespoke his corryn blood, while his height, honey-colored hair, and unusually muscular physique pointed to his human heritage.

Tonight his long hair was braided and his attire rich. His embroidered silk tunic was cut in the traditional corryn fashion, the delicate cutouts along the hem and neckline a counterpoint to the velvet edging that lay beneath them. The ease with which his left hand swung around his court sword was all that betrayed his station as a captain in Watchaven's Northmarch. It had been Morticai who had secured the invitations to the prestigious party that had caused him to dress so, but it was Morticai who had failed to join him there, as planned. And so he had returned to Northgate, and now paced in Morticai's room, as he had done so often before.

The door lock clicked a few hours before dawn. Coryden prepared to deliver his long-considered monologue of how he had spent his night awaiting the alley cat's return. The door opened, and instead he stared.

Standing in the doorway, Morticai stared back. His black hair, streaked with silver, was wildly loose and tangled. His crumpled street clothes appeared to have been slept in, and he seemed shorter than usual, as he clung to the doorframe for support. His complexion, pale even by corryn standards, could now compete with some corpses Coryden had seen. The deep blue eyes looked pained, but it was the two blackened circles beneath the eyes that reduced Coryden to speechlessness. It had been a long time since he'd seen Morticai so beaten. It was Morticai who spoke first.

"Some son-of-a-bitch stole my clothes."

"Wh-what?"

"My good clothes! What I was going to wear to the ball—the shirt with the imported Tradelenor lace, y'know?"

"Morticai, what happened to you? Who beat you up like this? Did someone beat you up for your clothes?"

Morticai looked puzzled.

"Oh. Uh, I'm sorry, Coryden. I guess I do look a little rough around the edges."

"A little!"

"I . . . uh, got into a bit of a scuffle at the tower and had to run. That was before I found out about my clothes. I hid them within sight of the palace! What's the world coming to? That shirt cost me a month's wages!"

Morticai stopped ranting and looked down. Coryden started toward him, expecting him to fall.

"I'm sorry . . . it took me . . . so long to get back," Morticai continued. "Gods, my head hurts."

Coryden helped him into the room, concern deepening with every step. He wanted to pick him up and carry him to the bed, but Morticai, stubborn as always, prevented him.

"I was right about Lord Aldwin, Coryden! I'm positive he's Droken. I found some coded papers. Better yet, I found the cipher key! I copied what I could."

"That's nice. Did anyone get a good look at you?"

"No, I don't think so. Only one human actually saw me." . . . *And lived through it,* he decided not to mention. "Besides, it was dark. I wish . . . things would stop spinning."

"I was wondering if I should search for you. By your appearance, maybe I should have."

Morticai sighed. "Yeah," he replied, "I was beginnin' t' think y' were goin' t' have t' come find me."

Coryden blinked in surprise as Morticai's old street accent emerged.

"I'm going to get Dualas, Morticai," he announced. "I think

he'd better have a look at you."

"Coryden," Morticai began, "I'm not hurt tha' bad. I mean, gods, th' guy barely drew blood."

Coryden paused at the door. "Stay put. That's an order."

Morticai sighed and nodded as Coryden closed the heavy door. *Gods, there'll be hell to pay tomorrow.*

CHAPTER THREE

Watchaven's human Northmarch commander, Kirwin McFerrin, scowled at the trio before him. Coryden and Dualas flanked Morticai, who looked as if he'd been in a brawl. Whether they were there for moral or physical support was difficult to tell. Morticai was avoiding McFerrin's eyes, which always meant trouble. Kirwin glanced at Phillip, his second-in-command; he had already fetched Morticai's file, and now sat waiting patiently at his small writing desk, quill in hand.

"All right, let's hear it."

Dualas and Coryden glanced at each other over Morticai's head, deciding who would be spokesman.

"Morticai?" Kirwin asked before they could start.

Morticai looked up, eyes innocent. The darkened circles beneath them almost made him look comical.

"I, uh, got into a bit of a tussle last night, sir."

"So I see."

"This guy stole my clothes."

Dualas's rolling eyes gave it away. "Is he lying, Sir Dualas?"

Sir Dualas, full corryn, with coal-black hair and deep green eyes, thought carefully before he answered. A Knight of the Faith, he had been assigned to the Northmarch by his Order, and whether it was because of the antics of Coryden's squad or his close friendship with Coryden, he had always chosen to serve with them. Kirwin knew he could depend on Dualas for a truthful answer.

"No, sir, someone did steal his clothes, but that is not the most important issue. And I do not believe he knows that it was a man who stole them."

"Why would some lady steal them?" Morticai asked.

"What? I don't know!" Dualas replied.

"Enough!" McFerrin snapped. "Let's hear it—all of it. From the top, Morticai! I've got to be out of here before the Sanctorium strikes the hour."

Morticai relayed a vague account of what had happened at Lord Aldwin's. Dualas added his expert opinion that Morticai would not be able to stay ahorse for several days. Kirwin's second-in-command faithfully recorded their words.

An uncomfortable pause followed. "Morticai," Kirwin suddenly bellowed, "*why* do you constantly get involved with things like this! This is the second time this year you've crossed swords with the nobility! I hadn't dreamed it was possible for you to get into more trouble than you did over that damned . . . courtesan!"

"But, sir," Morticai complained, "her lord was beating her. He would have killed her—you agreed with me that you would've done the same. . . ."

Kirwin's eyes narrowed. "No, mister! I said that I would have done what I could to help her run away—I would not have snuck her into Northgate to hide her! Besides, that's not the issue here." He stood and began pacing. "I ought to turn you over to the City Watch," he muttered.

"What do you expect me to do the day you're caught?" Kirwin continued. "What am I supposed to say to someone like Lord Aldwin? 'I'm sorry, Morticai is the only thief we have in the

Northmarch. He's had this problem for years.' "

"But," Morticai began, "if he's Droken—"

"And what proof do you have? Papers covered with gibberish?" Kirwin interrupted.

Morticai looked bewildered.

"That's the problem, mister! You may be right. But it's none of our business! Not unless we catch him wearing his robes outside the city. This is work for the Faithful."

He paused a moment, gazing suspiciously at Dualas.

"Dualas, were you involved in this?" he asked.

"No, sir."

"Did you know about it?"

"Not before last night, sir."

"Coryden?"

Coryden shifted his weight uneasily. "I knew he had some information, sir. I didn't know how he had gotten it. We were supposed to go to a ball last night."

"Um-hm." Kirwin shook his head in dismay. He walked to where his second-in-command sat and gestured for Phillip to hand him the page he'd been penning.

"We can't use this," Kirwin muttered. "If we put this in the official record, we'll have to turn him over to the City Watch."

"What should I put down, sir?" his second asked.

Kirwin sighed. "Pen the following," he instructed, " 'Morticai injured while off-duty, refused to say how. Confined to quarters until able to resume patrol duties, unexcused patrol absence.' That should do. Dock him for two cycles of patrol pay—and don't forget to charge him for this page and whatever you had to throw away."

"Hey!" Morticai complained. "That page'll cost me . . ."

Kirwin spun. "You'd better be glad that's all it'll cost you, mister! You should get public lashes for this!"

Morticai fell silent and stared at the floor.

Kirwin returned to his desk. "I'd like to give you the punishment this calls for. One more stunt like this, Morticai, and you'll be based at Mid-Keep instead of Watchaven!" he added, pounding his fist down on the desk.

"Yes, sir," Morticai mumbled. The short corryn began to sway and a moment later collapsed.

Coryden and Dualas caught him before he hit the floor.

Kirwin shook his head one last time.

* * * * *

Five days later, after an uneventful patrol, Coryden and Dualas paused before Morticai's heavy wooden door—on the other side, a thump-thump, thump-thump could be heard.

"Knives," Coryden whispered.

"I heard," Dualas whispered back, "that his insistent practicing was the only trouble he caused while he was confined to quarters—the men in the barracks below had difficulty sleeping."

Coryden shook his head and slowly opened the door. Morticai stood at the far end of the room, the table pushed back and his knife targets arrayed around him. He whirled toward the window, letting his last two knives fly toward a low target. He quickly spun back around.

"Thank gods, you're back!" Morticai greeted them.

"Morticai, we weren't gone that long," Coryden responded.

"Yeah, that's easy for you to say! You weren't cooped up with your head spinning for days."

"You do seem to be quite improved, however," Dualas noted.

"Well . . . yeah. Anyway, I've deciphered those notes I got at Aldwin's, and they just don't make any sense. I thought maybe you two could help."

Coryden and Dualas exchanged glances; Morticai seemed to have already forgotten Kirwin's threats. Meanwhile, Morticai had gone to his bed, flopped across it on his stomach, and was fishing beneath it.

A muffled "Ah" came from under the bed, and Morticai sat up with a small wooden chest in his hands. He promptly dropped the chest and grabbed his head.

"Unngh."

"Morticai?" Coryden asked. Dualas scowled.

Morticai reopened his eyes. "Oh, I'll be all right. I should have known not to turn upside down."

He opened the chest and pulled out a stack of papers.

"Morticai!" Coryden exclaimed. "Did all of that come from Aldwin's?"

"Well, I certainly didn't buy it," Morticai replied.

Coryden rolled his eyes. Morticai handed one of the pages to Sir Dualas. Dualas's scowl deepened.

"I think you should read this," Dualas said shortly, handing the note to the captain. "Are you certain you did this correctly?" Dualas gestured at the pile of papers that Morticai was digging through.

"Uh?" Morticai finally replied. "Oh, yeah, I think so." He handed the cipher key to Dualas, along with another note.

One by one, the notes were passed around.

"Hmm," Coryden muttered. "I don't know, Morticai. These aren't very coherent."

"See, that's my problem," the frustrated thief complained. "There's all this talk about voting, but who is voting, and what in Glawres's name are they voting on?"

"You can't even use these to prove Aldwin's involvement," Coryden said, tossing the last note back onto the bed. "He could claim they were discussing anything that required a vote by the nobility."

"It would be easier to understand if they had not used so many misleading terms," Dualas admitted. "But we should be able to figure some of it out. Let me see."

Dualas began pacing. "If we assume that your basic thoughts are correct, Morticai, and that Lord Aldwin, Lord Valdir, and Sir Ellenwood are Droken, then these notes could confirm that they are apparently working together on this council, whichever one it is, and voting in concert. And if they were Droken, they would obviously not be working for the best interests of the kingdom. Mention is made of Dynolva. . . ." Dualas stopped and stared hard at Morticai. He suddenly strode to the bed and seized one of the messages.

"That's it! It refers to the meeting . . . here"—Dualas

pointed—"as bimonthly. There is only one council that meets bimonthly—the Trade Council!" he finished triumphantly.

"The what?" Coryden asked.

"The Trade Council?" Morticai echoed dismally. "All this time I thought it was something important."

Dualas looked at them, surprised. "But, my friends, it *is* important. And, I do believe, it's beginning to make sense. Yes . . . Morticai," Dualas demanded abruptly, "how much does a goblet of good Dynolvan wine cost?"

"A few ferdhyn," he replied.

"Ah, that tells me you haven't bought any recently."

"Apparently not!" Coryden complained. "Last week the cost doubled from six to twelve."

"Twelve ferdhyn!" Morticai protested. "That's ridiculous!"

"Exactly!" Dualas replied. "And, that is a direct result of the Trade Council's tariff on Dynolvan wine."

"How do you know that?" Morticai asked suspiciously.

"Well," the knight admitted, "in truth, I would not know if Gunhar had not been complaining last week when I stopped by The Foaming Tankard. However, I know from what he said that most of the tavern owners in town are very upset about it."

"All right, so this means they've made the tavern owners angry—this is supposed to further the cause of Droka?"

"Somehow it must," Dualas replied. "Gunhar said Watchaven was retaliating because Dynolva had increased its tariff on goods shipped through our harbor. Why Dynolva would do such a thing, I do not know. However, I think it is unlikely our three Droken would be involved if it did not serve the Dark One."

"So?" Coryden asked. "We're back where Kirwin said we were—waiting to catch them wearing Droken robes."

"If they were not of the nobility, we could easily demand an investigation by the Faithful," Dualas responded.

"Well, maybe you can't ask for an investigation now, but if I can get some solid evidence, the Faithful will investigate—whether or not they're noble," Morticai said.

"Didn't you hear Kirwin?" Coryden said. "He was serious! If you get into trouble one more time he'll transfer you to Mid-

Keep. Then, what would you do? You'd go insane! No taverns, no ladies . . ."

"No I wouldn't. I'd jump contract."

"What? Morticai!"

"Oh, Coryden, I'm not serious!" Morticai shook his head. "But I can't just let this go." A wicked grin crept onto his face. "I mean, do you want to spend the rest of your life paying twelve ferdhyn for Dynolvan wine? Besides, if I find enough evidence Kirwin can't say a thing."

Coryden shook his head. He knew that Morticai was pushing him, teasing him—he also knew that there were times when Morticai's stubbornness was simply incredible.

"How do you propose we find this evidence?"

Dualas's question stunned Coryden. The knight was actually encouraging Morticai!

"Well, I'd start by following them, like before. The connections must go deeper. Maybe other council members are involved. Who is Aldwin getting his instructions from? He's not making these decisions himself, is he? And I haven't even had time to follow Ellenwood yet."

"I suppose that would be a good place to begin," Dualas agreed. "I could possibly find out who else is on the council. However, I do not suggest any further midnight investigations without us agreeing to it first."

"Hey! What kind of a thief do you think I am? I put serious thought into it, y'know."

"If you wish my assistance," Dualas growled, "you'll let me know what you are doing—more specifically, what you are doing that could get you into trouble. Do you agree or not?"

Morticai sighed. "All right, I agree."

Coryden could remain silent no longer. "You two are crazy!" he cried. "This isn't any small thing to be involved with, Morticai. You'll be dead in a sennight if they discover what you're doing!"

"That is precisely why I am willing to help, Coryden," Dualas interrupted. "Morticai is already involved with it. And you are correct: this is not a small matter. I did not say I approved of the methods he has used to get this far. But, I would rather help and know where he is than have him disappear into the hands of the Droken."

Coryden sighed. It was beginning to look as if it would be a long Light Season.

* * * * *

Dualas's footsteps fell with a steady rhythm, rebounding from the thick, stone walls with a deep, clear resonance. A thrumming intonation, rising and falling like the waves against the nearby cliffs, echoed faintly through the large structure. The long corridor contained many doors, but it was only the one at the end that interested him. The knight standing before it nodded a greeting before opening the heavy door.

Within, an ornate desk stood at the center of the large room. Rich tapestries covered the walls, their colors muted by the brilliant light that streamed through the two narrow windows behind the desk.

A man sat at the desk, intent on the papers that lay scattered across it. He was human, no more than forty years old, with brown hair and, for a human, delicate features.

"Sir Dualas, Your Blessedness," the knight announced.

The man looked up and smiled warmly. "Sir Dualas," he said, rising and coming around the desk.

Dualas dropped to one knee and bowed his head.

"Your Blessedness."

The Grand Patriarch gestured over Dualas's head, then offered his hand for Dualas to rise. "What brings our faithful knight here from the Northmarch?"

"A serious matter, Your Blessedness," Dualas began. "A Northmarcher has discovered a cell of Droken. A cell consisting of members of the nobility."

"Continue," the Patriarch replied, leading Dualas to a small seating area.

* * * * *

". . . That is how the situation now stands," Dualas finished.

The Grand Patriarch finished his second cup of tea. "You have done well to report this, Sir Dualas. This could be a very serious matter. I trust you do not doubt the authenticity of the information you have been given?"

"I have never known Morticai to lie about important matters."

"Is he . . . faithful?"

"He does not attend regular services; however, I believe he is quite devout."

"And why do you think thus?"

"He wears a token of Glawres, Your Blessedness. He has always worn it openly. Further, our captain, Coryden Lestryon of Menelcar, found him once at Glawres's beach. Morticai claimed he had gone there to think, but it seemed more important than that. I have observed him for some time. I suspect he worships there, as Glawres's earliest followers worshipped."

"You understand that we cannot begin an official investigation on such unsubstantiated information."

"Yes, Your Blessedness. Is there not a way to begin an unofficial investigation?"

"Your friend seems to have already begun one."

It was not what Dualas had hoped to hear. "I . . . see. Is there anything specific you would have me do?"

"Give the support you have offered. Lend your wisdom whenever possible. Lend your sword only if you must. You understand our position well enough to protect our interests. Report to me whenever you feel moved to, which I trust will be often." He rose, indicating the audience was at an end. Dualas rose and, bowing deeply, took his leave.

The Grand Patriarch allowed a slow count of ten before ringing the bell on his desk.

The door opened. "Yes, Your Blessedness," the knight said.

"Send for my scribe, Sir Thorald. Tell him to bring his writing materials."

The acolyte soon stood before him. "I need you to take a letter," the Patriarch began. "Address it to the Head of Inquisition at Abbadyr. . . ."

* * * * *

The yard of the Crestview Club was already crowded when the ornate coach pulled under the marquee. The owner of the coach emerged wearing a full cloak and Tradelenor-style hat—large brimmed and feathered. The man was in his mid-thirties, with long features, dark brown eyes, and long, light brown hair. The naturally curly hair would have been considered the height of current fashion in Tradelenor.

"Good evening, Lord Aldwin," the doorman greeted.

"Good evening to you, Wyborn. Is anyone of note here this evening?"

"Usual customers, my lord. Oh, a couple of merchants from Helgorn arrived a few hours ago, but no other foreigners. Should I watch for anyone in particular?"

"No, I am not expecting anyone," Aldwin replied.

Aldwin made his way through the club, nodding at acquaintances. Several Watchaven merchants were having an animated conversation in the main hall.

"Lord Aldwin!" one of the merchants called, rushing over to intercept him.

"Good evening, Master Ivar."

"We heard you had just returned from Dynolva. Does this nonsense continue?"

"I am afraid so. The Dynolvans have pledged to continue their tariffs and are threatening to use Locguard and Bridlington as their main ports."

"That's insane! Have all the world's corryn gone mad?"

"I certainly hope not. I have not spoken with any members of the other corryn kingdoms, however. If you will excuse me."

"But, lord, what will come of it?"

"I am not at liberty to say what the council will do next, Master. We shall soon have another meeting and consider the situation then."

He took his leave and smiled inwardly as the lively conversation continued behind him. Shortly he entered the private portion of the club—the Red Lion Pub.

The Red Lion's atmosphere was much quieter, with small groups of noblemen conversing in low tones. An ornate door, with stained glass representing leaves, stood in the back wall. Lord Aldwin was hailed before he could reach it.

"Lord Aldwin!"

Aldwin turned at the voice of Lord Orrick. The chubby nobleman approached him.

"Aldwin, have you heard about Lord Quinson?" he asked.

"Quinson?" Aldwin asked innocently. "No, should I?"

"Oh, dear," Orrick replied. "I feared that with you having been out of town you wouldn't have heard. Quinson lost his son this last week in a terrible hunting accident!"

Aldwin was genuinely confused. He knew that Quinson would have to come up with some explanation for his son's death—but a hunting accident?

"How?" he asked.

"Oh," Orrick replied, waving his hand, "you know how impetuous that boy of his was. Quinson went on a hunt and took the boy with him. Apparently the boy wished so much to go on the hunt itself that he tried to follow his father on foot. Well, the bear found the boy long before the hunters found the bear. They said it was a terrible sight!"

"I imagine so," Aldwin replied, wondering if Quinson had actually taken the boy's remains with him to back up this story.

"Just terrible!" Orrick reiterated. "Well, I just knew that you would want to know," he concluded.

"Indeed," Aldwin replied. "Thank you." And with a nod Aldwin took his leave and this time reached the door with the stained glass without further interruption.

A young woman with blonde hair and blue eyes met him just inside. Her rich, pale pink gown was decorated with white lace edging and delicate bows. Aldwin repressed a smile—such colors were usually reserved for virgins; he had personal experience that the color was inappropriate.

"Why, good evening, Lord Aldwin," she greeted him. "I trust your trip to Dynolva was enjoyable?"

"As enjoyable as one could expect, I suppose," he replied. "Is

Cwena available?"

"For you, always. I believe she is in the garden room."

He nodded thanks and headed toward the mentioned room. She was expecting him.

"My lord," Cwena said as he sat down beside her. He nodded in reply.

"Your trip went well?"

"It did," he replied. He had never been comfortable in her presence. She appeared to be in her early twenties. Her pale green eyes and exquisite figure were beautiful beyond compare. She was lovely, sensuous—and deadly. He had never seen her kill, but he had watched other jevano feed. She reached a hand toward the lace cuff of his shirt. He stood, not permitting her to touch him.

"Shall we?" he offered.

They retired to her room without further conversation. She sat on the bed, braiding her red hair, as Aldwin stepped into her dressing parlor. Removing his hat and cloak, he once again donned his Droker robe. Once properly attired, he opened a wall panel by Cwena's chifforobe with practiced ease. Before him, a narrow hallway led leftward. The only light came from a stairwell about twenty feet away. Lord Aldwin knew the path well.

The stairs led down to a small room, far beneath the club. Two guards, wearing full-faced helmets and chain armor, rose from their chairs as he reached the bottom. Aldwin smiled, remembering the boasts about the Dynolvan temple. *They would do well to visit ours,* Aldwin thought. *Perhaps they could even learn something about security.*

One of the guards approached him while the other maintained an easy fighting stance. Aldwin gave the sign of Droka; the guard nearest him returned it.

"The pass-phrase, Dyagon?" the guard asked, addressing Aldwin by his temple rank, signified by the ornate embroidery on the hem of Aldwin's robe.

"The harbor is empty."

"Evening service will begin in an hour." Without further

conversation, the guard turned and led him through a door and into a short hallway. Aldwin could feel the eyes of the guards behind the arrow slits. He stood behind a stripe on the floor as the guard approached the door at the far end of the hall and whispered his own pass-phrase.

The door opened, and Aldwin was allowed into a larger room. The four guards who were here nodded in respect to his rank, but said nothing. His guide left him and returned the way they had come.

From here, escort was unnecessary. Aldwin exited through the door opposite the one he had entered, traveled down one more short hall with arrow slits, and finally arrived in front of another door. He opened it, glad to be leaving the gatehouse.

"Good evening, faithful Dyagon." The man greeting him wore the red robes of an acolyte. This room was very different from the previous ones—the floor was black marble, and tapestries depicting Droka's battle with the Levani adorned the walls. However, it was the double doors on the opposite wall, intricately carved and leafed with gold, that dominated the room.

"I am to have an audience with the high priest before this evening's service."

"Please proceed then. I would not hinder you with idle conversation, Dyagon," the acolyte replied, gesturing toward the gilt doors.

Aldwin nodded politely and made Droka's sign before opening one of the large doors. Behind it, the temple bustled with hushed activity. The octagonal room was nearly fifty-five feet across. A fifteen-foot-tall image of Droka, purportedly made of solid gold, stood against the back wall—Aldwin had long suspected it was merely gilt.

Bas-relief scenes of Droka's triumphs covered the black stone walls. Inlaid gold defined the scenes. An acolyte was lighting the gold candelabra, which stood like soldiers around the perimeter of the room. Aldwin frowned behind his mask. Three weeks earlier the candelabra were to have been cleaned of old wax that had dripped down their sides, and still the chore had not been attended to. Had the acolytes been Aldwin's servants, they would have been soundly thrashed for such obvious inattentiveness.

In the center of the room stood an upraised granite platform, also octagonal and nearly fifteen feet across. Droka's sign, graven into the platform, was filled with dried blood. Two heavy chains ending in shackles hung from the high ceiling. More shackles were embedded in the platform itself. Currently, an acolyte was fastening the chains out of the way.

Aldwin watched as the acolyte finished his work. A small amount of mortar had crumbled from around the base of one of the ceiling anchors. Aldwin shook his head. It was sad to see his temple slowly sliding away from the high standard it had once held itself to. *I must remember to bring the issue up when the Dyagons next hold council.*

His gaze drifted to two more acolytes, also on the platform, standing at a small table. The table contained torture implements, which they covered with a black cloth. At least the implements appeared to have been cleaned. Once the table was covered, the acolytes moved it to the opposite side of the temple and placed it behind a door made nearly invisible by the intricate bas-relief. No holy day had occurred recently—a traitor must have been caught. Aldwin wondered if it had been anyone he knew.

The acolytes ignored Aldwin as he crossed the room to another, nearly hidden door. This one was not a closet, but led into the high priest's private section of the underground complex. It was a priest, not a mere acolyte, who greeted him this time.

"Dyagon, His Eminence awaits you." Without waiting for a reply, the priest turned, rapped lightly on a door, then opened and held it for Aldwin.

The office they entered was spacious—corryn furniture from Lorredre, a crystal chandelier from Tradelenor, and carpets from Bracar furnished the room as befitted the high priest's station.

Behind the desk sat the high priest. His red robe was broidered in black and gold. As with all whom Aldwin had seen, his silk mask was in place. As they entered, he closed a large book that lay before him. Aldwin noted it was one of the Books of Prophecy.

"Sit down, Dyagon."

Aldwin sat. Nothing more was spoken until the priest left them.

"Your report, Lord Aldwin?"

Aldwin shifted uncomfortably. The high priest's habit of using his name in private had always unnerved him.

"Everything went as planned. The Dynolvan Council was furious with our proposal. They are threatening to use the Locguard-Bridlington route as an alternative to Watchaven."

"Excellent. Did you give my message to Ambassador Volney?"

"Yes. He returned this." Aldwin deposited a sealed letter on the desk. The high priest opened it and read it silently.

"Very good. Not only are things proceeding well, but they are proceeding on schedule."

"Your Eminence, I . . . must report one other small incident."

The high priest's head tilted slightly. "Yes?"

"Someone broke into my estate while I was in Dynolva."

The high priest held up a gloved hand, interrupting him. "Perhaps you should remove your mask before you proceed, Lord Aldwin."

Aldwin licked his lips. There was no way around the command. Knowing the high priest knew your identity was one thing—withstanding his scrutiny, not knowing his identity, not seeing his reactions to your words . . . Slowly, Aldwin slid the silk mask to the rear of his hood.

"Lower the hood."

He did so.

"Now. Continue."

"Someone broke in. My blacksmith was coming from the coach house and encountered the thief attempting to leave. They wrestled, but the thief escaped. The alarm was raised and chase given, but once in the city . . ."

"And you dared to come here?"

"I had . . . he couldn't have discovered anything to connect me with the Droken," Aldwin stammered. "I had my robes."

The high priest's tone softened, "I see. Was much stolen?"

Aldwin looked down. "No," he said softly.

"Did your servant describe this thief to you?"

"My blacksmith is human, Your Excellence, and it was difficult for him to see him in the darkness. He said the man had a slender form, but seemed of human height. Another servant who saw the man flee thought he was corryn."

"Very well. You have increased the watch at your estate?"

"Yes, Your Eminence."

"Then, we shall consider the incident closed for now, Lord Aldwin. You will be careful, I trust."

"Yes, Your Eminence."

"You may leave. Service begins shortly."

Aldwin took a deep breath and pulled his hood and mask into place.

The high priest gave Droka's sign as Aldwin stood to leave. Aldwin returned it and with relief left for the comfortable anonymity he always found when surrounded by others at service.

* * * * *

Once Aldwin had gone, the high priest turned toward the wall. *He* had to be there, had to have seen and heard. He could feel His presence, as he always did when either of the two Droken princes were nearby.

The wall panel slowly opened. The corryn who emerged was anything but ordinary for his kind. He stood nearly seven feet tall. Even the exquisite silk Lorredre tunic could not hide his tremendous musculature. His silver hair was braided into a warrior's knot and although he was not dressed for battle, Ducledha—Black Sword, hung at his side. His ice-blue eyes demanded the high priest's attention. The high priest resisted, ever so slightly, before being helplessly drawn into that deadly gaze.

"Have Aldwin followed. See who is following him."

"Yes, Prince Luthekar. Thy will be done."

CHAPTER FOUR

The squalid section of town was teeming with peasants and filthy animals. Despite the noonday heat, Lord Aldwin pulled his summer cloak tighter about him. The stench was horrid. His guards led the way, shoving through the mass of people. *Curse these streets, too narrow for coaches!*

Finally, his guards turned down an alley that was, incredibly, even narrower. *Gods, how does the Watch patrol here?* They stopped before a small doorway. The door was missing, and in its place hung a faded cloth.

"Are you certain this is the place, Garric?"

"Oh, yes, m'lord. Madam Luvena has cured me of several curses. She's said to be one of the best in the city."

Aldwin sighed, wondering if he'd taken leave of his senses. Well, he had come this far. . . . "Wait here."

Beyond the cloth door a narrow hallway led into the dim depths of the building. It turned twice before ending at another doorway—this one curtained with colorful shells, strung like beads.

The shells announced his entrance, despite Aldwin's efforts to pass through quietly. He stood within a small room cluttered with the odd paraphernalia of Madam Luvena's craft. Strangely shaped, stoppered bottles were lined neatly along a small shelf, seeming to contain . . . He decided he did not need to know.

A large bowl filled with inky liquid sat in the center of a lace-covered table; Aldwin had seen a similar bowl used at the king's court. Others had claimed to see pictures in the wizard's bowl. Aldwin strongly suspected the others of too much enjoyment of the king's fine wines prior to the wizard's demonstration.

Before he could explore further, however, a small girl ran into the room through another seashell-strung doorway. She was dressed in a silk blouse and several layers of colorful long skirts. Aldwin noted that she wore a surprising amount of gold jewelry. Before Aldwin could fashion what to ask the child, she was gone, running back the way she had come.

"Mamma, mamma, a lord is here!"

Aldwin sighed. *Surely, all I shall gain here is a lighter purse.*

When the shells rattled again, a lovely dark-haired woman stood in the doorway. She was dressed much like the child. She did not speak, but leveled her dark eyes evenly at Lord Aldwin.

"Madam Luvena, I presume?" he began.

"Yes, Lord Aldwin, how may I help you?"

Aldwin jumped visibly. "I, ah, need your services."

"Please," she gestured into the next room. It was furnished much like the previous one, except that the shelves in this room were crammed with books. This surprised Aldwin but bolstered his opinion of Madam Luvena. The books showed her wealth more than her jewelry.

She led him to a small settee and set about making them tea. Aldwin recognized the scent of it and wondered if she intended it for them both. While he drank vallemo, he did not advertise his use of the mild, illegal spice. Most of his friends who dabbled with such things used moonflower—also illegal, but much stronger and highly addictive.

"Tea, Lord Aldwin?"

"No, thank you, I don't drink vallemo." He withdrew a cloth from inside his cloak and unwrapped the daggers and rope he had carefully preserved.

Madam Luvena looked at him questioningly. Aldwin's nervousness eased, as it became apparent that there were limits to her knowledge.

"My estate was broken into several days ago," he began. "The thief conveniently left me these mementos. I would like to know more about this thief. I was told you could help."

Madam Luvena carefully examined the items. "How many people have handled these?"

"My blacksmith, myself, and now, you."

"How long ago did this episode occur?"

"Six days."

Madam Luvena sighed. "This would have been easier if you had brought them sooner."

"I was out of town."

"Well, we shall see. It may not be too late. I cannot work with this one." She pointed to the dagger that had killed Aldwin's servant. "It has recent death upon it." Using a handkerchief, she gave it back to Aldwin.

She produced a black silk cloth, embroidered with odd markings. She laid the cloth across a low table and then fetched several candles and jars of powders. Aldwin watched with fascination as she prepared the items. The magicians at court had never seemed to take this much effort. Perhaps it was part of her act.

"You must be absolutely silent while I perform the spell."

Aldwin scowled. *I am not a child, Madam,* he thought, but refrained from telling her so. Madam Luvena began to chant as she sprinkled the remaining dagger and rope with various powders. She then began to sway, her eyes closed, while she chanted and gestured over the table.

Gods, this is trite! Does she think this will impress me?

The dagger slowly floated upward to hang a few inches below Madam Luvena's hands.

Aldwin blinked. *There must be a thread!*

She lowered her hands. The dagger remained floating. Continuing to chant, she cupped her hands, palms up, a few inches beneath the dagger. The dagger floated softly into her hands. She stopped chanting and opened her eyes.

Aldwin let out a held breath. Madam Luvena stared strangely at the dagger. Finally, she spoke.

"Your thief belongs to the Northmarch."

"What?" Aldwin asked incredulously.

Her dark eyes caught his but revealed nothing of what she felt within. "You heard me correctly."

"Anything else?"

"Yes. He is an orphan."

Aldwin snorted. "Do you know how many 'orphans' have joined the Northmarch? Half of them, I imagine!"

Her stare became icy. "If that is so, we may thank the Droken for it."

Aldwin returned the stare. *Just what does she know?*

"There is more. But first, we should discuss price. Do you know more now than when you came here?"

"Well, yes, of course."

"Then I ask you for one thousand korun."

Aldwin pulled his purse from beneath his cloak.

"And I shall ask you for another thousand if you would hear the last of the information I obtained."

Aldwin stopped and scrutinized this strange woman.

"Very well. What is it?"

"Your thief is corryn."

Aldwin settled back in his seat and considered it.

"And he is a Watchaven Northmarcher? Based here? Not in Dynolva?"

"Yes."

"And he's a corryn orphan. Do you know how many corryn there are in Watchaven's Northmarch?"

"No."

"Neither do I. But I know there are not many. Do you know if this thief was working alone?"

"No. No, I do not know that. Do you think he may have been in your estate on behalf of the Northmarch?"

"Ah, no, of course not. That wouldn't make any sense." *Damned witch! What's she doing, reading my thoughts?* "No, I just wondered if he had other friends who might have been involved."

"I see. No, I do not know that, I am afraid."

"Well, I thank you. You are quite correct, the full information is worth two thousand korun."

He laid the coins on the edge of the table.

Madam Luvena bowed her head toward him in thanks and rose to show him out.

After he had gone, she returned to the table. Aldwin had left the thief's belongings without a single thought to their disposal. Madam Luvena picked up the dagger and slowly turned it over in her hand.

* * * * *

Twenty days had passed since Morticai's assault on Aldwin's tower. Due to his confinement, patrol, and gate duties, only three of those days had been off-duty time. He had followed Lord Valdir those three days but discovered nothing more than where his mistress lived.

He had decided to follow Lord Aldwin tonight, but so far it had proven equally boring. Morticai's attention drifted from Lord Aldwin to the buxom maiden taking drink orders. She glanced his direction; he automatically smiled. She returned the smile and began drifting his way. He blinked and straightened in the booth. He hadn't wanted to talk with her now.

Sir Ellenwood walked through the door, stealing Aldwin's attention, which had also been on the young lass's sweet form.

Morticai sighed with relief.

"Get ya somethin', darlin'?" she asked.

" 'Fraid not, hon. I've already had enough," he said. Aldwin got up and began moving toward the door.

"Ah, surely you'd like more than jus' a couple o' brandies?" She smiled seductively, but Morticai wasn't watching.

Ellenwood passed Aldwin without so much as a nod of recognition. Morticai would not be able to slip out behind Aldwin without causing a scene with the barmaid. A brawny sailor threw some coins on the bar, drained his glass, and shouldered his way out the door. Ellenwood sat down in the booth Aldwin had vacated.

"Well, darlin'?"

Morticai settled back on the bench. "Maybe you could bring me another brandy. Thanks."

She scowled at him briefly. "If that's all ya want, then that's all you'll get!"

Morticai looked up, but she was already heading to the bar. Had he missed something?

His attention drifted back to Ellenwood. The former street urchin watched with increasing fascination as Sir Ellenwood slid his hand along the edge of the bench. The noble was attempting to be discreet, but to Morticai, trained in sleight of hand, the attempt was as clumsy and obvious as if he had gotten on his knees and looked beneath the bench. Ellenwood retrieved a paper and slipped it inside his cloak. Then, without even ordering a drink, he rose and moved toward the door.

Sorry, hon, Morticai thought, leaving a korun on the table.

* * * * *

Ellenwood traveled north from Black Horse Tavern, crossing Mainway into an area of the city filled with small shops. Morticai knew that Ellenwood was not heading home—his estate lay to the northwest. Of course, the fact that he was not traveling by coach was, in itself, unusual.

He eventually crossed Shipwright's Road and then surprised Morticai by turning east, toward the docks. The dockside of the city was extremely dangerous at night—not an area a nobleman would wish to frequent.

Ellenwood soon stopped, however, and reversed his fine cloak. Morticai smiled with understanding as Ellenwood wrapped himself in a coarse woolen cloak any dock worker would be proud of. Morticai was suddenly at a disadvantage. He had dressed well, expecting to follow Lord Aldwin to his usual haunts.

Ellenwood continued east for about a mile and then turned north again. If he continued, he would soon be in the poorest section of Watchaven. The area was riddled with long alleys, which would make the nobleman easy to follow, but its byways also contained some of the city's roughest gangs.

Several blocks later Ellenwood came to one of the area's major intersections. He crossed it diagonally and continued on. Not wishing to attract additional attention, Morticai stayed next to the buildings.

Three young humans suddenly stepped directly into Morticai's path from a nearby doorway. They blocked his path deliberately, with knives drawn. The Northmarcher automatically fell into a fighting stance, his new dagger in his left hand, a throwing knife in his right. The three looked at each other with raised eyebrows.

"What's this, a knife-fighting noble?" the tallest of the group asked.

"Ya' gotta' be kiddin'," another grumbled.

"Hey, he's a corryn knife-fightin' noble!" the third added, laughing.

Morticai edged closer to the wall and said nothing. He could probably take them but would lose Ellenwood. The rest of the street was empty, save for a beggar watching casually from across the street.

"You speak human, corryn?" one of them sneered.

"We got sharp claws, y'know," the tall one said, gesturing to his blade. "Why don't you jus' make this easy and give us your purse, uh?" When Morticai did not reply, the youth repeated his threat in extremely poor corryn.

Morticai considered his best route out of the situation—if he targeted the tall one and caught him off-balance before they moved in he might be able to slip back a few feet, then . . .

He heard footsteps behind him. Morticai glanced behind to see four more gang members. Now he was in trouble.

"Hey, Mika, we spotted him first!" one of them called.

"Yeah, but we stopped him," the tall one in front retorted.

"Split with us."

"We'll talk about it when we're finished."

"I'll wager!"

The beggar was still watching, but with increased interest as Morticai saw his slim chance of escape evaporate. There simply was no place to run. Slowly, Morticai reached out his right hand and dropped his knife. While the three men watched it fall in surprise, Morticai quickly gave the beggar a hand signal for help.

The men reflexively jumped back about a foot at the sudden hand sign. It was a signal used only by members of the Arluthians, a group feared by all the gangs, and while Morticai was a member of the elite group, he had not intended to involve them in this current affair. With Sir Dualas already involved, the risk of exposing Arluthian secrets was too high—and the penalties for revealing such secrets were not to be taken lightly.

The gang members stared at each other, wondering if the hand sign had been a bluff, but the beggar straightened and immediately whistled loud and long. A street urchin ran out of a nearby alley. The beggar repeated the hand sign to the urchin and pointed at Morticai.

Although he'd not known the beggar, Morticai recognized the boy as Tagger, one of the many urchins with whom he maintained casual contact. Tagger stared at Morticai openmouthed; Morticai smiled and shrugged. The boy turned and ran like the wind.

Cursing, the leader of the group before Morticai spat at his feet.

"That's what I think of you and your 'society,' Arluthian!"

Morticai smiled. "Ya gotta watch out for us corryn nobles," he replied.

The tall one glared at him and snarled more curses before both groups turned and ran. Now that all doubt had been removed, the gang members knew that if they spilled any of Morticai's blood they would repay the Arluthians with every drop of their own.

Morticai retrieved his dagger and quickly crossed to the beggar. He was lucky the beggar was an Arluthian—not many beggars were.

"I owe you my life, brother. Be at the next meeting and I shall gratefully repay you," Morticai told him.

"Perhaps. If not, you'll remember me. Now, catch up to your friend." The beggar motioned in the direction in which Ellenwood had gone. "And tell him to change his shoes the next time he comes to this side of town."

Morticai waved the beggar a goodbye and ran after Ellenwood. At last he spied the nobleman ahead of him. Luckily, he encountered no other gangs, although Ellenwood did skirt the worst section of town, known as the Snake Pit; even Morticai was thankful he had not entered that section of the city. Not long after passing the pit, the nobleman came to the Cobblesend Pub. Without pausing, Ellenwood entered the low-class establishment.

Morticai laughed aloud at the irony of it. He could walk in wearing his current attire and draw the attention of Ellenwood and every cutthroat there. But if he were dressed in his usual street clothes, Ellenwood's attention would still be drawn as the pub's patrons hailed him. After all, this had once been Morticai's side of town, his place of refuge with its narrow alleys and abandoned buildings. But Morticai was not one to give up easily. . . .

* * * * *

"Kithryl, open up," Morticai whispered.

Nothing. He rapped again, lightly. "Kithryl, come on, open up."

"Who's there?"

"Dyluth."

The back door of the Cobblesend opened a crack.

"Dyluth? Truly?"

"Yes, now let me in!"

"Dyluth!" A corryn woman with black hair and pale violet eyes opened the door. She wore a peasant's apron over her drab frock but still took Morticai's breath away with her beauty. She hugged him to herself before he had made it inside.

"Dyluth, I thought you had died! I considered going to Northgate and asking after you, but all I could remember was your street name."

"I'm called Morticai in the Northmarch—don't laugh now!"

She had already begun to snicker. "And I thought Dyluth, Lord of Shadows, was silly."

Morticai looked down, embarrassed.

"Oh, I'm sorry, Dyluth! I didn't mean it that way. I remember Dyluth was a very good name at the time—but Morticai's a human name! Why don't they call you by your birth name, Moranekor?"

"It's a long story," he mumbled.

"All right, I understand. You can tell me some other time. Why haven't you come by?"

Morticai shrugged. "I . . . guess I've been busy." He sighed. "Look, Kithryl, I'm sorry. I hadn't realized it had been this long. But, I'm doing something kinda important right now, and I need your help."

She frowned. "Are you in trouble?"

"No, I'm not in trouble! I'm following someone, but I didn't think he'd come this way, as you can see." He gestured to his clothes. "May I borrow a cloak so I can sit in the pub without being noticed?"

"Well . . . I suppose so. Is this dangerous?"

Morticai shrugged again. "I don't know. Maybe." He gave her his most innocent smile.

Kithryl shook her head. "Some things never change, do they?" she asked, fetching him a cloak.

* * * * *

The pub was crowded. Morticai stayed close to the wall as he worked his way to a booth. Ellenwood was already engaged in conversation with another cloaked figure. A few patrons wore their cloak hoods thrown back, but most, such as Ellenwood and his companion, did not. At this time of year, it would have been thought odd anywhere else in the city. Here however, the desire for anonymity often ran deeper than the desire for comfort. Morticai also kept his hood up.

Kithryl came and took Morticai's order as though the conversation in the kitchen had never occurred. She went to the bar and spoke with her husband, Breslen. He glanced toward Morticai and briefly nodded. This may have been the best place Ellenwood could have led him. Where else could he enjoy such cooperation?

He turned his attention back to Ellenwood and concentrated on reading the noble's lips, but it was a skill he had never fully mastered. He could discern only a few words; they seemed much like the messages he had stolen. He could distinguish "Dynolva," "Watchaven," and finally, "Trade Council." At least they were discussing something other than invitations to the Grand Ball.

Kithryl returned with his drink and nearly jumped when Morticai paid her with a royal—the drink was worth only a few ferdhyn. Morticai's knowing smile told her he would refuse any change. It was the least he could do for this woman who had harbored him during some of his darkest times. She shook her head and pocketed the coin that would easily pay their rent for several months.

He continued watching Ellenwood, but the conversation had apparently turned the other direction, with Ellenwood listening. Morticai wondered who Ellenwood's companion might be. He believed it was a man, but he was too tall to be Lord Valdir. No, this must be yet another player in this strange game.

Ellenwood finished his drink and rose. Now Morticai had to decide which of the two he would follow. It was the stranger who currently intrigued him. Morticai remained, sipping his drink, as Ellenwood left the pub.

Shortly after Ellenwood left, the stranger rose. He was tall, with fluid movements. Morticai suspected he was corryn, but then, neither height nor grace was necessarily an indicator;

Morticai's own height showed that height could not be trusted.

Now, as he followed Ellenwood's mysterious companion, Morticai's height and borrowed cloak made him indistinguishable from those who continued to roam these streets. Despite the hour, the streets here were still crowded with Watchaven's restless poor.

The stranger traveled southwest, directly toward Shipwright's Road. After a mile, he turned down an alley. Morticai immediately ducked into one himself. He felt certain he had not been spotted, but the alley the stranger had taken was a dead end, the perfect place for an ambush. Morticai loosened his sword in its scabbard and checked his daggers, making certain they were still positioned under the tailored slits in his only remaining Tradelenor shirt.

Suddenly, a coach came clattering out of the dead end. Morticai froze as it wheeled past and traveled toward the main road. Morticai ran down an alley, jumped a low wall, ran down another alley, and finally stopped, listening for the clippety-clop of the horses' hooves. It had been years since he had tried to follow a coach on foot, but the twisting streets gave him a chance. There were only a few streets here that were wide enough for a coach.

He heard the hoofbeats then, a little north of his own location. He could visualize the route the driver would be forced to take if he were heading for Shipwright's Road. Morticai was on the run again, down another alley, then across a narrow street that led to the main road. This was the street Morticai thought the driver would take, but there was no place along it to conceal himself. He gambled that the driver would turn right, toward Northgate. He crossed the main road and started north.

As expected, the coach emerged and turned right onto Shipwright's Road. Morticai had gambled that if Ellenwood's companion had enough money to hire a coach, he would most likely now return to the wealthy section of town. The quickest way there would be to travel northwest and then take the tight turn in front of Northgate and travel due south on Northgate Road.

The coach was traveling at a normal pace, and Morticai knew he would have a chance of catching it as it made the turn in front of Northgate. He had not seen any coachmen when it had first wheeled past him. It had been years since he'd hopped a coach; he hoped he still could.

He made it to the turn a few seconds before the coach. He stopped, panting, and hoped the Northmarchers guarding the gate were busy, and that Kirwin was not out taking some evening air.

He didn't have long to worry about it. The coach approached the corner, slowing for the turn. It slowed even more as it entered the three-way intersection, and Morticai ran from the shadows.

Catching the back of the coach was easy, although Morticai worried about the jerk he caused as his weight settled onto it; he'd been much lighter when he'd last done this. As expected, the coach took the tight turn down Northgate Road. Morticai allowed himself a brief glance back; no Northmarchers chased after the coach to inform it of its unwanted passenger.

He had time to catch his breath as the coach traveled toward the center of the city. Obviously, the coach's passenger was, like Ellenwood, affluent. Why had they chosen the Cobblesend for their meeting? What was so crucial that they had to go into Watchaven's roughest areas to meet? More to the point at the moment, just how close to the palace was this damned coach going?

The coach had almost reached Royal Way, and Morticai considered whether to jump off. He had just decided to do so when it turned right and began to slow. Morticai disembarked and moved quickly into the shadows at the side of the road.

He was shocked when he realized his exact location. He stood only one block north of the palace itself on the street that carried the nickname "Accent Alley," earned because the street contained the estates of the ambassadors who represented the rest of the Confederacy.

The coach was entering the large, circular drive that led to the Dynolvan Embassy. Morticai cautiously ran closer. It was risky, but now his curiosity was afire—he had to see who was riding inside that coach. The coach stopped, and servants ran out to greet it.

The door opened, and a tall, elegantly dressed corryn with silky white hair stepped from the coach. Morticai searched his memory for the name; he had seen the man several times from a distance and knew he had heard the name. Lord Danvek! That was it! Lord Danvek—Dynolvan ambassador to Watchaven.

CHAPTER FIVE

"Thank you, Hadley. You may leave now." Lord Aldwin sampled the appetizers his butler had brought to the library.

"You know," Valdir suggested, "you would have better luck with your hawks if you varied their diet." He nervously brushed his long, brown curls from his eyes and assaulted the appetizers. Lord Valdir's sharp, birdlike features matched his eating style, as he picked and plucked the appetizers from the tray.

Aldwin waved a hand. "I have heard varying opinions."

The butler closed the door behind him.

"Well, now that that is out of the way," Ellenwood proposed, "shall we get back to more pressing business?" Sir Ellenwood was older than either Aldwin or Valdir and more conservative in dress and manner. His straight black hair was short for a nobleman, barely touching his collar. His dark eyes were serious, his rare smiles humorless.

"Yes," Aldwin agreed. "As I was saying, Helgorn merchants

are already in the city, spreading their lies. I tell you, every kingdom in the Confederacy will be ruled by the merchants if we don't stop it now!"

"That is why we are here," Ellenwood replied. "Once the Droken control the northern kingdoms, the other kings will see that only by joining with us can they save their own kingdoms from the fate that has befallen Helgorn."

"Surely you don't think that, Sir Ellenwood?" Valdir asked.

Aldwin glanced toward the ceiling as Ellenwood took a sip of his drink. Ellenwood set his drink down, stood up, and began pacing slowly.

"Dear Lord Valdir," Ellenwood began, "you must try to understand what we are about and why, for your own good. We must not fall as Helgorn has fallen! As you know, Helgorn was once a monarchy, as the rest of the Great Cities are. But the merchants slowly gained more and more power—and power is the same as money—until they overthrew the king. They let the king live, but only because he signed that damnable charter that abolished the nobility in his kingdom and, in its place, established the Council of Merchants.

"Now, if we do not keep tight control over the merchants in our own kingdom, the same will happen to us," Ellenwood proclaimed, stopping and staring hard at Valdir. Valdir swallowed and nodded.

"On top of the problem of the merchants, we have our own Droken agenda. As you know, our poor people who have had to live outside the Confederacy in distant Cuthaun live most pitifully due to the weak soil, not to mention the hideous weather. Additionally we would, of course, like to be able to stand up, without fear, and proclaim our love for the Dark Father. But how can we do this? We certainly cannot do it as long as the Faithful have control of the kingdoms, can we?"

"Of course not," Valdir replied.

"And so, the first step to gaining our own freedom is to take control of the northern kingdoms—both to give our people a safe place to come and live, and to have strongholds from which we can launch our blessed war against the other kingdoms.

And *this*, Lord Valdir, is where the merchants come back into play."

Valdir looked puzzled.

"You see, Valdir," Ellenwood continued, "the best way for us to accomplish both goals—that of saving our kingdom from the merchants and taking it for ourselves—is for us to stir up the trade issue between Watchaven and Dynolva until the two kingdoms go to war. This is the perfect solution for us.

"First, it keeps the merchants busy worrying about other merchants and too busy to think about taking over our kingdom. Second, it makes the merchants look very, very bad. The citizens are already complaining about the high cost of good tea, wine, and drink, and they are blaming everyone for the problem—the merchants, the nobility, and the king. But the merchants see it as more than a mere inconvenience. They *will* push us into war if they feel that it is hitting their purses, and hitting them hard! And let us imagine that it does lead to war. . . .

"The populace will be further set against our current leaders, who have obviously been ineffective in controlling the situation and the merchants. If, at that crucial point, the Droken move in, stop the war, and we set up our own, more efficient structure, the populace will be grateful to us. So grateful, in fact, that the Faithful will have lost control. So grateful, that we should be able to maintain our hold without having to kill the bulk of the populace. In their eyes, we will be heroes. *Now* do you understand?"

"That's why we are stirring up the merchants!" Valdir replied with new understanding.

Aldwin suppressed a groan. "I was about to say," he began, attempting to reclaim control over the meeting, "the high priest is very pleased with how things have gone so far. He even remarked that things appear to be on schedule."

"Well, I suppose that is good," Valdir remarked, sighing. "I still wish they would let us know a little more about who is helping us. I was so afraid that we would not be able to secure the backing we needed in Dynolva. Have they told you who from

Dynolva has joined us in this? My curiosity has been driving me mad."

"No, they have not said," Aldwin admitted.

"They will tell us when it is safe to do so," Ellenwood replied.

"Nonetheless," Aldwin interjected, "things apparently are on schedule and that can only be good. Now, we have already covered the agenda for the next Trade Council meeting. Are there any questions on how we are voting? Good. As I mentioned before, we must be prepared for the onslaught of questions this will bring from the merchants. Thus far, they have seen us as acting in their best interests. We are simply responding to the 'unrealistic demands the corryn are placing upon us,' as Lord Orrick so aptly stated at the last meeting."

"Yes," Valdir smugly agreed, "he has been one of our strongest allies, hasn't he? He would absolutely die if he knew he was supporting the Droken."

"True. However, as I was saying about the merchants, we must be prepared for anything," Aldwin repeated. "They are near the breaking point and will be very upset. The Helgorn merchants will undoubtedly stir them further, to their benefit. We must make certain they continue to see the Trade Council as working in their interests. The nobility have taken it all rather well, considering it will also hit their purses."

"We can be thankful Dynolva is a corryn kingdom," Valdir added. "Our nobles would not be so cooperative if it were the throat of another human kingdom we were cutting."

"You are probably quite correct," Ellenwood agreed. "Well, are we finished then? I must be leaving."

"What?" Valdir asked. "Are you not interested in hearing about Lord Aldwin's burglar? I could not wait for us to finish with business so he could tell us about it!"

"In point of fact," Aldwin replied, "we are not quite done with business. It seems that a little information has come from, shall we say, higher up, concerning my burglar. I now know that he is both an orphan and a member of Watchaven's Northmarch."

Valdir and Ellenwood exchanged startled glances.

"You do not know his name?" Ellenwood asked.

"Not yet. There is one more bit of information I have been given, however, that should help us locate the fellow—he is corryn."

"Are you serious?" Valdir asked. "Gods, how do they find these things out? That is incredible!"

"Yes, one wonders . . ." Ellenwood agreed.

"Yes. Well, we all know how effective the Droken are—after all, look at us," Aldwin replied, chuckling.

"Quite," Valdir agreed.

"Of course, you must pass this information to your own cells and have it passed down the rest of the chain. By the time it has reached the bottom, surely someone will be able to give us a name."

"Absolutely!" Valdir replied. "My own cell will be meeting quite soon. Shall we place a bet as to which of us can supply Aldwin with the name of his burglar first, Ellenwood?"

Ellenwood smiled. "I suppose I should take you up on this, Lord Valdir, but you know I do not gamble."

"Ah well, I thought I might convince you, knowing how confident you are of your chain's abilities."

* * * * *

A block away, the "burglar" in question waited impatiently for Ellenwood's coach to leave Aldwin's estate. In the distance, Grandhaven Sanctorium chimed the half hour.

"That'll be another korun, mate," the hack said.

"Okay, okay," Morticai replied.

He sat beside the hackman on the driver's seat of a rented coach. Grudgingly, he gave the hackman another korun. Ellenwood had best hurry—this was expensive!

Following the Droken noblemen had become increasingly difficult. Aldwin and Valdir tended to frequent the same places, which made guessing their stops easy, but they also seemed to do nothing of interest. Ellenwood and Danvek were much more interesting to follow but were extremely random in both their haunts and their transportation.

Morticai had toyed with the idea of following Ellenwood on his patrol horse, until he realized how obvious a lone horseman would be. Sir Dualas had suggested hiring the coach. Perhaps Dualas should come along and pay for it!

"Dyluth!"

Morticai jumped and checked his left hand, which was halfway to his dagger.

"Blessed Benek, what was that!" the hackman exclaimed.

Morticai peered over the edge of the coach. The ground—in fact, the entire alley—looked deserted.

"It's a friend of mine," Morticai said softly. "I'll be right back." He quietly lowered himself to the ground.

"Tagger?" he whispered. He had recognized the boy's voice and knew where he had to be. A moment later the urchin's shaggy mop of hair appeared from under the coach, followed by a dirty, but grinning face.

"Did I scare the old geezer?" Tagger whispered.

"I think so," Morticai replied. "But if you'd clean your ears out, you'd realize you're whispering too loudly."

"Aw, Dyluth."

"Aw, nothin'." Morticai sat down. "So, what'cha need?"

The boy crawled over and sat beside him. "Well, I was jus' wonderin' what was goin' on. You've been runnin' all over town after those frilly shirts."

Morticai's eyes narrowed. "You've been followin' me?"

Tagger's eyes widened in innocence. "Nah. I-I mean, not till t'night."

Morticai smiled slyly. "And what about the others?"

"What others?"

"C'mon, Tagger," Morticai said threateningly. "You know exactly what I mean."

Tagger chewed on his lower lip. "After I told 'em what happened, some of 'em have been keepin' an eye on ya."

"Who?"

Tagger shrugged. "Slip, Tubby, Nailer, Boskens. A few others, maybe."

Morticai released a heavy sigh. "Tagger, you've gotta stop followin' me."

"But y'might get hurt!"

"I'm a lot more apt to get hurt if I've gotta keep an eye out for you and your friends!"

"Then it *is* dangerous!"

Morticai smiled. "You're just afraid you won't have me around for an easy meal."

Tagger looked hurt. "That's not true."

"I know," Morticai replied, still smiling. He became serious. "Look, Tagger, I know that y'mean well. But, well, this could be dangerous, possibly very dangerous. I can take care of myself pretty well, but it could be a problem if I have to defend myself and you or one of the others."

"Yer not gonna tell me what yer doin', are ya?"

"No, I'm not. Let's just say . . . this is special Northmarch business and I could get in trouble if I told you 'bout it," he lied.

"All right . . ." Tagger replied, sullenly.

"And you'll tell the others to stop following me?"

"Yeah, I'll tell 'em."

"And if they keep followin' me, I'll round up the whole bunch of you an' take you to the orphanage."

Tagger's eyes filled with fear. "You wouldn't!"

"Of course not. But if y'keep followin' me, I may think about it. Understood?"

"Yeah."

"Here." Morticai dug into his boot pocket and pulled out a korun. "You fetch the others that've been followin' me an' go buy some food." He shook his finger at Tagger. "And if I hear that you didn't . . ."

"I know," Tagger replied.

"One more thing, Tagger." Tagger, who'd already started getting up, sighed and sat back down. "Do y'know what they call me in the Northmarch?"

"Yeah. Uh, Morticai, isn't it?"

"That's right. Please, when you see me with strangers, use that name instead of Dyluth, all right?"

Tagger looked confused. "They don't know you're Dyluth?"

"Some of them do. But some of them don't, and I'd just as soon keep it that way."

Tagger nodded knowingly. "All right. An' I'll tell that t' the others, too."

"Good. Now, off with ya."

Tagger grinned and ran down the alley. Shaking his head, Morticai climbed back onto the coach. The hackman eyed him suspiciously.

"Anythin'?" Morticai asked.

The hackman shook his head. "Not yet, mate."

* * * * *

A few minutes later, Ellenwood's coach emerged from Aldwin's estate and traveled the few blocks to Dynolva Way. As the coach turned east onto the main thoroughfare, Morticai's hired coach pulled out of the alley. Coach traffic was light, but sufficient to keep Morticai's hired coach from being obvious. They stayed at a comfortable distance, following the glow of the lamps on Ellenwood's simple, but elegant, coach.

"I think he's goin' t' the docks, mate."

"Then I guess we will too," Morticai replied.

The hack threw him another suspicious glance and continued driving without further conversation. Morticai hoped the hack would keep his tongue quiet after tonight. Of course, the royal Morticai had in his pocket should help. The coach turned northwest onto Shipwright's Road.

"Ah . . . mate," the hack began. "Y'didn' say anythin' 'bout us travelin' t' the nor'east side o' town. Y'know, many a man has died up that way."

"Well," Morticai said, pulling out the royal, "would this make it worth the risk?"

The hack looked at Morticai in surprise. "You're a mite bit serious 'bout this, aren't ya?"

" 'Fraid so."

"This mus' be pretty important, eh?"

"Is to me."

"A'right, mate. You're on."

They had just reached the turn. As they made it, Ellenwood's coach turned off the main road.

"Did you see him? He turned north!" Morticai said.

"Wha'? Where? I was busy with m' team."

"Slow down. I think it was—here. This is it! See him?"

"Aye. Let's take it easy here." The hack slowed his team to a lazy walk and turned to Morticai. "If you're truly serious, mate, I sugges' y'blow out our lamps." He gestured to their own burning coach lamps. "Can ya get 'em while we're moving?"

Morticai smiled in answer and scrambled over the topside of the coach. He returned quickly, and the hack picked up speed down the darkened street.

"Didn' think you'd find that a problem," the hack said. "We'll still need t' be careful, though, or he'll hear us."

"We shouldn't need to get that close. As long as we're careful so we can see when he stops."

"You're the one with the corryn eyes, mate. That'll be yer job." After a couple of miles, the hack pulled his team to a halt. "Y'see where he's headin'?"

Morticai sighed. He could see very well where Ellenwood was heading—straight for the Snake Pit. This was the third time Ellenwood had led him toward this section of the city. The infamous section of town had once been the palace district. Centuries ago the palace relocated after a hurricane ravaged the area; the shipping companies built warehouses—and then abandoned them when the south docks opened; and then the poor moved in and rebuilt the area countless times as the generations passed. Now even the poor did not want to live in its snaking alleys and narrow streets. The Watch rarely entered it—even by daylight.

Morticai dug along the top of his boot and produced another royal.

"Would this be enough?"

The hack considered it. "Y'know m'coach can't travel those narrow streets—if I was crazy 'nough t' want t' travel 'em."

"I'm not asking you to—his coach can't either."

"Right, mate." The hack cautiously accepted the coin and continued on. Finally Ellenwood's coach stopped.

"What now, mate?"

Morticai sighed. "Well, I guess we part company."

"Are you daft, man? Y'don't really want me t' let y'off here, do ya?"

"Well, actually I'd like you to wait. But I don't think I have enough left in my purse to make it worth your while."

The hack strained to look at him in the darkness. "Y'seem like a nice 'nough chap, for a corryn. Can't figure what you're doin' followin' this noble. Course, I can't figure what a nobleman's doin' on this side o' town. Tell y'what . . . I'll wait for ya—but not too long. If I think trouble is headed m' way, I'll leave. But, if things stay quiet like they are now, I'll stay as long as I can. Can ya handle that thing?" He pointed to Morticai's rapier.

"Had plenty of practice."

"Somehow that doesn' surprise me. Don't forget how."

Morticai grinned and quickly climbed to the ground. "Thanks." He grabbed his old cloak from inside the coach and raced toward Ellenwood's coach.

Two blocks from his quarry's coach Morticai turned into an alley, took the first right, and then cut back to the street the coaches had parked on. As he'd expected, Ellenwood had disembarked from his coach and was now on foot and wearing his tatty cloak.

Morticai cautiously followed. A scrawny cat purred beside him briefly before deciding the stranger had no food to offer. Farther on, a rat—nearly as large as the cat—sauntered leisurely out of his path. As a boy, Morticai had made a game of using such rats for knife practice. More than a few had run off with his knives. Morticai and Ellenwood traveled another block north before the noble turned left.

"Pssst."

Morticai jumped and swung leftward, dagger ready, hand to his sword.

"Gettin' jumpy in your old age, Dyluth?" The words were corryn.

Morticai relaxed.

"That's a good way to get cut, Calsen," he replied, also in corryn.

The corryn standing in the doorway laughed softly. To a human, only a shadowy form would have been visible standing in the darkness, but Morticai's eyes could still make out most of Calsen's features. Calsen's shoulder-length black hair was pulled back, and his corryn ears were effectively hidden by the shadow cast by his tattered, large-brimmed black hat.

"Come on," Morticai said as he resheathed his dagger and ran down the street to catch Ellenwood. Calsen followed as another cat dashed madly out of their way.

"What'cha doin' here? I haven't seen you on this side of town in years."

"I'm following someone."

"No wonder you're in a hurry. Anyone I know?"

"I doubt it. He's a nobleman."

"What? Here?"

"Yep."

"Good gods, is he insane?"

"Shhh! There he is—slow down."

Ellenwood had already passed several side alleys, but continued to follow the main alley as it bent rightward. A figure ducked back into a nearby doorway and was gone by the time the two corryn passed the same door.

"I followed him to the Cobblesend one night," Morticai continued. "He doesn't seem to have any problems. Have you seen him before?"

"No. He ought to change his shoes."

Morticai laughed. "You're not the first to make that observation."

"No one bothers him? That's odd. He certainly seems to know where he's going."

"So I notice."

Ellenwood had turned off into a side passage and now negotiated a series of jogs in the tangled web of alleys.

"Someone hire you to follow him?"

"Yeah, his last mistress," Morticai lied.

"Good money in that?"

"You'd have to ask her."

"Nice t'see you haven't changed," Calsen replied, chuckling. "You still in the Northmarch?"

"Yeah, how about you?"

"Oh, a little of this, a little of that. I've been workin' the docks kinda regular here of late."

"Really? That's good to hear."

"You still tryin' to talk all your old friends into honest jobs, uh?"

"No, I gave up. Of course, a lot of them have died."

The faint sound of singing drifted toward them, but the echoes from the old stone walls made it impossible to tell where it came from. The cobblestones became scarce, as the crumbling pavement quickly turned into dirt.

"Yeah, I know," Calsen admitted. "That's why I'm workin' the docks now. It's safer. How come you never come around anymore?"

"Most of the time the Northmarch has me. I get off three days out of ten. As you've mentioned, this isn't the safest side of town. After seven days of duty, I'd rather have three days when I don't have to worry about whether my sword is in reach."

"Like now," Calsen said with a smirk. "You ever see Heather?"

"Oh yeah, she still gets me invitations to some of the better parties."

"She still Lord Ullock's mistress?"

"No, she's with Lord Jendall now."

Calsen studied Morticai closely. "That's too bad. I always thought, y'know, you'n her would maybe get matched."

Morticai shrugged. His long-running on-again, off-again affair with the silver-tressed corryn courtesan had become an item of common gossip among all of his old companions. Long ago he'd tired of his friends' meddling attempts to keep them together.

"I don't know that we were ever meant to match," he answered slowly. "It's true that in some ways we match, but in those ways we're almost too much alike. And in other ways, we're too different. Besides, all that matching stuff is for the upper class and merchants—I don't know that it means anything for us."

They lapsed into silence then, as Ellenwood turned yet another corner. Despite the lengthy walk, they were still within a couple of miles of his coach. They turned the corner. Ellenwood had vanished. The two corryn quickly moved back to back. Calsen had produced two long, narrow knives, while Morticai held both his sword and dagger.

"He wasn't that far from us," Calsen whispered.

"I know. He could have seen us."

"I don't think so. We both kept to the shadows."

"Talked too much."

"Maybe, but I don't think so. Backtrack, or go forward?"

"Let's go forward."

Morticai carefully moved forward; Calsen stayed at his back. They turned the corner to once again face the deserted alley. There were no doorways Ellenwood might have entered. As they edged down the alley, Morticai chided himself for letting himself be drawn into idle chatter with Calsen. Maybe Coryden was right; maybe he would get himself killed this time—the Gods knew, he'd deserve it if he kept making mistakes like this. They reached the next intersection. There was no sign of Ellenwood—nor anyone else for that matter.

Morticai lowered his sword. "Well, that's that! Damn! This is the second time in three days I've lost him!"

"Hidden door?"

"Back there? I wouldn't think so—would you?"

"I don't know. They're gettin' better at it."

The two corryn went back and began checking the alley's walls for inconsistencies.

"You know how dumb we must look?" Morticai observed.

"Who cares?"

"I had a coach waiting for me outside the Pit. He's probably gone by now."

"Hoy! Travelin' in style now, aren't we?"

"Yeah, and costing a fortune! I hired it to keep up with the noble's coach."

"Dyluth." Calsen stopped and lowered his voice, despite the fact that they were still speaking in corryn.

"Yeah?"

"What's this about? You wouldn't waste your time followin' a nobleman for an ex-mistress."

Morticai sighed and turned to his old friend. "Dangerous stuff, I'm afraid. I've found a Droken cell."

"Good gods, Dyluth! And you think I'm crazy to keep livin' in the Pit?"

"Look, Calsen, have you seen anything suspicious here lately—anything at all?"

Calsen pondered Morticai's question for some time before answering. "Well, since you're talkin' Droken, I can think of one rumor I've heard that might fit their style. Remember the old Burnaby Manor?"

"How could I ever forget? Gods, we had some good times there!"

"Yeah, we did, didn't we?" Calsen replied, chuckling. "Well, if you remember, it's just a few blocks from here. There's been some rumors lately that it's haunted."

"Oh, come on, Calsen! We both know what that means. Some thief or gang has decided to use it as a cache."

"Yeah, I know. But there's been some odd things goin' on there. I haven't heard that much, myself. You ever talk to Fenton, the spice merchant?"

"I know him, but it's been a few years since I've seen him."

"I've heard that Fenton knows somethin' about what's goin' on at the manor," Calsen continued, "but I haven't bothered to talk with him about it."

"Hmm. I may have to arrange a meeting with Fenton. Does he still work out of the Lower Bazaar?"

"Last I heard."

"Well, it's obvious I'm going to have to try something other than this." Morticai gestured to the deserted alley.

"I'm sorry to hear you're doin' this type of work, Dyluth. There's not much future in it, y'know."

"I know. Well, I guess I'd better get back to my coach, if it's still waiting. If the other coach is still there maybe I can pick up the trail again."

"You want me to walk back with you?"

"Don't be silly. I haven't forgotten how to walk these alleys. Besides, it seems pretty quiet tonight."

"Yeah, sometimes it is. Well, take care, Dyluth."

* * * * *

They parted company, and Morticai began backtracking his way to the coach. Despite his disappointment at losing Ellenwood, he found his thoughts drifting back to his conversation with Calsen. It pleased him to know that his friend was still alive—it had been too long since he'd lifted a mug with his old crony.

He found it puzzling that Calsen still lived in the Pit. If he was working the docks, he should be making pretty fair wages—unless he wasn't working regularly. He could see that in Calsen.

A low whistle interrupted his thoughts. He spun to see four rough-looking young men eyeing him from the opposite end of the block. The human group exchanged glances among themselves.

"Hey!" the tallest one shouted at him. "Corryn!"

The corryn thief took a cautious step backward and found himself regretting he'd not accepted Calsen's offer to walk him back to his coach. With a quick flash, the gang's knives came out; no one wasted time with talk. Everyone here was prey, even Arluthians. Morticai drew his sword and dagger, spun, and ran in the other direction; the four men gave chase, as he knew they would.

The former urchin took the next turn, hoping he still remembered the area. One of the four whistled now in odd, interrupted bursts. Years ago Morticai would have understood the calls, but too much time had passed. He knew they were calling for the rest of their gang, informing them that they were in pursuit.

The alley turned and ended at another, running crosswise. Morticai heard the rushing footsteps coming from the right before he entered the turn. His right hand flew upward, his dagger's crossguard blocking a downward knife thrust; he immediately followed with his sword, thrusting it easily into his unarmored opponent.

Using the sword as an anchor, Morticai spun to the right, placing his back to the wall before withdrawing his sword from the chest of the gang member. The would-be attacker crumpled. Behind the human, two more toughs began yelling as they tried to pull the dead man's form out of their way.

Morticai was already running. He was glad that knives were still the popular weapon here—his sword would help even the odds. He passed the next side alley and fifteen feet later regretted it—his alley turned right, but went no farther. The ex-street urchin made it back to the intersection, but now the gang members were close and entered the intersection as he did.

Only two could reach him in the narrow confines. The gang member standing before Morticai's sword tried blocking with his knife. The Northmarcher easily disengaged and thrust his sword through the man's chest and then blocked the left-handed knife thrust of another youth with his dagger.

A knife shot forward, driven by the youth's other hand; abandoning his sword in the dead man's chest, Morticai grabbed the knife hand. The youth's face showed surprise, but he recovered quickly and tried to disengage his other knife from Morticai's dagger. Before the maneuver was complete, Morticai brought his left knee up hard, catching him in his privates; the youth doubled over.

A dagger struck the wall a couple of inches from Morticai's head, thrown by a gang member standing behind the man wearing Morticai's sword. The dead man had been caught by others and was being let to the ground as they tried to shove past.

Morticai grabbed his sword. As he recovered it, he used his right wrist to block the arm of the bent-over youth—and the knife thrust aimed at his stomach. Morticai had spotted the thrust too late; the knife tip raked lightly across his chest.

This one wouldn't give up. Morticai's block had brought the youth's right arm up high; with the arm still blocked, the corryn brought his own dagger back, slashing cleanly through the youth's throat. The Northmarcher left the intersection blocked by the dead and quickly dying.

By the time he made two more turns the remaining gang members were again on his heels. At the third turn he risked a glance behind—he'd killed three; four were still in pursuit. Two turns later the number had dropped to three. Morticai continued on, trying to guess where the missing assailant would reappear. The realization came a few steps before the opening—it was a shortcut he himself had once used. The man leapt toward him only to land on Morticai's ready sword.

Pleased to leave another obstacle in his pursuers' path, Morticai continued on. He heard shouting ahead of him—four more were coming straight on. He took the side alley he'd just reached, and the chase continued.

There was no place to face them and no way to shake them. It had been easier as a child, when there were places he could fit that adults could not. Morticai continued and prayed that the coach was still waiting—by the time he reached it, if he did, he would be too winded to continue running. He thought of looking for a place to make a stand but knew it would mean certain death. Eventually they would bring him down with sheer numbers.

He was within a quarter-mile of his destination when they finally trapped him. He turned a corner to see three more gang members coming from the other direction—these fresh from little running. He spun, back to the wall, and dropped his dagger to toss a throwing knife at those behind him while they were still distant enough for the throw to be valuable.

The thrown knife caught one of them in the stomach—not an instant kill, but enough to slow the others. Morticai ducked to retrieve his dagger as a knife sailed over his own head. It bounced off the wall and elicited curses from the three approaching from the other direction.

The three moved in quickly. Morticai parried a knife thrust with his sword, blocked another with his dagger; he spun to the other side of the alley as he sidestepped a third thrust and brought his sword across an unlucky man's stomach. The rest were nearly upon him. He would have it to his credit that he had killed half of them before he died.

He blocked another thrust and then watched in surprise as the man gasped and crumpled to his knees; his compatriot fell in neat imitation. Behind them, Calsen withdrew his long knives.

"I sure wish you'd kept to the main alleys," Calsen panted. "You were hell to catch."

There was no more time for talk as the others charged. Morticai spun leftward, punching one in the face with his sword's guard, catching another across the face with the blade and barely missing Calsen.

"Be careful with that damn thing!" Calsen shouted over the screams of the man caught by Morticai's blade.

"Sorry."

They turned and ran the opposite direction. At the corner they were met by two more.

"Did you have to take on the Pit's largest gang?"

"Hey, how was I to know?"

They moved back to back and stayed in the intersection where they could both fight. Morticai blocked with his dagger and brought his sword in from the left, catching his first opponent in the side.

Another moved in before the first could fall, and only the crossguard of Morticai's dagger kept the blade from gutting him. Instead, the blade was pushed leftward to slide up Morticai's left arm. Gasping, he brought his sword in, pulling it across the man's side as he kicked the man back into his companions.

"Let's go!" Calsen called.

Calsen had dropped the two facing him, but the blood running down Calsen's side was his own. They ran the last three blocks, turning the corner to see the coach still waiting. The hack had turned the coach around and now looked, open-mouthed, over the top of it. They jumped onto the back. Morticai wrapped an arm around Calsen.

"Get us movin', man!" Morticai shouted, but his words were lost in the sound of tack and hooves.

"Dyluth, why does . . . this kind of thing always happen . . . whenever I see you?" Calsen gasped.

"Just lucky, I guess."

They moved at full speed down the narrow street and did not slow until the coach turned onto Shipwright's Road. The coach quickly sped up again; Morticai feared the hack would drive his team full speed across the entire city without realizing the jarring ride he was giving his passengers.

Calsen slipped in and out of consciousness, and Morticai feared he would not be able to hold him. Finally, the coach slowed as the hack turned onto Mainway. Just after the corner it pulled to a stop. Morticai stepped off but mismanaged Calsen's weight and landed behind the coach with the barely conscious Calsen atop him.

"Mate, are ya a'right?" the hack asked.

". . . Don't know," Morticai gasped.

The hack knelt beside him and stared.

"Look," Morticai continued, "do you know where the Dappled Stallion Inn is?"

"Of course!"

"Then, help me get him inside the coach."

* * * * *

By the time they reached the inn, Morticai had stopped Calsen's bleeding and wrapped his cloak around his own bleeding arm.

"We're here," the hack said, opening the door.

"Good. Look, go ask for Paxton—he's the owner. Tell him that Dyluth needs some assistance and is out in your coach.

Wait." Morticai stopped the hack as he started to leave. "Here."
He pressed his last royal into the hack's hand.

"Mate, y'don' need t' . . ."

"Yes, I do. You don't know how good it felt to see your
coach when I turned that last corner."

For the corryn, the next hour faded from his consciousness.
He felt his body drifting on a great river . . .

"Dyluth? Morticai?"

The voice was Paxton's. Morticai opened his eyes, realizing
he'd drifted off to sleep. The aged owner of the Dappled Stallion sat down and laid a gentle hand on his arm. Morticai's
chest and arm had been cleaned and wrapped and he lay on the
inn's best bed—Paxton's.

"Can you spend the rest of the night here? Or do we need to
get you back to Northgate?"

"Unfortunately, I've got gate duty tomorrow."

"I presume that means we need to get you back."

"Yeah. How's Calsen?"

"He lost a bit of blood, but I think he'll be all right. Is he
a . . . Brother?"

"No. He's suspected me of being an Arluthian for years, but
that's all it is—suspicion. It's almost a joke between us."

"Will he suspect anything when he wakes up?"

"No, I don't think so. He knows I have a lot of friends in
odd places. I hate to admit this, but the last time we got
together I had to board him at an inn for similar reasons."

Paxton shook his head and laughed. "I'm glad I didn't run
with you when I was younger, Morticai. I don't think I'd have
survived it!"

"Hey!"

But Paxton just laughed harder.

* * * * *

Dualas insisted on checking Morticai's wounds. Apparently
satisfied with his condition, the knight rewrapped his arm.
Coryden, surprisingly quiet, sat next to the bed.

"That should do," Dualas said as he finished. "You are fortunate the cut was vertical. If you are careful with it, it should heal in a few days."

"Well, that's good," Coryden replied. "I don't know if I'd have been up to facing Kirwin again." He leveled an exasperated stare at Morticai.

"So, what have you learned while I've been running from street gangs and spending every royal I own on coaches, Dualas?" Morticai asked quickly.

Dualas shook his head. "I have learned quite a bit, but it does not look as though it will help us. I checked the list of decisions made by both the Watchaven and Dynolvan Trade Councils. This has apparently been developing since last Light Season. It all looks very innocent. In fact, it looks very much as though the Dynolvans started it. However, all of the damaging decisions that have fueled this affair have been proposed by one of our three Droken."

"I'm worried about Lord Danvek," Morticai observed. "If he's in their camp we've got real problems."

"It would explain some of it, if the Droken were being aided by someone, or several someones, on the Dynolvan side of things," Dualas agreed. "You have not had much to say about any of this, Coryden. Do you still think this is an affair we should not be pursuing?"

Coryden stared thoughtfully at the window.

"No. No, I think it needs to be pursued," he finally replied. "I wouldn't have said that a sennight ago, as you both know. But I'm not blind. I never thought I'd see corryn and humans set so against each other. I helped break up a fight in our own hall last night. If the Droken can set corryn Northmarcher against human Northmarcher, what's to keep them from setting Dynolva against Watchaven?"

"Well, I'm tired of losing nobles where they shouldn't be able to go," Morticai announced. "Calsen said that some odd things have been happening at old Burnaby Manor. I intend to find out what."

"How do you propose to do this?" Dualas asked evenly.

"First, I'm going to set up a meeting with Fenton. Calsen said that he knew more about it. Then I might just pay a visit to the manor."

"What do you think is there, Morticai?" Coryden asked.

"I don't know. When Calsen first mentioned it, I thought he was crazy—he said rumors have been circulating that the manor is haunted. But since then, I just don't know. I keep coming back to it. Something feels strange about it."

"Morticai, do you mean to imply that you feel guided in this?" Dualas asked.

"I dunno, Dualas. Maybe."

CHAPTER SIX

Morticai stood on the battlements and gazed across the city, his thoughts drifting over recent events. He heard the door open behind him but didn't bother to turn around—it was just about time for Evadrel to relieve him.

"Morticai!" Kirwin's voice snapped.

Morticai's heart skipped a beat—he knew that tone. Making certain his movements were casual, he swung to face his commander. Evadrel stood behind Kirwin.

"Yes, sir?" Morticai asked, innocently.

"What have you gotten into?" Kirwin demanded.

Morticai was honestly confused.

"Dammit! Don't give me that damned innocent look of yours! I've got a man from the Inquisition sitting in my office who says they've had 'reports' about you! What the hell have you done to bring the Inquisition here!"

Morticai's mouth dropped; Evadrel's eyes widened.

"I-I," Morticai blinked, swallowed, and tried again. "I don't know, sir."

Kirwin scrutinized him, and gradually his features began to soften.

"You truly do not know?" he asked.

"No, sir."

"You've done nothing at all to break the law of the Faith?"

"No, sir." Morticai's confusion compounded as he quickly thought things over. He'd never done anything to violate their laws.

Kirwin sighed. "Don't ask me why—I probably shouldn't. Morticai—I believe you. But, so help me, Aluntas, if you're lying to me. . . !"

"Wha-What do they say I've done?"

"They won't tell *me*," snorted Kirwin. "They've asked a lot of questions and haven't answered a single one of mine. Their man is waiting in my office with a whole list of people he wants to talk to, starting with you. Come on, let's go see what it is they think you've done."

Evadrel stepped aside for them to leave, his amber eyes full of concern. Once Kirwin started through the door, Morticai turned and quickly shrugged, indicating to Evadrel that he really didn't know what was going on.

Evadrel returned him a sign for luck.

* * * * *

Evadrel was the last to be interviewed. Morticai sat outside Kirwin's office, waiting for permission to leave. Coryden, Dualas, and Berret Heimrik waited with him. Berret, one of the few humans who served in Coryden's patrol, had been the sergeant of Morticai's squad for several years now.

The interviews had lasted ten hours; Morticai had watched his entire squad file through, one at a time. Kirwin had taken over Phillip's office in an attempt recover at least a portion of the day.

News that the Inquisition was at Northgate had spread like

wildfire. The large structure was, at the same time, too quiet and too much abuzz to be normal. Because of the patrol schedules, the news would reach Dynolva in just a few days. Morticai was thankful he did not have to patrol to Dynolva himself—the Levani only knew what the story would be by the time it reached the corryn city.

At last, Evadrel emerged. Some squad members had come out obviously shaken, but most had walked out defiantly—Evadrel smiled reassuringly as he passed them.

The human who had introduced himself as Geradon Kinsey, Faithful from the Inquisition at Abbadyr and aide to Inquisitor Rylan Glaedwin, emerged just behind Evadrel. He was of average height and build, with distinguished features and a closely cropped beard. His hair was dark blond, his eyes a brilliant blue. He was well dressed, looking more like a merchant than an aide to an Inquisitor.

His eyebrows raised as he surveyed the three who had remained to wait with Morticai.

"I should not need to speak with you further . . . today," he said to Morticai. "I understand you have two more days off duty before you are scheduled to patrol again. I do not know yet if we shall allow you to continue patrolling or not—that is a question the Inquisitor will address when he arrives in a few days. In the meantime, be certain that you remain in Watchaven. Good night."

Geradon nodded curtly and walked out, without so much as a word to the others. Morticai visibly slumped in the chair.

Soon they were climbing the stairs to Morticai's room, ignoring the glances they received from those they passed. It was Berret who finally broke the silence.

"I sure wish you had let me in on these things earlier, Morticai."

"I didn't want to involve you, Berret. It's not that I don't trust you. Really."

"I suppose that I should be thankful. I'd still like to hear what the hell is going on, though."

"Yeah, upstairs," Morticai replied despondently.

Berret threw an arm around Morticai's shoulders as they passed through the attic storage rooms.

A buzz of noise filtered toward them as they approached Morticai's door. The four stopped and exchanged knowing glances—Coryden's patrol had apparently gathered in Morticai's room, as was usual when times were troubled. Coryden opened the door.

More than just Coryden's patrol had crowded into the room. Apparently, anyone who considered himself a friend of the patrol had gathered here as well. Coryden addressed them.

"I know you've all got questions, but they'll just have to wait a little longer. I'd like everyone to leave except those who were actually questioned by Brother Kinsey."

The crowd reacted as expected and filed out of the room muttering softly among themselves. Coryden's mouth dropped as he watched a human in the exiting group pass. The man stood almost seven feet tall; even Dualas was staring up at him. He had short, curly hair, dark brown eyes, and tremendous musculature. The man ducked under the doorframe as he left.

"That's Richard, one of the new men who joined last week, sir. He's from Briarwood." One of Coryden's men had stepped up beside him.

"I hope you don't mind that I brought him here," he continued. "He'd like to join our patrol if Alvis decides to move back to Dynolva. I thought it better for him to hear rumors from us than rumors from the rest of Northgate."

Coryden blinked. "Can he fight?" he asked.

"Who cares? Do you want to spar with him?"

"Hmm. I guess we'll see. Gods, he's big."

It was hours later when the squad left for their own quarters, leaving only Coryden and Dualas behind. Morticai sat crossways in an old, large chair, having pulled further and further within himself as the evening had progressed.

Coryden walked to the liquor trunk, retrieved a bottle, and poured glasses for the three of them. He knelt beside Morticai's chair.

"You going to come back to the world?"

Morticai smiled crookedly and took the drink.

"What for?"

"So we can decide what we're going to do."

Dualas pulled up chairs for himself and Coryden.

"So, what do we do now?" Dualas asked softly.

"Well," Morticai began, "I happen to have a meeting scheduled with Fenton tomorrow, and if you gentlemen are willing to accompany me, we might just gain some useful information."

Both Dualas and Coryden stared at him in surprise.

"What's wrong?"

"You're going to continue? After today, you're going to meet with Fenton?" Coryden asked.

Morticai threw his hands up in the air. "Why not? What else can happen—the Inquisition show up? They already have!"

* * * * *

The Hilltop Tavern was crowded with patrons, both local and foreign, enjoying the music and food the famous tavern offered. Geradon Kinsey moved through the crowd, barely avoiding being caught up in a circle-dance. These Watchaveners certainly seemed to enjoy enjoying themselves.

The mood was quieter on the back side of the **L**-shaped tavern, where the private booths were located. Moving to the far back booth, he knocked lightly before opening the door. A man in his early thirties smiled up at him. His straight hair was dark brown, his eyes a warm hazel. The smile looked comfortable, as though it were worn often.

The table was already set with food, though the dishes were covered. Geradon sat down as the man lit a candle. The white candle was ringed with narrow gold bands—one band every inch—and stood in an ornate candlestick in the center of the table. As the candle burst into flame the noise outside the booth died. It was as though the tavern itself had ceased to exist.

"We do not have to worry about our neighbors?" Geradon asked, gesturing to the booth behind them. He lifted a dish cover and began serving himself.

"No, I have already paid the bartender to make certain we are left alone and no one allowed back this far."

Geradon gestured to the food. "Have you eaten, Rylan?"

"Yes," the Inquisitor replied. "Well," he asked eagerly, "how did it go?"

Geradon leaned back in the booth and sighed loudly. "It looks like it's going to be interesting, I'll grant that. . . ."

* * * * *

"So his hatred of the Droken is not well known?" Rylan asked, setting Morticai's Northmarch file down on the table.

"Not known at all," Geradon replied as he placed his now empty plate to the side. "And once I learned he had grown up in the streets, a few things did fall into place—it explained his cocky attitude."

"Yes," Rylan agreed with a knowing smile, "never show weakness in front of your enemies."

"Precisely. I am very sorry to say that he reminds me of that vagabond we dealt with last month in Tradelenor."

Rylan's brow furrowed. "How?"

"My fear is that he will get himself killed before we can track down Aldwin's superiors. I tried to convince him of the danger in what he is doing, but danger is too much a part of his life in the Northmarch. I really doubt my little speech had any impact. How about you? What did you learn?"

"Well, he has rubbed against the Watch a few times but has never actually been jailed. It seems that Captain Coryden has intervened when needed."

"What kind of trouble?"

"Primarily problems resulting from women and gambling—fits very nicely with what you heard. Lord Ullock tried to jail him concerning a lady, but the charges were dropped. He has fought a few duels. When he was a child he was caught several times picking pockets and stealing food. He was sent to the orphanage but apparently ran away before he ever reached its doors."

Geradon shook his head. "Can it be this straightforward? Is this a simple case of revenge?"

"It may be just that. Did you find out how he came to suspect Aldwin?"

"Yes, Dualas told me. Apparently he just stumbled onto it. He found a coded note at a party and watched two noblemen." Geradon pulled out his notes; "Sir Ellenwood and Lord Valdir . . ."

"Those are the two Sir Dualas reported to the Grand Patriarch," Rylan interjected.

Geradon nodded. ". . . retrieve the note, copy it, and return it to where it was hidden. Morticai decided to retrieve the note at the end of the evening, but it was gone. So, listen to this: because he was curious about it, he broke into Valdir's estate while Valdir was out of town and supposedly found Droken robes in his closet."

Rylan shook his head. "Unfortunately, I would be inclined to believe his claims about the Droken robes. I looked over some of the recent Trade Council records today. The three noblemen in question are certainly up to something, and it does not look good for king or country. Did you stir up the Northmarch appropriately?"

"Oh, yes. Any Droken spies in the Northmarch are certainly aware that the Inquisition has arrived and should think we suspect this Morticai of being Droken."

"Did you notice any friction between the corryn and humans in the Northmarch?"

"No. Do you think the situation is that volatile?"

"It is quickly getting that way, I am afraid. Not much blood has spilled yet, but the Watch's reports do show an increase in fistfights and the like between humans and corryn. I suspect it would be worse, except that many from Dynolva and Menelcar are deciding this is a good time to travel home to visit friends and relatives. Apparently the Watchaveners, in Dynolva at least, are doing the same. Our innkeeper told me this morning that the amount of business we are seeing here is very unusual; he said it is almost as though Dark Season had not ended."

"Hmm. That is not good to hear. The kingdoms are polarizing."

"Yes, although so far, Menelcar has managed to stay out of it. And all of this is because of manipulation of the Trade Council."

Geradon shook his head. "It is truly frightening. I might have expected something like this between Tradelenor and Lorredre, but here? What about the monarchs? The Trade Council cannot pass any new regulations or tariffs without their approval, can they?"

"You are right, the monarchs in both kingdoms must approve the actions of their councils. But the nobility hold so little power that the nobles would consider it a dire threat if the monarch interfered. And I believe the monarchs are aware of that. In any event, the manipulation is occurring on such a subtle level that I doubt they have any quarrels with how their councils are proceeding."

"What of the Confederacy? Is there any talk of involving the Great Council?"

"Not yet. The Great Council will stay out of it if at all possible. Dynolva and Watchaven have been stable for so long, I believe they think this is nothing more than a minor trade squabble. Thanks to Locguard, these frontier kingdoms have a reputation for a lot of shield-thumping.

"Unfortunately," Rylan continued, "that has never applied to these two kingdoms, but I doubt that any on the Great Council, particularly the southern kings, realize that they are any different from Locguard. And of course, the Great Council will not meet until the Day of Aluntas, so who can say what will happen between now and then?"

"How can we stop it?" Geradon asked.

"The question is not how can we stop it, but how can we prove it? There is the problem. How is Richard doing?"

"He joined the Northmarch about a week ago and has taken up with one of Morticai's squad members. He is trying to stay as close as possible. The problem is that Morticai does not bunk with the rest of his squad."

"What? Why not?"

"I never really found out why, but Morticai sleeps in the attic."

Rylan laughed. "Why not? You were right; it looks like it is going to be interesting. I just wish it were not so serious."

With that, Rylan blew out their candle. The noise from without instantly resumed.

CHAPTER SEVEN

Prince Luthekar waited impatiently for evening service to end. At last the door opened, and the high priest entered.

"This had best be important," Luthekar snapped.

The high priest stopped, midway to the chair before his desk, and tilted his masked head.

"Do you think I would bother you with something trivial?"

"I have much to tend to, and coming here is awkward. I presume something has developed since our last meeting."

"Yes." The high priest sat down in the chair before his desk—Luthekar already sat in the chair behind it.

"Something about Lord Aldwin I thought you would want to know: he has passed some information down the chains in hopes of learning more about his thief."

"He withheld information?"

"Well, let us say he has not been as honest as he should have been. He apparently recovered a dagger and some rope that the thief left behind. Rather than share that bit of information with us, he went to a local witch named Madam Luvena. He learned from her that the thief is a member of Watchaven's Northmarch, and that the man is a corryn orphan."

"The Northmarch? Indeed, this is troublesome news. This witch needs to be visited again."

"That has already been seen to."

The high priest rose and went to the door that led to the temple. A lovely, dark-eyed woman came into the room. She smoothly slid into the chair before the desk and smiled seductively at Luthekar.

"Cwena?" Luthekar asked, smiling.

"What do you think, my lord? Is this form not pleasant?" She flipped her long hair behind the chair.

"Yes, it is, Cwena. Quite different from your usual form. Does the witch still live?"

"Unfortunately not. I would have liked to have kept this form, but now I can make it last only a few days."

"Do not worry, Cwena. As you gain more experience, you shall find that you can retain the shapes of those on whom you feed for longer periods of time. Eventually, you will be able to recall any of the forms."

Madam Luvena/Cwena smiled again, but now it was a cold, feral smile.

"Were you able to learn more from Madam Luvena as you fed, Cwena?" Luthekar continued.

"Yes, my lord, but only one small thing, I am afraid. The corryn thief was working alone."

"Are you certain? He was not working on behalf of the Northmarch?"

"Yes, I am certain. He was working alone. It was something the witch determined after Lord Aldwin left her. Aldwin had been fearful that the Northmarch was behind it, or so Madam Luvena believed, so she recast the spell, looking for that particular thing."

Luthekar leaned back and laughed a cold laugh.

"Good news, is it not?" the high priest asked.

"Yes, very good news. So the man must truly be a common thief—if Madam Luvena was correct."

"Indeed, 'if,' " the high priest agreed.

"And our man in the Northmarch?"

"Unfortunately, he is out on patrol. He should be returning from Dynolva now and arrive back in Watchaven in three days. As soon as he arrives I shall set him to discover the name of the thief."

"Excellent. We have fought far too hard to reach this stage. It has taken too long to convince the nobility to fight against the yoke that the Faith has placed upon them. I shall not tolerate even a small blemish on this campaign."

"However, this still leaves us the problem of Lord Aldwin. Should we deal with him now?"

Luthekar waved a hand. "Let it wait. The man has been barely competent through this whole affair. It will be a pleasure to see him die, but it can easily wait. Before long, the Trade Council will cease to be important—Watchaven and Dynolva will be at war."

* * * * *

Morticai tried to hail the serving girl. She moved back to the bar, oblivious to his signaling. Morticai sighed.

"This is ridiculous! How do you ever get served here, Dualas?"

Dualas raised his eyebrows in surprise. "I have never had any difficulty. But, of course, I do not normally come this time of day."

Coryden tapped his glass impatiently. "I don't understand why you had to wait until now to eat, Morticai. You should have eaten in the mess hall, long before we came here."

"Are you kidding? I walked in there this morning for breakfast. You'd have thought I was Glawres himself! Everyone stopped eating so they could stare. At least here I'm not being treated as though I'm a condemned man."

"No, here you're just being ignored," Coryden observed.

Dualas raised his hand. Immediately the serving girl rushed over to their table, smiling sweetly.

"Can I get somethin' for you, Sir Dualas?" she asked.

Morticai rolled his eyes and rested his chin in his hand.

"My friend here," Dualas said, indicating Morticai, "would like some of that delicious chowder your sister makes."

Morticai straightened, but the girl rushed off.

"What do you mean, chowder? I hate chowder, Dualas!"

"But that's what the Foaming Tankard is famous for, Morticai. Besides, how can you live in Watchaven if you don't like fish?"

Morticai sighed in exasperation.

"So what is it we're supposed to do?" Coryden asked, interrupting their banter.

"Huh? When?" Morticai asked.

"At Fenton's! Why do you want us to go with you?"

"Oh. Uh, well, Fenton, as I said, is a merchant—a, uh, low-class merchant—and he doesn't have the best sort of customers." Coryden and Dualas were looking at him suspiciously. "Anyway," Morticai continued, "I thought that with all this Inquisition business it might be nice if the two of you came along. You could, y'know, keep an eye out for anything suspicious."

Coryden and Dualas exchanged glances.

"Morticai," Coryden began, "there's nothing wrong with coming out and saying that you don't trust the man, y'know?"

"Well, it's not that I don't trust him."

"Uh huh," Coryden said, unconvinced.

"When are we supposed to meet him?" Dualas asked.

"At six o'clock."

"Morticai," Coryden complained, "it's almost six now! If we're going to make it, we need to get moving."

"But I haven't eaten," Morticai complained.

The clock at Grandhaven Sanctorium struck the quarter hour, punctuating his comment.

"See?" Coryden continued. "We've only got fifteen minutes. Come on!" With that, Coryden rose from the table.

Dualas rose also and threw enough money on the table to

cover the cost of the chowder. Grudgingly, Morticai rose and followed his two friends.

* * * * *

Fenton's shop lay at the far end of one of the twisting underground tunnels that comprised Watchaven's Lower Bazaar. Centuries ago the merchants discovered that shops built underground were easier to heat; thus, they could enjoy a healthy business even during Dark Season. The Lower Bazaar was born. During Light Season, however, it was less expensive to operate out of aboveground shops, which did not require lamps; consequently, most merchants had shops both below and above ground and opened their Lower Bazaar shops only during Dark Season. Now the tunnels were largely deserted, and light came from only a few widely scattered shops.

"I can see why you wanted us to come along. How much farther is it?" Coryden whispered, as though the quiet tunnels would have protested any louder volume.

"We're almost there," Morticai replied. "I think it's at the end of this tunnel."

"Don't you know for sure?" Coryden asked.

"Well, it's been a long time since I've seen him. But I'm almost positive this is the right tunnel."

Coryden shook his head, wondering why he let himself get dragged into these things.

Soon, dim lamplight was seen emanating from a far doorway. Morticai held up his hand for them to stop.

"Okay. I think the best way to do it would be for Dualas to come with me, and you"—he indicated Coryden—"to wait out here."

"Yes, sir!" Coryden replied.

"Oh, Coryden," Morticai complained, "you know I don't mean anything. Besides, we're not on patrol."

Coryden smiled and nodded, knowing that he'd made his point.

"We shouldn't be too long," Morticai continued, handing their lantern to Coryden.

* * * * *

"No matter what happens," Morticai whispered to Dualas as they approached the door, "let me do the talking. Fenton is a little strange."

Dualas would have liked to ask how Fenton was strange, but Morticai had already gone through the door. He followed, as a cord attached to a metal wind chime announced their entrance into the small shop.

Worn tapestries and strung shells adorned the upper walls. Below them, every section of available wall space was lined with narrow shelves holding row upon row of small jars. Dualas moved closer to look at the jars. Herbs.

A short, fat, balding man had come through a back doorway smiling broadly. His arms were outstretched.

"Friend Dyluth," he greeted, "it has been far too long since you have honored me with your presence in my humble abode!"

Dualas realized that it was Morticai the man was referring to, as they grasped arms in greeting.

"And who is your friend?" the man said in a tone much less friendly.

"Fenton, I'd like you to meet Dualas. Dualas is a man I would trust with all that I have," Morticai said with a grand gesture toward Dualas.

Dualas thought the formality odd; perhaps this was what Morticai had meant about Fenton. Picking up on the cue, Dualas bowed deeply before the man.

"I am honored to make your acquaintance, dear sir."

It seemed to suffice. With a pleased smile, Fenton gestured to the back doorway.

"I know that Dyluth would not come here without reason." He went to the front door of the shop and locked it. Dualas looked at Morticai to see if the corryn were as alarmed as he that Fenton should be so quick to close their means of exit. Morticai, seemingly unconcerned, was gesturing for him to come along.

The room they entered was even smaller than the shop had

been, although the furnishings were rich. It was styled in the Bracarian tradition—thick carpets, low tables, and a large number of pillows. Newer tapestries hung on the walls, but much of their beauty was lost in the dim lighting. A single lamp sat in the center of a low, round table. Dualas noted the chimney was in desperate need of cleaning. Morticai had moved to where he could watch the doorway, which Dualas suspected was not an accident. He followed suit and sat on the floor beside him. He had never been fond of Bracarian customs and felt awkward sitting on the floor.

Fenton entered and closed the door behind him. The room was stifling; Dualas hoped they would not have to be here long. Fenton moved to a samovar that sat on a nearby table—Dualas had not noticed it before.

"Well, Dyluth," Fenton began, "it has been a long time since we have talked. Are you still in the Northmarch?"

"Yes," Morticai said, chuckling.

"That is funny?" Fenton asked.

"Well, I've seen a few old friends lately, and they all ask me the same thing."

"Ah. I suppose it's because you've never seemed to, how shall I say, belong in the Northmarch. I have never been able to imagine you sitting on a horse in chain armor swinging a sword."

"I'll have to come by sometime in my armor."

"Please, don't. And your friend?" Fenton gestured to Dualas. "Are you also in the Northmarch?"

Luckily, Dualas caught the slight dip of Morticai's head before answering.

"Yes, I am."

It was not a lie, but normally he would have answered that he was a knight of the Faith in service to the Northmarch.

Fenton brought cups to the table nearest them. He was about to pour into Dualas's cup when Morticai quickly placed his hand over it. Fenton stopped and looked sharply at Morticai.

"What's this?" Fenton asked.

"I am afraid that my friend Dualas will not be drinking with us," Morticai explained.

Fenton gave Dualas a suspicious stare.

"Why?"

"Because he is a knight of the Faith."

One would have thought Morticai had told Fenton it was Droka himself sitting on his floor. Fenton jumped back and seemingly from nowhere produced a knife, which he held in his free hand. Dualas could see that the hand was shaking.

Morticai stretched his hands out, palms upward.

"Friend Fenton, I mean you no harm, and neither does my friend Dualas. You know that you do not want to cross blades with me."

"Dyluth, what is this trick? Why would you bring such a person here?" The man was almost in tears.

"I say again, we mean you no harm. Please, put your knife away. You know my skill with the blade."

"I know."

"I shall drink with you."

"You will?"

"Yes."

Slowly, Fenton sheathed the knife. Dualas watched him replace it in the wide sash wrapped around his waist. Fenton poured himself and Morticai cupfuls of what Dualas now suspected was vallemo. Fenton immediately picked up his cup and downed it. He poured himself another, but now waited, watching Morticai. Morticai drank, and then Fenton began to sip from his cup normally.

"Why have you come?" Fenton asked.

"To ask about Burnaby Manor," Morticai replied.

"Who told you to ask me about Burnaby Manor?"

"I will not tell you. It is privileged."

"What do you want to know?"

"What has been going on there? Why was I told that you might know something about it?"

Fenton sipped from his cup and watched Morticai suspiciously. Morticai drained his cup. As though it were a signal, Fenton began to talk.

"The man that used to provide my vallemo used Burnaby

Manor as his home for a long time."

He began pouring Morticai another cup. Dualas glanced at Morticai in alarm. Morticai did not look happy either but returned Dualas an even stare and said nothing. Again Fenton drained his cup, poured himself another, and waited for Morticai to drink. Morticai drank, and the conversation continued.

"One day, I went there to find the door locked, which was not right," Fenton said. "I spoke with some people in the Pit and was told that it was haunted. Of course, I laughed."

Fenton stopped talking and again the ritual with the cups was performed. Dualas noticed that Morticai appeared as he did when he had drunk too much—it took him too long to blink, and he swayed ever so slightly. The knight wondered how far this could go, and when, or if, he should try to intervene. Fenton continued.

"So, I hired some boys from the Pit, good ones, mind you, tough, and told them to investigate the manor for me. They did. And they died."

"They . . . died?" Morticai asked.

"Yes. They were found the next day on the docks. Every one of them. Cut to pieces. Me, I don't need to be told twice—Burnaby Manor is haunted."

Again Fenton poured for them, but this time Morticai did not drink.

"Fenton," he asked, "is that it?"

"That's it. All of it."

"Are you sure?"

Fenton pointed to Morticai's cup. Once again, Morticai drank.

"There is one small thing, but I swear that I'll have you killed if ever it comes back to me."

"And that is?"

"When people whisper about Burnaby Manor at night, they say that it's haunted with Droken."

Morticai nodded, a little too deeply, in reply.

"You have my word, Fenton, that it shall not come back to you."

"Your word has always been good, Dyluth."

Fenton rose. Dualas did likewise, glad to be off the floor, and then had to help Morticai to his feet.

"I would have thought you could hold vallemo better than that, Dyluth," Fenton said, eyeing Morticai.

"Out of practice," Morticai mumbled.

Fenton led them to the front door.

"I am curious why you ask such questions, Dyluth. And I am curious why you feel that you must bring a bodyguard from the Faith with you. But I do not know if I wish to hear the answers."

"You don't."

"So be it."

Fenton unlocked the front door. As they left, Fenton reclosed the door, and locked it behind them. Morticai took a few unsteady steps and then fell against the tunnel's wall for support.

"Oh, Glawres, my head," Morticai muttered.

"You used me, friend 'Dyluth,' " Dualas said acidly. "How long have you been using vallemo?"

"You assume too much, Dualas. I used it first as a child. I have never used much of it, never had to have it, and do not use it now. I bought it from Fenton when Coryden and I were helping Lewis quit using it. As you can see, it wouldn't have helped if he'd had to buy it for himself."

Coryden ran up the tunnel toward them.

"Morticai! What happened? Are you all right?"

"Well, not at the moment. I'll be fine in a bit."

"What happened?" Coryden asked Dualas.

"He drank four cups of vallemo in exchange for information."

"*What?* And you let him?"

"It's not his fault, Coryden," Morticai interrupted. Cautiously, Morticai began moving down the tunnel, using the wall as an anchor. "It was an unusual situation. I thought I could get by with two cups, but it took longer because Fenton was scared. I would be in a lot better shape if someone had let me eat first."

"You knew this would happen?"

"I knew it was a strong possibility."

"Damn!"

Dualas moved to Morticai's side. Morticai gratefully accepted the additional support.

"Oh, quit worryin', Coryden," Morticai continued. "You and I have crawled back to Northgate in worse shape after drinkin'. Besides, wait till you hear what we found out."

* * * * *

The main reception hall of Dynolva Manor filled slowly. The crystal chandeliers did not cast their scintillating light on the exquisite attire of Watchaven's nobility but on the livery of the manor's servants. Many had their spouses and children with them. The group spoke in hushed murmurs, and parents kept a tight rein on the children, but nonetheless, the noise level was steadily climbing.

Lord Danvek stood at the far end of the room on the raised platform that usually held a table laden with appetizers. The table had been moved, and the lord of the manor stood quietly with his hands clasped loosely behind his back as he watched the last of the servants enter. As expected, when the doormen closed the large doors a momentary silence fell across the crowd. It was his cue.

"If I might have your attention," he began. "There has been a great amount of concern among all of you these past few weeks. There have been many questions as to what has, and is, transpiring between Dynolva and Watchaven. It is much to your credit that rumors concerning recent events have been kept to a minimum. Unfortunately, the trade war with Watchaven not only continues but worsens."

A murmur rose and fell among the crowd. As it passed, Lord Danvek continued.

"Because of the deteriorating situation, I have found it necessary to request your presence here this evening. Until this situation resolves itself, I am requesting that all the staff remain at the manor."

Again, the crowd reacted, some with gasps, some with nods of fulfilled expectation.

"I know that this will be difficult. Unfortunately, we all know that humans can be terribly unpredictable. It is my belief that the city is no longer safe. You are welcome and encouraged to bring your families here. Those of you who are currently living in the city have possessions to be concerned with. I am afraid I must ask you to leave your furniture behind, but you are welcome to bring all of your other goods here. We are preparing the stables to provide a place for storage.

"The underground storerooms are empty now that Light Season has come upon us," he continued, pacing the length of the platform. "It shall be up to all of you to help us fill it again. All food that you bring shall be placed in the storerooms. We must be prepared to stay here for a long while—or to leave hurriedly, if need be. We have worked out rooming arrangements, which you will find posted beside the doors." He gestured toward the back wall. "Are there any questions?"

"Lord, are we going to war?"

"We do not know. Not yet. Hopefully, not ever. But, we must be prepared, and I shall not permit any of you to be injured."

"What about supplies other than food?" another asked.

"We shall send special groups out tomorrow to gather what we need, but they will be armed and will number no less than ten. Any other questions?"

The crowd murmured amongst themselves, but no more questions appeared forthcoming.

"Thank you for your service and attendance tonight."

Later that night, Lord Danvek sat in his study, quill in hand.

Your Majesty, I regret to inform you that I have had to require that all our personnel remain at the Manor. The situation within Watchaven is becoming untenable, and several injuries have already occurred. I have been informed by my inside source on the Trade Council that Watchaven plans to continue its current policies. I have noticed a tightening of security about the city and cannot help but wonder if it is a prelude to war. Has any word been received concerning where the Northmarch will stand if it should come to war? We cannot stand against both Watchaven and the Northmarch, but then, neither could Watchaven stand against us if the Northmarch were to side with us. Please keep me advised as to your wishes.

Your humble servant,
Danvek.

His next letter was more difficult, but then, Lord Danvek had always found the Droken codebook a great bother.

CHAPTER EIGHT

Rylan Glaedwin had just laid the results of his research on the table, when a knock sounded at the door. Geradon returned with a frown and a piece of paper.

"What is it?" Rylan asked.

"A message from Richard," Geradon replied. "This is the second night in a row that our three Droken hunters have left together. I tell you, Rylan, those three are up to something."

"You think Sir Dualas withheld something?"

"No, he told me what he knew—at the time. My thought is that they are pursuing something new."

"Surely not!"

"I would not put anything past Morticai."

"Perhaps you should go to Northgate and have a little chat with them when they return this evening?"

"I suppose I should. I am sorry, Rylan. I was hoping to work with you this evening."

Rylan smiled, "Well, in a few days the Inquisitor will officially arrive, and then I shall have a few words with Morticai and Dualas myself. Be careful. I shall wait up for you."

* * * * *

"You actually grew up in this section of town?" Dualas asked as he cautiously eyed their surroundings. They walked toward Burnaby Manor, skirting the edge of the Pit. Ahead, shadowy figures ducked into doorways as they approached.

"Yeah," Morticai replied. "Of course, it wasn't this bad then."

"How much farther to this place?" Coryden asked.

"Oh, uh, just a few blocks now. Ya see, Burnaby Manor isn't really in the Snake Pit, it's on the edge."

"That is comforting to hear," Dualas noted as he eyed the rat pacing them along the top of a nearby wall.

The alley before them suddenly narrowed. The rat disappeared into a hole. Morticai stopped.

"All right, we're getting close. The alleys around the manor are tight, and there are a lot of turns. That's why this was such a great place when I was small—it was good for hiding from big folk. With the current rumors about the manor, I doubt anyone will bother us."

Coryden glanced heavenward. Dualas nodded in silent agreement and blessed himself. They had taken only a few steps when Morticai stopped, looking back at them disapprovingly. Coryden and Dualas exchanged glances, uncertain why he had stopped.

"Think you could put your hoods up? It's bad enough that your armor can be heard three blocks away; let's not flaunt it any more than necessary."

Coryden and Dualas raised their cloak hoods. "I wish you'd worn more than that damned Tradelenor armor!" Coryden complained to Morticai. "It won't stop anything—it's women's armor!"

"You are wearing armor?" Dualas asked in surprise.

Morticai smiled and raised his shirt cuff. Beneath, a finely wrought chain mail shirt shimmered in the moonlight. "Yes. And Coryden is wrong. It's not 'women's armor.' It's true it won't stop a sword, but that's not what it's designed for—it's designed to stop thrown knives, and it does quite well."

Morticai turned and started away again. Coryden looked at Dualas and shook his head in disagreement.

They passed quickly through the tangle of alleys. Morticai put an arm out and stopped them as their alley opened onto a small plaza. Ahead, the manor lay washed in Bemalor's moonlight.

It was as large as the finest manors that stood by the palace. Years of neglect had destroyed much of its former beauty, but the carved pillars and intricate architecture cried out in memory of the majesty the structure must have once had. The gate was a pile of rotted wood, but the granite pillars to which the fence had attached still stood as silent sentries. Despite the crowded conditions within the Pit, none had dared build on the manor's lawn of rubble and weeds. Coryden and Dualas both stood surprised by the unexpected sight.

"It must have been tremendous in its day," Dualas whispered.

"Yeah, so they say," Morticai replied. "Come on, I want to see if something is still here."

They cautiously circled the manor, ducking in and out of the alleys that led toward it. The streets began to slope, and it was only then that Coryden and Dualas realized that the manor was built on a bluff. With the crowded buildings surrounding it on three sides, they had not noticed the night sky behind it. Its upper floors must have a grand view of the harbor.

As they came to the back side of the manor, their view of it was obscured by the wall of rock that rose up beside them. Rock had fallen from the edge of the bluff, and loose piles of rubble and brush choked the narrow alley. Several times Morticai stopped and looked around carefully. Finally, Coryden could stand it no longer.

"Are you lost, Morticai?" he whispered.

Morticai looked back, surprised. "Of course not!"

Coryden did not know whether or not to believe him. They eventually stopped, however, as the short corryn turned his attention to the bluff beside them. With a flourish he brushed aside the honey-star vines to reveal a rough-hewn tunnel stretching away into the rock. Broken hinges were all that remained to declare that there had once been a door to protect it.

"Aha! It is still here!"

"You're not going in there, are you?" Coryden asked.

"It's better than knocking on the front door."

Coryden and Dualas exchanged uncertain glances.

"This leads to the manor itself?" Dualas asked.

"Well, it used to. I honestly don't know if it still does or not. It's been about fifty years since I used it."

"Did you bring light?"

"Light is easy." Morticai reach down and quickly wrapped a bundle of dried brush together. Pulling out his tinderbox, he quickly lit it and remarked, "See? Instant torch. Now, I promise I won't go into the manor. I just want to see if the tunnel is still clear. Y'know, it may not be worth our time. But, if it is clear, it will not only save us a lot of time, but it may be a lot safer than how Fenton's friends went in."

"How do you know they didn't use the tunnel, too?" Dualas asked.

"I don't. But I doubt it. It's amazing how few people have ever known about it. And this alley still looks as abandoned as ever."

"Can we hear Grandhaven clock from here?" Coryden asked.

"I heard it," Dualas announced.

"Then," Coryden continued, "if it chimes twice and you're not back, we'll come in and find you."

Morticai sighed. "Okay. This shouldn't take long."

The corryn orphan entered the musty tunnel as Dualas and Coryden watched. He'd taken only a few steps when he stopped and looked back at them.

"Watch out for falling rocks." Then he turned and continued down the tunnel.

"How heartening," Dualas remarked, glancing upward.

"You know, Dualas," Coryden said as he let the vines fall back over the tunnel's opening, "I used to think I was mad for letting Morticai involve me in things like this. At least now I know I'm not the only one," he finished, smiling.

Dualas regarded him a moment, but before he could answer, the ring of swordplay issued from within the tunnel. The ring of metal on metal was quick and sharp—someone was pressing a strong attack. They both tore the vines aside to enter, but Morticai was already at the mouth of the tunnel, quickly backing toward them and desperately defending against his attacker. As Morticai came into the moonlight, he threw his makeshift torch to the ground to draw his dagger.

It was a corryn who emerged behind the sword that flashed quickly about Morticai's blade, and without hesitation he included the waiting Coryden and Dualas within his fast sword strokes. The man was taller than Dualas, with silver hair pulled back and braided. He wore no armor but carried a shield on his well-muscled left arm, which he flicked up and down, easily blocking Dualas's blows.

Coryden watched for an opening as he and Morticai pressed in, but the silver-haired corryn not only defended against their attacking swings, but replied, keeping them as much on the defensive as the offensive. Coryden had seen many a knight lose in battle to Dualas's smooth style; this man acted as though they could fight no better than children.

Then the warrior took a step forward. Instantly, Morticai slid to the left to move behind the tall corryn. Coryden's blow struck solidly against the warrior's shield; apparently in a planned move the tall corryn had pivoted, his shield solidly defending against Dualas and Coryden as his bright blade swept down in a fast arc toward Morticai's right side.

Morticai brought his dagger to the right. Coryden saw the blade connect with Morticai's side even as Morticai's dagger tried unsuccessfully to parry it, and an instant later Coryden himself was flying backward—the shield had been slammed into his face with a force he'd not thought possible.

Head ringing, he scrambled to his knees to see the silver-haired warrior running like the wind down the alley. Morticai was on his knees, leaning against the rock wall, holding his side. Dualas had leaped over Morticai with apparent thoughts of giving chase.

"Dualas! Morticai's been cut!"

Instantly, Dualas turned to Morticai, abandoning thoughts of pursuit; Coryden was there an instant later. Morticai's eyes were squeezed shut, and he breathed in small, shallow gasps.

"Morticai, let me see," Dualas said as he tried to pry his friend's hand away from the wound. Finally, Morticai complied. Dualas quickly inspected the wound and then clamped his own hand over it.

"It does not appear very deep. It does not look fatal, but it is bleeding freely. We need to bind it—soon."

They helped him to his feet, and with both of them supporting him, started to turn to go back the way they had come.

"No . . . other way . . . it's quicker," Morticai whispered.

They turned around and began slowly moving north.

"Don't get us lost, Morticai," Coryden cautioned. "We can't afford it."

"Go to . . . the . . . Cobblesend. . . . It's close."

"The what?" Dualas asked.

"The Cobblesend," Coryden replied. "I've never been there, but I've heard him talk about it—it's a tavern."

"How far is it?" Dualas asked Morticai.

"Not . . . too far. Take . . . the first left. . . ."

* * * * *

Kithryl jumped when the sharp rap sounded at the back door.

"Who's there?" she asked through the closed door.

"A knight of the Faith, very much in need, madam," came the muffled reply.

A knight of the Faith? Here? she thought. She cracked the

door. "Dyluth!" she cried, flinging the door open.

Morticai looked up and tried to smile. The pain in the dark blue eyes was obvious; the attempted smile didn't quite come off.

"Need . . . some help . . . I'm afraid."

Kithryl clasped her hands to her mouth and ran back inside the Cobblesend, leaving the door open.

Dualas and Coryden carefully maneuvered Morticai through the back door. Kithryl returned and threw a blanket on the kitchen floor.

"I'm sorry, but we have no beds here," she apologized.

"This will do quite well. Thank you, dear lady," Dualas replied as they moved Morticai onto the blanket.

Coryden supported Morticai's head as Dualas laid Morticai's cloak open—the bandages were blood soaked. Kithryl gasped.

"Quickly!" Dualas directed at Kithryl. "We shall need something to use for bandages! Hurry!"

Kithryl jumped like a startled rabbit and ran from the room. "He should not be bleeding," Dualas whispered. "He would not have made it to Northgate."

Coryden sat back as the implication sank in. Dualas was quickly undoing Morticai's bandages. Kithryl ran back into the room, her arms laden with what appeared to be new table-cloths.

The bandage was off now and Coryden saw for himself that the wound was not deep, although it was over a hand's width in length. It was still bleeding easily and had not slowed from when he had first glimpsed it in the alley—or perhaps that was just his imagination. Dualas's words still rang in his ears. Dualas grabbed a tablecloth without hesitation and clamped it over the wound.

A black-haired corryn came bounding into the kitchen. "Kithryl, where have you . . . ?" the man was saying. "Almighty Aluntas!" he exclaimed at the scene before him.

"Hi . . . Breslen," Morticai said.

The man stood frozen a moment before replying, almost in a whisper, "I shall close the pub."

Dualas applied pressure to the wound, but the cloths continued to fill with blood. Dualas held a folded cloth tightly against the wound, then covered it with another, and another, as the cloths became soaked. When it was obvious the bandages were not slowing the flow, Dualas would toss them all aside except for the one on the bottom, and again repeat the sequence.

By the time Dualas threw aside the third set of cloths, Morticai was slipping in and out of consciousness.

"Let me switch with you," Coryden said.

"Very well," Dualas replied, and quickly they changed places. And so, they continued.

It was not until Dualas took Coryden's shaking hands away from the cloths that he realized the bleeding had stopped. Or, at least, it no longer soaked through.

"Coryden. Coryden." Dualas was shaking him gently. "You can stop now."

Coryden glanced sharply at Morticai. His chest still rose and fell—slowly. Dualas left him and began wrapping yet more bandages around Morticai's chest, though not as tight as before. Dualas checked Morticai's heartbeat.

"I am going for help, Coryden," Dualas said. "See if you can find another blanket; I fear Morticai's blood has stolen much of his body's warmth. But, most important," Dualas said, grabbing Coryden's arm, "should he awaken—and he might—*do not let him move!* He must remain still."

"I understand."

"I shall return as quickly as possible; Breslen bought a horse from one of his customers."

"Is Dyluth gonna die?"

Everyone in the kitchen jumped at the unexpected question. Only now did they realize that Kithryl had left the back door open; a crowd of children peered in at them.

"Shoo!" Kithryl cried, running to the back door. "You children should not be here."

"But Kithryl . . ." one of them complained.

She bent down to the child and took him by the shoulders.

"No, Tagger, Dyluth is not going to die." She wiped a tear from her face. ". . . Unless the Levani insist on taking him—and we all pray that they will not. Now, you and your friends go on. I'm sorry I can't feed you tonight, but you understand."

"Will it help Dyluth if we pray?"

Kithryl smiled. "Of course it will. Now, go on." She herded them away from the door before returning to close it.

* * * * *

Coryden pulled out Morticai's dagger and inspected it while he waited. A notch as wide as his thumb was cut in the side Morticai had used to parry the warrior's blade. It was no wonder he'd not been able to stop it. Coryden shuddered as he thought about what would have happened if Morticai had not had the dagger to parry with. He wondered what the silver-haired warrior's blade had been made from.

Finally, he heard voices from the front. Kithryl and Dualas entered, followed by Kirwin; Ivan, the Northmarch's surgeon; Berret; Evadrel; and . . . Geradon Kinsey. Coryden quickly glanced at Dualas, but the knight seemed unruffled by Geradon's presence.

Ivan and Geradon moved quickly to Morticai's side. Ivan gently shook Morticai's shoulder. Immediately his eyes snapped open and he jumped—and then immediately gasped; both Coryden and Dualas grabbed him to prevent any further movement.

"Easy, Morticai," Ivan said.

Ivan and Geradon carefully began removing Morticai's bandages. Coryden glanced at Kirwin, but Kirwin was apparently assessing the severity of the situation as he surveyed the kitchen.

"Describe this swordsman to me," Geradon suddenly ordered.

"He was approximately two hands taller than I," Dualas began.

"Blessed Levani!" Berret exclaimed.

"He was corryn, with silver hair. I do not know how long the hair was—it was braided. I could not tell his eye color in the moonlight. He . . . fought very well."

"I've never seen anyone fight like that," Coryden said.

The bandages were loose now, and Ivan and Geradon both closely inspected the wound. The wound was still oozing blood, the flow of which began to increase again. Ivan promptly clamped the dressing back on the wound.

"It is as I feared," Geradon sighed. "Did you notice how smooth the edge of the cut was?" he asked Ivan.

"Yes," Ivan replied.

Geradon slowly surveyed the room and then turned his steady gaze on Kirwin.

"This wound is not deep, Commander, and should not be still bleeding. It bears the taint of sorcery."

"Which means?"

Geradon bit his lower lip in thought. Finally he replied, "I have dealt with sorcerous wounds before. It is very difficult; he has already lost much blood. But we may be able to save his life."

For several long seconds no one said a word.

"Great. Just great," Morticai finally muttered weakly.

"Dualas, relieve Ivan, and keep pressure on this dressing," Geradon ordered. "Berret, put as much wood on the fire as possible—I need it as hot as you can make it. Lady." He turned to Kithryl. "Have you needle and thread?"

"No, brother, not here."

"Can you fetch some?"

"Yes, I believe so," she replied, puzzled.

"Then do so. Do you have strong drink in this tavern?"

"Yes," Breslen replied.

"We shall need two bottles of your strongest spirits. Coryden, when he returns, lean Morticai up against you and have him drink one of the bottles—as much of it as possible. We shall have to cauterize the wound to stop the bleeding. . . ."

* * * * *

It was near dawn when Geradon unlocked the door to the room he shared with Inquisitor Glaedwin. As promised, Rylan sat waiting for him.

"Thank Aluntas you are all right!" Rylan exclaimed as Geradon relocked the door. "I sent a message to Richard, and he replied that you had left with Commander McFerrin and several others. I almost went to Northgate myself."

"I am glad you didn't," Geradon replied, moving to pour himself a drink. "It will be much better for you to stay out of sight as long as possible."

"Why? What happened?"

Geradon sank into a chair with his drink and took a long draught before replying.

"Our three novice investigators fought Luthekar tonight."

"*What?* Here, in Watchaven?"

"Yes, here in Watchaven. Morticai was wounded by Ducledha." Blessing himself, Rylan shook his head.

"He is still alive," Geradon said evenly.

Rylan brought his eyes up to lock with Geradon's.

"He was wounded by Ducledha and yet lives? Tell me all of it, Geradon."

"I still do not know all of it . . ." Geradon began.

* * * * *

Rylan shook his head again. "So what, besides the bleeding and physical description, convinces you it was Luthekar they fought?"

"Two things. First, this . . ." Geradon handed Rylan the dagger he had taken from Kirwin. "That is the dagger Morticai tried to block the blow with."

Rylan nodded slowly. "That does look like the work of Ducledha."

"And secondly," Geradon continued, "Morticai apparently stumbled onto this corryn inside a tunnel—I still have many questions about that, mind you—and Morticai remarked that this corryn had no light with him."

"A tunnel?"

"I know that it supposedly goes to an old manor—I do not think it leads to the Dark One's temple, I am afraid. I stopped by the Sanctorium on my way back here and notified the Grand Patriarch; by dawn a contingent of knights will be ready to go there with us."

"Good." Rylan nodded. "Will Sir Dualas be coming?"

"No. He requested that he be allowed to stay with Morticai and, under the circumstances, I granted that."

"That was the best thing to do," Rylan agreed. "I must agree with you, Geradon. It all looks like Luthekar—the wound, the blade's sharpness, the description, no use of light. Blessed Aluntas, what is going on here?"

"To bring one as highly placed as Prince Luthekar here? I don't know."

"We should have used the candle," Rylan said, glancing about the room.

Geradon shrugged. "I think we are safe—for the moment. But I agree, we should use it from now on."

"Did you pack extras?"

"Yes, just in case."

"Good. So, Morticai lies injured at Northgate. I do not like that; he is too much of a target."

"I am afraid I agree. But there is not much we can do about it at the moment, beyond my permission for Sir Dualas to remain with him. Unless, of course, you wish to officially arrive."

"No, that would tip our hand too much. If Luthekar is involved, it is best that he not know I am here."

"I agree. I hinted that they should keep a close eye on Morticai, and I shall check on him as soon as we are finished at the manor. In fact, I just might move in for a while. I think I could manage that. Morticai's wound will need daily tending anyway. What do you think?"

"I think it would be wise. I fear that as soon as they discover he has not died from Ducledha's wound, they will try to kill him. Be careful, Geradon."

"And you, as well," Geradon replied. "It has been a long time since we faced Luthekar."

"Indeed," Rylan replied. "Tomorrow I will notify the Grand Patriarch. If we should die, someone needs to know that Luthekar is involved."

CHAPTER NINE

Service had been well attended. Droka's high priest remained on the upraised platform, as the masked congregation made their slow exodus from the temple. There was some talk among them. Behind his mask, the high priest smiled. It was the sign of a good service; Droka's worshippers were so aware of their hunted status that talk was usually kept to a minimum.

A worshipper slowly worked his way forward to kneel silently before the platform. He could have been praying, though the high priest doubted it. Although faithful to their cause, Udall had never been overtly devout. By now, most of the congregation had exited. The high priest walked over to the kneeling form.

"Udall, arise," the high priest whispered.

The man's head jerked upward and then he nervously glanced behind him.

"I would not compromise one of our most faithful servants, Udall," the high priest assured him.

The man stood but bowed his head. "Your humble servant begs forgiveness for his shallow and needless fears."

Again the high priest smiled behind his mask. That's what he liked about Udall: he abased himself so well.

"Forgiveness is granted. So, you received my message?"

"Yes, Your Eminence."

"And are there any corryn orphans in Watchaven's Northmarch?"

"Yes, Your Eminence. We have few corryn here in Watchaven. It is well known that one of them grew up in Watchaven's streets as an orphan—they call him Morticai."

"Morticai? That is not a corryn name."

"I know, Your Eminence. I do not know where the human nickname came from, but Morticai is full corryn. I tried to discover his corryn name, but none I could ask without raising suspicions knew it."

"You have done well, Udall. I would not have wanted you to endanger your position. You are very valuable to us."

"There is more, Your Eminence."

"Oh?"

"Yes, Your Eminence. When I returned from patrol all of Northgate was astir. An emissary of the Inquisition has arrived from Abbadyr. All of Morticai's patrol have been questioned— he is under Inquisitorial investigation."

Despite his efforts to conceal his surprise, the high priest gasped audibly.

"That is . . . very interesting, Udall. And why are they investigating Morticai?"

"No one seems to know, Your Eminence."

"Is anyone else under suspicion?"

"None seem to be, Your Eminence."

"You have, indeed, brought me very valuable information, Udall. Such information deserves a reward. We may yet have more work for you to do. I would like to introduce you to someone."

"Thy will is mine."

"I shall introduce you to Prince Luthekar."

Udall bowed deeply. "Your servant is very honored, Eminence. Much I have heard of Prince Luthekar; I never hoped to meet him."

"We reward good service, Udall—always."

The high priest motioned to his subordinate, standing patiently at the edge of the room. The red-robed priest quickly came forward.

"Has Prince Luthekar arrived?"

"Yes, Eminence."

"Good. Follow me," the high priest directed.

They proceeded to the anteroom outside the high priest's office. Prince Luthekar wheeled to face them; he had obviously been pacing.

Udall gasped. The high priest froze, then consciously let his breath out easily, naturally. Luthekar's eyes were as red as the sun falling into Dark Season.

The high priest knew it to be a manifestation of Luthekar's power, a thing that marked Droka's two princes—when they wished, and sometimes when they didn't. It was something no mortal ever wished to see.

"Well?" Luthekar spat.

"We have the name of the Northmarch thief," the high priest began.

"It is Morticai," Luthekar snarled. "Who is this?" he demanded, pointing at Udall.

"This is Udall. He is our Northmarch agent."

Luthekar gazed at Udall, calm beginning to creep back into his being. His eyes gradually faded back to their normal, cool blue.

"There were two corryn with this Morticai," Luthekar said. "One wore a helm that bore markings of the Faith; he was called Dualas. The other appeared to have mixed blood. What can you tell me of these two?"

Udall swallowed before he began. "The one called Dualas is a knight of the Faith who serves the Northmarch. The mixed-blood corryn—d-did he have light hair?"

"Yes."

"Then that would have been Coryden, Morticai's captain. Coryden and Morticai have long been close, and Dualas and Coryden are known friends, but I have never before known Morticai to keep the company of the knight."

The high priest interrupted. "Udall says the Inquisition has arrived at Northgate and is investigating Morticai."

Luthekar stared at him a moment before returning his attention to Udall.

"Tell me what you know."

"It is said at Northgate that the Inquisition arrived two days ago. I just arrived from Dynolva today."

"What are their names."

"There is only one man. His name is Geradon Kinsey."

"Halt. You say there is only one man?"

"Yes, Your Royal Highness."

"You may call me lord. That is strange. Continue."

"H-he questioned Morticai's patrol. Those who are willing to talk about it say that the man asked a lot of questions about Morticai's past and his religious habits."

"So what do people think the investigation is for?"

"I have heard several theories, lord. Some say that Morticai must be Droken. Some think that he is suspected of being Droken because he has never attended service regularly. Yet others think it is because of something his parents did that he does not know about. Most think that a nobleman has arranged it for revenge because Morticai dallies with the ladies of court."

"And what do you think?"

"I-I do not know, lord. I do not know much about him. I once watched him win over a thousand korun in wagers by throwing knives, and I have heard many stories about him. They say he likes the ladies too much. He likes to gamble. He likes Tradelenor styles. I've heard he frequents noblemen's parties, though how—for one of such low station—I do not know. That is all I know of him." Udall audibly gulped in a breath. He hoped his information was sufficient; it was truly all he knew about the strange corryn orphan.

"What of the other two?"

"I know little about Sir Dualas, except that he lives for the Faith. I think he was born in Dynolva. He has filled in on other patrols but serves primarily with Captain Coryden. Because he is from the Faith, he serves in whatever patrol he wishes and can come and go when he pleases, although only once that I know of has he been called back by the Faith."

"And Captain Coryden?"

"He is a half-breed and comes from Menelcar. I've heard his father is a shipwright there and that Coryden would have much money if he would give up the Northmarch to help his father with his business. He spends more time with his men than most captains—his men are very loyal to him. He spends much of his free time with Morticai."

"Not any longer. I wounded Morticai tonight. If he is not yet dead, he shall be by the morrow. Go back to your duties at Northgate. Watch and listen to everything that is said by and about Captain Coryden and Sir Dualas—but be very careful not to be caught. Report back in six days."

"Yes, lord."

Luthekar turned to the high priest. "I would have finished the other two as well, but was uncertain how many more were about. Now, I am beginning to suspect it was just the three of them."

The high priest turned to Udall. "Thank you, Udall. You may leave now."

Bowing deeply, Udall took his leave. As soon as the door shut, Luthekar turned to the high priest.

"We have much to discuss."

"Indeed. What happened?"

"I was attacked leaving the manor!" Luthekar slammed his palm down on the desk. "This Northmarch orphan of yours was in the tunnel as I left to come here. We fought, and when we emerged, the other two joined in. I wounded the thief and left. As I stated, at the time I was not certain the entire patrol was not present."

"Father of Darkness!"

"I heard the two names, Morticai and Dualas, as I left. This is grave news about the Inquisition, although perhaps this incident tonight will save us."

"Why do you think they have come?"

"Isn't it obvious? This thief had to be working for them. Somehow he determined that Aldwin was Droken."

"Everything could be compromised!"

"I think not. I suspect their investigation is still in the early stages—else would I not have been met by an entire contingent of knights?"

"I suppose you are correct."

"I do not think they were expecting me. But something led them to the manor, which now is useless!" Luthekar again slammed his hand onto the desk. "I do not understand why the Inquisition has come to the Northmarch so visibly. Nor do I understand why there is only one man—I have never known the Inquisition to send lone men."

The high priest shrugged. "Perhaps this man's help has yet to arrive. Perhaps they were detained."

"Perhaps. Or perhaps the other man is hiding. Whichever it is, we can no longer afford the luxury of Aldwin's stupidity."

"I agree."

"We can restructure the cell with Valdir in command," the Dark Prince said, as he once again began to pace.

"Do you not think he will be a liability as well?"

"Actually, I do. But we need him to remain active in the Trade Council. As you know, we are not quite done with our work there. Have the next four in the structure killed—that will break the chain, assuming the Faith's agent discovered them. Then we can isolate Valdir's cell until we know things are secure."

"With times this volatile, would it not be easier to move those beneath? Would the Faith not see the deaths as a purge?"

"It is precisely because these times are volatile that I would rather kill them. The Faith will not know if it is related to us or to the general unrest. At this point, we cannot risk their being picked up and interrogated. Although I suspect very little information has been passed on, we cannot be certain. We think that this thief started out working alone. I am very glad that he tasted Ducledha's edge."

"Indeed. I shall make the necessary arrangements."

"And I will need to base my command here. Much more inconvenient, but necessary."

"I shall have quarters prepared for you," the high priest replied, backing out of the office.

Luthekar slowly shook his head. So much was at stake. It had taken them years to lay in the supplies between his homeland of Cuthaun and the northern kingdoms. They desperately needed these warmer lands. Cuthaun had grown slowly, but steadily, over the years until its people had reached the limit of how much they could grow in the poor soil.

Too many Droken, trying to flee to the safety of the hidden country, died on the long trek there. Few of the common followers had any real knowledge of where Cuthaun lay. Too many Droken fled toward Cuthaun without preparation, not knowing how to make the proper connections, and with the vile Faith on their backs.

And now? Now, after years of subtle corruption and infiltration into the nobility, years of piracy and work to raise the funds and gather the supplies needed, now one man was attempting to unravel it all. It was unthinkable. He could not allow it.

* * * * *

Morticai moaned softly. With a sigh, Dualas opened his eyes for the fifth time. His thoughts had barely begun to roam in waking-rest when Morticai had moaned—each time. Dualas had unbent his legs to once again check the sleeping corryn.

The wounded thief appeared to still be sleeping, despite the apparent discomfort. Dualas glanced to Coryden—Coryden had abandoned thoughts of wake-resting and slept like the humans in a large chair on the far side of the room. Apparently it was more successful, but Dualas would not leave Morticai that unattended.

A light rap sounded on the door.

"Good day, Sir Dualas," Geradon Kinsey greeted softly.

"Indeed, brother," Dualas replied, "it is good, thanks to your ministrations of last night."

"Thank you."

Dualas noted that Geradon carried a covered pot, ladle, and cup.

"How is our wounded Morticai this morning?" Geradon asked.

"Still sleeping, though apparently in some distress."

"Yes, I fear he will be uncomfortable for several days—until the burn heals and I remove the thread holding his wound closed."

Geradon moved to where Dualas had sat and, setting his armload down on the nearest table, bent over the sleeping Morticai. Geradon felt his forehead and then, brushing the corryn's hair aside, gently grabbed his shoulder.

"Morticai, wake up. You must wake up, for just a little while." Geradon gently shook his shoulder.

Morticai moaned and finally opened his eyes into a painful squint.

"Uugh. Oh . . . gods!" He moaned and promptly attempted to roll into a ball.

Dualas and Geradon both moved to keep him flat, which proved easy to do. Dualas found Morticai's weakened state frightening. The knight glanced at Coryden. It surprised him that Coryden was sleeping through this much noise—he certainly wouldn't have while on patrol.

"Stay flat, Morticai," Geradon soothed. "I know it hurts, but you should lie flat as much as possible. Easy, easy. That's it. Take it easy. The less you move, the better. I have brought something to help with the pain. I have also brought something to help you regain your strength."

Geradon went to the table and ladled a thick, dark liquid into the cup.

"Raise him up, Sir Dualas. Be very careful. Do it slowly.

That's good. Morticai, this is a special broth. I won't lie and tell you it tastes good, but it is not terrible either. I have added something to it that should ease the pain. Here."

Geradon held Morticai's hands in place around the cup and helped him drink. Dualas noted that Morticai did not seem to notice the taste. He drank very little of it, however.

"Come on, Morticai. Just a little more. The more of this you can manage, the better."

The process was repeated, and this time Morticai drank longer.

"That's good. I think that will be enough for now. Easy."

Geradon set the cup on the table and then gently grabbed Morticai's hands.

"Morticai, can you hear me?"

"Yeah. My ears usually keep workin' when I'm in pain. Don't seem any different now."

"I am sorry we had to hurt you so last night, but you must understand that you would not be alive now if we had not done what we did."

"Yeah, I know. When'll the pain stop?"

"It may take a couple of weeks."

"Oh, Glawres!"

"Easy. In a little while, you should feel a bit better. I want you to squeeze my hands as hard as you can—that's it. Can you squeeze any harder? That's enough."

Dualas had seen dying men with greater strength.

"Is the pain easing any?"

"Yeah, maybe."

Morticai appeared to be slipping back into sleep.

"Good. Rest now. Get all the rest you can."

Geradon then carefully loosened Morticai's bandage and looked beneath it.

"Ah, good. It appears the bleeding has truly stopped. I am certain there will be some difficulty with the healing, but it does not look unmanageable."

Geradon carefully retightened the covering. Dualas noted that retightening the bandages did not elicit any moans from the sleeping Morticai.

"Later this evening I shall cleanse the wound and redress it. Could you be here then, Sir Dualas?"

"Yes, brother."

"Good. Lay him back down. That's good. You have been trained in the healing arts?"

"Yes."

"Here in Watchaven?"

"In Dynolva."

"Well, I like your touch. I have seen men die for no other reason than that they were handled too roughly. Could we make it warmer in here? I fear this draft will not be good for him."

"I shall start a fire."

Dualas moved to the closer fireplace and began laying the wood. Geradon followed him over and sat on a footstool beside the hearth.

"I have never seen a wound so difficult to manage," Dualas observed.

"Well," Geradon replied, "to my knowledge, few men have fought Luthekar and run away to tell of it, let alone survived a wound given by Luthekar's sword, Ducledha. Morticai will be the first."

Dualas stopped and stared at Geradon.

"Luthekar—Prince Luthekar of abomination?"

"You did not know?"

"No."

"I thought not. Everything fits, however—the physical description, the difficulty with the wound, the fact that the warrior met Morticai inside a tunnel carrying no light."

Dualas laid the last log in the fireplace and struck the fire.

"But I must ask you to give me your word not to tell anyone," Geradon continued, "including Morticai and Coryden. The situation is delicate. It would be disastrous if this became general knowledge at Northgate."

"You have my word."

"Tell me," Geradon asked, "why is Morticai obsessed with this? Is it because of his parents?"

"I had not known about his parents until you told me two days ago, but I suspect that is at the heart of it." Dualas shrugged. "I think he harbors a great hatred of the Droken—but unlike most, he is not afraid to try to bring them to justice. I know you disagree with Morticai's involvement, but you must admit he has uncovered a great deal of information."

"That cannot be denied, but he may die for it yet."

"Perhaps. But then, any of us might die on our next patrol."

Geradon nodded. "I wondered how much of this was due to the Northmarch. So you see this as no different than your patrols?"

"No, I did not say that. This is more dangerous, to be certain, but is it more dangerous than the prospect of war between Dynolva and Watchaven? I think you must agree that war seems to be the inevitable goal. And, if war is the goal, then is it actually separate from our Northmarch duties? The Northmarch was created to preserve the safety of the borders and highways of both Dynolva and Watchaven. Even from Droken."

Geradon smiled. "You argue a good case, Sir Dualas. When is Coryden's patrol to leave again?"

"The day after tomorrow. Brother, if I might ask, did you visit the manor this morning?"

"Yes, I did. All we found, however, was an old abandoned manor."

"I feared that would happen."

Coryden coughed and, apparently unable to shift positions, woke up. Straightening, he stretched before climbing out of the chair to check on Morticai.

"Damn, it's hot in here," he complained. Turning, he spotted them and nodded curtly at Geradon.

"Good day, Captain," Geradon said. "I am sorry, but if you will feel Morticai's hand you will see that he is quite cool—that is the reason for the fire this warm summer's day."

Coryden lightly touched Morticai's hand and then lifted the cover of the nearby pot.

"Yuck! What is that?"

"That is a broth for Morticai, with a few special ingredients.

Yes, it smells horrible, but it honestly does not taste as bad as it smells. Taste it, if you like. It serves two purposes. It contains belladonna mixed with vallemo to ease his pain so he can sleep and minced beef liver, beef heart, and scurvy grass to bring back his strength."

"I think I'll just eat in the mess hall, thank you. Belladonna, did you say?"

"Do not worry; it is a very small quantity. I promise you it will do him no harm."

A knock sounded on the door, but before Dualas could reach it, Kirwin and Phillip entered. Kirwin eyed Coryden's rumpled clothes disapprovingly but spoke to Geradon.

"Your things have been moved into Captain Coryden's quarters, Brother Kinsey."

Coryden's eyes widened in surprise.

"Thank you, commander," Geradon replied.

"You can sleep with your men in the barracks until you leave on your next patrol," Kirwin told the stunned Coryden.

"Ah, commander," Geradon interrupted, "I am afraid that Captain Coryden must remain in Watchaven."

Now it was Kirwin's turn to stare. After a moment of stunned silence, Kirwin muttered between clenched teeth, "For how long?"

"I am afraid I do not yet know," Geradon replied smoothly.

"And I don't suppose Sir Dualas will be able to go either, eh?"

"I am afraid you are correct."

"That means the entire patrol stays!" The volume of Kirwin's voice was gradually creeping upward.

"I must apologize for the inconvenience, but I have not even begun to investigate last night's events."

Kirwin was obviously trying to stay calm. His second-in-command shifted his weight from foot to foot several times before finally clearing his throat.

"Sir," Phillip suggested, "perhaps this would be a good time to get the west wing of Northgate painted. You have talked about assigning a patrol to do it."

Kirwin glared at Phillip a moment before spinning toward Coryden.

"So be it! Coryden, your men can report to Phillip for assignment."

With a final glare at Geradon, Kirwin spun and marched out. Phillip followed, albeit reluctantly.

"Dear me," Geradon said softly, "I do believe I've upset him."

* * * * *

The angry crowd packed tighter as the doors to the Guildhall opened. The meeting had at long last ended. Now they would learn how their grievances had been received. Several of their senior masters emerged, their faces grim and set. A space was cleared at the top of the stairs, and it became obvious that an official announcement would be made.

The crowd's bitter shouts diminished to a soft growl as a nobleman with light brown curls, dark eyes, and angled features emerged to command the attention of all those packed before the building. He appeared ready to begin the announcement when his eyes focused on something beyond the crowd. His eyes widened in fear, and as he opened his mouth wordlessly, he spun as though to flee into the building.

A few in the crowd had turned by then, and some in the back could hear the pounding hooves. By the time those still emerging from the building realized the nobleman was trying to reenter it, the corryn horseman was even with the door, releasing the arrow that sped unerringly to its target. Shock, followed by shouts, ensued, as Lord Aldwin crumpled into the arms of his still-emerging delegation.

The rioting lasted far into the night. It would be a night the corryn of Watchaven would always remember.

* * * * *

Udall waited nervously outside the high priest's office.

Finally, the high priest's aide emerged, holding the door open.

"Enter," he said.

The high priest sat behind the desk; Prince Luthekar sat before it. The door quietly closed behind him.

"Udall, please, be seated," the high priest said.

Udall carefully made his way to the chair. He noted, with a good deal of relief, that Luthekar's eyes were normal. Luthekar's mood also seemed better than when Udall had first met him. He feared that the Dark Prince's mood would soon worsen.

"So," the high priest began, "what has transpired at Northgate since Morticai's unfortunate demise?"

"I f-fear I have grave news to report, Your Eminence." Udall inwardly cursed his trembling voice. The masked priest and unmasked Luthekar both stared at him intensely. He found the courage to continue. "M-Morticai still lives."

"Impossible!" Luthekar snapped.

"How?" the high priest asked.

"Th-the Inquisitorial priest has moved into Captain Coryden's quarters and has been tending Morticai daily. Captain Coryden has moved in with Morticai. Coryden's patrol has been ordered to remain in Watchaven by the Inquisition."

"The man is a curse to me," Luthekar muttered.

Relieved, Udall took a deep breath. Luthekar was not as enraged by the ill news as he had expected.

The high priest shook his head. "What have you learned of the Inquisition's investigation?"

"It is at a standstill. Kinsey is waiting for his master, the Inquisitor, to arrive."

"I believe it is time we make certain the Inquisitor is disappointed when he arrives," Luthekar said to the high priest.

"I agree," the high priest replied, rising. Without another word, the high priest left the room. Udall studied his clasped hands and prayed that his nervousness was hidden from Luthekar by his hood and mask.

"Have you heard what the condition of the wound is now?" Luthekar continued.

"I have heard it said that he is healing very slowly. It is said that the priest brews a special potion each day and makes Morticai drink it. I talked with some of those who have taken it to him, and they say that the brew smells more like sorcery than the Faith."

"Good," Luthekar replied. "That should help us, then." The Dark Prince produced several small jars, each containing a different colored powder. He pushed them across the desk to Udall.

"Udall, when you have completed this new assignment, you shall return here and never again have to patrol with the Northmarch. . . ."

CHAPTER TEN

The main hall was filled to capacity. The bar had been shut down, to the displeasure of more than a few Northmarchers. Kirwin McFerrin walked easily through the crowd. As he reached the far end of the hall he gestured to a table; four men grabbed it and placed it before the main hearth.

He climbed onto the table and surveyed his men as a hush quickly spread through the room. He noted that Brother Kinsey stood near the door. Kirwin had actually begun to look forward to the Inquisitor's arrival—the quicker he arrived, the quicker Kirwin could get the Inquisition out of his fortress. He had enough worries without the Inquisition meddling in Northmarch affairs.

"May I have everyone's attention," he began needlessly—a dropped needle could have been heard in the large hall. "I have recently received important orders from Mid-Keep. All patrols are canceled until further notice."

A loud rumble of exclamations swept through the crowd. Then, silence fell again. Kirwin smiled; considering the magnitude of his announcement, his men were reacting with a good show of discipline.

"The patrols that are still out will be informed of the situation as soon as they return. To answer some of your questions, let me state a few basic facts as they currently stand. We are not at war. We do not know if war will occur. The Northmarch does not and cannot side with either Dynolva or Watchaven. And, no, I do not know what we will do if it comes to war—that is a decision for High Command; however, we *will not* bear arms against fellow Northmarchers under any circumstances.

"You are free to enter the city; however, the following rules are now in effect. Anyone entering the city must have at least one companion; before leaving Northgate you must tell the gate guard where you are going and at what time you expect to return; we are on alert status—therefore, no one is allowed to stay out longer than four hours.

"I strongly suggest our corryn Northmarchers refrain from entering the city at all. I shall pass on information as I receive it from Mid-Keep. Some of you may be assigned to special messenger squads who will carry messages from here to Mid-Keep. Questions?"

A corryn close to the front waved a hand.

"Yes, Serlias?"

"Sir, my wife and son live in the city, and, well, sir, I've become concerned for their safety. What should I have them do?"

"I wish I could tell you to bring them here, but as you realize, we just don't have the room. I understand that the embassies of both Dynolva and Menelcar, as well as Grandhaven Sanctorium, are taking in refugees. Phillip will set up escort units; any of you who wish to have your families escorted to safety in any of those locations may let Phillip know, and we'll assign them an escort unit. Yes, next?"

"Sir," began a burly human, "I've heard that people in the city are starting to stockpile food—that the shelves are as bare

as at the end of Fading Season. Will we have supply problems
here?"

"I have also heard that people have begun hoarding. However, I anticipate no difficulties maintaining our supplies."

The questions continued for several minutes. Finally, Kirwin climbed down from the table, allowing himself to be swallowed up by the crowd. A group was beginning to cluster
around Phillip. Others wandered off, talking softly among
themselves. Kirwin suspected there would be a lot of talk at
Northgate this night.

* * * * *

It was time for Morticai's midmorning serving of broth.
Having heard Grandhaven's clock, Morticai was gingerly working his way back to his bed. Geradon would be furious if he
discovered that he'd been getting up every day to throw knives.
He had just made it onto the bed when the door latch began to
turn.

"Mornin'," the Northmarcher said when he saw that Morticai was awake.

"Hi, Udall. Don't tell me, you've brought me this wonderful stuff that I'm just gonna love—right?"

Laughing, Udall set the broth down on the table beside the
bed.

"You're not tired of this, are you?"

"Well, it tasted pretty good the first few times. But six
bowls a day seems to do something to the flavor."

"Well, drink up. I don't think you'll find any of us willing
to drink it for you!"

"Yeah, I'll wager you're right. Thanks."

After Udall left, Morticai carefully maneuvered into a sitting position. He picked up the broth, stared at it a moment,
and set it back down.

Yuck, he thought. *Not this morning; lunch will be here soon
enough!*

Taking a deep breath, he slowly pulled himself up beside

the bed. Picking up the broth, Morticai worked his way to the window using furniture and walls for extra support. The small window opened onto the northern roof of Northgate's eastern wing.

He opened the window and nonchalantly poured the broth onto the roof. A dingy gray cat quickly ran across the roof toward the spilled broth.

"Enjoy it while it lasts," Morticai told the alley cat. "It's not gonna last forever—I hope!"

He had made it back to the bed when the door latch began to turn again. *Must be Geradon,* he thought, closing his eyes. Silence. He lifted an eyelid enough to see Udall closing the door. *What the Levani is he doing back so soon?* Udall picked up the wooden bar and placed it across the door.

Morticai quickly moved his arm off the far edge of the bed. *Damn! Where's my dagger?* Udall turned around and drew his sword. Morticai feigned sleep as Udall advanced. He was almost within sword reach. . . .

With a yell, Morticai flung his chamber pot into Udall's face and rolled off the opposite side of the bed; Udall howled in rage. Morticai gained his feet but feared he'd be unable to keep standing—the room spun around him, as searing pain shot up his side.

Clearing the bed, Udall rushed toward him. Morticai staggered back, colliding with a stack of chairs. He grabbed at them for support; the unsteady stack toppled into Udall's advancing sword strokes. The spinning room became a blur, as he fought back the panic rising within him.

Morticai could hear Udall advancing. He careened into an empty wardrobe and tried to pull it over. He succeeded but crashed to the floor with it—and then heard Udall's cry of anger from underneath the destroyed furniture.

For a moment, he lay frozen—listening for Udall's movements. His vision cleared, and he saw the human pulling himself from the debris only a few feet away. His pile of practice knives also lay close. He scrambled toward them on his hands and knees as, again, the room began to spin.

Reaching the knives, he rolled into a sitting position; the room reached full speed. Panting, he tried to focus—unsuccessful, he threw two knives with his eyes closed. He heard them as they struck . . . furniture.

Morticai regained his feet and reeled against the room's northern wall. Someone pounded on the door. Leaning against the wall, Morticai tried again to focus; he could see a vague blob moving toward him. The pounding on the door became rhythmic. Udall let out a cry and charged. Morticai could no longer wait for his vision to clear; he threw his last knife and prayed his aim was true.

The blob fell and lay still. Gasping, Morticai closed his eyes and held his head. The dizziness subsided. Remaining frozen, he opened his eyes. Udall lay in a growing pool of blood about five feet away. He heard the door burst open, but looking up made his head spin again.

* * * * *

The door gave with a loud crack, as Richard threw his large form against it for the third time. Coryden charged past, as Richard cleared the doorway. It took the captain a moment to spot Morticai, leaning against the opposite wall of the large room. Broken furniture lay everywhere. It wasn't until he was halfway to Morticai that he saw Udall.

"Morticai! Are you all right?"

"Coryden? Uh, yeah. I think so."

A crowd of stunned Northmarchers filled the room. Everyone in the barracks beneath Morticai's room had heard the noise.

"Udall!" someone cried.

Coryden reached Morticai's side but decided against moving him back to the bed. Dualas appeared, and then Berret, and, as Coryden watched, his patrol quietly maneuvered themselves between Morticai and Udall's angry patrolmates. Coryden noted that Richard had moved over with his men. The crowd began yelling questions.

"Udall's dead!"

"How?"

"Who? Morticai?"

"Udall!"

"What happened?" Udall's captain demanded.

"He, uh, he attacked me," Morticai said.

The noise level climbed, and more questions were shouted; Morticai didn't respond.

"Bastard corryn!" someone shouted.

"This is crazy," one of the humans responded to the insult. "What're we talkin' about here anyway? We're all North-marchers—this has nothin' to do with Morticai bein' corryn."

The room seemed to growl, as the crowd argued amongst themselves.

"Why would he attack you?" Udall's captain demanded, but before Morticai could answer, another voice commanded everyone's attention—Kirwin's.

"What's going on here?"

The room fell silent. The crowd parted as Kirwin walked through. He paused when he saw Udall.

"Morticai murdered Udall," someone said.

As one entity, Coryden's men tensed and moved a step closer to Morticai and their captain.

"It was self-defense," Evadrel said.

Most of Coryden's patrol stared at Evadrel—their quiet scout rarely talked if more than two or three people were present.

"Udall had no reason to attack him—he didn't hate corryn. Morticai must've provoked it," someone else yelled back.

Kirwin spun; Coryden expected him to order the room cleared, but before the order could be given, Geradon's voice rose above the murmuring crowd.

"The Droken have eyes and ears everywhere. And more than a few reasons to send an assassin against Morticai."

"Droken!" The whisper floated through the crowd as Geradon came forward.

Kirwin commanded everyone's attention. "I want everyone

out of this room except Captain Coryden, Captain Williams, Sergeant Heimrik, and . . . Brother Geradon."

Reluctantly, the crowd dispersed. The last to leave the room, Richard extracted the wooden bar from the iron bracket he'd pulled from the wall and drew the half-broken door closed after him.

"All right, Morticai," Kirwin demanded, "what happened?"

"Udall brought me my broth and—"

"Where is it?" Geradon interrupted. "Did you drink any of it?"

Kirwin glared at Geradon, who ignored him.

"I, uh, I poured it out the window," Morticai admitted.

"What?" Geradon asked.

Coryden went to the window, opened it, and then paused before looking back at Morticai.

"Did you drink any of that broth, Morticai?" he asked softly.

"No, why?"

Reaching outside the window, Coryden turned around with the lifeless alley cat in his hands. Kirwin's mouth dropped.

"Blessed Levani!" Captain Williams exclaimed.

Geradon nodded. "As I said, the Droken have eyes and ears everywhere. I suggest we check this man's belongings carefully and quickly."

"Captain Williams," Kirwin ordered, "secure Udall's belongings before anyone tampers with them."

"Y-yes, sir," Williams replied.

"You expected this?" Kirwin demanded of Geradon when Williams had left.

"I expected some sort of an attempt, though I had not considered poison, because I have been preparing the broth myself. I am sorry, Morticai. This was a grave error on my part. Thank the Levani, your patron Glawres watches over you."

"Are you all right, Morticai?" Kirwin asked.

"I, uh, think so, sir."

"I had better check his wound," Geradon told Kirwin.

Kirwin nodded. "Captain Coryden," he instructed, "remove Udall's body to the sanctum and get this room cleaned up."

"Yes, sir."

"Carry on," Kirwin replied with a sigh.

As Kirwin exited, Morticai slumped against Berret.

"Glawres, my side hurts," he mumbled.

"Well," Geradon began, "let's go take a look at it."

* * * * *

Morticai awoke the next morning to find Sir Dualas sitting beside the bed.

"Good morrow!" Dualas greeted cheerfully.

"Ugh. If you say so," Morticai replied. "Gods, I'm stiff. How long before I can move like a real person again, Dualas?"

"Brother Geradon has said that a few more weeks should have you feeling normal again."

"A few more weeks!" Morticai sighed. "I've never had a wound like this."

"This was a sorcerous wound."

"Yeah, I know. That's what Geradon said. So, what happened with Udall? The last thing I heard was Kirwin telling someone to check his gear."

"Indeed. They found nothing in his trunk, but when they searched his body they discovered a vial of powder that Brother Kinsey says is the poison that was used in your broth."

"I never thought I'd have to kill a Northmarcher," Morticai said solemnly. "What's happening in the city?"

"There is an ill wind that smells of war, I am afraid. I understand you were told about Lord Aldwin's assassination and the rioting."

"Has there been more?"

"No, but then not many corryn are braving our streets, either."

Morticai shook his head. "And no one is trying to find out who we fought or where he is, are they?"

"I believe the Inquisition is looking into it."

"Yeah, I'll wager!"

A soft knock sounded at the door. The door had been repaired and the bracket reattached to the wall. Brother Kinsey and a shorter human with soft brown hair, wearing the robes of one of the Faith, stood without.

"Good morrow, Sir Dualas," Geradon greeted.

"Good morrow, brother."

"Sir Dualas, if you could come with me, I have something to discuss with you," Geradon continued. "My associate here will tend Morticai's wound this morning."

Morticai sighed. So much for practicing with his knives—they weren't going to give him any privacy.

"Good day," the man of Faith greeted as he began unpacking bandages.

"Yeah, that's what they're sayin'," Morticai replied.

The human stopped and looked at him thoughtfully.

"I am sorry. I suppose you do not see it as a 'good day' at the moment." He finished unpacking and began carefully undoing Morticai's bandage.

"Well, let's just say I'm gettin' awful tired of lookin' at the ceiling."

"I understand you actually had a rather busy day, yesterday."

"Yeah, that was terrible."

Morticai automatically held his breath as the last of the bandage was removed. Yesterday's activities had reawakened his nerves near the wound.

"Do you hunt Droken officially for the Northmarch?" the human asked.

"No. In fact, Kirwin isn't too fond of it. I'm afraid that when this is all over, he's going to ship me to Mid-Keep."

"Kirwin, that's your commander?"

"Yeah."

"So, you think Kirwin will send you to Mid-Keep—because you have been hunting Droken?" the human said as he inspected the wound.

"Well, actually because I keep disobeying orders. Not that I mean to. But this is important, y'know, and he just doesn't understand that."

"What about the Faith? Shouldn't the Faith be able to handle this?"

"Well, they're supposed to. No offense, but the Faith just doesn't use the right tactics. If I hadn't gone to the Pit, I wouldn't have found out that the Droken were using the abandoned manor. I just can't see agents of the Faith going into the Pit."

"Hm. It's time to get these stitches out."

Morticai inhaled sharply. "It is?"

"I promise you, it will not hurt as much as when they were put in. I understand this was lanced a few days ago?"

"Yeah. That certainly hurt!"

"Well, let us see what we can do here. I believe you will find that the wound will feel better once the thread is removed. Roll over a bit more. That's good. Now, hold steady. I shall do this a small piece at a time. There."

Morticai winced.

"That was the first piece of thread. That wasn't too bad, was it?"

"No. Just get it over with, will ya?"

"If you are ready." The priest carefully removed the remaining stitches.

Geradon Kinsey entered the room. Without looking up, the human addressed him.

"Yes?"

"The knights from the Sanctorium have arrived, Inquisitor."

"Thank you, Geradon."

Morticai jumped. Geradon exited the room again.

"I'm sorry, did I hurt you?" the Inquisitor asked.

"Uh . . . ah, no. S-so you're Inquisitor Glaedwin?"

"Yes. You may call me Rylan, if you wish. I am sorry I was unable to visit with you earlier, but I had a lot of work to do. All things considered, it looks as though your wound is healing very well." Rylan began to redress the wound. "I must tell you something about this wound that you do not know. You were told that the wound was sorcerous?"

"Yes."

"Well, the sword that wounded you has quite a reputation. In fact, the sword even has a name—Ducledha. Because of the way the wound acted, and the physical description you gave us, we are fairly certain we know who it was that you fought in that alley in the Snake Pit."

"You do?"

"Yes. Have you ever heard of Prince Luthekar?"

"No. What's he prince of?"

"The Droken."

"Wh-what?"

"That's right. The Droken. And I am very pleased to say that you will survive this wound from his sword, Ducledha—despite the fact that no one before you has ever survived such a wound. All those before you have bled to death."

Morticai stared at this strange man who sat beside him and talked so calmly about such things.

"I fought the prince of the Droken?"

"One of them, yes. There are actually two princes, Luthekar and Mortern. They have only been sighted a few times in the thousand years that the Faith has attempted to keep record of them."

"A thousand years?" Morticai asked incredulously.

"Yes. Of course, they are not mortal in the normal sense. As you saw, Luthekar is corryn. And as you know, a corryn is at the end of his days at five hundred years—and yet Luthekar seems to be in his prime. Mortern is human. Oh, what dread price they shall pay for such favors from foul Droka!"

Morticai stared at Rylan as his words sank in. Before he could respond, however, the door opened again and Geradon reappeared, this time with Kirwin, Phillip, Coryden, and Dualas in tow.

"Inquisitor Glaedwin," Kirwin seethed, "I have been told by Brother Kinsey that you intend to move Morticai from Northgate. For two weeks now I have allowed Brother Kinsey as much freedom within my stronghold as possible."

Morticai paled. *Move me?* He fought back the urge to run, even though the thought was ludicrous.

Kirwin had stalked to the large table and pounded his fist on it. "I have even suspended my normal reprimand procedures. But no one, understand me, *no one* takes one of my men without my permission! So why don't you tell me what this is all about?"

Inquisitor Glaedwin turned and addressed Kirwin smoothly, "Indeed, Commander, I find it commendable that you feel so strongly for your men. You have every right to be informed of our wishes and to approve them. There are several reasons we believe it would be in Morticai's best interest, and yours, I might add, for him to be moved.

"First, there is security," he continued. "With the strained relations between Dynolva and Watchaven and the burden this has placed on you, it is unfair for you to have to deal with the additional threat of Droken assassins attempting to reach Morticai. I am quite certain that if he remained here, more assassination attempts would be made—unfortunately, it is the Droken way.

"Second, moving Morticai to Grandhaven Sanctorium would give him the added benefit of expert care givers to aid his recovery. Mother Edana is quite famous for her skills in healing.

"And finally, we could continue our investigation without being a further nuisance to you. I understand how involved your duties must be and am certain that it would ease things for you if we were not in the way."

Commander Kirwin appeared stunned. Finally, he spoke, "I see. So, you believe that Morticai would be safer at the Sanctorium?"

"I am afraid so. Your fortress here is very strong, but, as Udall demonstrated, one can never know who might be Droken. But more important, and safety aside, Morticai can receive care at the Sanctorium that is impossible to give here."

Kirwin's eyes scanned the room, falling last upon Morticai. "Inquisitor, if you wouldn't mind, I would like to discuss this in private with my men."

"Certainly. Geradon?"

Geradon helped Rylan gather up the contents of his bandaging kit before they headed toward the door.

"Sir Dualas," Kirwin said, "would you please show them to my office."

Dualas smiled ruefully. "Yes, sir."

When they had left, Kirwin turned to Morticai.

"Well?"

"Yes, sir?"

"Well, do you want to go?"

"You're letting me decide?"

Kirwin shrugged. "You know I don't approve of your methods. If you were on special assignment and working with the City Watch, it would be different. As it is, this would all be an incredible disgrace—were it not for the fact that you were apparently correct. It does appear that the Droken are involved in this disruption between Watchaven and Dynolva."

Morticai couldn't believe what he was hearing; Kirwin continued.

"I have spoken with Brother Kinsey at some length. The Inquisition does not hold you at fault for any of this although they, too, are not in agreement with your methods. But you have certainly suffered for your involvement with this. So, yes, I think you should make this decision. Mind you, we will have a fight on our hands if you decide to stay here. But the Northmarch stands by its men."

"Morticai," Coryden interjected, "before you decide, I've talked with Dualas, and his words echo the Inquisitor's concerning the Droken sending more assassins. I know you've never been fond of the way the Faith works, but this would be for only a short while. I think you should consider it."

"You're serious."

Coryden's concerned eyes met his. "I don't want to walk in here and find you dead. You haven't been downstairs. I've never seen Northgate this crowded. I've met Northmarchers I've never seen before—just from patrols that are out when we're on leave. I can post a guard, but that's no guarantee if the Droken use poison again. Even Dualas could be overcome. So what can I do? Move our entire patrol in here? I know how much rest you'd get then."

Morticai considered it. "Could you come and visit?"

"I don't know why not."

Morticai sighed. "All right. You know, I've always worshipped Glawres on the beach," he sheepishly admitted. "I've never even seen the inside of Grandhaven Sanctorium."

CHAPTER ELEVEN

The coach ride from Northgate to the Sanctorium proved grueling. By the time they'd reached the Watchaven landmark, Morticai couldn't have cared less what the inside looked like. The coach turned into one of several private courtyards attached to the great building. Geradon hopped out of the coach to go to fetch something; the Inquisitor gently pulled Morticai against himself. The change in position relieved a surprising amount of the pain.

"We shall have you settled very shortly, now. I am sorry the ride was so jarring. When you are feeling better, I have a great deal to discuss with you. I think you will be quite interested to hear what I've learned about your Droken nobility."

"You mean, you believe me?"

"Of course. We never actually doubted you—once we read your decoded notes. And it is obvious that something is wrong between Dynolva and Watchaven. The problem is determining what their next move will be and proving it to the king. By the way, you might be interested to know that when we stormed Burnaby Manor it was empty—but of course, we expected it would be."

Morticai looked at him in surprise, but before he could say anything the coach door opened and a human woman climbed in. She appeared ancient, so much so that Morticai was surprised at how easily she entered the coach. She wore the full robes of a Matriarch. She immediately fixed her entire attention on him.

"You dear child," she began and stroked his hair as one would a cat. Morticai tried not to smile. As old as she was, the ex-street urchin had probably been stealing apples on Watchaven streets before she had been born.

"They have made you ride in this coach with such a wound. Look at me," she said and caught his face with her hand, forcing him to look into her eyes. Her eyes looked deep; Morticai found himself wanting to look away and yet unable to do so.

"You have seen too many woes, little one," the aged Matriarch concluded as she let him go. "We shall give you some rest from them here." With that, she left the coach as quickly as she had entered.

"That was Mother Edana," Rylan informed him, "but I suppose you gathered that."

"Yeah. She's gonna take care of me?"

Rylan laughed softly. "Don't worry, she is not usually that intense. She will, however, have you on your feet much faster than you would expect."

"Does she talk to everyone like that?"

"Not everyone. She is, shall I say, very perceptive. She is a living Levani in the fullest definition."

"Huh?" Morticai asked.

Rylan did not explain further, however, and Morticai soon found himself in a small, cozy room in one of the Sanctorium's quieter wings.

On their way to his room Morticai had been astonished at the number of corryn refugees crowded into the long halls.

Although he had been told of the recent events, until now he had seen no evidence of them himself.

Once moved into the room, he was surprised at how comfortable the bed proved. Although he intended to stay awake, sleep quickly claimed him, as the quiet security of the Sanctorium settled about him.

* * * * *

Morticai woke suddenly, every muscle tensed, every instinct fully engaged—and unable to act. A strong hand was clamped over his mouth while others held his wrists. The knife he expected to feel at his throat was absent, however, and his eyes were met by the light blue eyes of a middle-aged corryn wearing the hood of a monk. The corryn smiled as Morticai relaxed.

Still keeping his hand in place, the monk whispered, "Sorry to wake you so rudely, Dyluth, but we don't break into Grandhaven Sanctorium every day, y'know."

Morticai nodded, and the hands holding him down released him. Morticai could see that two others, a man and maiden of the Faith, were in the room as well.

"Nelerek, what the Dark One are you doing here?" Morticai asked.

"Trying to find out if you're all right, ya vagabond. First I hear you've nearly died at Burnaby Manor, then I hear you're locked up at Northgate, then I learn the Inquisition's after you and that they're bringing you here. What the Dark One are you doing! And never mind that you don't call on your Arluthian Advocate for help."

"I couldn't involve you, Nelerek," Morticai defended himself. "Coryden and Sir Dualas were involved from the start. I wasn't about to put you or the Arluthian Society at risk."

Morticai's gaze kept drifting to Nelerek's companions. Suddenly, he recognized one of them and burst out laughing, and then promptly held his side.

"Dammit, Dyluth!" Nelerek scolded, "with most men I'd have to worry about yelling—with you it's laughing!"

"I'm—I'm sorry, Nelerek," Morticai said as he tried not to laugh again. "It's just that I recognized that cute maiden of the Faith you've got with you. I never realized you looked so good in a dress, Scatla!" Morticai said, pointing to the "maiden."

Scatla put his hands on his hips. "Try to help a Brother and what do you get? He flirts with ya."

Now, the monk watching the door started laughing as well. Nelerek shook his head.

"And I thought you'd retired, Paxton," Morticai teased, recognizing Paxton's easy laugh.

"Well," the monk replied, "you're not going to stop by this Brother's house wounded and not have him worry. Calsen told me a little about that fight you and he were in."

"Dyluth," Nelerek interjected, "we don't have much time. Come now, I need some answers and quickly."

"Sure."

"Do you want us to get you out of here? I've got a dozen more Arluthians in position to break you out."

"What?"

"You heard me, we're here to break you out."

Morticai shook his head. "But I don't need to be broken out."

"They're not holding you against your will?"

"No. They moved me here to protect me from Droken assassins, though I can see how good their security is. I might as well be at Northgate."

Nelerek exchanged glances with Paxton and Scatla.

"Then the Droken are truly trying to kill you?"

Morticai sighed. "It's beginnin' to look like it."

"And why are the Droken trying to kill my ward?" Nelerek asked evenly.

Morticai shrugged. "I discovered that some of our nobility are Droken. They're involved in this Dynolva-Watchaven thing, and I fought some prince of the Droken, and now they're upset."

"What!" Nelerek and Paxton cried simultaneously.

"Shhh," Morticai admonished. "And you were worried about me making too much noise."

"What do you mean you fought 'some prince of the Droken'?" Nelerek whispered sharply.

"Well, that's, uh, what Inquisitor Glaedwin said. He said that the corryn we fought outside Burnaby Manor was some type of Droken prince."

Nelerek looked at Paxton. "Luthekar—if he was corryn."

"What is this? Everyone knows about this guy but me?" Morticai asked irritably. "I didn't even know the Droken had nobility."

Paxton abandoned the door to come and sink down beside the bed. "Dyluth," he began, "you don't seem to understand what this means."

"Never mind now, Paxton," Nelerek interrupted. "Grandhaven Sanctorium is the best place for him—at the moment. Unlike us, the Droken won't enter these halls. Dyluth, you are recovering from this wound?"

"I seem to be."

"A time may come when we shall have to free you from here and take you someplace safer. You do not fear the Inquisition?"

"You know I've always feared the Faith, Nelerek. I was very uncomfortable about it at the beginning, but they seem to mean me no harm."

Nelerek sighed. "Very well—for now." He paced to the small window and, studying it, worked it to see if it opened. It opened smoothly to reveal a small, private courtyard. "Scatla, you know the layout here. What does this courtyard attach to?"

Scatla moved to the window and briefly studied the flowered garden. "The private sitting room for the maidens is to your left, the Matriarch's rooms are straight ahead, and the Grand Patriarch's are to your right."

Nelerek tapped on the stained glass, "Hm, I don't think a crossbow bolt will penetrate this. Unless it is at very close range."

"Maidens' sitting room?" Morticai asked.

"You can't get out this window, Dyluth," Nelerek said slyly, "and you're in no shape to be chasing maidens."

Paxton looked heavenward. "Grandhaven Sanctorium may not be ready for Dyluth, Nelerek."

Nelerek smiled crookedly. "Any protégé of mine, it had better not be—else I or the Faith have failed." Closing the window, he returned to the bed and began to examine its wooden frame. "Paxton, do you think a sliver of this bed would suffice for Webspinner's sorcery?"

Paxton tilted his head. "What type of sorcery?"

"I'd like to send Dyluth a pigeon each day. Webspinner will have to cast a spell to teach the bird to home on this room."

"Ah, I see." Paxton nodded. "Well, I think a sliver from the windowsill would work better, if we can find a spot that's unpainted. The bed can be moved, you know."

"You're right," Nelerek agreed, returning to the window. "Ah, I think this should do." He carved a small piece of wood from the sill's outer edge. "Hm, I probably should get him a lock of hair, as well."

"You're gonna cut my hair?" Morticai complained.

Nelerek sighed. "You've got enough hair for two people, Dyluth! I'm not going to cut it where anyone will see." Nelerek cuffed him lightly in jest and then quickly obtained a lock from the nape of Morticai's neck. "Each day, between the hours of noon and one, open your window for my bird. Should you need us to come, all you need do is attach a note to it."

Morticai smiled. "It's nice to have friends."

"It's nice to have Brothers," Paxton corrected him.

"I fear that you'll need all the help your Arluthian Brothers can provide," Nelerek cautioned as he raised his cowl. "Now, Sister Scatla, if you would be so kind as to lead us out of here."

* * * * *

Morticai soon discovered that Mother Edana was all that Inquisitor Glaedwin claimed. She fussed over him and at him, made him walk up and down the hall thrice daily—and enabled him to move again. Although he still had to rest frequently, he was amazed at the progress he made.

Currently, Morticai sat on his bed wondering how he might gain more freedom about the large Sanctorium; so far, he had been allowed to roam only the hallway outside his room. A light knock sounded on the door.

"Enter."

Inquisitor Glaedwin entered the room.

"Good day, Morticai."

"Hello, Inquisitor."

Glaedwin sat down beside the bed and smiled.

"I do wish you would call me Rylan."

The corryn shrugged. "Whatever you wish."

"I understand that you are doing well."

"Yes—you were right about the Matriarch. It wasn't easy the first day, but I must admit I feel much better now. How long am I going to have to stay here?"

"Well, that is part of why I've come to speak with you. I've spent a good deal of time talking with Sir Dualas and Captain Coryden, as well as doing some research of my own. I have developed a theory as to why Udall was sent to kill you."

Rylan paced to the open window and gazed into the courtyard beyond.

"I am operating on the assumption that the Droken were unaware of your activities until the night you fought Luthekar. On that night, Luthekar could have heard two names, yours and Sir Dualas's—this is according to Sir Dualas's recollection.

"Luthekar would have recognized Dualas as a knight of the Faith from the insignia he was wearing. And although you were not wearing insignia, your captain was wearing his Northmarch cloak brooch. Now, if you had been Luthekar, what would you have thought?"

Rylan turned to gaze at Morticai.

"I don't know," Morticai began. "I guess that he'd been found."

Rylan nodded.

"Indeed. Perhaps he would have thought that you were working for the Faith; after all, a knight of the Faith was there.

Or, more likely, he would have thought that the Northmarch was working with the Faith."

Morticai considered the strange concept. A pigeon flew to the window and landed on the sill.

Rylan turned to stare at it a moment before remarking, "They don't do that very often."

Damn! Morticai thought as the Sanctorium's bells began chiming the noon hour.

Rylan walked to the window, obviously expecting the bird to fly away. The bird eyed him suspiciously as it strutted back and forth along the sill.

"How unusual," Rylan remarked. "Perhaps it is someone's pet?"

He reached out his hand to stroke the bird's back. The bird hopped away from him and fluttered to Morticai's knee. Morticai lightly swatted at it; it fluttered a few feet away and then returned. Now Rylan was eyeing him suspiciously.

"Friendly, isn't it?" remarked Morticai innocently.

"It seems to be," Rylan said slowly.

Morticai picked the bird up and walked to the window. "Shoo! Get out of here!"

The bird quickly flew away. Morticai turned to find himself still facing Rylan's suspicious gaze.

"Uh," Morticai said, "you were saying something about Luthekar thinking the Faith and Northmarch were working together."

"Yes, I was," Rylan replied. He shook his head and continued. "So, why should the Faith work with the Northmarch? As you yourself have noted, the Faith sometimes has difficulty gathering information—particularly when someone as obvious as, dare I say, Dualas, is involved. It would seem reasonable for the Faith to work with the Northmarch and someone like yourself, who could gather information more efficiently.

"You should also understand," he continued, "that Luthekar would not be here unless something extremely important to the Droken were involved. Your finding him would be seen as a grave threat to the Droken operation. Luthekar would decide that you were the most versatile, unorthodox, effective member of our 'team'—and the most dangerous element."

Morticai scowled, not liking where Rylan's logic was heading. Rylan continued.

"Therefore, he would decide that he must remove you, and do so as quickly as possible—even if it meant risking a valuable agent in the Northmarch, like Udall."

Rylan paced back to the bed.

"Unfortunately, there is an additional problem that has resulted from this. If you had fought anyone but Luthekar, you would have been at risk only until the plot was complete. But, because you survived the wound dealt by Luthekar's sword, you have received an honor that is usually reserved only for men of the Faith. The Droken will hunt you for the rest of your life—and, I am very sorry to say, you will never again be truly safe."

"You mean they're going to keep sending assassins?" Morticai asked slowly.

"Yes, that is exactly what I mean. The miracle, of which you were the object, will be seen as a direct insult to Luthekar and Droka."

"Miracle?" Morticai asked. This was the first he'd heard anything about miracles.

"Yes," Rylan explained patiently, "surviving the wound from Luthekar's sword. And the miracle will be seen as an insult, a challenge, against which he must retaliate."

"Wait a minute! You mean because he couldn't kill me the first time, I've insulted him?"

"Don't you understand, Morticai?" Rylan asked. "No one has ever survived a wound from Luthekar's sword, because the sword was given to Luthekar by Droka. Only by your patron's intervention could you have survived—otherwise they would not have been able to stop the bleeding. Your patron Glawres consciously chose to let you live. And because he has done this, it will be seen as a direct challenge—by Droka and by Luthekar, his champion."

Morticai's head spun with the implications.

"Why did Glawres do something like that for me?"

Rylan laid a hand on his arm. "Who can say? But are you unhappy because he did?"

"No, of course not. But, what does it mean? That you won't let me leave here?" he asked suspiciously.

"No, that is not what it means. The Inquisition has always faced the wrath of the Droken—against those who help us and against our own ranks. I, myself, have a price on my head."

Morticai looked at him in surprise.

"My choice has been to continue on," Rylan explained, "although I must admit I am more cautious than before. I often travel under a different name, and I have a bodyguard, as well.

"You fall into the category of an informer," Rylan continued, "although I know that is not how you view yourself. The Inquisition helps informers change their identity. It involves a name change, perhaps hair dye. I would think that would be particularly important in your case," Rylan said, eyeing Morticai's silver-streaked tresses. "And, you would need to move to a smaller town, someplace far from here. Some of our informers become a part of the Faith—they join the clergy and move to a distant monastery."

Morticai looked at him, aghast.

"You're asking me to leave Watchaven and the Northmarch!"

Rylan shook his head. "I am afraid there are not many options, Morticai."

"What about you? You've 'continued on': why can't I?"

Rylan furrowed his brow before heaving a heavy sigh. "The Droken will be waiting for you if you return to Northgate, Morticai. . . ."

"But I have friends who have disappeared before, right here in the city," Morticai complained. "Watchaven is big. I don't have to go back to the Northmarch right away." His mind raced. He had to make certain he wasn't moved from this room—tomorrow might well be the day he returned Nelerek's bird with a note calling for help. "Besides," he added, realizing that Rylan was staring at him, shocked by his outburst, "we still have to find Luthekar!"

Rylan blinked. "You still want to continue with this?"

"You're damned right I do!" Morticai's anger erupted. "This is the second time the Droken have destroyed my life! I ran the first time, all the way from . . . from Lorredre. I'm not running again!"

Rylan's brow furrowed again. "I don't know, Morticai. We shall talk more about it—later. For now, however, I have something to show you."

Morticai hesitated, fearful that if he went with Rylan now, he might not be returned to this room.

"Coming?" Rylan asked.

Sighing, Morticai rose—he could see no way around it. They walked down the hall, turned down another, and finally stopped before a closed door. Rylan smiled as he theatrically gestured for Morticai to open it. Morticai hestitated a moment before complying.

"Well! I was beginning to wonder if my four hours would run out and I'd have to get back to Northgate without seeing you!"

Coryden's familiar voice came from the middle of the large room, where he stood with his hands on his hips. Berret and Dualas were also in the room, sitting at a small table not far from the door.

"Coryden!" Morticai cried.

He entered the room and then stopped abruptly; his knife targets were hung at various heights against the room's right-hand wall, his knives piled on a nearby table.

"I told you it'd surprise him!" Berret said, laughing.

Morticai spun around to Rylan, who stood leaning against the doorjamb, his arms crossed and a warm smile across his face.

"You approved this?" Morticai asked in astonishment.

"Of course," Rylan replied. "I would not deprive you of one of your favorite hobbies." His tone became serious, "Besides, if I agree to what you have proposed today, you will still need your skills."

Morticai smiled. Maybe he wouldn't need to see that bird again after all.

* * * * *

Morticai stood with his eyes closed, his arms stretched upward, and his wrists crossed. He consciously relaxed and counted slowly as he lowered his hands. Each hand held three knives. He had been working for months on this one throwing maneuver; he took an easy breath and slowly opened his eyes.

With a snap, both arms flicked outward, a knife leaping from each hand toward targets on opposite sides of the room; as they sank solidly in the soft wooden targets, he threw two more knives, striking the target in front of him, and finally he spun to embed his last two knives in the target behind him. The entire maneuver had taken less than two seconds. Each knife had struck center of the **X**s painted on the targets.

Soft applause rose from the doorway. "You should have joined the carnival," Rylan observed.

Morticai shrugged. "Why? I make more money with it this way."

"Yes," Rylan agreed, "but from what I've heard, your methods have the unwelcomed side effect of often angering those you wager with."

Morticai smiled wickedly. "Rylan, that's half the fun."

Rylan shook his head. "Maybe you can survive the Droken, Morticai. Come." Rylan gestured to the table. "I have good news for you."

Morticai certainly hoped so. He had been here only a week and a half and had already tired of it. He had unsuccessfully tried flirting with a few of the maidens; they had all smiled and quietly gone about their business.

"You expressed a desire to continue your investigation of Watchaven's Droken. Are you willing to do so under my command?"

Morticai thought a moment before replying, "I suppose so. It would be better than moving to some monastery."

"Excellent. Geradon is packing my things now. He has rented us a larger room at the Hilltop Tavern. As soon as you are packed, we can move into it. I will allow you to move about the city, as long as I have some idea what you are about—you understand the risks?"

"Oh, yeah," Morticai hastened to reassure him.

"Good. I am going now to Northgate to tell Commander McFerrin that the Inquisition will be keeping you for a while—I expect you will want to explain things to Captain Coryden, but I strongly suggest we let the rest of the Northmarch wonder."

Morticai was beginning to understand where those stories he'd heard about the Inquisition had originated.

"Will you take Coryden a note from me?" Morticai asked.

"Certainly." Rylan's eyes narrowed. "That reminds me, you can tell whoever has been sending you the bird that it is no longer necessary."

Morticai started to say, "What bird?" and thought better of it. Rylan rose.

"I shall leave for Northgate shortly. Will it take you long to compose your note?"

"No, not at all," Morticai replied.

"Good."

* * * * *

Coryden paused in the middle of the street. He reread Morticai's note and wished he had spent more time teaching him to write neatly. He couldn't quite decipher the name of the tavern at which they were to meet.

"Let me look at it," Berret suggested.

Coryden handed it to him. "Please do."

Berret moved the paper closer and farther away as though it would improve the script. Evadrel looked over his shoulder.

"It's the Dappled Stallion," Evadrel remarked.

Coryden and Berret both stared at him. Evadrel shrugged; Coryden sighed. "Well," Coryden said, "let's go."

Morticai's entire squad had insisted on escorting Coryden to his "secret" meeting with Morticai. Even Richard, the squad's new man, had come along. Coryden really couldn't complain—

after all, they were as concerned for their captain's safety as they were eager to see Morticai.

Incidents in the city had become sporadic, but journeying in groups was still the safest form of travel. There were days when nothing seemed to happen and days when a corryn was beaten or killed. Coryden could not remember a time when Watchaven had felt so foreign.

The group turned a corner to see a squad of the City Watch standing in a cluster at the next intersection. Coryden heard a voice saying that he had his orders, and surprisingly, the Northmarch captain recognized the voice. It belonged to Captain Trahern, a longtime drinking friend.

Another voice rose from the center of the watchmen.

"You can't do this, Trahern! I haven't done anything!"

As one, Coryden's group came to a stunned halt.

"Morticai!" Coryden yelled and then ran up to the squad of watchmen.

The ex-street urchin was, indeed, in the center of the group.

"Thank Glawres!" Morticai exclaimed in corryn. "Coryden, they say they're gonna take me in. I haven't done anything!"

The watchmen stepped aside enough to let the Northmarchers approach Captain Trahern. More than a few startled glances were thrown at Richard, who stood taller than half the corryn in Berret's squad.

Berret replied, also in corryn, "Morticai, I don't know how you do it, but I swear you get into more trouble than the rest of the patrol put together!"

"Stop that!" Trahern ordered. "Quit speaking in corryn! What did you say?" He glared suspiciously at the human Berret, whose corryn was surprisingly fluent.

"Wait a minute," Coryden said quickly in human. "Just what is going on here, Trahern?"

Trahern straightened authoritatively. "I have orders from the palace to pick up Morticai."

"What!" half the patrol exclaimed at once.

"What I need," Morticai said in corryn, "is a diversion."

Trahern spun and soundly backhanded Morticai, who was

knocked into a shocked Evadrel.

"I said to stop speaking in corryn!" Trahern yelled, but he had already unwittingly begun the diversion Morticai had requested.

Everyone began speaking at once. Coryden was aware that his men were turning it into a confrontation, but at the moment, he couldn't have cared less.

Coryden had stepped up close to Trahern. "*Nobody* strikes one of my men without good cause! Since when has speaking corryn become unlawful in Watchaven?"

"He's getting away! Stop him!" someone yelled.

Coryden looked up to see Morticai, half a block away and running. He watched in horror as a watchman, beyond his reach, raised a crossbow and sighted on Morticai.

"*No!*" Coryden yelled.

Richard was already shoving watchmen aside. He knocked the crossbow upward as its bolt left the stock. Coryden could not help but wince as Richard followed with a full strength punch to the middle of the watchman's stomach. The bolt flew wild and embedded in a nearby wall; the watchman went to his knees.

Swords were drawn, and the street echoed with the sound of steel on wood. Coryden quickly sized up the situation: there were about twenty watchmen, while Coryden had twelve; the Northmarchers had more experience—they could take them, but it would be messy.

"Do you really want to test your men on us?" Coryden said softly.

Trahern glared at him without answering, but both sides paused, waiting for their commanders to sort things out. Coryden counted the seconds. The longer Trahern hesitated, the better the chance that blood would not be shed.

"Resheath!" Trahern finally ordered. Slowly, both sides dropped away from each other, the watchmen resheathing their weapons, the Northmarchers lowering theirs.

* * * * *

It was several hours later when Coryden and his men straggled into the Dappled Stallion. The proprietor was expecting them and quickly ushered them into a back room. Morticai sat with his chair tilted back, his feet on the table, and a tankard in his hand. He sported a dark bruise on his left cheekbone.

"Hi!" he greeted them cheerfully. "What took you so long? You guys didn't fight back there, did you?"

Coryden glared at him. "No, we didn't fight! But we might well have. Morticai, he really did have orders from the palace to pick you up. What is going on?"

Morticai lowered his feet. A serving girl came in with a large trayful of tankards. Everyone settled in around the table.

"You're serious? He really did have an order?" Morticai asked.

"Yes! Now, what the Levani is going on?" Coryden demanded again.

"Hm. I don't know, Coryden. I haven't had time to cause any trouble—honest. I just got out of the Sanctorium this morning."

Berret remarked, "Well, you certainly got your diversion, all right. You must have done something to cause this."

Morticai shook his head emphatically. "No. It might have something to do with what Rylan has been telling me, but I didn't expect it from the palace."

"Morticai," Coryden said, "you're not making sense. What in the Benek's name are you talking about?"

Morticai sighed. "Well . . ."

It was late that night, and well past their four-hour time limit, when Coryden and his men left for Northgate. They had sent several messages to the gate guard, explaining that they were being detained by the Inquisition. After all, Morticai was working for the Inquisition now.

* * * * *

The elaborately decorated coach pulled slowly to a halt. They were still very close to Watchaven, just north of the city on a narrow wagon path that led to Dunder, a tiny village that lay ten miles north of the huge city.

To the east was a magnificent view of the ocean. The cliffs here were high; the roar and crash of the waves to resounded hollowly on the jagged rocks. The coachman hopped down and opened the door of the coach with a well-practiced flourish.

He held out his hand. The white-gloved hand that accepted his help was slender, elegant, and feminine. The lady landed lightly, her ornate gown softly rustling. She was corryn, but petite for her race, with pure silver hair and deep green eyes. Her hair wound elaborately around her head, ending in cascading curls.

"Thank you, Nevin," the lady offered graciously.

"M'lady, we are miles from any habitation," the coachman began. "Will you not allow me to accompany you?"

"Thank you, Nevin, but absolutely not," the lady replied firmly. "Please, I will be quite safe. I need for you to wait here—and be patient! I expect I shall be gone for some time, but you must not worry."

"Yes, m'lady," Nevin replied resignedly.

The lady lifted her skirt an inch off the sand and carefully made her way down the trail that led to the small stretch of beach, far below.

She stopped as she reached the base of the cliff, where the trail ended in a small circle of upthrust rocks. The rocks were carved with ancient, intricate designs. In the center of the protected spot stood a large stone basin, formed from a single boulder. It, too, bore elaborate carvings. It was a solemn place, where the weight of the ages could not be ignored.

The lady stopped before the basin and removed her gloves. She offered up her prayer as she dipped her hands into the water and withdrew them cupped full of the hallowed liquid. As the ancients had done, she took a sip and then scattered the remaining water in a circle about herself. The ceremony performed, she continued on.

Now at the level of the ocean itself, the sound of the waves was either tremendous or muted, depending on where one stood. The rocks caused odd echoes, and small caverns abounded. The lady walked slowly, expectantly, as she came onto the beach itself. Before her, a few yards away, sat a lone figure. Not wanting to intrude too quickly, she approached cautiously.

"Dyluth?" she spoke softly.

Morticai turned. His lopsided smile came slowly, ruefully.

She moved closer and knelt beside him on the sand, abandoning her concern for the dress she had so carefully tended on the trail. She touched his face lightly, turning it, and frowned as she inspected the bruise on his left cheekbone.

"I'm glad you were able to come, Heather," Morticai said. "I wasn't certain you would be able to get away."

She released his face, and gave his hair a single, soft stroke, letting her hand linger at the back of his head. "I would have come under any circumstances. It has been a long time since we have met here. What troubles you, Dyluth?"

Morticai sighed, and then an ironic smirk crept onto his face. "Heather, you're going to tell me that you've warned me of this for years." The smirk faded. "Just don't tell me that I deserve it. Please?"

He looked away and gathered his thoughts; she remained silent, her face filled with concern.

"I have come upon a Droken plot. What would you think if I told you that it is the Droken who have driven Watchaven and Dynolva so close to war, and that the Droken doing it are Watchaven nobles?"

"Were it anyone else," she answered, "I would laugh. But you, my love, would not lie about such a thing. Do I know them?"

Morticai shrugged. "I suppose so. Lord Aldwin, Lord Valdir, Sir Ellenwood?"

Heather nodded solemnly. "I could see such a thing from Aldwin, but Valdir? How odd. I do not know the other. But wasn't it the Dynolvans who assassinated Aldwin?"

"I don't know how that happened," Morticai admitted. "I know for a fact he was Droken. Maybe their plans to stir up the

Dynolvans worked too well. I don't know. I was kind of tethered down at the time."

"As in?" Heather asked suspiciously.

Morticai sighed. "Well, it's part of why I asked you to meet me here. Do you remember Burnaby Manor?"

She smiled seductively. "How could I not?"

"Yeah." Morticai returned the smile. Becoming serious again, he continued. "Well, I was wounded in the alley outside the tunnel by a corryn knight of some kind—at the time, that was what I thought he must have been. I've been told that the 'knight' was Prince Luthekar. Ever hear of him?"

"No,"Heather answered slowly. "It is familiar somehow, but I don't know why. Where is he prince?"

"I don't know if there is a 'where,' but he's a prince of the Droken."

Heather stared at him a long while, horror slowly filling her eyes. "Now, I remember where I've heard the name. I've heard the court bards tell stories about him. Oh, Dyluth! He is a foul, wicked creature! You fought him?"

"Yeah. Almost died, too."

"But Dyluth, the stories say that no one can survive against him!"

"Well, the Inquisitor tells it a little diff—"

"Inquisitor!"

"Uh, well, yeah . . . Heather, let me get through one thing at a time. Please?"

She sat beside him and involuntarily shuddered. Morticai continued.

"Anyway, this Inquisitor told me it's Luthekar's sword that no one is supposed to be able to survive. Y'see, Heather, my problem isn't the Inquisition. They came to investigate and are generally on my side of things. In fact, I'm kinda working for them now. My problem is the Droken."

"*You* are working for the Inquisition?"

"It was either that or move to a monastery somewhere. See, the Droken are after me because I survived that damned sword. A Northmarcher tried to kill me, for Glawres's sake! Of course, he turned out to be Droken. But I can't go back to North-gate—at least, not until this is over. I wanted to talk with you because someone at the palace has put out an order to have me picked up, and I want you to find out who ordered it."

Heather cradled her forehead in her hand and shook her head. "Oh, Dyluth!" she said disgustedly.

He looked away. "I thought that would be your reaction," he said glumly.

Heather moved to kneel in front of him. She took his hands in hers, bringing them together before her. She waited until Morticai looked back at her before speaking.

"Dyluth, what are you going to do? If the Droken have truly singled you out for death, what can you do?"

"Nice of you to put it so clearly," Morticai replied cynically.

"Dyluth, listen to me! Don't you understand? I know what it is like to be hunted! You should remember, too: you helped me hide. You should run from here—far, far away."

"I am hiding, Heather! That's why I didn't meet you in town."

"What of the Arluthians? Have you heard from Nelerek?"

"Yes, I have heard from Nelerek."

"And?"

Morticai sighed. "He thinks I should leave town."

"See? Even Nelerek agrees," she pointed out needlessly.

Morticai looked away. When he turned to her again, his dark blue eyes brimmed with unshed tears. "Do you know what you're asking? I-I don't want to leave Watchaven." He blinked the tears back. "I don't want to run again! I'm old enough now to do something I couldn't when they killed my parents, Heather. Now I can fight back!"

Now it was Heather's turn to look away. The smugness had left her voice when she spoke again.

"Dyluth. Morticai," she began and then stopped. She turned back, catching his eyes easily with hers. "Moranekor," she said softly, using his true name, "I know that we have had many differences. But there is much that cannot be denied, either. I would not have you fall to the Droken!"

He stared at her a moment before pulling her into his arms. She cried softly as he rocked her back and forth.

"Heather."

"Please, we can leave here, Dyluth," she said. "We should have done it long ago. I will go with you. We can begin a new life. I am ready to find out the truth about my heritage. We could go to Tradelenor, while I learn about things in Lorredre. If I could clear my family's name, I would have all the money necessary to protect you. We could even be matched. Let us be gone from this human place, where corryn are not welcome."

Morticai held her away from him. "Heather, are you crazy? Be gone from this human place. And go to Tradelenor? You can't get any more human than Tradelenor!"

"Then, we'll go to Cuthedre! Anywhere but here, Dyluth! As long as we go together."

Morticai shook his head. "No!" He let loose of her shoulders; she continued to sob softly. "Heather, really now," he chided her, "think about it. Think about us. You know it wouldn't work. The first time I got into a fight, you'd be gone. And if that didn't do it, you'd leave when your fine clothes wore out and I couldn't replace them for you."

She stopped sobbing and looked at him, hurt. "Is that all you think I care about?"

He sighed. "No. But I won't have you match with a dead man, either."

She fumbled for the slit in her outer skirt, retrieved a kerchief from her purse, and dabbed at her eyes. Afterward, she laid a hand along Morticai's face. Now it was his eyes that filled with hurt.

"So now I know what it takes for you to agree to matching," he said. "Finally, I know."

"That's unfair," she said accusingly, dropping her hand.

"Probably. I'm sorry." He picked up a pebble and threw it toward the water. Sighing, he continued, "Besides, Heather, there's more to it, I think."

She looked confused. "More to what?"

"More to what's going on. I've felt odd about this. Ever

since it started. It's like . . . it's like it's something I've got to do." He paused awkwardly. "Y'know, the Inquisitor said it was a miracle that I lived. He said that only by Glawres intervening could I have survived. I still don't know what to think about that."

Heather looked at him, her tears dried now. "This Inquisitor really said that?"

A smirk came over Morticai's face. "Yeah, he couldn't figure it out either." He laughed openly, throwing his head back. "Miracle performed on Watchaven street urchin—maybe it does sound like Glawres. Aluntas knows, the patron of the sea has never been predictable."

"You underrate yourself, Dyluth," Heather replied. "You always have. Glawres should be proud of you. After all, you have never been predictable, either."

Morticai smiled weakly. "I'm sorry. I didn't want to meet with you to argue." He looked down.

She lifted his chin. "I am sorry too. I'll get your information—and fret myself sick worrying about you, I am certain."

"Y'know," he said slowly, "I still love you."

She smiled. "And I, you."

They embraced again, this time allowing it to turn into long, remembering kisses.

* * * * *

Morticai glanced at the threatening sky. Dark clouds billowed in rapidly from the southeast, a sure sign of rain. He grabbed his hat, as a gust of wind tried to snatch it from his head. The first drops of rain began to fall as he entered the side door of Carlton's Cabinetry Shop.

Inside, amid the benches and woodcrafting tools, a corryn was busy lighting oil lamps, which were already chasing the darkness from the dim corners of the shop. The Northmarcher removed his hat and cloak and placed them on a carved wooden cloakstand.

"That's some storm," Morticai observed.

In the lightening room, Nelerek's features became visible. "I'm not surprised," he said, lighting the last lamp. "Word from the docks has it that it hit Menelcar first."

"I'm glad it didn't come ashore here," Morticai responded. Outside, the rain began to pound against the door.

A table, set with two mugs and a bottle, stood in the center of the room. Nelerek sat and began pouring their drinks.

"Aye, we don't need bad weather," Nelerek agreed. "Aluntas knows we corryn have enough problems at the moment." He glanced up then, and scowled at Morticai.

Morticai blinked, and then realized that Nelerek was scowling at the bruise that was still fading from his left cheekbone.

"Uh, City Watch," Morticai said.

"Ah." Nelerek nodded, as though it was sufficient explanation. "Speaking of trouble, have any more Droken come to visit?"

"No, thank Glawres," Morticai replied, taking a seat.

Nelerek raised his mug. "Here's hoping it remains that way."

Morticai joined him in the toast.

"I have spoken with the council," Nelerek announced.

Morticai leaned forward expectantly.

"You will be pleased to know," Nelerek continued, "that they have officially approved of your current, ah, connections, with the Inquisition."

"Thank you," Morticai replied, sinking back in the chair. "It would have been tough if they hadn't."

Nelerek nodded. "Agreed. Of course, the Arluthians are as eager as the Faith to defeat the Droken. The council's main concern was whether our Brotherhood would be compromised should the Inquisition decide to 'test your merits.' "

Morticai blinked in surprise. "You mean, as in 'hurt me'; do you truly think they would do something like that?"

Nelerek shook his head. "No, I think they'll leave you alone. These three seem to mean you no harm, but I have had experience with others from the Inquisition who were not so gentle."

"Three?" Morticai asked, tilting his head.

"Aye, you heard me—three. Y'see I've done a little of my own research. That new man that recently joined your squad, Richard, is also working for the Inquisition."

Morticai considered the new information.

"But," Nelerek continued, "they seem to be an honest group. By the way, the council was very interested in what you've uncovered and were quite pleased that you've used your skills so effectively. You just might gain a rank, if you can survive long enough," he added, with a wink.

"You're as cheerful as Heather," Morticai said, shaking his head.

Nelerek raised an eyebrow. "Are you two . . . ?"

"No," Morticai snorted. "She's going to help me do a little research, that's all." Morticai solemnly studied his drink before taking a slow swig.

Nelerek cleared his throat and abruptly changed the subject. "Well, as expected, Luthekar seems to have vanished, but I have learned that the haunting of Burnaby Manor began over a month ago. I'm afraid that is all I've discovered so far."

"That's all right, Nelerek," Morticai said glumly. "I don't want to drag you into this, anyway. It's bad enough that they're after me; no sense endangering you further." Morticai drained his mug.

Nelerek reached across the table and grabbed Morticai's free arm. "Is that self-pity I hear, Dyluth? Y'know, just because you've finally locked horns with the Droken doesn't mean they're going to take all of us. And if you don't get rid of such ridiculous notions, I'm going to give you a good flogging, the likes of which you haven't had since you slept in doorways."

Morticai's mouth opened wordlessly. Then, dropping his gaze, he sat silently.

"Hit the mark, didn't I?" Nelerek said gently.

"There have been more 'ridiculous notions' than I care to think about," Morticai admitted slowly.

"I'm not surprised—I suppose it's normal. But if you continue thinking they are going to get you and all your friends, they will get you," Nelerek admonished softly.

Morticai sighed and settled himself for the coming lecture; however, his Arluthian advocate did not give the expected litany.

"I always knew that you'd be up against the Droken sooner or later—your parents' deaths sealed that fate," Nelerek began. "I'm just glad that it waited this long. Y'know, I've put a lot of effort into your training, and not just because you've got talent. I chose to train you because you are an idealist, a true Arluthian—and because I knew that someday you'd have to fight the Droken. Everything I've taught you can be used against them and for your own survival.

"You've given me a lot of pride, y'know. Think about it— you've passed each Arluthian trial by a grand degree. Hell, you've never even been scratched!" He sat back down and leaned across the table.

"It's a sign that you can take on the Droken—that you've got the skills to do it. There's a lot of training in there." He tapped Morticai on the head. "It has kept you alive this long— there's no reason for it to fail you now. This doesn't have to be any different than the Arluthian ordeals you've already passed through."

Morticai smiled weakly. "The ordeals don't last day in and day out, Nelerek. They last only a few hours. This is different."

Nelerek nodded. "But they are life and death—just like this. Give it time, Dyluth. A day will come when you'll realize that keeping an eye open for the Droken has become second nature. Just like your knives or your rope work, practice will make it seem simple."

Morticai smiled again, this time with a little more conviction. "Yeah, I guess so. I hope so."

Nelerek smiled. "That's better. So, just what exactly do you and the robes plan to do about this plague of Droken infecting our two beloved cities?"

Morticai sighed. "Well, Inquisitor Glaedwin has sent for more help, but we don't think it'll get here before war breaks out. He's already met with King Almgren."

Nelerek raised his eyebrows. "My, my."

"Yeah, but it didn't do any good," Morticai complained. "King Almgren wants solid proof, and my deciphered notes aren't enough. And now that Aldwin is dead, the notes carry even less weight."

"So?" Nelerek asked, refilling both of their mugs.

"So, Glaedwin and Kinsey are both shuffling through Trade Council voting records to organize some sort of report they can show King Almgren—I don't think it'll help."

Morticai took a swig from his mug. "I've been lying low and putting out all the contacts I can, but so far nothin's turned up. My other choices are to sniff around the Snake Pit some more, go back to following people, or maybe break into Ellenwood's or Valdir's to see if I can locate more evidence. All I know is I've got to do something, or I'll hang myself and do the Droken's work for them. This inactivity is driving me crazy."

Nelerek nodded. "No wonder you've been brooding. Sounds like you need to move about more. I don't know if the Snake Pit is the place to do it, though. Promise me that if you decide to go there, you'll let me know so I can go with you."

Morticai nodded, if not too enthusiastically. "Yeah. Usual message drop?"

"Aye."

"Y'know, Nelerek, I think that's part of what's bothering me so much—having to be so damned dependent on other people. It was bad enough before all of this began."

Nelerek's brow furrowed. "What are you talking about?"

"Oh"—Morticai waved a hand—"my damned patrol—and Heather. I guess I just never noticed it before, but Coryden's patrol has turned me into some kind of mascot they think they've got to protect. I'm tired of them constantly watching out for me. And Heather treats me like a stray pet that she wants to chain. Only now, I'm gettin' it from all sides—the Inquisitor, my patrol, Heather. Everybody is tellin' me to stay off the streets, to let them be my eyes and ears. I hate this helpless feeling."

Nelerek nodded. "Oh, I understand that—especially coming from you. But things have a way of changing, Dyluth. It won't stay like this forever."

Nelerek began packing up the table's contents. "Well, Carlton's apprentice should be arriving before too long, and I suppose we should be gone before he arrives. Carlton hasn't decided if he should make his apprentice an Arluthian Brother or not."

Morticai stared out the window as Nelerek packed up. Maybe it was his destiny to fight the Droken. Wasn't that what he had been trying to tell Heather? So why was he so upset? Wasn't it what he'd always wanted?

And Nelerek was right. Things did change. It was the one constant—and one of the strongest precepts of Glawres, the unpredictable, ever-changing Levani of the sea.

"Dyluth? Are ye all right lad?"

"Oh, uh, yeah, I'll be all right," Morticai replied. "I was just thinking about what you said."

Nelerek smiled and blew out the last lamp.

CHAPTER TWELVE

Two days later Watchaven finally began to dry out. The western night sky still flashed with a spectacular display of lightning as the storm rained its last against the Great Mountains west of Dynolva.

The sloped roof upon which Morticai lay gave a grand view of the lightning, as well as Sir Ellenwood's manor. For more than an hour, Morticai had lain watching the sky and waiting for Ellenwood's household to be fully claimed by sleep.

The decision to come here tonight had been a sudden one. He had been faced with another dull evening once Rylan and Geradon had left for evening service at the Sanctorium. In frustration he had decided to go out and had left Rylan a note saying just that—that he had gone "out." He had been wandering aimlessly when one of his favorite urchins, Slip, had found him. Slip had overheard a conversation in a tavern—a conversation between Ellenwood and some other corryn. Ellenwood had complained about having lost Burnaby Manor as a base of operations; indeed, he had complained because the base had been moved into his own home, but had said that it wouldn't be a problem by the end of the evening. At that point they had spotted Slip, but Slip, as his name indicated, was very good at getting away.

Morticai had paid Slip a royal for the information and given him a note to take back to the inn telling Rylan that he would hit Ellenwood's before any evidence was removed. He had almost expected Rylan to be here by now with his own people, but there was a chance that Rylan was still at the Sanctorium. Morticai actually hoped that Rylan was still gone—he much preferred being able to do this his own way.

It would be an easy assault. The two-story house wrapped around a combination garden/coachyard. No wall surrounded Ellenwood's small lot; no guards were apparent. Morticai could enter through a ground-floor window, or easier yet, he could hop the four-foot-gate that led into the coachyard and take his pick of the several doors that opened onto it.

Deciding he had waited long enough, Morticai grabbed his pack and carefully slid down the roof. He silently walked along the top of a garden wall to a large tree and stepped onto a sturdy branch.

A violent fluttering erupted near his head; he jumped, but avoided falling, as the bird he'd surprised took flight. Cursing to himself, he climbed to the dark alley below.

He paused in the alley, listening and watching for any sign that the bird's panicky flight had been noticed. He could not be too cautious here—this was a human neighborhood. With emotions running so high, Morticai doubted the humans would allow a corryn thief the pleasure of making it to the gallows.

The Arluthian reached the coachyard gate without incident and within moments was over it. He decided to enter the house through the most ornate door—it had the highest chance of being maintained, oiled and silent. The lock was an old style but one of the first he'd been taught to pick. It clicked softly and opened silently.

Once inside, the Northmarcher let his eyes adjust as he listened to the sleeping household. He had apparently entered through Ellenwood's formal sitting room. He jumped as something touched his leg and then smiled as he recognized the soft shape that rubbed against him.

Reaching down, he scratched the now-purring cat behind the ears and then, picking it up, placed it on a nearby chair. It wouldn't do for him to step on it, after all.

The room was sparsely decorated with traditional furniture. Everything was in its place. *A perfectionist*, he thought. He quickly searched the room.

He found nothing of interest but had not truly expected anything incriminating to be kept in the formal sitting room. The petty noble's bedroom, study, or library, if he had one, would be the most likely locations for such things. The corryn hoped to find something in the study or library—he had never been one for rummaging around in a room while someone was sleeping in it.

The doorway that led from the sitting room opened onto a rectangular foyer. Halls stretched away to both Morticai's right and left, and stairs swirled up from both sides of the front door. Marble statues adorned both sides of the room.

The corryn stood still and listened. The house seemed almost too quiet, but then some were that way naturally. His ears picked up the faint ticking of a clock, somewhere to his right. The sound of the clock surprised him; for a petty noble with such a small manor, Ellenwood certainly seemed to have furnished it well.

The ticking simplified Morticai's decision about which direction to choose. From the outside, he had guessed that the kitchen and dining areas would be on the left. The ticking reaffirmed his conviction that anything of interest would be to the right.

The Arluthian cautiously made his way down the hall. The first room proved to be the library. Its door stood open, which Morticai found uncomfortable. He preferred to search with doors closed; however, closing the door behind him, if it normally stood open, would be disastrous should someone come downstairs.

The library was more ornate than the sitting room, but once again, everything was in its place. The corryn thief began his search. The cat had followed and sat on top of a reading table, cleaning its paws. The first search produced nothing.

"Well?" Morticai whispered to the cat. "Where is everything? The study?" The cat nudged forward to be petted. "That's not what I asked!" Morticai whispered.

The thief eyed a closed door that stood in the room's far wall, wondering if the library had an attached study or if it were merely a closet. He went to it, and carefully examined the knob and hinges.

Suspicious of the hinges, he quietly rummaged in his pack until he produced a small bottle. Carefully unstopping it, he used the glass rod attached to the top to oil the door's hinges.

A door opened upstairs somewhere and then closed again. Morticai paused only briefly before using the door he had so carefully oiled. It swung open without a sound. As the thief closed the door behind him, the cat, in a fit of madness, dashed through behind him. Morticai sighed with relief that he'd not caught the damned thing's tail. The door had led into yet another room, as the cat had obviously known.

Just what I've always wanted, he thought wryly, *a stupid cat to follow me while I thieve.* "You'd best not be a demon!" he whispered to the cat. The cat, however, had already jumped into a chair, chosen a plump cushion to shape into a bed, and ignored him.

Morticai surveyed the dark room. It was, indeed, the study, and contained baroque Lorredrian furniture. His attention, however, was immediately caught by the clutter filling the room. Several large pieces of paper were scattered across the desk, a nearby chair, and a couch.

His curiosity pulled him to the papers, which turned out to be maps—of Watchaven, Dynolva, the coast north and south of Watchaven, and the area north of both kingdoms. The map showing the area to the north appeared to contain some type of markings.

The Arluthian listened a moment for footsteps; hearing none, he took the northern map to the window to better examine it. The still-moonless sky provided just enough light for him to make out the symbols.

He swallowed hard, as comprehension sank in. The map showed the movement of an army—a Droken army. His hands began to tremble as the pieces of the puzzle fell into place. He took a deep breath. This was evidence.

A floorboard squeaked in the hall. The thief glanced at the window's lock; the key was missing—he couldn't count on having the time to pick it. Throwing the map back on the desk, he scanned the room. His best concealment would be against the opposite wall, in a space between a bookcase and a chair. As the corryn thief crossed to the wall, he nearly stumbled on something leaning against the far side of the desk—a sword.

Even in its scabbard he recognized Ducledha; without hesitation the thief picked up the vile sword and unsheathed it. He positioned himself close beside the bookcase, flattened against the wall, with the sword held upright before him. *Don't let it slip!* his mind screamed at him. And immediately after, *Oh, Glawres, if this is here. . . .*

The wall behind him suddenly gave way. Morticai jumped full circle, automatically landing en garde. A dark shape stood before him; the Northmarcher instinctively thrust with the sword, even as his mind recognized the shape's features. Luthekar did not move as the sword thrust cleanly through him, sinking up to the hilt. Slowly the Dark Prince smiled.

Morticai gaped at the embedded sword. Luthekar grabbed the short corryn by the throat and slammed him against the bookcase.

"You didn't think I could be hurt by my own sword, did you?" Luthekar asked, his voice dripping with contempt.

Gagging, Morticai struggled.

Still impaled by the sword, Luthekar pulled Morticai away from the bookcase and slammed him against it again.

"Stop fighting, or I'll kill you here and now!"

Morticai's head rang. The room, still swimming before his

eyes, brightened with lamplight. Morticai tried to kick out, but his limbs seemed to desert him, his legs failing him midway as Luthekar tightened his grip.

"Guards!"

The voice was Ellenwood's.

A strong backhanded blow landed across Morticai's face; the room darkened. As his vision returned, Morticai realized his feet were on the ground, though his legs had seemingly lost their power to hold him up. It was Luthekar's strong grip, still around his throat, that supported him.

Suddenly, there were other hands, and again Morticai struggled. He was shoved facedown onto the desk, his arms pulled roughly behind him. There was shouting and talking, but it blended into a monotonous buzz as the room faded in and out of existence.

Someone pulled him back by his hair and onto his knees. His wrists had been bound behind him, and his arms had also been tied, above the elbows. Something cold hit him in the face, and he realized it had been water. He blinked and gasped, as the room slowly began to, once again, take shape around him.

Ellenwood stood before him, his arms crossed and a scowl on his face. A guard stood beside him with an empty bowl in his hands. Morticai blinked against the pain in his head and wished whoever was pulling his hair would let go. Luthekar leaned against the desk, casually wiping his sword. Squinting, Morticai could see a clean cut in Luthekar's silk tunic——the only sign that he had been stabbed by the sorcerous blade.

Morticai's hair was released. The corryn wanted to shake the water out of his eyes, but knew the movement would be one he'd regret. He looked around the room. Several more guards, in chain armor and full-faced helms, stood about the room. *Where in Glawres's name did the guards come from?*

"Well, what now?" Ellenwood asked, turning toward Luthekar.

Oh, Glawres, where's Rylan? Morticai thought.

Luthekar looked around the room at the guards.

"Leave us," he ordered.

Two of the guards began to move toward Morticai.

"Leave him," Luthekar commanded. "I will call you when we need you to get him."

Without a word, the guards moved out of Morticai's sight. He assumed they left through the secret passage he had so unfortunately hidden in front of. Luthekar carefully inspected the edge of his sword. Then, in a sudden flash of movement, he swept down to his knees before Morticai and brought the edge of his sword up, underneath the thief's chin. Gasping, Morticai automatically drew away from the deadly sword.

The corners of Luthekar's mouth lifted in a sly smile. "Your memory seems to be working well, little Northmarch thief," he said. "I think we shall see just how well."

A light knock sounded on the door.

"Come," Ellenwood ordered.

A servant and yet another armored guard entered the room. "There are none outside, Your Eminence," the guard announced.

Morticai closed his eyes briefly and fought the fear that gripped him. His desperate situation was becoming painfully apparent.

"Good," Ellenwood answered.

"You are certain you checked thoroughly?" Luthekar asked.

"Yes, Prince Luthekar."

"Go then, and tell the others to prepare the temple platform. When it is ready, return here with three others."

"Yes, Your Highness." The guard moved out of Morticai's sight.

Ellenwood walked to the desk and emptied the contents of Morticai's pack.

"There is nothing here," the petty noble announced, rummaging through the pile of gear. Ellenwood handed the now-empty pack to the servant. He gestured to the pile. "Take all of this down to the docks tomorrow and toss it away."

"Yes, m'lord." The servant hastily repacked the thief's bag and left them.

"Perhaps it is time for Sir Ellenwood to drop out of sight?" Ellenwood asked Luthekar.

"Perhaps. Perhaps not," Luthekar replied. "Let us not jump too quickly. We know that we have at least an hour, perhaps longer. Let us learn what we may and then decide."

The noble moved to a section of wall behind the desk and opened yet another secret panel. Morticai was aware of Luthekar's cold stare, but concentrated on watching Ellenwood. *Stay calm!* he repeated to himself. Ellenwood pulled a red Droken robe, embroidered in black and gold, from the secret closet and slipped it over his head. *Red?* Morticai wondered.

"Do you really think we can get useful information in such a short time?" Ellenwood asked Luthekar.

Luthekar caught Morticai under the chin with his hand and forced the corryn to gaze at his face. The thief stared into the ice-blue eyes and found his fear subsiding, as his mind filled with hatred.

"I think we shall need the jevano, but, yes, I think we can learn a few things," Luthekar said, releasing his hold.

Jevano? Morticai thought, briefly closing his eyes again. When he reopened them he found Luthekar still before him, smiling coldly. Once again, Morticai shoved the fear aside, allowing his hatred to take its place.

Guards reappeared and hauled Morticai roughly to his feet. They took him into the passageway, which traveled only a few feet before ending in a flight of stairs, going down.

Morticai looked down the stairs and suddenly found his head spinning and his legs giving way. He felt himself pulled back by his collar and then a brief cry of pain escaped him as he was lifted off the ground by his numb arms.

"It shan't end that easily," Luthekar whispered to him. The Dark Prince had slipped an arm under Morticai's bound arms and now carried him, like a shield, down the stairs. At the bottom, Luthekar released him; Morticai promptly sank to his knees and squeezed his eyes shut against the pain as his arms relocated themselves.

He was hauled up by his collar and pushed ahead. The tun-

nel seemed to go on forever; Morticai felt that his unsteady legs
would desert him at any moment. They finally stopped before
an oaken door, and he was shoved through the doorway—into
an office. *An office?* Morticai looked around at the oddly normal
room. He had expected a dungeon, anything. But an office? It
soon became apparent, however, that the office was merely on
the path to wherever they were going.

The thief was shoved through another doorway on the
opposite side of the room. They had now entered a small
entrance hall. Despite the knot of fear in his stomach, Morticai
found himself looking at the doors and wondering how easy
they might prove to unlock, memorizing how many doors
stood in each room, in each wall. They pushed him through
yet another door—and the small hope he had begun to build
vanished.

Morticai stood in a large octagonal room. He was aware of
the large golden idol to Droka, the black walls covered with
carvings, and the gold candelabra, whose light danced off gold
that wrapped around the carvings. But it was the center of the
room that froze the Arluthian, that caused him to pull in a
ragged breath, not caring if Luthekar was watching—it was the
platform that dashed all hopes and affirmed all fears.

The guards had moved on both sides of him now, and
though Morticai knew he could not hope to escape, he could
not help but struggle as they dragged him toward the blood-
covered platform and the chains that hung down to it. It
wasn't until they had dragged him onto it that he realized Droka's
symbol was graven into it.

"No-o-o!" The cry escaped his lips even as the other two
guards joined in, holding him facedown, on the platform.

They quickly released him, but the corryn thief found he
could not move. He lay, panting like a trapped animal, as the
armored shapes moved around him. He discovered that it was
his legs he could not move—the irons he had glimpsed as he
had been dragged onto the platform were now securely holding
his lower legs, just below the knees and at the ankles.

He managed to turn his head from right to left but immediately turned it back after rediscovering where Luthekar had backhanded him. He felt the guards unfastening his arms; fleeting thoughts of escape danced uselessly through his head. Even if his legs had been free and usable, his arms were so numb as to be useless in a fight or even in opening a door.

His arms were quickly pulled above his head, and two guards held each arm as the shackles that hung from the ceiling were lowered. Another cry escaped him as the shackles were affixed, and pain burst through the numbness to run down his arms; short spikes within the shackles had pierced his wrists. The room momentarily blackened; small rivulets of blood trickled down his arms.

When the dizziness had subsided, he found himself completely immobile. His knees were a foot apart on the platform, his lower legs securely fastened; his arms were stretched taut, up and out toward the ceiling, his wrists about three feet apart. He tried to look up at his wrists, but the dizziness reclaimed him, and he had to close his eyes until it stopped.

When he reopened his eyes, they were met by Luthekar's cold gaze. Other shapes were moving behind the prince, and Morticai realized that they all wore Droken robes. Although some wore the usual black that Morticai was familiar with, others wore solid red, and yet others had one color or another embroidered about the hem.

A red-robed figure came to stand next to Luthekar and when he spoke, Morticai remembered that it was Ellenwood, wearing the red robe with the black-and-gold trim.

"Cwena has arrived," he told Luthekar.

Taking his eyes from Morticai, Luthekar replied, "Good. Bring her in." Luthekar returned his gaze to Morticai. "I have someone for you to meet."

A green-eyed, red-haired woman came into Morticai's field of vision.

"Is this he?" she asked, demurely.

"Yes. Cwena," Luthekar continued formally, "I'd like to introduce you to the Northmarch thief, Morticai. Thief, I'd like you to meet Cwena, one of our most faithful, if young, jevanos."

She smiled at him, seductively. Morticai felt his stomach knot in fear.

"He's cute," she said. "His form might be fun . . . for a while."

"Now, Cwena," Luthekar admonished gently, "it is very important that we keep all of his information intact, so you must leave his soul. I want you to feed, but do so carefully. Did the high priest tell you what information we are seeking?"

The sultry redhead sighed. "Yes, he told me. You want me to feed now?"

"Yes. The entire temple could be in danger, and we do not know how much time we have. So be quick, but be careful."

Morticai found his breath coming in quick shallow gulps. Despite his immobility, he found his arms could still tremble, and as she approached him, he fought back the urge to scream. *Oh, Glawres, why didn't I send a note to Nelerek, as well?*

She came close in front of him and caught his head between her hands with a strength she should not have had. Morticai felt a sickly warmth about him and then a strange, alien thought touched his inner self. The scream came from deep within him, as his fear enveloped and consumed him. . . .

* * * * *

His eyes slowly focused. He was still shackled on the platform, his body drenched in sweat . . . or was it blood? He didn't know. At first, he couldn't hold up his head. Sounds filtered into his consciousness. Finally, he found the strength to look up.

A few feet away, Luthekar held Cwena in his arms. The redrobed Ellenwood knelt before her. Had he somehow hurt the wicked thing? Luthekar looked over at him, an odd look of curiosity in his eyes. Cwena stirred, as though she had also been asleep. The jevano sat up and looked at Luthekar, then at Morticai. After a moment's study, she spat at him.

"Did you learn anything?" Luthekar asked.

She looked down and closed her eyes a moment before replying. "Yes, but very little. His mind is fear, chaos, madness."

"What did you learn?" Ellenwood demanded.

She looked at Morticai before replying evenly, "He is working with the Inquisition, but no one knew his whereabouts tonight."

"Thank Droka!" Ellenwood exclaimed.

Morticai blinked in surprise. He had hoped that he could hide the truth from her and had concentrated on the fact that, as far as he knew, Rylan still hadn't received word of where he was. Apparently, it had worked. The only problem was that it *was* true—he didn't know why Rylan wasn't here yet. If Rylan didn't show up soon, it probably wouldn't matter. There would be nothing left for him to do.

"What else?" Luthekar asked Cwena.

The jevano seemed to be thinking, remembering, as though it were a thought from long ago. Finally, she replied.

"He did not know about the temple. He did not know that you," she nodded to Ellenwood, "are the high priest."

Morticai blinked in surprise. *That's what the robe colors mean!*

"He worships Glawres." Cwena spoke the name distastefully. "And he is an Arluthian."

Automatically, Morticai spat, "She lies!"

"I doubt it," Luthekar said, the cold smile returning.

Glawres, what did they learn from me? Morticai thought. He wanted to sob. He knew he could not deny what she had plucked from his mind, knew they would believe her.

Luthekar came before Morticai and knelt down, picking up the symbol of Glawres that hung around his neck.

"So, you serve two masters, then."

"Arluthes is not a god," Morticai replied, irritated at the assumption.

Luthekar raised an eyebrow.

"Truly? There are Arluthians who would argue it." He jerked the symbol from Morticai with one quick pull and then, turning back to Cwena, he asked, "Did you learn what rank he holds?"

Morticai took in a sharp breath.

"No," she answered.

Morticai released the breath. It was small comfort, but comfort, nonetheless.

"We should let her feed again," Ellenwood said.

"No!" Cwena cried. Then, calmer, "I-I am sorry, Your Eminence. I did not wish to burst out so. I doubt that I could learn more."

"I agree with her," Luthekar said. "No, you need not feed again, Cwena. You may leave us now."

Morticai sighed with relief. Cwena quickly left, as though she, too, was relieved.

Luthekar turned to Ellenwood. "You must be gentle with her—she is still very young. When she has been a jevano for a few centuries she will become a great asset to us. But until then, her skills must be honed gradually. You took your last jevano for granted—now that he's been killed you must be patient until Cwena can develop. Besides," the prince added, turning again to Morticai, "now we know that we are not limited to a few hours."

Ellenwood came over to Luthekar. "I presume you have something in mind?" he asked.

Luthekar rose and slowly walked around Morticai. Morticai reflexively tensed as he passed behind him, out of his view. When the prince had come full circle, he stood with his hands on his hips, in apparent thought.

Morticai licked his dry lips, wishing they would get it over with.

Unfastening his dagger, Luthekar approached the corryn thief.

Morticai stiffened; Luthekar casually slipped the dagger under Morticai's shirt, ran it up the front, and bared the thief's upper body.

"This is something I wanted to look at," Luthekar said, gesturing for Ellenwood. "Hmm. See? You can tell by the scar—they cauterized it." He pointed at the wound Morticai had received from Ducledha.

"But," Ellenwood replied, "they should not have had time to cauterize it. Correct?"

"Correct. You see, as I suspected, he could not have survived without help." Luthekar tapped the medallion of Glawres he held in his hand.

"Glawres?" Ellenwood asked, surprised.

The Dark Prince looked at Morticai thoughtfully. "Have you ever performed a Ritual of Retribution?" Luthekar asked Ellenwood.

"No. We have never before been able to lay hands on any worthy of it," Ellenwood replied. "The Ritual of Retribution is rather long, isn't it?"

Morticai blinked and tried to follow their conversation.

Luthekar shrugged. "It lasts three days." He smiled. "And perhaps, during that time, we might learn some things about the Inquisition, or perhaps the Arluthians."

Ellenwood's red hood nodded. "We might, indeed."

"I think you will find it good for your congregation. It stirs one's faith to see what is done to such an anathema."

"I must read up on it, I fear."

"Do not worry, I will help you with it. I know this is a rare ritual here, but in Cuthaun at least one is performed each year."

"It would be an honor, Prince Luthekar."

Luthekar came close, in front of Morticai; the thief did his best to stare back defiantly.

"I want you to think very carefully, Arluthian," Luthekar began. "Tonight, you shall be allowed rest, but starting tomorrow night, you will wish that you had allowed Cwena your mind and soul.

"I do not expect you to talk with me tonight," he continued. "That will be better saved for tomorrow night, or perhaps the day after, once you've had a taste of how you shall die. I will allow you a choice, however. If you give me the information I am seeking, I shall make your death as painless as the ritual allows. If not . . ."

Morticai spat in Luthekar's face. Luthekar's eyes narrowed. With his jaw set, he wiped it away. His muscles flexed in anger as he drew his hand back and repaid Morticai with another backhand, given full force. Morticai's world filled with blackness.

* * * * *

The doorkeeper at the Hilltop Tavern greeted Rylan and Geradon with a pleasant smile.

"Good evenin', mates!" he hailed. "Do ye need a lamp or would ye be joinin' the evenin's entertainment?"

He gestured to the side door that led into the tavern; lively singing could be heard from the other side.

"I am afraid we must take a lamp, my friend," Rylan replied, returning the smile. "We have much to do on the morrow."

Nodding, the doorkeeper quickly lit a lamp and handed it to the waiting Geradon.

"Ah, well, then I wish ye a good night's sleep, mates."

"Thank you," Rylan replied as they headed upstairs to their room.

"Locguard accent?" Geradon asked when they were beyond the doorkeeper's hearing.

"Correct, almost," Rylan replied, pleased.

"Almost!" Geradon exclaimed. "How can it be 'almost'?"

"There was something else there, as well. Can you tell me what it was?"

They climbed several steps without conversation.

"Are you referring to his usage of 'mate'?" Geradon finally asked.

"Indeed! Locguardians rarely use the term; however, here in Watchaven it is quite common. So either the man picked it up from living here, or perhaps one of his parents came from here and one from Locguard. Geradon, I do believe that in a year or so you will be fairly good at distinguishing accents."

They had reached their door. Geradon held the lamp up as Rylan unlocked it.

"Then," Rylan whispered, "once you have learned to distinguish human accents I shall teach you how to distinguish corryn accents."

Geradon grimaced, but Rylan didn't notice. Turning to Geradon, he placed a finger over his lips, reminding him to be quiet. Geradon nodded and handed the lamp to Rylan, who was now in the lead.

Rylan turned the lamp down and cautiously entered the room, heading for the door that led into their bedroom.

"He's not here," Geradon announced.

"What?" Rylan asked, turning the lamp up.

The door to Morticai's room stood open, the bed still made. A note lay in the middle of Rylan's worktable.

"What a waste of paper," Geradon muttered, before reading it aloud. " 'I have gone out. Should be back by morning. M.' Good gods, who taught him to write?"

Rylan came and looked over his shoulder.

"Hm. Considering his background, you should be surprised he *can* write. And I would wager that he did not learn how in a Sanctum."

"I suppose you're right," Geradon grudgingly agreed. "But he could have told us more. 'Should be back by morning.' Now that is a lot of information!"

Rylan scowled. "I agree. The city is far too dangerous now for him to be about at night."

"And don't forget," Geradon grumbled, "King Almgren had no idea who issued the order to pick up Morticai. The king may have rescinded the order, but we have no guarantee that whoever issued it will not issue another."

"You are correct, of course, Geradon. Do not worry. I shall speak with Morticai about it first thing on the morrow."

* * * * *

Morticai awoke with an involuntary moan. The temple was deserted, the tall candles several inches shorter than he last remembered. His entire body ached, his head pounded, his shoulders occasionally spasmed, and his arms were painfully numb. He was certain that had the chains not been holding him upright, he would have been too weak to do so alone.

He tilted his head back to look at his wrists, stretched above him. They had stopped bleeding, and only an occasional throb penetrated the numbness to remind him of the spikes. One thing was certain—he wouldn't be slipping his hands through these manacles.

He found that by grabbing the chains above the manacles he could relieve a little of the pressure. Then he discovered that he could rotate his arms slightly at the shoulders; at least the chains would allow that much. It seemed to help awaken his arms so he turned his impaled wrists back and forth, gritting his teeth until tears ran down his cheeks. Finally he was assured that, should they lower his arms for some reason, he would not find them totally useless.

He carefully surveyed the rest of the temple. Everywhere were carved pictures of Droka. It wasn't until Morticai spotted Glawres's likeness that he realized the scenes were of Droka fighting the Levani. He scrutinized the scene with Glawres and finally determined that Droka was supposedly drowning Glawres, the patron Levani of water and the sea. *Hmmph!* Morticai thought.

The only doors the thief could see were the huge golden doors he faced. He knew his captors had brought him in through a smaller door somewhere behind him, but he could not turn his head enough to see it now; besides, the effort increased the pounding in his head. He was glad he could not see the large idol of Droka that stood behind him—the bas-relief carvings were depressing enough.

Morticai sighed. There was no way to escape his current bonds. Had he been able to slip his wrists through the manacles, he could have reached the small pick sewn into the hem of his pants—assuming it was still there. No, his only hope of escape would depend on the Droken releasing his wrists, which seemed unlikely. Perhaps they would let him eat a last meal.

The likelihood of rescue seemed even more doubtful. Morticai cursed himself for not having told Nelerek his plans. At the time it had seemed too much of a bother. Heather would miss him in the morning and would certainly tell Nelerek. By now, he had to assume that his note had not reached Rylan. Assuming that to be the case, the Inquisitor would also miss him by morning but might or might not tell Coryden.

There was a chance that Nelerek would remember his mentioning Ellenwood's estate at their last meeting—a chance. . . . Again and again, Morticai turned the thoughts over in his head. His emotions swung like a pendulum from meager hope to despair and back, over and over.

His arms began to grow numb again. Taking a deep breath, Morticai again grabbed the chains and began to twist his arms awake. He felt a small trickle of blood on his right forearm. He found himself wondering if he could commit suicide by twisting his wrists inside the manacles and then quickly pushed the thought from his mind.

The trickle was small, and he realized that it would be close to impossible to move his wrists enough to catch a vein. He thought about the slaughtered cows hanging from hooks in the market and shoved that thought away, too.

White specks danced before his eyes. He blinked, realizing that they had not come from within his weary mind. He looked to the ceiling, scrutinizing the anchors that held his chains. He twisted the chain again—and was rewarded by a few more specks of dust drifting past him to the floor.

Morticai twisted harder and, this time, pulled. His effort, however, was rewarded with a searing agony that shot down from his wrist, eliciting an unwanted cry and plunging him close to unconsciousness. He gasped in ragged breaths as the pain slowly ebbed. Luckily, his cry seemed not to have been heard by any guards—he assumed that some were posted outside the doors.

He tried twisting again, more gently, but again, pain traveled down his arm, though not as severely as before. *Damn!* Blood flowed more freely now down his arm, and he began to fear he might, after all, be able to bleed to death from the small punctures. His arm trembled and, in apparent sympathy, his shoulders spasmed.

This time he was able to stay quiet, though tears ran down his face with the effort. He had squeezed his eyes shut so tightly that the headache returned. For a long time, he just hung onto the chains and tried to relax and reclaim some strength. Finally, he was able to again twist the chains.

He twisted until he was once more claimed by despair, brought on by the pitifully small amount of mortar his efforts had gained him, and the exhaustion that was quickly claiming his body. Eventually, he fell into sleep, only to be awakened by the agony that claimed his wrists as his weight settled fully within the manacles.

He thought about trying to wake-rest, but quickly threw the thought away. Even under perfect conditions he'd been unable to master the skill; it would be useless to try to use it now. And so the pattern continued, and as the candles burned ever lower, he lapsed in and out of sleep.

CHAPTER THIRTEEN

Rylan paced the makeshift study, while a maid cleared the remains of breakfast from their table. Geradon impatiently thumped his quill against the edge of the inkpot as he waited for the maid to leave and Rylan to continue his dictation. At last, the maid closed the door and Rylan continued.

". . . if he is not at Northgate, then come here *immediately*. Underline 'immediately,' Geradon. Sign it and have that sent now. No, better still, I want you to hop a coach to Northgate. I want to make certain this gets to Richard now and not six hours from now, if he is on duty."

* * * * *

Nelerek had just finished his morning chores when the pounding began. He stepped out of his just-cleaned mews and onto the expanse of flat roof he used for weathering his hunting birds. Looking over the edge of the roof he could see a coach parked below but could not see the insistent knocker.

"I shall come down," he yelled over the edge of the roof. The pounding ceased. He traveled back through the mews, into his upper loft, and downstairs. Opening the front door's spy-shutter, he peered outside.

"Heather?" he asked, surprised, and promptly opened the door.

"We have trouble, Nelerek," she immediately began. "Dyluth was to meet me at dawn this morning—he never arrived. . . ."

* * * * *

Rylan had just started a list of places to search when he heard a key in the doorlock. As the door opened, he realized that he had been holding his breath in expectation—he released it as Geradon entered the room.

"I suppose it was too much to hope that you were Morticai, and your expression tells me he was not at Northgate," Rylan said.

"Correct, I am afraid, on both points," Geradon replied. "I came ahead of the others so I could have a few moments with you alone."

"The others? Captain Coryden?" Rylan guessed.

"Coryden, Dualas, Berret," Geradon listed. "We shall be lucky if the whole patrol does not come," he said cynically.

"Now, Geradon," Rylan chided, smiling, "you must admit, their camaraderie is commendable."

"It will at least give us a goodly number for searching, though I fear the worst."

"I hate to hear you speak so, friend," Rylan replied.

"I hope to be proved wrong. If you will permit, I shall sequester in our room for a short while."

"By all means," Rylan said.

Geradon was still absent when Richard's strong knock echoed from the door.

"Come," bade Rylan.

Richard entered, followed by Captain Coryden, Sergeant Heimrik, Sir Dualas, and someone Rylan did not know.

"Inquisitor," Richard began, bowing his head in respect, "I believe you know everyone who has come with me except Evadrel." He gestured to the stranger. "Evadrel is the scout for Morticai's patrol."

Rylan nodded politely. Evadrel smiled, and returned the nod.

"Brother Geradon?" Richard asked.

"Is sequestered at the moment, seeking insight. He will join us shortly," Rylan explained.

"I have told them about my allegiances," Richard apologized.

"That is all right, Richard," Rylan assured him. "I hope you will forgive our small deception," Rylan turned and addressed the unusually silent Coryden. "It was the only protection I could give Morticai while he was at Northgate. Richard is my personal guard."

Coryden smiled ruefully. "I'm not offended. I just wish we could keep him," he finished, looking up at Richard.

"I feel terrible," Rylan said, gesturing for them to sit down. "I fear I became so caught up in our research that I allowed Morticai too much reign over when and where he might go. He had been informing me in advance of his activities. This note caught me entirely off guard." Rylan handed the sparse note to Coryden and continued, disheartened, "He was my responsibility, and I have failed you."

Coryden shook his head. "If there is anything I have learned from my years with Morticai, it is that you can not tether him in one spot. It just doesn't work." He passed the note to Berret.

"Yep," Berret agreed, looking at the note, "that's Morticai, all right. Gave you plenty of information."

"Morticai has always had a habit of coming and going as he pleases," Coryden explained. "If you thought he was conforming to your wishes, I'm afraid that it was probably because it did not conflict with what he wanted at the time."

"To my knowledge, however, I do not believe he has ever missed a patrol," Dualas noted.

"No," Coryden agreed, "but then, that has always been important to him. No, Inquisitor, you have no reason to feel guilty."

Rylan smiled, "You are very forgiving. Have you any idea where we should begin searching?"

Berret laughed. "Do you know how many taverns and ladies there are in this town?"

Coryden scowled, "I don't agree, Berret. Not this time. If things were different I'd wager you'd be right, but too much is at stake. I'm thinking something may have happened to drive him into hiding—I've seen him do it before, y'know, especially if he's been hurt."

"As long as it wasn't by that damned sword," Berret replied softly.

Coryden sighed, and an awkward moment of silence ensued. It ended abruptly when the door to the bedroom opened and Geradon emerged. Rylan scrutinized his associate closely.

"He is still alive," Geradon announced.

Rylan and Richard both sighed with relief. The North-marchers exchanged confused glances among themselves.

"Geradon has a special gift for divination," Rylan explained. "Could you discern which direction we should search?" the priest asked his associate.

Geradon's bright blue eyes clouded. "I could not get a direction."

Rylan straightened; Richard opened his mouth as if to say something, but then he shut it again without speaking.

"There's a significance?" Coryden asked.

"Geradon," Rylan began, "Captain Coryden has suggested that Morticai might be hiding somewhere, perhaps for his own safety. Could that be possible?"

Geradon shook his head and sat down with them. "Only if he has found an ensorceled place to hide." He searched the eyes of the others in the room. "In most cases," he explained, "I am able to discern which direction the person is from me—not distance, but at least a general direction."

"And in the other cases?" Coryden asked suspiciously.

Geradon sighed. "Although he is still alive, it must be somewhere that is ensorceled against divination. In the past, this has usually meant the temple of Droka."

Silence claimed the room. Finally, Geradon broke the mood.

"Sorcery would have the same effect whether or not a temple to Droka were involved, of course," he said. "I know that is not much of a comfort, for in either case, it supports the thought Morticai is being held somewhere against his will. But he is still alive, and I would stake my life on that. We may have time to find him."

"Geradon," Rylan said softly, "what of Morticai's friend, or friends, with the bird? Could they have convinced him to go into hiding?"

Geradon shrugged. "Who knows? Only if his friend is a sorcerer—or has enough money to purchase such services."

"What of the sorcery used to tell the bird where to fly?"

Geradon shook his head. "You are correct that sorcery was used to train the bird. But that was very modest sorcery. Whoever it was . . ."

"What the Levani, uh"—Coryden paused a moment, embarrassed by his exclamation, "are you talking about?" he finished. "What 'bird'?"

Rylan smiled. "Someone was sending Morticai a bird while he was healing at the Sanctorium. I never did find out who it was, but from the one message I intercepted it appeared to simply be a concerned friend. Whoever it was, Morticai was apparently cooperating in the communication."

"Hmmph!" Berret muttered, "probably one of his ladies."

"Well," Coryden said, "if Morticai was hiding with a friend, he would have found some way to let us know he was safe."

"Yeah, you're probably right there," Berret agreed. "Otherwise, he'd know you'd tear the city apart looking for him."

"So, gentlemen," Rylan finally spoke, "I am afraid this unfortunately brings us back to the supposition that he has been captured. I believe it is time that the temple of Droka in

Watchaven be exposed. Tell me everything you can about this city."

* * * * *

It was dusk when Coryden returned to Northgate. Berret had set up their command post in Morticai's room; the entire patrol had been searching since noon.

"Anything?" Coryden asked as he entered the old attic.

"Nothing yet," Berret replied.

Coryden sank wearily into Morticai's favorite chair. Without asking, Berret poured him a drink.

"There's still hope, Coryden," Berret said. "The Inquisitor came by less than an hour ago and said that Brother Kinsey had repeated his divination—Morticai is still alive, wherever he is."

Coryden threw his head back against the chair and slowly shook it.

"I'm getting too old for this, Berret," he said.

"We'll find him, Coryden—we'll keep looking until we do."

"Yeah, I know, one way or another." Coryden sighed. "Y'know, this happened a few times when Morticai was young. Not with Droken chasing him, of course; but there were times he simply disappeared. That's when I discovered just how big this city really is. It hasn't gotten any smaller."

"But you apparently found him then."

"Yeah. All of this was, I guess, before you were born. Once he was hurt pretty bad."

Coryden sat up and rubbed his neck. "Well, I can see what I'd be like if I stayed here," he said.

"You're not going out again so soon, are you?" Berret asked. "You should at least go downstairs and have something to eat with your team."

Coryden smiled. "Thanks, Berret. I'll be all right. And I will eat, whether or not I'm hungry—but it'll wait till later. Let me look at that list."

Berret handed him their master list of areas to search.

"Hm." Coryden scrutinized it. "When did you hear from Dualas last?"

"His team checked in a little over an hour ago," Berret said, picking up another list.

"So, you're keeping track of check-ins?"

"Yep. And where everyone is searching, too. If a team comes up missing, by Aluntas, I plan to know which area of town they were in!"

"Good idea, Berret—very good."

A knock sounded on the door.

"Come," Coryden said.

The door opened, and a Northmarcher, wearing his guard duty insignia, stood in the doorway.

"Captain Coryden, there is someone downstairs to see you," he informed Coryden.

Coryden and Berret exchanged glances.

"I'll be right down."

* * * * *

The corryn waiting at the postern gate of Northgate's eastern wing studied Coryden as he approached. Likewise, Coryden took in as many details as he could about the stranger who stood beside the guard.

The stranger appeared to be about two hundred and fifty years old, early middle age for a corryn. His hair was coal black, the most common corryn hair color, and his eyes were a light, dusty blue—not as common. His clothing was expensive, but conservative. He could have been a minor Dynolvan noble, or a merchant, neither of which were particularly popular in Watchaven at the moment. His serious eyes followed Coryden carefully.

"I am Captain Coryden. You wished to speak with me?"

"Ah, yes," the corryn said, glancing at the guard.

Coryden inclined his head, and they moved a few steps away from the human guard. The corryn stranger dropped his voice to a whisper before continuing.

"I know that you do not know me," he began, "but there is much I would discuss with you. You and your patrol are search-

ing the city for your friend, Morticai. I am also a friend of Morticai's, though to me he is known as Dyluth—which tells you
how long I have known him. I have a coach waiting outside, if
you would speak with me. . . ."

"I would—were you not so hasty," Coryden said suspiciously. "You have not even told me your name."

"I am sorry," the corryn said, shaking his head. "My name is
Perlagus."

"And why should I believe you are a friend of Morticai's?"

Perlagus threw his hands up in exasperation. "What can I
do to prove such a thing? Ask me anything you wish, but
please, let us not tarry."

Coryden realized the corryn had a point—what could he ask
that only a friend of Morticai's would know? Finally, a question
came to mind, but Coryden knew it would be an unfair one;
few of Morticai's closest friends knew the answer. Unable to
think of anything else, Coryden demanded, "Tell me Morticai's
name at birth."

"Moranekor of Lorredre," Perlagus replied.

Coryden blinked and after a moment of stunned silence
replied, "I'll be right back."

He returned shortly wearing his sword and cloak.

"Let's go."

Nodding, Perlagus led him to the waiting coach. They
climbed inside, and the coach proceeded toward the north gate,
much to Coryden's surprise.

Noting his reaction, Perlagus explained. "I felt that I might
as well combine our discussion with some useful travel. There
is a beach that is special to Dyluth just north of town. I have
not had time to search it. I do not expect to find him there, but
I would like to see if there are any signs of him having been
there recently."

"You are, indeed, a close friend," Coryden said, nodding, "if
you know not only Morticai's true name but his connection to
Glawres's beach. I had not thought of the beach, myself. Why
have I never met you before?"

Perlagus shrugged. "I stay very busy. It has been many years since Dyluth and I have been able to spend much time together. You may know me by another name, however—Dyluth usually calls me Nelerek."

Coryden shook his head. "It sounds vaguely familiar, but I do not recall it directly."

"It does not matter now. Please, let us get to business. . . ."

* * * * *

It was much later when Coryden stepped from the coach at Northgate's postern gate.

"Coryden!" Berret called, rushing up to him.

Hope suddenly welled up inside the captain.

"News?" he asked anxiously as Berret grabbed his arm.

"No, Coryden." Berret shook his head. "No word of Morticai."

Coryden sighed, his weariness reclaiming him.

"I was worried sick about you," Berret was saying. "You've been gone hours."

"I'm sorry, Berret. There turned out to be a lot to talk about." *Like Morticai belonging to the Arluthians,* Coryden thought. Nelerek had made him swear on his life that knowledge would remain secret. Of course, Nelerek had also informed Coryden that by the same knowledge, Coryden, too, was now Arluthian, and would eventually be brought fully into the secret society.

"And . . . ?" Berret prodded.

"Nothing yet," Coryden confessed. "But Morticai apparently has a lot of old friends who are also looking for him."

Berret's expression sank, and then he shrugged. "Well, it can't hurt. I am afraid we have other problems, though."

"What's happened?" Coryden asked anxiously.

Berret sighed. "Kirwin called an assembly while you were out. . . ."

"Damn!"

"Nothing to worry about there, Cor; Kirwin never even missed you. The problem is that we're supposed to move out in twelve hours."

"Twelve hours! Are we at war?"

"No, not yet. But the whole bloody Northmarch is supposed to meet at Mid-Keep. Dynolva is moving out too. Come on, the rest of the patrol is waiting for us up in Morticai's room. I knew you'd want to hold a meeting."

"You bet I do!" Coryden exclaimed as they headed up the stone steps.

CHAPTER FOURTEEN

Morticai let the murmuring flow in and out of his mind, not caring where it came from or what was being said. He hoped he would be well before next patrol. Seemed like a long time since he'd been well. But Rylan said it shouldn't take long. Who was Rylan?

With a gasp, Morticai jerked awake. His hands trembled with the effort of grabbing the chains, but his wrists demanded it. He squeezed his eyes shut and fought back the sob that threatened to escape from deep in his throat.

The murmuring stopped. Morticai opened his eyes. Before him stood two black-robed figures.

"Well, this should make things easier," one of them said.

The voice was feminine, as was the voice of the other, who now approached him.

"Can you hear me?" she asked.

"Yes," he replied, barely managing a whisper through his dry lips.

She walked to a nearby table and returned with a bowl of liquid. *That wasn't here before—was it?* he wondered, staring at the table. He looked at the edge of the room to see how far down the candles had burned, and realized with a start that fresh candles had been placed in the tall candelabra. Only alternating candles had been relit, leaving the temple much darker than before.

"Here, drink," the Droken urged, holding the bowl up to his lips.

He looked at it suspiciously; it looked like water. He wanted it.

"It will not harm you," she assured him, tilting the bowl upward.

The liquid touched his lips. It did seem to be water, and he shut his eyes and took as much of the soothing liquid as she would allow. She took the bowl away long before he was ready, however.

"Tsk, tsk," she said, waving a finger in front of him, "if you drink too much, you will get sick."

"Wh-what time is it?" he asked.

"It is night," she replied matter-of-factly. "And we must prepare you for tonight's ritual."

His heart sank. Hopes that the small mercy she had shown him might be enlarged upon began to vanish.

"Will I be allowed a last meal?"

The robed figure giggled.

"Silly, you shan't die tonight."

Morticai blinked. *Shan't die tonight?* Her companion came over with wet cloths and a knife. The one who had spoken to him set about removing the remains of his shirt while the other began washing his right hand and arm.

They worked quietly, and for a time Morticai closed his eyes and let the feel of the soft, moist cloths soothe his weary muscles.

"Tilt your head back," he was instructed, and they washed his hair, too.

He found the courage to ask the other questions that plagued him.

"But they will kill me."

"Of course," the Droken female replied, still matter-of-factly. As she spoke, she softly stroked his face. "And it is a shame, for you are very pretty." A note of sadness entered her voice.

"Then why don't you free me?" he whispered.

She lowered her hand, as her companion finished braiding his hair. "Because you hate my beloved Droka," she said sweetly. "Glawres has claimed your soul and possesses you, and for that, you must die."

Morticai had his own thoughts about who was possessed.

"Now," the other Droken said, "if you could reclaim yourself from Glawres and convert . . ." Morticai decided this quieter one sounded older.

"Do not tease him!" the younger female complained.

"I am not teasing," she replied evenly. "If he converts, I believe Prince Luthekar will spare him." Then, to Morticai, "Will you not consider it?" she asked. "For my friend here?"

Morticai's stomach turned at the very thought.

"Never!"

"Then you shall die," the older one replied. "See?" she admonished her companion. "This is one truly possessed. He may be pretty, but his heart is wholly controlled by Glawres."

Silence fell then, as they gathered up their supplies. The older Droken started toward the gilt doors but stopped when the younger one lingered behind.

"Are you coming?" she asked.

"In just a moment," the second girl replied.

"Be careful. Remember, he is possessed."

"I will. I shan't be long."

The older one left them, with several backward glances.

"Free me!" Morticai whispered.

"I cannot," the Droken whispered back, shaking her head. "I would not," she said with conviction.

"Then why do you stay behind?"

"To ask you to consider conversion."

"I cannot."

The Droken sighed. "Then I shall watch you die," she said.

"Have you watched others die?" he asked.

"Oh, yes!" she replied with relish.

Morticai's skin crawled.

"How-how long?"

"Will it take?"

He nodded slowly.

The robed figure shrugged. "I do not know. Usually it takes only one night, but the ritual to be performed on you will take longer. They say, three or four days."

He looked at her blankly, his soul numbed by the finality of her tone. She bent close and kissed him before turning to run up the aisle to the doors.

When the gilt doors reopened, Morticai could see that the area beyond was packed with Droken. Soon, several red-robed Droken entered the temple and began lighting the unlit candles.

Morticai glanced to the small pile of mortar his most recent efforts had dislodged. The former pile had been scattered by the feet of the Droken women; this pile lay painfully apparent. With a sudden thought, Morticai directed a fabricated sneeze toward the pile—the mortar promptly scattered. The Arluthian sighed with relief.

He heard footsteps behind him and automatically stiffened. It was Luthekar. The Droken prince walked into view and examined Morticai as though he were a painting or a statue. He wore golden Droken robes with elaborate embroidery. His hood was thrown back, his silver hair unbraided.

"Are you ready?" the Droken prince asked his captive.

Morticai glared back, saying nothing.

Red-robed Droken were now bringing items to the dais and filling the small table. Morticai looked at the implements and repressed a shudder.

"Move the table closer," Luthekar directed. "Put it there." He pointed. The Droken quickly complied. A brazier was brought to the edge of the dais, and then the Droken scattered like leaves before the Darkness, some exiting through the gilt doors, and some disappearing from Morticai's sight to exit, he assumed, through the door Luthekar must have used.

Luthekar walked up close and dropped to one knee.

"I make you an offer, though I expect you will not take it," he began. "You shall die here, and die slowly."

Morticai swallowed, but maintained his even stare.

"However, if you die, it is your own doing. From you, Droka will accept repentance. This is not something that I offer lightly—most are not offered a chance to repent. You are being offered this because Glawres has used you. Droka demands retribution. It can come by your death, or by your faith—given to Droka."

"No," Morticai whispered.

Luthekar shrugged. "That is what I expected to hear. I must warn you, though, that should you try to lie, thinking that it will be a way for you to escape . . ." Luthekar tilted his head. "I would know. I think that should not surprise you, however."

Luthekar raised his hood and pulled his mask forward. It was an elaborate mask, with embroidered and gem accents in a hideous design. Luthekar turned toward the gilt doors, and a red-robed figure walked to stand beside Luthekar on the platform. Morticai noted the black-and-gold embroidered hem and assumed it was Ellenwood.

"Are we ready?" the red-robed Droken asked. Now the captive thief knew for certain it was Ellenwood.

"Almost," Luthekar replied. He picked up a black silk cloth from the table and advanced toward Morticai. Morticai said nothing and expected it to be placed over his eyes. Instead, Luthekar pulled it across his mouth, forcing it between his teeth, and tying it tightly behind his head; Morticai coughed.

"I shall offer you several chances to convert," Luthekar told him. "At those times, a nod will suffice."

"Surely you do not expect him to convert!" Ellenwood exclaimed.

"No, I do not," Luthekar replied. "But I was instructed to offer it."

Ellenwood paused and then signed himself. Morticai had never seen the sign—he assumed it was Droka's.

"Let us begin," Luthekar said, and turning toward the gilt doors, he clapped his hands loudly.

The doors promptly opened, and black-robed Droken quickly filed in. Morticai's palms began to sweat. He stared at the wall carving of Glawres and prayed for strength.

The room soon filled to capacity. Morticai stared at the large number of black robes and wondered how many of them were people he knew. If any of them did know him, they were not talking about it. The silence was uncanny. *Kirwin should see such discipline*, danced madly through his mind. Then, in horror, he realized that the heights were too varied and that there were children under a number of the robes. *Oh, Glawres! Don't let them be raised into this horror!* he prayed. Luthekar began.

"You are brought here tonight to witness a Retribution. This corryn"—he gestured to Morticai—"stands accused of the highest offenses. This faithful servant of Droka"—Luthekar gestured to Ellenwood—"stands as witness to the following crimes."

Luthekar unrolled a scroll with a flourish.

They're going to run it like the bloody court! Morticai thought.

"This corryn, called Dyluth and Morticai, has purposely and wantonly searched us out to do us harm," Luthekar read.

"Yea, this is so," Ellenwood replied.

"He, through his efforts, has caused one of our own, a faithful Dyagon, to be slain."

"Yea, this is so."

"He, with others whom he enticed, attacked me, Droka's own prince, with intent to kill."

A gasp escaped the congregation.

"Yea, this is so."

"He has given his own soul to Glawres and allowed Glawres to possess him so that he could survive Ducledha's edge."

"Yea, this is so."

The crowd stirred, their robes rustling softly.

"He has worked with the vile Faith, indeed, with the Inquisition itself, and done all that he could to aid Glawres against our beloved Droka."

"Yea, this is so."

"And yet, there is more. Not only has this corryn given himself to Glawres, not only has he fought us through the wickedness of the Faith; this corryn"—Luthekar gestured again to Morticai—"is an Arluthian, sworn to the utter destruction of Droka."

Another gasp swept the room.

"Yea, this is so."

"And thus does this corryn, called Morticai of the North-march, stand accused of the most vile crimes. Is there hope for one so wicked? Can there be any repentance?" Luthekar turned to Morticai. "Wouldst thou repent thy crimes and throw thyself upon Droka's mercy?"

Morticai stared at Luthekar, his eyes blazing hatred, wishing he had not been gagged so that he could spit.

"Then these are thy crimes."

Luthekar moved to the brazier and withdrew a rod of some sort. Morticai tensed and tried to see the end of it, but Luthekar had turned to face the congregation.

"Is there any denying that this corryn is a worshipper of Glawres?" Luthekar asked the congregation.

"No!" they replied in unison.

"Then let *him* not deny it."

Luthekar turned to Morticai, who could now see the branding iron held by the Droken prince. Luthekar approached him; Morticai tried to look away but found he could not help but stare at the end of the rod in morbid curiosity. The brand was the token of Glawres, glowing red from the heat of the brazier.

Ellenwood moved behind him and grabbed his right arm at the elbow and just below the manacle. Luthekar stood close now, and Morticai forced himself to look away. Despite his best efforts, his body trembled; he thought of Kithryl's eyes when he had lain on her kitchen floor. He felt the first touch of the hot iron on his inner forearm—and screamed. . . .

The scream gradually became sobs. His body shuddered uncontrollably; he had emptied his bladder, though there had not been much in it. He choked back a sob and tried to concentrate on whatever it was that Luthekar was saying. He couldn't concentrate past the burning in his forearm. *Oh, Glawres!*

He didn't feel Ellenwood grab his other arm, but he saw the red-hot brand that Luthekar was bringing toward him. He was shocked to recognize the Arluthian symbol.

He started screaming even before it touched his left forearm, while a distant portion of his mind scolded him for carrying on so. Blackness engulfed him, and as it swept over him, he prayed that he'd never wake up.

He dreamed he'd been sent to hell. He didn't know what he had done but had been sent here nonetheless. With a jerk, he awoke, and the nightmare became reality again. His arms still burned, and, as a new sob escaped him, he realized that water had been thrown in his face and on his arms.

His vision began to clear. Ellenwood stood before him, an empty bowl in his hands. Luthekar was leading the congregation in some kind of responsive prayer. Morticai blinked against the tears in his eyes and realized belatedly that it was his own sobs that still echoed in his ears.

The prayer was apparently complete, for Luthekar had turned toward him. Suddenly, Luthekar backhanded him; the Droken prince spoke, and Morticai heard his words as though from a great distance.

"Shut up!" Luthekar had commanded.

Amazingly, Morticai did. Dizziness swept across him, but with it came a calming, and as his vision cleared again, he was able to stay quiet, to somehow detach himself from the searing pain in his forearms.

". . . and so shall ye all partake," Luthekar was saying to the congregation, "for it is your right; it is your duty."

It made no sense; he had missed too much of it. *You'd best stay awake,* he thought wildly, *or you'll miss your own death!* And then the words of the Droken female echoed back to him: *Silly, you shan't die tonight!* He wondered if the girl were in the crowd, wondered if she'd have any regrets that she'd not freed him.

The congregation was lining up before the dais. Morticai tried to bring his mind back to concentrate on what was happening, to see if he could figure out what they were about. Snap! He jerked as he felt the braided leather on his back. Snap! It came again, and suddenly concentration was not a problem.

He tried to turn his head. Snap! This time he cried out. He had glimpsed the pile of whips behind him. Crack! He let out another sob. The congregation was filing past, circling behind him, and as they came to the front of the dais each passed his whip to another advancing Droken. Snap! *Oh, Glawres, please let me die!* Each member of the congregation was apparently going to have a chance.

Crack! *There must be over a hundred of them!* Snap! He cried out freely again. The congregation began singing, with Luthekar directing them. Snap! The singing covered a good deal of his cries. Morticai wondered how many lashes a man could survive; he'd heard stories of such things from the docks while growing up. Crack! And so, it continued. *My wrists, perhaps . . .*

He tried to twist his wrists in the manacles. Crack! His wrists were so numb, he couldn't tell if he'd moved them or not. Snap! He looked up as he tried to move his arms. Crack! He had moved them some, but not enough to catch a vein. Blood trickled down both arms, stinging as it hit the fresh burns on his inner forearms.

Snap! The whip had snaked around his side; his cry echoed above the singing. Snap! The next lash landed on his side as well. Crack! Morticai had begun tensing with each stroke. Snap! He cried uncontrollably. His strength was fleeing. Crack! *How long can this continue!* Snap! He prayed for unconsciousness, for insanity, for anything. . . .

* * * * *

Rylan stared at the small fire and slipped another prayer bead through his fingers. They'd still gained no clues to Morticai's whereabouts. One of Morticai's urchin friends had been found murdered, but there was nothing to suggest that it was connected. Nonetheless, it had disturbed Rylan greatly. He had said an entire set of prayers for the unknown child. Geradon came over and sat down beside him. Rylan looked up.

"Captain Coryden is here to speak with you."

"Have they. . . ?"

"No, they have not found him yet," Geradon said softly.

"What is it, Geradon?" Rylan asked evenly.

"I shall let him tell you."

Rylan walked into their study. Coryden stood at the window, looking out into the night, his body tense. Dualas stood by the unlit fireplace, also tense, his eyes concerned.

"Captain?" Rylan asked.

Coryden turned to him. The half-breed sighed and gestured to the chairs. Rylan sat down. Coryden also sat, and Rylan noted the slightest tremor in the first words to leave his lips.

"I have some bad news," he began.

"Yes?" Rylan sat patiently. Whatever Coryden had to tell him was upsetting him terribly.

"The Northmarch is to move out at dawn."

Rylan considered the news. "I am sorry to hear that. Are we at war?"

"No, not yet."

"Geradon shall continue the search. I must unfortunately continue with our research, but there is still hope, Coryden—"

"We're not going."

Rylan looked at him, stunned.

"You are not going?" Rylan asked.

"No." Coryden looked away from him. "We—the patrol, that is—we've talked about it. Berret's squad, and myself, and of course Dualas—we're going to stay behind. The other two squads will go with the Northmarch."

"Isn't that desertion?"

Coryden looked at him evenly. "That's what it's usually called, yes."

Rylan looked at Dualas. He seemed much calmer than Coryden, though still concerned.

"Are you certain you wish to do this?" Rylan asked Coryden.

Coryden's eyes locked with his. "It's Morticai's only chance, now, isn't it?"

"I—I do not know," Rylan replied. "You know it is no guarantee that we will find him."

"I know. But it certainly wouldn't help if we left, now, would it?"

Rylan sighed. "Are you asking for my approval?"

"No. I'm just asking that you not turn us in," Coryden finished evenly.

"I can not lie, if I am asked, but I will not turn you in," Rylan said. "Where will you and your men stay?"

"We don't know yet," Coryden admitted.

"I could suggest that you seek sanctuary at the Sanctorium," Rylan said with a twinkle in his eye. "You know, political refugees are never turned away."

Coryden slowly smiled. "We just might do that, Brother Glaedwin."

Rylan nodded and returned the smile.

* * * * *

Morticai jerked reflexively at the touch of the cloth on his face.

"Hold still." The voice was Luthekar's.

He moaned in reply; he couldn't have said anything if he wanted to. Luthekar's hood was again thrown back, and he supported Morticai's head while he wiped his face. Morticai closed his eyes. The cloth was taken to his back, and again he moaned.

He became aware of a tugging, and realized that the gag was being untied. It was Luthekar, and Morticai was surprised at the gentleness in his touch.

Why all the concern? Morticai wondered vaguely.

He felt a hand under his chin.

"Can you hear me?" Luthekar asked.

Wish they would lower my arms . . . he thought and then realized he would be unable to use them if they did.

"You may speak now," Luthekar said, as though Morticai

might not have noticed that the gag had been removed.

"I hate you," Morticai whispered.

A rueful smile crept onto Luthekar's face.

"And you have not even seen my anger," the Droken prince replied. "Here, drink this: it will give you some sustenance."

Luthekar held a cup up to his lips; Morticai thought about trying to resist, then decided to drink, hoping it was poison. The liquid tasted sweet, and he wondered what was in it.

"You provided quite a spectacle tonight," Luthekar said. "I was surprised. I would have thought you were stronger than that."

Morticai spat at him, but Luthekar easily dodged it.

"I do wish you didn't have such nasty habits," Luthekar said, and then lightly backhanded him, almost as in jest. "You must have learned such things in the streets," he continued.

Morticai's head rang, and for a moment, he thought he would lose consciousness.

"You know, my offer to you still stands," Luthekar told him. "Tonight was mild compared to what tomorrow night will be. If you do not convert before then, you will most certainly die."

Luthekar held a key up before Morticai. "This is all that stands between you and death. One word, given sincerely, would allow me to use this key to free you. Think about that tonight." Luthekar laid the key on the table that still contained the bloody implements, and then, without another glance back, he left him.

Morticai stared at the key and several minutes later realized that tears were running down his face. "Stop it!" he cried, but the tears continued. He had actually been considering Luthekar's offer. *Oh, Glawres, forgive me.*

If you want the key, then take it.

Morticai jumped at the strange thought that echoed in his mind. He swallowed, and forced himself to look at Glawres's carving. Nothing on it had changed. Morticai looked again at the key. It was within arm's reach—if he hadn't been shackled.

He tilted his head back to look at the chain's attachment. He couldn't tell much about it; he knew it was loose but couldn't get a good look at it. He thought about twisting the chain; he wasn't certain he was up to it.

If you want the key, then take it!

Morticai jumped, involuntarily jerking his chains and inviting his muscles to spasm. He gritted his teeth until it passed. *Damn! You cry out less when there's no one around!* he chided himself. *If I am alone . . .* He tried to look behind him. He saw no one. He shuddered and then chided himself for being scared.

He looked at the chain and sighed. He tried gently to twist it. The effort seemed to drain his last energy. *Blessed Aluntas, I hurt!* He let the chains support him and for a while allowed himself to float on the sea of pain, aware only dimly of his surroundings.

Eventually, however, he twisted the chain again, and this time managed to produce a small amount of mortar. He continued twisting, keeping at it until it caused such pain that he couldn't keep from moaning. He panted with the effort but began again, as soon as he was able.

Finally, he could no longer make his arm move, as exhaustion claimed him. Awareness began to fade in and out, his nightmares mixing with reality for what seemed an eternity.

CHAPTER FIFTEEN

Nelerek paused. The small delivery wagon was parked at the mouth of the alley. The shadowy form of its driver intently watched the busy intersection that lay beyond the alley's entrance. The sun had just risen, and though small carts and wagons were already traveling Watchaven's main streets, the dim alleys were still quiet, as cats looked for quiet places to curl up and dogs scuffled playfully in the dirt with the children already emerging from quiet houses.

Nelerek whistled softly.

The wagon's driver turned and dipped his head in greeting. Nelerek approached and climbed onto the seat next to him.

"Morning," Nelerek offered.

"Yeah, it is, isn't it," Paxton replied, allowing himself to stretch.

"Any activity?"

"Not last night," Paxton replied, shaking his head. "I think this one's a dead end, Perlagus. Valdir is laying as low as the ebb tide. From what I've heard, he's been that way ever since Aldwin was killed."

"You could be right," Nelerek agreed. "How are you doing?"

Paxton shrugged. "I've slept more, but I wouldn't be able to sleep easy as long we think the Droken have Dyluth."

"What of the Dappled Stallion?"

Paxton waved a hand. "Don't worry about the inn; my oldest boy's been wanting to run it by himself for years. I think he's looked forward to a chance to show his younger brothers that he can do it. Have you heard from Heather?"

"Not since yesterday morning."

Paxton shot him a concerned glance.

"You think she's all right?"

"Yeah," Nelerek replied. "She's been seen around the palace. I think she's still trying to learn something there. Now that's an area I think is a dead end!"

"How about the urchins? Have you talked to any of them?"

"Yeah," Nelerek replied, "but only to convince them to be careful."

"Ha! Urchins? You'd have better luck if you paid them to give up looking for Dyluth."

Nelerek shook his head. "I don't think so, Paxton. Dyluth has always been very generous to the orphans of this city. I don't know if you knew that."

"No, I didn't know—but it doesn't surprise me."

Nelerek nodded. "I don't think I could pay them enough to keep them from looking. So I settled for the next best thing and have tried to convince them that if they're going to work with the Arluthians, they must be careful."

Paxton smiled. "That's what I've always liked about you, Nelerek: you're always the one in there making the best of any given situation. So, you going to let me move to Ellenwood's?"

Nelerek looked at him in surprise.

"Don't you think you ought to get some sleep, first?"

"Very well," Paxton grudgingly agreed. "I'll get some

sleep—but you come and get me if anything happens!"

"Don't worry," Nelerek replied. "I will."

* * * * *

A light knock sounded on the door of the booth. Geradon grabbed the unlit candle and stuffed it in his bag.

"Yes?" Rylan asked, unlatching the door.

Coryden and Berret stood just outside the booth.

"May we join you?" Coryden asked.

"Please do," Geradon replied, moving the bag so there would be room.

The two weary Northmarchers sank down beside the clergymen. Coryden relatched the door.

"Will you be ordering anything?" Rylan asked.

"No," Berret replied, "we ate at the Sanctorium."

Rylan and Geradon exchanged glances. With a nod from Rylan, Geradon withdrew the candle he had so hastily repacked. Coryden looked at it and raised his eyebrows.

"Ah," Rylan began, "this is a rather special candle. Are you expecting to be joined by any of your men?"

"No," Coryden said.

"Then, if we might demonstrate," Rylan said, gesturing for Geradon to light the candle. He quickly did so, and the noise in the rest of the tavern promptly vanished.

"Blessed Levani!" Berret exclaimed, jumping.

Coryden smiled. "That's a pretty handy trick. I assume that no one can hear us?" he asked.

"You are quite correct. In fact, we pay the bartender extra to keep the booths around us empty," Rylan explained.

"And," Geradon added, "we always sit in this far booth."

"Does the bartender know about this?" Berret asked, pointing suspiciously at the candle.

"No," Rylan replied. "But it is essential to our work—Geradon and I have lost important secrets to Droken sorcery in the past. We have burned more such candles on this assignment than on many, I fear."

Coryden shook his head. "I've never seen much sorcery. When I do see it, it always amazes me."

"'Tis a very dangerous thing," Geradon cautioned. "There is a fine line between sorcery that furthers the cause of the Faith and that which furthers the Dark One's wickedness."

"Don't worry," Coryden replied wearily, "I have no desire to learn any of it. Besides, I've always heard you have to be born with the skill."

"So," Rylan said, changing the subject, "has any more information surfaced?"

Coryden looked dejectedly at the drink he had brought with him to the booth. "No."

"Have . . . have you prayed about it recently?" Berret asked Geradon.

"Yes," Geradon began.

Coryden glanced up sharply at his troubled tone.

"He is still alive," Geradon assured him.

"But?" Coryden asked.

Geradon paused. "Morticai's life-force is not as strong as it was."

"He's been hurt," Coryden stated evenly.

"That is probably safe to assume," Geradon confirmed softly.

Coryden pounded a fist down on the table.

"At least we know he is still alive," Rylan soothed.

"I'm not certain that knowing doesn't make it worse," Coryden complained. "No, no, I don't mean that. I'm sorry. I'm glad we know he's still alive——I just feel so helpless. And now we know that if he wasn't hurt before, he is now. That's just great!"

"I'm afraid I have additional ill news," Rylan said.

Coryden threw up his hands.

"I believe the Dynolvans will declare war by tomorrow," Rylan continued.

Berret shook his head. "Well, at least that was bad news we were expecting."

"What has happened, Rylan?" Geradon asked.

"As you know, I spent some time at the palace this morning. While there I heard that Watchaven has seized a shipload of goods bound for Dynolva from Menelcar."

"Almighty Aluntas!" Berret exclaimed. "You're right, that will do it!"

The others nodded in grim agreement.

* * * * *

The touch on Morticai's face was light, and for once, he awoke without a jerk—his arms were numbed beyond that capability. Pain was certainly still present, however, and the captive thief pulled in a ragged breath as his body's senses reminded him of the previous night's torments. A cup touched his lips; a firm hand supported the back of his head.

"Drink."

Morticai's eyes snapped open at the sound of Luthekar's voice. The Dark Prince tilted the bowl upward, and, unable to resist and uncertain if he should try, Morticai drank. It was the same sweet liquid Luthekar had given him the previous night.

"Can you speak?" Luthekar asked.

"Yes," Morticai replied, though it came out a hoarse whisper.

"This evening's service shall begin shortly. Did you think about my offer?"

"Yes."

"And?"

"May you freeze in the Wastes with Droka!"

Luthekar nodded. "That was what I expected." He shrugged. "But I have made the offer. The offer will continue to stand until you die, though I suspect that after tonight you will not be sane enough to choose."

"Leave me alone."

Luthekar smiled coldly. "As you wish, Arluthian." The silver-haired corryn moved behind his chained captive and with a sudden jerk the silk gag was, once again, pulled tightly into place. "Pray to your god," Luthekar whispered into his ear. "See if he will save you—in one hour you shall learn for yourself how easily Glawres abandons those who worship him."

Morticai did, indeed, spend the hour in prayer—praying that

somehow the Droken army would be discovered, that the plot would be broken, that his death would not be meaningless.

The main doors opened and, as before, the large room filled with masked Droken. Ellenwood stood with Luthekar on the dais, but unlike the previous night, Luthekar began with a responsive prayer and a hymn.

The mere sight of the lit brazier reawakened the pain in Morticai's forearms, and the Northmarcher fought the knot of fear that threatened to overwhelm him. *Oh, Glawres, should I go mad, please keep me from telling them about the Arluthians. Please.*

The hymn came to an end.

"We have sung our praises to the Almighty Droka," Luthekar began. "Now, we must turn our attention to the dispensing of his justice."

Luthekar moved out of sight; Morticai tensed. A pair of strong hands grabbed his head and with a jerk, snapped it back so that Morticai looked at the distant ceiling. Morticai gasped, thinking the Dark Prince planned to break his neck. Instead, he found himself looking into Luthekar's cold eyes, unable to free himself from the prince's iron grip.

"It is proven," Luthekar said to the quiet congregation, "that this abomination is a worshipper of Glawres, an Arluthian, and a Northmarcher. It is proven that he has actively fought against us. For these crimes, justice must be done."

Luthekar bent down and whispered to him, "This is the last time I shall ask. I will allow your head to move enough to answer me—will you repent?"

Morticai shook his head.

"Then so be it," Luthekar whispered. He straightened, but kept Morticai's head in his iron grip.

The evil prince nodded to someone out of sight. A body moved against his arm; it proved to be Ellenwood. Then Morticai saw the glowing iron rod. Ellenwood slowly lowered it toward his eyes; Morticai's scream filled the temple. He nearly wrenched his hands through the manacles, and would have doubtless broken every bond that held him, had it not been for Luthekar's unnatural strength.

* * * * *

A heavy veil of silence hung over Grandhaven Sanctorium.
War had been declared and the Sanctorium's doors closed; the
fortress could be entered only by those deemed faithful by the
knights who now guarded the famous landmark and the hun-
dreds of corryn refugees who were sheltered within it.

The Inquisitor and his assistant moved with purpose
through the great structure. At every intersection, a knight of
the Faith waved them through. Rylan paused as they passed the
section that sheltered the refugee families. A woman's muffled
sobs echoed toward them from somewhere within the great
chamber. Geradon gently laid his hand on Rylan's arm, and
with a sigh, Rylan continued on.

They stopped at an intersection, and the knight standing
guard nodded in silent greeting; Rylan addressed him.

"The Grand Patriarch has reassigned you to our service, Sir
Dualas. Please, come with us."

"At your service," Dualas replied, dipping his head in
respect.

They continued through the structure and eventually
stopped before a plain wooden door. The knight standing
before it smiled warmly at Dualas.

"Welcome aboard, Dualas," the knight greeted, opening the
door for them.

"Thank you, Richard."

Inside, Geradon gestured for Dualas to sit down as he
cleared a space for Rylan. The small room's sparse furnishings
were littered with books and papers.

"Please excuse the mess," Rylan apologized. "We are still
unpacking. As soon as we heard that war had been declared, we
returned here. I trust that Captain Coryden and his men
returned safely this evening?"

"Yes," Dualas replied. "After last night's riot they decided
not to search past midnight. They had just returned this
evening when the news that war had been declared reached us."

"Thank the Levani," Geradon whispered.

"Sir Dualas," Rylan said slowly, "has Captain Coryden resented the fact that I have continued my work and not helped with the search?"

"No, I do not believe so. Coryden has always understood that it was Morticai's own choice to face danger. Pardon me, Inquisitor," Dualas spoke softly, "but do you ask me this because Morticai has died?"

Rylan looked at Geradon.

"No," Geradon replied. "He was not dead when I last sequestered myself. However, the force of his life is fading. I fear that he has been grievously injured—I should not be surprised if when I next seek his spirit I find that it has fled this world."

"I see," Dualas said heavily. "Would you have me speak with Captain Coryden?"

"No," Rylan replied. "I shall do that myself, but I wished to speak with you before I did."

Dualas nodded slowly.

"Do you know where the captain is now?"

"I believe so—or if need be, I can locate him."

"Then I must ask you to lead me to him," Rylan said. "I think it would be best if he is prepared before Geradon discovers that Morticai's spirit has left this world."

* * * * *

Coryden stood alone, gazing from the battlements across the city's predawn landscape. Rylan had left him over an hour before, and for the entire time, he had not moved. Dualas approached slowly, wondering what he could say to his friend to ease his grief. His captain glanced his direction and then surprised him by starting the conversation.

"Dualas, how many men have you seen die?" Coryden asked thoughtfully.

Dualas tilted his head in thought. "About two score, if I count only those I've seen die in the Northmarch."

Coryden nodded. "We have all seen death come. So why do we continue to believe that we cannot die?"

"We may not continually dwell on the fact that we can die, but I do not believe that either you or I believe that we will not die."

"But Morticai?"

Dualas frowned.

"Do you think that Morticai has ever truly considered his mortality?" Coryden continued.

"Do you think that he has not?"

Coryden sighed. "I don't know."

An uncomfortable pause followed as Coryden returned his gaze to the city. Dualas knew that his friend had more he wished to say. He waited patiently for his captain to continue.

"What is truly odd," he finally continued, "is that I think you're correct—I know that both you and I have considered our own deaths. But despite that, I'm only now realizing that I have never accepted that Morticai would someday die."

"How can you say that?" Dualas asked. "How many times have I heard you caution Morticai to be more careful? How many times have I watched you pace his room, concerned that he may not return to it?"

"That's true, Dualas," he agreed, "but I've never actually accepted the possibility that he might not return. He might return wounded, or I might need to go into the city to find him, or straighten things out with the Watch—but actually die?" Coryden shook his head. "And I, of all people, should know better. Why can't I learn to let go of my people, Dualas? Why is it that I grieve like an old woman every time I lose a man? The other captains don't."

The barest hint of a rueful smile crossed Dualas's face. Here was a subject about which he had thought much in recent days, indeed, a subject he had been wanting to breech with the captain. He regretted that the opportunity to do so had not come before this moment.

"My friend," he began gently, "I believe that there are misunderstandings in your perception of things."

Coryden turned toward him, and, for the first time, Dualas could see that he'd been crying.

"That you feel more for your men than most captains is not a fault," Dualas continued. "For all that it may cost you, your men respond to it and serve you more faithfully because of it. It is true, however, that you have been grieving Morticai's capture more than I have ever seen you grieve. But there is nothing wrong or unnatural about your sorrow for Morticai. Have you not realized that Morticai is different?"

"He's different all right."

Dualas smiled at the touch of exasperation in Coryden's tone. "That is not what I meant," he replied. "I have heard many stories through the years but paid little attention to them until recently. You had just joined the Northmarch when the two of you met, had you not?"

"That's right."

"And although you were old enough to have left home, Morticai was still a child."

Coryden nodded.

"I have heard stories about his childhood. That when he became ill, it was you who sat by his bed; that it was you who would go into the city to look for him when he was overdue to work in the kitchen. That it was you who helped defend him when you learned that several groups of youths sought to kill him; indeed, that this was when you taught him to use a sword. Are not these things true?"

"Well, yes," Coryden admitted, "but what I did was nothing more than anyone would have done had he been given charge of Morticai."

"I have even heard that it was you who took him to his first brothel—that it was your present to him when he came of age to join the Northmarch."

A faint smile crept onto Coryden's face. "Well, I don't know how much credit I can take for that. He never would admit it to me, but I was told by some of the ladies at that brothel that he'd been dabbled with by a few of them in their own kitchen."

Dualas blinked in surprise but forged ahead to make his point.

"Yes," he continued, "but nonetheless, you were the one

who watched him become a man. I know that you never thought of yourself as Morticai's adopted father, Coryden, but for all purposes you were the closest thing to a father that he had."

Now it was Coryden's turn to blink in surprise. Dualas continued, ere the captain could deny his claim.

"When Morticai became older, the two of you began to go drinking together—you know that I have heard many of those stories, and you have told me that many of them are true. It seems to me that as Morticai grew older, you changed—no longer were you a father, but more of a brother to him."

Dualas continued, adding his final blow.

"Then you became his captain, and this, I believe, is where you lost the clear vision of your friendship. You somehow decided that you should feel no more for Morticai than any of your other men. I suppose you were afraid that it would be seen as favoritism. But this is why you grieve so, Coryden. You *should* grieve for Morticai, though I wish with all the power of the Levani that there be no reason to grieve."

Coryden closed his eyes and for a long while stood silently. At last, he sighed deeply and turned again to lean against the battlements and stare at the city. Dualas remained where he was, once more waiting patiently for his friend to speak.

"You're right," Coryden whispered. He shook his head. "I guess I've just never wanted to admit it. I can remember being teased about Morticai, when he first came to the Northmarch. Maybe that's why I fought it."

"Teased?" Dualas asked.

Coryden nodded. "They used to say that Morticai was my 'pet street rat.' For a while some of the men called me 'Uncle Coryden.' " He shook his head. "That was so long ago, I'd almost forgotten it. But it made an impression. It's strange, but that's part of the reason I've always thought that I would die before Morticai—it's why I never believed I'd have to go through this."

"Pardon?"

Coryden shrugged. "Because I'm a half-breed and have

always felt older than Morticai. I mean, look at me, Dualas. I'm approaching my middle years already. You can tell just by looking at me that what they say about half-breeds dying young is true. I shall surely live longer than a human—but live as long as a corryn, as long as Morticai? Even though Morticai has grown as quickly as a human to manhood, he's practically stopped these last ten years!" Coryden sighed and kicked his boot against the battlement. "It doesn't matter now. Brother Kinsey says that he doesn't think he'll live another day."

"I know that what Brother Kinsey has told you does not bode well, my friend, but Morticai would say that there are still game pieces to be played. I have noted that some of Morticai's best wins have come when the odds were against him. You must hold onto your hope, Coryden—for as long as Brother Kinsey says that he still breathes."

Coryden drew a ragged breath and shut his eyes tightly. "I know you're right. I've got to play it out all the way to the end." Reopening his eyes, he gestured toward the city. "Somewhere out there, Morticai's playing it out too."

CHAPTER SIXTEEN

It was beautiful—the crisp air, the warm sun. Moranekor snuggled into the warm hay and listened as the birds sung their praises to the new Light Season. It felt so much better to ride in the supply wagon than the rattling old caravan wagon that had served as his family's shelter in Lorredre this past Dark Season.

He'd pleaded with his parents to let him ride in the supply wagon. His mother had thought him too little, but his father had taken up for him, making Moranekor proud when he'd argued that his boy was old enough to know how handle himself in an open wagon. With a soft laugh his mother had relented, admonishing him not to play too near the edge.

Tilting his head back, he could see the back of his father's hat as he drove the wagon; behind them, his mother drove the beat-up caravan. Before long, the soft rhythmic thump of the horses' hooves lulled him into a unplanned, but peaceful nap.

He awoke with a gasp as he slid against the front of the

wagon. The horses were neighing wildly; they had obviously been pulled up hard. His father let out a fearful yell, and the team turned and broke into a run. Moranekor's heart thumped at the fear in his father's voice as he urged the horses ever faster. They were running over rough ground now—they must've left the road.

All Moranekor could see was hay—he'd slid under most of it. Frantically, he fought his way upright to try to see over the top edge of it. They were no longer on the road; they raced across an open field. Behind them, he could see his mother, her eyes full of fear as she whipped the caravan's team to the same pace as the supply team.

Panic grabbed him; what was wrong? He knew his father had purposely left the road. He called to his father but couldn't be heard over the thunder of the horses' hooves. The hay continued to fall over him. He fought to shove it from his face so he could see what was going on. Finally, he caught a glimpse of horsemen, wearing strange black robes, racing behind them.

Bandits! his mind cried. *Oh, no! It must be!*

He'd never seen bandits before but had heard terrible stories about them. A jolt knocked him from his feet and back beneath the hay once more.

But, they can't be bandits, he thought as he struggled to regain his feet. *Bandits don't have horses.* In all the stories, only the leader of the bandits had a horse. *And what are those funny clothes they're wearing?*

Suddenly, the world seemed to disintegrate around him. He was in the air, along with the entire contents of the wagon. The horses were screaming, but he couldn't tell if they were above or below him. He hit the ground hard, the impact forcing his breath from him. Then he was rolling. Some kind of hill—a steep one, it seemed. He couldn't stop his roll. The brush scratched at him, and he tried to grab at it. The last memory of trying to stop the roll was abrupt—a bone-wrenching thump along his back and head.

* * * * *

He heard screams. He recognized the voices; he lay frozen in fear, with a fist shoved into his mouth. His parents . . .

Madly wiping away the tears that ran down his face, he pulled himself up onto his knees by the tree that had stopped his downhill roll.

"I'm coming!" he cried, but his cry was lost in their screams.

Above him, all he could see was brush, scrub, and the steep incline he'd rolled down. He was about to call out again, to tell his mother and father he was coming, when he heard the laughter.

He froze. *S-someone's* making *them hurt*. . . .

His body was wracked with stifled sobs; his mind filled with an overwhelming fear that threatened to make him sick. He had to go see, had to help, somehow. He started to climb back up the hill. Every few feet he had to stop, his body shaking uncontrollably.

Oh Aluntas, please, please do *something!*

An eternity seemed to pass as he tried to reach the top of the hill. The screams were lessening.

No!

He was close to exhaustion—from the climb, the shaking, fear. At last he reached the top, only to lie sobbing and shaking as he tried to find the courage to look over the edge. Stifling his sobs, he pulled himself up beneath a broad bush. He lay flat on his stomach as the tears flowed freely.

He couldn't see his parents—too many people, all of them wearing the strange black, hooded robes, were in the way. They laughed and taunted their screaming victims; Moranekor felt sick as wave after wave of the horrible sounds washed over him. He couldn't make himself move; it was all he could do to keep his cries from drawing attention to where he lay hidden.

Oh, please, please blessed Levani! Come save them. make them stop. Please. . . .

The Levani never came; and at last, the screams died away.

The black-robed people talked among themselves; their words were nothing more than a buzz to the still-shaking child. He watched them as they slowly mounted their horses.

The sun was setting. As they rode away, he finally saw his parents. They'd been nailed to the trees; he could not recognize them.

With a scream, Morticai broke from the nightmare. He followed the first scream with another, and another. And then, like a wounded beast, he cried. It had been a truth he'd never been able to face, a memory he'd blessedly blanked from his mind. The pain and darkness that now surrounded him was nothing compared to the memories that had broken from whatever dark tomb in which he'd hidden them. For untold hours he suffered through the memories—over and over again.

Then the agony that lay where his eyes had been took hold of him, as flashes of color and brightness replaced the darkness. He writhed in his bonds, heedless of whether any could hear his agonizing cries. At last, when his body had wrung itself to numbness, thoughts returned; insanity, hoped for, proved unattainable.

His thoughts were distant, detached. He thought about all that he had been driven to—Watchaven, the Arluthians, the Northmarch. And now, to his certain death. The corryn thief chided himself for being sloppy in his work; he, an Arluthian, deserved such an end for being so stupid. And what of the Northmarch? Had all of Coryden's efforts been lost on him? Couldn't he remember something as simple as the importance of telling his commanders what he was about?

Or was his fear of the Faith still so great that he feared what Inquisitor Glaedwin would have done, had he informed the man of Faith of his plans? The ex-street urchin now knew that however the Inquisitor might have reacted, it would not have cost him this.

Coryden and Nelerek would be ashamed that they had wasted their time on such a worthless waif. Perhaps he should have gone with Heather, his first friend in the streets, and hid behind her fancy skirts. Or stayed in the Pit, with the gangs, as Calsen had done—in those days he had had the sense not to interfere with things Droken. He wished for tears that could not come.

The memories from long ago returned again to haunt him. To think that he had run, all this distance and all these years, to die by Droken hands, as his parents had died. He laughed at the irony of it. And then came the anger.

"Glawres!" he shouted into the deserted temple. "Is there no justice? What was the purpose of my living? Was it your will, all along, for me to stay with my parents and die?"

Silence was the only reply.

"You didn't help me survive Luthekar's sword! They were wrong! Why should you help me? It was nothing more than a cruel joke by Droka!" Morticai's voice dropped to a whisper. "Why didn't I give it up, long ago? Foolish street rat, Heather would say. Goin' t' go out an' defeat th' Droken."

Luthekar's words echoed in his mind. . . . *The offer will continue to stand until you die.* . . .

"*No!*" Morticai cried in anger at the thought. He grabbed the chains above his wrists and jerked. "No!" he cried and jerked again. With a pop, the right chain dropped an inch.

Morticai froze. Pain shot through his arms, but he couldn't deny it—his right hand was lower. He took a few deep breaths to calm himself. *Damn!* he thought. *I wish I could see the ceiling!* He tilted his head back, as though the movement could somehow let him sense what lay beyond his blindness.

For an instant he was gripped by the fear that someone might be watching. But all remained quiet—no doors were slammed, no alarm raised. No, he must still be alone. Biting his lower lip, he twisted on the chain. It felt . . . strange. Morticai sighed. He couldn't tell anything. He guessed that one side of the anchor must have pulled loose. But what of the other side? He continued twisting, as new thoughts tumbled through his mind.

What if he pulled it down? What good would it do? Was the key still on the table? For that matter, was the table even still there? Even if it was still there and he could reach it, how far could he hope to get? How could a blind man hope to find his way out, avoiding the guards?

He stopped. Despair suddenly overwhelmed him, and with

a sob he found himself praying to Glawres, as his anger of moments before quickly faded.

Forgive me, Glawres, he prayed silently. *I just wanted it to be simple. I wanted it to be over with. But I-I've wanted to fight them for so long. I can't just give up. Please, I hope it's what you want. Maybe I am a fool—but I can't help it. I hate them, Glawres. Please, don't let them defeat me, please.*

He took another deep breath, and repositioning his hand on the chain, he started to twist.

* * * * *

The dawn air was still cool. Nearby, a mourning dove cooed softly. Paxton paused in the alley, easing the large pack he hauled to the ground. A servant walked toward him carrying a basket loaded with vegetables and a woven rope bag, filled with fresh eggs for her master's breakfast.

Paxton opened his pack. The servant turned in at a gate several houses away and vanished. Paxton straightened.

Well, mate, all's clear this far, he thought as he ran a hand through his gray hair. *Hmm.* He checked the ragged clothing he wore and, picking up a handful of sand, brushed it down the side of his right pant leg. Then, reaching into his tatty vest's inner pocket, he retrieved a flask and took a small sip. *There, that should do it,* he thought with a wry smile. *Old peddler Jenkins would laugh to see me now!*

He looked behind him and gave a final nod to Nelerek, who sat with the wagon at the far end of the alley. Nelerek nodded in reply. The aging innkeeper picked up the pack and continued on at an easy pace. He noted that traffic was beginning to pick up as he reached the main road. More servants were walking his way, chattering amongst themselves.

"Ladies," he greeted, nodding deeply. "Would ya perhaps be needin' a new egg bag on this fine day?"

They shook their heads, mumbling amongst themselves.

"Or a new spoon, perhaps?"

One of the women stopped. "Do ye have any pot lids, peddler?"

"What size of pot, madam," he said.

She blinked and slowly replied, "Oh, abou' this big." She held her hands a few inches apart.

"Sorry," Paxton replied, "I've no' got any tha' small."

She smiled and nodded. "Ah, well, I'll jus' keep lookin'."

Paxton raised his hands, gesturing that he was sorry he couldn't help her. She turned and trotted off to catch up to her friends. Paxton let out a sigh. *Dammit, ya ol' geezer,* he chided himself, *you've got to watch your tongue! You know a peddler doesn't talk like an innkeeper!*

He found that he was thankful for the encounter, though, as he continued on. It wouldn't do to make that type of mistake where he was headed. A young man sat on a doorstep, whittling a piece of wood; the man winked at him as he passed, and Paxton had to repress a smile. *Scatla's gonna turn out a lot like Dyluth,* he found himself thinking.

Still, it was good to know he was being covered by the half-dozen Arluthians who were discreetly watching—they had already lost one Arluthian too many. He was surprised that Nelerek had gone along with his crazy plan to gather information, but their informants on the streets had found nothing, and Nelerek's concern was quickly turning into desperation.

Paxton stopped before Ellenwood's open court gate. Everything appeared normal. *Well, 'ere goes,* he thought. Soon, he was standing before the servant's door to the kitchen, rapping lightly. A rotund woman, her size magnified by the large apron she wore, swung the door open. She looked Paxton up and down, frowning.

"We don't need anything, peddler," she said sternly.

"Ah, but, m'lovely lass," Paxton quickly replied, "I'm new t' this port an' have some marvelous things here—" he gestured to his pack—"things tha' ya canno' find 'round here. Things from Bracar." With a smooth flourish he swept a tiny alabaster box out of a top pocket in the pack and under the woman's nose.

She blinked and, despite herself, sighed admiringly. Paxton opened the box lid and held it up for her to sniff.

"That is a lovely scent," she admitted. "But we've no money here for trinkets the likes of that," she finished, a hint of disappointment in her tone.

"For a lady whose eyes sparkle like th' sea itself," Paxton cooed, "it would be m'pleasure t' give it t' ya." With another flourish, he pressed it into her large palm.

"Oh," she said, startled. "Oh, I . . . I couldn't."

"Ah, m'dear lady, o' course ya can. 'Tis only a little thing."

A smile crept onto her face. "Come in, peddler!" she snorted. "I suppose we could at least look at what you've got. But you'd best not slow down my kitchen," she warned, shaking a fat finger at him.

"Never come 'tween a master cook an' 'er kitchen," Paxton replied wisely. Smiling, she led him inside.

The kitchen was large and busy. A young woman, a single long braid hanging down her back, stood before a counter, plucking a chicken; a child sat on the floor working with a bowl of fresh, unshelled peas; and a man, dressed in chatelaine's livery, sat at the heavy worktable smoking a pipe. All activity ceased as Paxton entered. The man frowned.

"Do you need something, Hilda?" the man asked the cook. "I thought you bought all you needed from the last peddler."

"Well, I thought it wouldn't hurt to take a look," she retorted. "This peddler has things from far away. After all, if you'll remember, it was a peddler who gave me that bethroot that stopped that awful hacking of yours!"

The man wrinkled up his nose. "Well, be quick about it," he snapped at Paxton.

"Certainly, m' lord."

Paxton opened his pack and began to show the cook his wares. Unfortunately, the chatelaine remained; the child and servant silently returned to their chores.

"Ah yes," Paxton said, hoping to start a conversation, "I've come through many a port t' reach this fair city." He pulled out more imported wares. "Have ya ever seen such a marvelous work of art?" he asked, as he handed the cook an intricately carved Lorredrian spoon.

"Never known peddlers to travel much by sea," the chatelaine replied.

"I was a sailor in m' younger days," Paxton replied. " 'Tis a good way t' find some beautiful an' useful things! An'," he added sheepishly, "when ya get t' be my age, 'tis much easier t' gain passage with an old friend than t' walk 'tween 'ere an' Menelcar."

The man straightened and stared intently at Paxton. "Will you be returning to the docks, peddler?"

"Aye, in a couple o' days," Paxton replied. "I'll peddle m'wares here an' then head back down th' coast."

"I've got something to sell you, if you're looking to buy as well as sell," the chatelaine said.

"O' course!" Paxton replied.

The chatelaine left the room.

"Oh!" the cook exclaimed. "Isn't this pretty, Miranda?" She held up a carved wooden bowl for the servant to see.

"Yes, ma'am, it is."

"How much would you take for this?" she asked Paxton.

"Well, m'lady, I'd be 'appy t' let ya have it for twenty ferdhyn."

She wrinkled her nose, "Seems a bit much."

The chatelaine returned carrying a black silk pack. Tossing it onto the table, he said, "Take a look at that, peddler, and tell me what you'd give me for it."

Paxton took in a sharp breath, and then coughed, long and loudly, to cover the mistake. The ploy seemed to work, as the room's occupants politely glanced away.

" 'Scuse me, m'lord," Paxton said. "I'd be 'appy t' look at your pack."

The aging Arluthian picked it up and opened it. Inside, the pack contained the full accoutrements of a thief—rope, dismantled grapple, oil, a pouch that Paxton knew would contain lockpicks. Paxton looked at the chatelaine and raised his eyebrows.

"We were fortunate enough to catch a thief a few days ago," the chatelaine explained. "It will be a long time before he sees anything outside of Gull's Cliff Prison!" he added, chuckling.

I'll wager! Paxton thought acidly, but he replied, "Aye, ya were lucky t' catch 'im. Hmm. I could resell th' pack, an' th' rope. I'll give ya a korun for it."

"Excellent!" the chatelaine replied.

Paxton dug into an inner pocket of the vest and drew out a korun. " 'Ere, m'lord," he said, handing the coin to the chatelaine. "Is there anythin' 'ere m'lady would like?" he asked the cook.

"Yes," she said. "I'll take this spoon, and those bowls. How much will that be?"

"Fifteen ferdhyn."

The cook went to a small crock and dug out the coinage.

"You know, peddler," the chatelaine remarked, "if I were you, I wouldn't try to sell that pack here in Watchaven."

"Oh?" Paxton asked innocently.

"Well," the chatelaine explained, "that thief might have friends in the city, you know."

"Ah," Paxton replied, "aye, right ya are, m'lord. Thank ya for th' warning." *Indeed, he does,* he thought.

With the transactions finished, Paxton reloaded his pack, placing the silk pack on the top. Then, closing it up, he nodded politely to the chatelaine.

"Well, m'lord an' ladies," he said, taking his leave, "I thank ya an' pray that Glawres's blessin's fall upon ya like the spring rains."

The door shut behind him, and, gritting his teeth, he made his way back the way he had come. Scatla saw the look in his eyes; hopping to his feet, he crossed the street and headed the same direction as the Arluthian innkeeper. Nelerek saw the look, as well.

"Paxton?" he asked anxiously as the "peddler" reached the coach.

"Take a look at this!" Paxton hissed, opening his pack. Scatla trotted up as Paxton tossed the black pack to Nelerek.

"Blessed Benek!" Scatla exclaimed.

"You've checked Gull's Cliff Prison, haven't you?" Paxton continued.

"Yes," Nelerek replied evenly.

Paxton nodded. "I expected you had. According to Ellenwood's chatelaine, the thief they caught is in Gull's Cliff. He sold me the pack for a korun."

Nelerek checked the pack's contents.

"Is it Dyluth's?" Scatla asked anxiously.

Nelerek bit his lower lip. "I'd say so," he replied softly, holding up the small container of oil and examining it.

"I'm sorry, Perlagus," Paxton replied. "I didn't expect to be handed his pack."

Nelerek leveled a stare at him. "Don't be sorry," he said. "We're going to go and get him."

Paxton blinked.

"Yeah!" Scatla said eagerly. "That man of the Faith says he's alive, so let's go get him!"

Paxton's worried eyes met Nelerek's. Apparently, Nelerek hadn't passed the word around that "that man of the Faith" had told Dyluth's captain he expected Dyluth to die at any moment.

"I know he might be dead, Paxton," Nelerek said softly. "I'm prepared for that. But we've got to try. And if he's dead, they'll pay," he finished coldly. "Scatla," he directed, "unhitch this horse and take a message to Captain Coryden."

* * * * *

The chain crashed to the floor. Morticai cried out involuntarily and then tried to stifle the moans that threatened to escape him. He was only partially successful, and as he panted from the exertion, he moaned in short, hiccupy bursts; dizziness seized him and threatened to plunge him into unconsciousness.

"Well," he said softly, once he had regained his remaining senses, "I guess no one heard. Glawres knows, I gave them plenty of time to call for help."

The thief gingerly tried to move his right arm. The pain was excruciating, and he desperately fought back a sob.

Damned lot of good this has done me!

He took a deep breath and tried again. This time, he was able to lift his arm, though the dizziness tried once more to take hold of him. He fought through it, and did not stop the movement until his hand lay on the edge of the table.

Thank Glawres! he thought. *It's still here!*

But would the key still be there? A sob escaped as he slid his hand along the edge of the table and pain shot up his arm; he began to tremble as his hand slid over two cold, metal items—they were not the key—he could tell by the feel, they were other . . . things. At last, he found the key.

He stopped, and for a while just let his hand lay atop it as, again, he panted. Trembling, he commanded his fingers to close around it and he was suddenly seized by a new fear—that he would be unable to work his fingers—but his numb fingers obeyed and he soon had the key in his grasp.

Wild thoughts tumbled through his mind. Surely someone had heard . . . and they were watching from the edge of the room. Or, maybe the key didn't even work the manacles—Luthekar could have laid any key on the table. He pushed the thoughts away. There was only one way to find out if any of them were true. He had to keep going.

Bringing his hand back to his body was easy, though noisy. The thief pulled his hand off the table, and with a thump it fell to his side. Then, with his heart pounding, he gritted his teeth and drew the key up to his left wrist.

He couldn't get it into the lock; not because it didn't fit—he couldn't keep his hand steady enough. Unsuccessful, he had to let his hand drop again. A couple of minutes of rest and an anxious prayer later, he tried again.

This time, he got the key in and, after another short pause, turned it. He heard a click, but the manacle remained shut. Morticai inhaled sharply, thinking at first that the key had broken in the lock but then realizing what had happened—he had unlocked the manacle; the spikes were keeping it closed.

Damn!

Morticai's right hand still clung to the key in the lock. With more effort, he pulled the key out and slid his hand up to the manacle itself—and instantly regretted it. As the weight of his right hand settled, the left manacle popped open. The spikes tore free, and even as Morticai cried out from the pain, he felt himself toppling forward. With a thud, he landed face down on the platform, and the blackness that filled his vision exploded to fill his mind.

* * * * *

Morticai awoke with a start. He still lay on the platform, could still feel the cold stone beneath him. As soon as his pounding heart quieted, the Arluthian held his breath and listened. He could have been in a tomb, for all the silence. He slowly released the breath and began, once more, to assess his situation.

He was shocked to realize that he still gripped the key—loosely, but at least it still lay in the fingers of his right hand. His body was both numbed and filled with pain; thinking through all the sensations proved difficult. He knew he had to reach down to his calves and ankles if he were to truly free himself. It all seemed so useless.

He told himself to give it up; a moment later, he was mustering the strength to move his hand down to his right knee. His mind ran wild with insane thoughts, and he spent as much time fighting them back as he did fighting the pain. As his hand reached his knee, he dropped the key. Panic seized him. He frantically patted the floor beside him but soon found it—the key had not fallen out of reach. After a few moments of painful fumbling, he released the iron on his right calf.

He needed to transfer the key to his left hand to remove the manacle from his right wrist. He fought back his fear as he made the transfer; he couldn't afford to drop the damned key again. At last he freed his right wrist from the spiked manacle and his legs from the irons.

With more effort, he rolled onto his back and, for a time, he lay still. He knew he should keep moving—and yet he wanted to lie quietly, just a little while longer. Just a . . .

Morticai started, and wondered if he had fought his way back to awareness as quickly as he felt he had, or if he had, in fact, fallen asleep. He panicked; how long had it taken him to pull the chain down and free himself? It had to have been hours.

Trembling, he rolled over and tried to orient himself. He knew that the way out lay behind him somewhere. He tried to crawl. It was an effort, but he found he could pull himself forward.

Gods, you must be a sorry sight!

He bumped into something, and fear gripped him—and then he sighed, realizing it was the table. He must have gotten turned around.

Just great! Now, wouldn't they laugh if you crawled to the front doors!

He turned around and began again. It seemed to go quicker than he thought it would, or maybe he had just lost all sense of time—he couldn't tell. But at last he found the edge of the room. He suspected that he had gone off course; he edged along, searching for a crack that would tell him he had found the door.

The pain was beginning to fade into an odd numbness, and Morticai began to fear that his wounds would kill him after all.

No! Please, please, not after getting this far! Oh, Glawres!

He continued, but he knew his speed was slowing—exhaustion was finally claiming him. Hoping he was not leaving an obvious trail of blood, he stopped for a moment and felt the ground behind him. He couldn't tell for sure—he didn't think so, but he wasn't certain he could trust his numbed fingertips. Nothing could be done for it, so he continued on.

That's it!

He had found a crack. He ran his hand up it, looking for a knob or lever; he didn't find one. He began to despair and then remembered that he hadn't seen a knob on the door they had brought him through—they had just pushed it open.

He pulled himself into a sitting position. Dizziness swept over him. As soon as he was able, he slid over the crack. He prayed there were no guards on the other side and pushed.

With ease, the door opened. His heart racing again, Morticai gathered enough strength to pull himself through it. There was a wall of some sort on the left—he dragged himself to it and slid along it.

A wall?

He didn't remember a wall like that. The door swung shut as he cleared it, causing him to jump.

Probably just as well, he thought. *No sense in leaving open doors for them to follow.*

He found another wall, butting against the one he had slid along. Realization flooded in—he had found a closet. A damned closet! He wanted to cry. Anger welled up, and with more effort than he knew he had left he pushed himself from the back wall to the door again.

He pushed against it—it wouldn't open. With a sob, he tried to fit his fingertips into the crack to pull it open. His trembling fingers betrayed him—he had to fight to relocate the crack, and when he did find it, he couldn't use it. He let himself slide to the floor—maybe there was a good space at the bottom of the door.

There wasn't. Morticai panted—with fear, exhaustion, and anger. His mind reeled with emotions; his body was numbed by pain.

It's not fair! Oh, Glawres, I kept going—why did it have to be a closet! It's not fair! Is this what you wanted? Is this your will? I did my best. I don't want to die, don't want to die. Not in a closet. A damned closet . . .

And finally, the despair and frustration gave way to exhaustion. Finally, sleep came.

CHAPTER SEVENTEEN

Paxton nervously readjusted his mask. The silk half-masks had been developed for Arluthian ceremonies and ordeals—not to be worn in public. Still, it was the only way they had of protecting their identities while storming Ellenwood's manor.

The innkeeper stole another glance at the leaders of the operation. Nelerek and another Arluthian stood a dozen feet away, speaking softly with Dyluth's captain and the man of Faith he had been told was the Inquisitor. Knights of the Faith had blocked off the mouth of this alley, while the last-minute arrangements were made.

Paxton's skin crawled at those arrangements—who had ever heard of Arluthians working with the Faith? Not that the Arluthians were against the Faith, but they weren't accustomed to working side by side with them, either. The Arluthians, the Faithful, and the Northmarch—what a combination.

The meeting was apparently over. Paxton sighed with

relief—he worried that word would spread to Ellenwood's household that the Faith was in the neighborhood. Nelerek came over to him.

"Ready?"

"I suppose so," Paxton replied. "Uh, brother?" he whispered.

Nelerek edged closer. "Something wrong?"

"No. I, uh, I was wondering if you'd sent word to Heather," he finished.

Behind his mask, Nelerek's pale blue eyes locked solidly with Paxton's. "Not yet," he replied. "Not until I know if he's alive or not."

"Do you think she'll complain? I mean, she is an Arluthian after all, and with Dyluth being her Advocate, she has the right."

Nelerek shrugged. "If she complains, I'll just say that I couldn't reach her. It's what she gets for not working with us the way she should." Nelerek's whisper became a hiss. "You'd think she'd be honored to be the only female Arluthian in Watchaven! Her disrespect for Dyluth is inexcusable—it's a disgrace!"

Paxton looked down. "Dyluth might disagree with you," he said softly.

"Perhaps. We need to get into position."

Nelerek moved away and, with a sigh, Paxton followed. He knew that Nelerek was under a lot of pressure. Yet, it worried Paxton to see him so emotional. It was dangerous—very dangerous.

* * * * *

Dualas drew his sword; standing just in front of him, Coryden did the same. They both watched the Inquisitor, waiting for him to give the signal. The last of the knights were still positioning themselves; it would be just a bit longer.

Dualas scrutinized Coryden's rigid form. Although now assigned to the Inquisitor, Dualas had requested he be allowed to stay with Coryden during this raid. Dualas knew that the previous night had been hard on the Northmarch captain. Dualas reached up and gently laid his left hand on the captain's shoulder. Coryden sighed and relaxed, ever so slightly. Still, he did not turn or speak—his eyes remained on the Inquisitor. At last, the signal was given.

They fell in behind Rylan as he ran up to the manor's front doors. The street echoed with the thunder of hooves as mounted knights charged from the nearby alleys, positioning themselves to cover the exterior of the house; crossbows, legal only in the hands of the Faith, were leveled at the windows.

"Hear ye—open your doors!" the Inquisitor shouted forcefully. "The Faith demands entrance!"

Traffic came to a standstill, and while some of Ellenwood's neighbors peered from nearby courtyards, still others grabbed curious children and rushed them inside. Ellenwood's doors remained closed.

Glaedwin did not repeat his order. He stepped aside, and nodded at Richard; the Inquisitor's huge bodyguard charged the doors. Crack! They remained shut. Dualas moved forward, and together they charged into them. Crack! Someone must have barred them.

The sound of swordplay rang out from behind the manor. The hand-held ram was brought up, and Richard, Dualas, Coryden, and Berret quickly took positions on it. Two swings and the doors gave way.

Inside, battle had already been joined. Dualas moved in behind Coryden as he viciously pressed an attack against an armored guard. The masked Arluthians, some in armor and some not, had apparently gained entry from the back.

"The guards are coming from back here!" someone shouted from a hallway.

Dualas moved in on a guard and easily blocked his opponent's first swing. Soon, a rhythmic pounding echoed through the halls—the ram was being used again.

"Yield!" Dualas demanded of his less-skilled opponent.

"Never!"

With ease, Dualas dispatched him. He glanced around the

room for another opponent, but the fighting was already finished here. The unarmored Arluthians were tying up the servants, some of whom were crying. Coryden headed in the direction they had heard the ram. Dualas and a half score of the Northmarchers fell in behind him.

He's too quiet, Dualas thought.

The ram had been used on what had, apparently, been a hidden door. Echoes of clashing swords floated eerily from beyond the broken doorway. Coryden came to an abrupt halt. An Arluthian stood before the door with an armload of unlit torches.

"Here," the Arluthian said, "it's dark down there." He held a bundle of the torches over an oil lamp, apparently lit for the purpose; they burst into flame. He handed one to each of them as they passed by.

"Those folks are strange," Berret muttered behind Dualas as they entered the dark hallway.

* * * * *

The cry echoed quickly through the halls.

"Attack! Attack! We're under attack!"

Ellenwood looked up sharply as a priest ran into his office.

"Your Eminence!" he cried. "The Faith has taken your manor!"

"Father of Darkness!" Ellenwood cried, jumping to his feet. Of the four different passages that led to the temple, only the one from his manor was not defended by a gatehouse.

"Guards have already been sent to the western tunnel," his assistant informed him.

"Go kill the prisoner, and then meet me in my private quarters," Ellenwood ordered.

The priest rushed from the room. Ellenwood found himself thankful that this had happened *after* Luthekar had left to join his forces to the north.

The high priest slid his desk chair aside and pulled back the carpet. He drew a small wooden chest from the small compartment; everything appeared as it should.

The priest dashed back through the door. "He's gone! Eminence, he's gone!"

Ellenwood blinked. "Impossible! Have they gained the temple?"

"No, Eminence!"

With the chest tucked under his arm and his dagger drawn, Ellenwood rushed to the temple on the heels of the priest. The platform was empty. The chain lay in a pile beneath the table. Guards rushed through, taking the shortest route from the eastern gatehouse.

"Someone must have helped him escape," Ellenwood intoned evenly, "and thanks to that, we now have the Faith on our doorstep. Come with me. We've no time to waste!"

* * * * *

The fighting was at the bottom of a steep staircase. Armored Arluthians and several knights were trying to break through a wall of guards holding the tunnel. These guards seemed better trained than the ones they had first fought—even the knights were having difficulty prevailing against them. Unable to move forward any farther, Coryden's group had stopped on the stairs.

"Move aside! Let us through," came a muffled cry from behind them.

Dualas looked over his shoulder; the Inquisitor and Brother Kinsey were inching their way down the crowded stairs. The two men of Faith stopped just above Dualas; Dualas flattened himself against the wall so they could move past, but they remained on the step above him.

"Do you have enough room?" Rylan asked Geradon.

Geradon narrowed his eyes and scrutinized the situation ahead of them.

"I believe so—it does not look as though we shall gain much ground, otherwise."

Dualas was puzzled; what could they do from here? Geradon began to mutter. At first, Dualas thought he was still speaking to Rylan, but the knight could make no sense of the words.

Geradon brought his hands together, as in prayer, and then, with a graceful sweep of his hands, gestured to the base of the stairs.

Dualas's eyes automatically followed the gesture, and then widened—with a flash, the protective padding beneath the defenders' mail burst into flames. With a cry of alarm, the Arluthians and knights leapt backward; everyone backed up several steps to give himself the room and protection he needed.

Then, for a time, it was impossible to speak, as the screaming Droken tried unsuccessfully to rid themselves of the mail and burning padding. Coryden turned and looked over his shoulder at Geradon; the smile on Coryden's face sent chills up Dualas's spine.

They had to drop to one knee to stay beneath the smoke as it billowed past them to exit at the top of the stairs. Dualas prayed that, though Droken, the enemy would die quickly. As unconsciousness claimed the dying men, the knights moved forward to end their misery. Once again, the group moved forward.

The tunnel was long and took several turns; at each, those in the lead prepared themselves to meet ambushers, but they encountered none. Coryden was pressing forward; Dualas had to trot to stay up with him.

At the tunnel's end they found a large wooden door. It appeared locked, and word was passed to bring the ram, but before it could be brought, one of the masked Arluthians moved up to the door. Within seconds it was open.

Everyone, save the Inquisitor and Brother Kinsey, seemed surprised by the office on the other side of the door. "They usually have quarters attached to the temple," Rylan explained as the group pressed on.

"They're already gone," Geradon said, disappointedly.

Indeed, it was becoming obvious that any remaining Droken had fled. They ran through the office and through another small room and into the temple.

A universal gasp escaped the group at the site of the temple, with its large idol to Droka and bloodied platform. Never before had a Droken temple in Watchaven been discovered. Dualas guessed that, like himself, none of the knights present had seen one until now. He moved closer to Coryden.

* * * * *

Ellenwood and his assistant trotted down the eastern tunnel. They passed quickly through the deserted eastern gatehouse to the door beyond it. When they had closed the door behind them, the high priest paused—he rarely used the sewer entrance. They stood on a ledge above the confluence of three different subterranean channels.

Holding his nose as would a child, his assistant intoned, "Do you know where you are going, Your Eminence?"

Ellenwood looked at him disdainfully; the assistant dropped his hand.

"Of course," Ellenwood replied and took the sewer's northwest passage.

They continued on, and the assistant asked no more questions. They had traveled no more than a quarter-mile when they saw the first intersection ahead of them.

"Hold!" a voice cried, as a crossbow bolt flew past them in warning.

Three men, wearing black silk masks, had stepped onto the ledge in front of them. The crossbows they carried were cocked and aimed. One of the masked men addressed the two Droken.

"Nice afternoon for a stroll through the sewers?"

* * * * *

Paxton froze. He had thought himself prepared for the sight of the temple, but he had been wrong. He was not alone, however—around him, nearly everyone else had stopped moving as well. After a moment of stunned silence, his eyes sought Nelerek.

Nelerek had moved ahead of him, once they had passed the bottom of the stairs. Now, Paxton was surprised to see that

Nelerek was still moving—toward the platform. Others were beginning to move again, as well. Paxton ran after Nelerek, but by the time he reached him, Dyluth's Advocate was on the raised dais, kneeling near the center.

Paxton's stomach threatened to betray him, but he forced himself to climb onto the platform with the quiet corryn. As he reached him, Nelerek looked up.

"He has escaped," Nelerek announced, excitement edging into his voice. "He must still be close by."

The Inquisitor's assistant replied sadly, "Nay, I fear the Droken may well have taken him with them."

"Not so quickly, Geradon," replied the Inquisitor. "Why do you think thus, Arluthian?" he asked Nelerek.

Nelerek pointed to a chain, lying under the table. "This chain appears to be the one that once hung up there," he said, pointing. "And this,"—he picked up something that Paxton could not see—"I suspect fits these."

Now Paxton could see that Nelerek was holding a key. Nelerek clamped the bloody manacle at the end of the chain shut, and then opened it with the key.

"Start searching!" the Inquisitor ordered the knights. "Be careful," he warned them, "there may still be ambushers about."

A few of the Northmarchers came to the platform and began examining the floor, while others headed for the large gilt doors. Nelerek scanned the temple.

"Heavenly Benek," Paxton muttered, as he forced himself to survey the bloodied platform, "what have they done to him?"

"I don't know," Nelerek replied softly, "but we had best find him quickly."

A rumble issued from beyond the large doors, which were now open, and several knights came running back into the temple.

"Brother Glaedwin!" one of them exclaimed. "They have collapsed the tunnel beyond these doors!"

Rylan nodded. "Were any of our people injured?"

"No, brother," the knight replied.

"Good. It is a standard tactic, but I am surprised that they waited this long to collapse it. Should you enter any other tunnels, be wary—they apparently waited in hopes of catching us."

The Northmarchers talked softly and, slowly moving away from the platform, scrutinized the floor. Moving in the direction they were headed, Nelerek walked to the edge of the room. Paxton gladly followed and found his attention drawn to the bizarre wall carvings.

Nelerek also seemed interested in the bas-relief as he ran his hand along the wall. The Northmarchers had almost reached the spot where they stood. Suddenly, Nelerek pushed forcefully against the wall; Paxton jumped as the wall swung inward.

"A hidden door!" one of the Northmarchers exclaimed.

A muffled whimper came from beyond the door.

"Oh gods," Nelerek whispered.

"He's found him!" someone shouted.

Pandemonium erupted. The Northmarchers rushed forward; the word was shouted that Morticai had been found. Nelerek dropped to his knees in the closet and clasped Dyluth in his arms; Morticai whimpered and tried to pull away. Nelerek began to cry. Paxton was, himself, unintentionally shoved into the closet by the anxious Northmarchers.

"Do not move him!" the Inquisitor shouted.

And then, Paxton got a clear view.

Somehow, the Inquisitor pushed his way in. "Careful!" he cried. "Let me to him! We've found him alive—now, let those of us who are trained take care of him."

Nelerek slid out from behind Dyluth, leaving Coryden to cradle him in his arms. Trembling, Paxton grabbed Nelerek's arm and helped him to his feet. The Inquisitor and his assistant were shouting orders to those around them; Paxton and Nelerek emerged from the press.

Nelerek leaned against him, and Paxton pulled him closer.

"Oh, gods," Paxton whispered to him, "I'm sorry, Perlagus. Gods, I'm sorry."

"His eyes," Nelerek whispered. "His eyes."

Another of the Brethren approached them, one who Paxton

suspected was of higher rank.

"Brother," the newcomer said softly, "we all feel your loss. Your Ward's accomplishments will not be forgotten. You obviously taught him the path well."

"Don't speak of him as though dead!" Nelerek replied sharply.

"I meant no harm," the Arluthian replied, dipping his head politely, "but I ask your forgiveness. Dead or alive, we will not forget what has happened here. Nor will the Droken be allowed to so harm one of our own and not pay for it—thy vengeance is our vengeance."

"Thank you," Nelerek whispered.

The Northmarchers had been moved away from the closet as the Inquisitor prepared Dyluth to be moved to the Sanctorium. Nelerek approached Coryden, and for a moment they stood without speaking.

"They'll pay," Nelerek intoned softly. "It has always been our mandate." He gestured to the temple. "This is not payment enough. They shall pay dearly."

"It would be better if he had died," Coryden replied.

Nelerek blinked in surprise. "Nay! It is easy to think such now, Coryden, but you will not think so later."

Coryden sighed heavily. "Perhaps."

They were interrupted by a group of Arluthians, who entered the temple from the opposite side. Before them marched a group of Droken, with the hoods of their robes thrown back and their hands tied behind them.

"Prisoners!" echoed through the large room.

The Inquisitor emerged from the closet, as his assistant continued to work with Dyluth.

"Brother Glaedwin—crossbows," a knight addressed him, pointing to the illegal weapons the Arluthians carried.

"It is all right, Sir Vathan. They carry them in the name of the Faith," the Inquisitor replied, with a wink at the lead Arluthian.

"These decided to try to leave, Father," the Arluthian said. "We caught them in the sewers."

The Inquisitor walked up to a Droken with red robes, embroidered in black and gold.

"Ellenwood," Nelerek hissed softly.

"Well, Sir Ellenwood," Rylan addressed the quiet Droken, "I see that this foray is not a total loss. It appears that Morticai's suspicions of you fell short of even his imaginings. It will be a pleasure to report to the Grand Patriarch that we have apprehended Droka's high priest in Watchaven."

Ellenwood spat, "May Droka take you all!"

"I doubt it," the Inquisitor dryly replied.

"Rylan!" came Geradon's voice, shouted from the closet. "I shall be needing your assistance."

Rylan moved back to the closet. Coryden began to move slowly toward the group of Droken; Paxton touched Nelerek lightly on the sleeve, but the Arluthian shook his head, discouraging any interference.

It was not until Coryden stood before Ellenwood that anyone else realized what he was about.

"You son of a demon!" Coryden spat, as his dagger shot up from his hip. "Droka can have you *now!*" The knights rushed to grab him as Coryden plunged the dagger upward, under Ellenwood's ribs and into his heart; the surprised Ellenwood fell with Coryden atop him, still stabbing. It took six of them to pull him off the corpse.

CHAPTER EIGHTEEN

The first sensation was that of a woman's hand, gently stroking his brow. It was soothing, and Morticai sought to open his eyes to see who it was.

Morticai gasped. Suddenly, hands were upon him; he struggled. There was shouting, and then a woman's voice speaking firmly—it was a voice he knew.

"Peace, child! We will not harm you. Moranekor!"

Stunned, Morticai stopped struggling.

"Calm thyself, child. Lie still. You are safe. No harm will come to you. *You are safe!*"

His brow was stroked again, but the hand was different. He tried to put a name to the voice. He knew he'd heard it before.

"Mother?" another familiar voice whispered.

Mother Edana! And Heather! Morticai began to tremble.

"Shhh," Mother Edana's voice soothed. "It is all right, child. You are safe."

"M-mother Edana?" he whispered.

"Yes, child," she replied. "It is I."

He trembled all the more.

"Do not be afraid, child," she said, and he felt her take him into her arms. "You were rescued and are in Grandhaven Sanctorium."

"Truly?" he whispered.

"Truly," she said.

A moment later a hand lifted his. He felt skin, and realized that she had drawn his hand up to her face.

"Feel?" she asked. "It is truly I."

It seemed to be. "Heather?" he called.

"Yes!"

It had to be Heather. It had to be. He felt another's touch now, and a sob escaped him as he was moved into Heather's arms; she started to cry.

"Now, children," Mother Edana's voice said softly, yet firmly. "You must both stop this mourning. Hold each other and find peace. You are together, and you are safe. Be thankful for that."

Morticai realized that his wrists felt odd. He felt them and discovered that they had been wrapped. He brought his hand up and found that his head had also been wrapped.

"You must leave the bandages alone, Morticai," Mother Edana said. "I will be changing them shortly."

He let his hand drop, and now something else—something hard—hung around his neck. His hand closed around it as he tried to discover what it was.

"That is a very sacred relic, Morticai," Mother Edana informed him. "You are wearing the holy sign of Glawres that was worn by Levani Menahen. Patriarch Phelim had a dream that told him to bring it to Inquisitor Glaedwin. You must leave it on at all times until you are completely healed. Do you understand?"

"Yes," he replied. He lay against Heather, allowing the scent of her perfume and the sensation of her touch to encompass him.

"Perlagus?" Heather asked.

"Yes," Mother Edana replied. "I will bring him—and Captain Coryden—but not yet. First, the two of you need time together."

Coryden. There was something about Coryden trying to edge into his mind. He tried to push it away, but it kept returning to trouble him. He wanted very badly to hear Coryden's voice. He needed to . . . to *tell* him something?

"Dyluth," Heather whispered. "It will be all right." She hugged him closer in response to his tenseness.

"Coryden," he said. "There is something. Heather, I must see Coryden." He realized what he had just said, and a sound—part sob, part crazed laugh—escaped him.

Heather followed with a sob of her own. "Don't think about it," she cried. "Oh, my Dyluth!" She began to rock with him in her arms. "There will be plenty of time for you to talk with Coryd—"

"No!" Morticai exclaimed, as memories returned. "No! Heather, I must talk to him now! Oh, Glawres, I've got to warn him."

"I shall fetch him," said Mother Edana. Morticai could hear her robes rustling as she rushed from the room.

* * * * *

"Are you certain about this?" Nelerek asked Coryden.

Coryden paced to the end of the small room.

"I don't see that we have a choice," Berret interjected. The squad sergeant sat on the edge of a bunk in the small room in which Coryden's squad had been quartered.

"Good heavens, man," Nelerek replied, "what if they don't believe you? You may be taking your entire squad to the executioner!"

"I'm afraid I agree with Berret, Perlagus," Coryden said. "I don't see that we have any choice. We cannot convince King Almgren that a Droken army lies to the north—but the Northmarch . . ."

"Why should they believe you any more than King Almgren, Coryden? You deserted! You have no proof other than Dyluth's word of what he saw on the maps. Of course, you and I trust his word, but will they? If you had the maps to show them, you'd have a chance—but Ellenwood obviously destroyed them, or else Luthekar took them."

The door opened, and Sir Dualas entered.

"Good news!" he exclaimed.

He handed Coryden an envelope with the elaborate seal of the Faith.

"What's this?" Coryden asked, and started to break the seal.

"No!" Dualas caught his hand. "Do not open it. That is a letter from the Grand Patriarch."

Coryden looked at him, uncomprehendingly.

Dualas smiled. "It is for Northmarch high command. It informs them that the Faith has proof that a Droken army lies to the north and that you and Berret's squad were ordered into service with the Inquisition."

Coryden laughed. "Does this answer your fears, Perlagus?"

Nelerek shook his head. "I suppose so," he sighed.

Evadrel entered. "We're ready," he announced.

Coryden rose. "Well, this is it, then." He grasped Dualas's forearm in a soldier's farewell. "Thank you, friend, for this. He raised the sealed letter. "I wish you were coming with me."

A smile crossed Dualas's face. "But I am." The smile broadened. "I didn't have a chance to tell you—the Inquisitor has released me to go with you. This will add further weight to the letter, for I am the witness who saw the Grand Patriarch sign and seal it. Will they doubt my word that it is authentic?"

* * * * *

Coryden hesitated outside the door that led to Morticai's room. After a moment's pause he rapped softly.

"Who is it?" came Morticai's voice.

"It is I, Coryden," he replied.

He was about to open the door when Morticai himself opened it.

"Hi," Morticai said, clinging to the edge of the door. "I didn't think I'd get to see—you'd get to come by before you left."

"Morticai, you shouldn't be out of bed!" Coryden said, entering the room. He closed the door and wrapped an arm around Morticai to help him back to the bed.

Morticai sighed. "Oh, Coryden," he said softly. "Coryden, I'm sorry."

"Sorry?" Coryden looked at his friend, confused.

"I was so stupid," Morticai said, shaking his bandaged head. "I mean, I deserved what I got, y'know—I should have . . . I should have known better."

"Oh, gods, Morticai," Coryden said, shaking his head. He wanted . . . With a shock, he realized that he wanted eye contact with him. Instead, he grabbed Morticai's hands and moved closer. "Listen, I . . ." He didn't know what it was he wanted to say; he felt as if he were losing control. "Morticai," he began again, "it wasn't your fault. You didn't know what you were going into, that's all. I'm just glad you're alive," he finished in a whisper.

"Cor . . ." Now it seemed Morticai was the one lacking for words.

Coryden allowed his control to slip away and, apparently to Morticai's surprise, embraced him. The corryn thief relaxed and returned the embrace, and for a short while they sat silently. Coryden tried to think of something to say, but nothing seemed appropriate. After a moment, he released Morticai and fought to regain his composure.

"I've got to be going," he said slowly.

A slight smile briefly lit Morticai's face. "I know," he replied. "I'm going to worry about all of you, trying to sneak past Watchaven's scouts."

"Oh, we'll be all right. Will you promise me you'll do everything they tell you to? To take care of yourself?"

The smile returned. "Yeah, I'll stay outta trouble."

* * * * *

The itching was driving him mad!

"No!" Heather cried. "Don't scratch!"

Morticai stopped his hand before it reached the eye bandages.

"I'm sorry, Heather," he said. "But it's driving me crazy!"

She took his hands in hers. "I shall sit here and hold your hands all night, if it is what I must do."

Morticai smiled. "I can think of better things. . . ."

"Dyluth!" she scolded him.

Morticai sighed. "I know. But having you so close—so often. It's almost as bad as the itching!"

"Perhaps I should stay away?"

"No! Oh, Heather," he said.

She took him in her arms. "I was teasing," she said, "and you knew that very well."

Morticai smiled. "But it got you even closer."

She giggled. "What am I to do with you!"

"Well," Morticai said, "since you won't do what I'd really like, why don't you tell me what you found out today at the palace. Have the armies met?"

"No, not yet. They said that it would take five days for both armies to reach Mid-Keep."

"And they've been gone?"

"They only left yesterday morning, silly."

"I'm worried about Coryden," Morticai admitted. "I fear they'll be caught by Watchaven's scouts."

"You yourself said that if anyone could sneak past the scouts, it was Coryden," she replied.

"I know. But Coryden left after the army was already on the march. If he was able to get past them yesterday, he should be all right. There wasn't any word about spies being captured, was there?"

"No, not a bit."

Morticai sighed with relief. "Well, I can hope they made it through, then. Did Lord Jendall go with the army?"

"Of course," she replied. "You need not worry, if that is what is in your head, lover. You have nothing to fear from Jendall."

"Sure, as long as he's out of town," Morticai retorted.

Heather laughed. "No, that's not what I meant. I have already spoken to him. He knows that you are injured and that I am staying with you as much as they will allow."

"Heather!"

"There's nothing to worry about," she repeated. "You must trust me, I am afraid. He is very different from Lord Ullock, my dear. He would never harm you, just because we are close. However, I did find out something else that you might be interested to hear."

"Oh?"

"Well, my sweet, now that the king and most of his nobles have left with the army, I found people a little more willing to talk with me."

"You mean, about that order?"

"None other. You'll be shocked when you hear who issued it."

"Heather, don't tease! Who?"

"Prince Edris."

"Edris? Which one is he?" Morticai knew that Edris was one of King Almgren's many sons, but he had long ago stopped trying to remember who was where in the succession line.

"Almgren's fourth son."

"What have I done to him?" Morticai complained.

"I certainly wouldn't know," Heather replied. "I know it has nothing to do with me—he's never looked at me, and I'd have nothing to do with him if he did."

"Hmm. That is strange. I wonder if he confused me with someone else?"

"I wouldn't think that very likely," she said. "But, there is more. Once I found he issued the order, I thought to take a look through his chambers."

"Heather!" Morticai exclaimed. "That was a terrible risk!"

"Hush now," she replied. "If you can take risks, so can I!"

Morticai whispered, "And look what it's gotten me."

She stroked his hair. "Yes, but you have always taken such risks. I take them very rarely. As Nelerek would say, my odds are better. And besides, Edris, like all of the princes, has gone with his father and the army."

"So what did you find?"

"Well, actually, it was more what I didn't find."

"What?"

"Well, I knew that he would pack all of his clothes, which—isn't that silly? Just what he needs is his finest clothes to go to war in! But, what was truly odd was that all of his ivory was gone."

"Ivory?"

"He collects carved ivory. You know, little animals and such. Every bit of it was gone. He has always been frantic that it might be broken—anytime it has been displayed, like at his birthday party, he has hovered and fretted over it. Not something I would think he'd wish to take on an overland trip with an army, don't you agree?"

"How strange."

"Exactly my thoughts. Unfortunately, I have not been able to think why he would have taken it."

"Are you certain it was he who emptied it? It's possible that some thief has just been waiting for an opportunity like this, you know."

"I thought of that. But there's a little bit more. There wasn't a thing in his desk—except . . ." She paused dramatically.

"Except what, Heather? Don't tease me!"

"Well, I found an odd map. It was in the very bottom, as though it had fallen from the back of the drawer, if you know what I mean."

"Yeah," Morticai replied. "Did it show armies?" he asked, his excitement growing.

"No, it looks like one of the cities, but it's unnamed, so I am not certain which city. But I have a friend who is a mapmaker; I'll take it to him—I'm sure he'll know which one it is."

Morticai tried to pull himself up straighter, but a searing pain shot up his right arm. He gasped, and then doubled over as his right shoulder, and then his right side, spasmed.

"Dyluth!" Heather cried, pulling him closer.

"I-I'll be all right," Morticai moaned.

* * * * *

It was just past noon. At last, Coryden could see the tops of Mid-Keep's towers on the horizon. The Northmarch captain held his hand up, signaling his men to stop. The squad halted behind him, the sound of tack and hooves giving way to the sound of panting horses.

He had stopped them beside the small stream that wound lazily across the plain, providing water for the nearby villages as well as Mid-Keep. The weary band dismounted and immediately began tending the tired horses. Coryden did not like running the horses so hard—their good health would not continue if the men kept pushing them.

But now their destination lay only a few miles away, and they had made the good time he had hoped they would. They had cut half a day off of the usual two and a half it took to get to Mid-Keep from Watchaven. He signaled for Evadrel.

"Shall I scout ahead?" Evadrel asked, anticipating his captain's wishes.

"It would probably be a good idea. We both know there's not enough room inside the keep's walls for the entire Northmarch—I suspect most are camped outside."

"True," Evadrel replied thoughtfully.

"What's wrong?" Coryden asked. Evadrel tended to speak little, but when he did speak, his tone could speak volumes.

"I worry that there is no smoke."

Coryden blinked and scanned the horizon. He had not thought about it before, but Evadrel was correct. There should have been smoke from cookfires—especially this close to noon.

"Hmm. You're right. Be careful."

"Yes, sir."

Evadrel unslung his bow from the back of his pack and strung it. Then, notching an arrow, he trotted off in the direction of Mid-Keep. *I wonder if he could run without a bow in his hands?* Coryden thought distantly as he watched the scout disappear.

* * * * *

The horses had finally cooled off and drunk their fill when Evadrel returned. Coryden rose from underneath the tree he had claimed and walked to meet him as the corryn scout approached. Evadrel's eyes told him there was trouble.

"What is it, Evadrel?" Coryden asked, as soon as he could speak without shouting.

Evadrel did not answer until he reached his captain.

"Very bad news, sir," he replied, slightly out of breath. "They are gone."

"What!"

"The keep is deserted, sir, but there is more."

* * * * *

An hour later the squad stood before Mid-Keep's gate—or rather, what had once been Mid-Keep's gate. Coryden was stunned, even after Evadrel's warning. The keep was a burned-out husk. The gates had been torn down, the hinges purposely destroyed. Coryden shook his head.

"Incredible," Dualas muttered beside him. "It must have been a terribly difficult decision to make."

A piece of parchment was nailed up on the wall beside the gate. Coryden walked his horse up to the gateway to read the notice for himself.

Notice is hereby given, it stated, *that the mandate of the Northmarch is to serve the kingdoms of Dynolva and Watchaven. We are to protect the borders and highways, and their citizens as they travel. We cannot condone the killing of citizens from either kingdom—nor will we allow our soldiers or our fortresses to be used for such. Thus, has Mid-Keep been removed as an aid to either side in this senseless war. The Northmarch shall not desert either kingdom. We shall march to the north and camp on the border until this madness has passed. To this, we give our official seal.* It was signed and sealed by the Northmarch's High Commander, Lord Seabrook.

"How long ago did this happen?" Coryden shouted to Evadrel.

"At least three days ago," he replied.

"Three days," Coryden muttered.

"They'll have reached the border by now," Dualas replied, having ridden up beside him.

"We'll have to keep going," Coryden said. "We have no idea how far that Droken army is from them."

Berret had ridden up to them by now, returning from the small town that stood just north of Mid-Keep.

"Evadrel is correct, Cor," he said. "Quite a few of the townspeople have left, but those still here say they burned it four days ago."

Coryden shook his head. "They must have decided to do it before giving the order for everyone to gather."

"Well, I suppose they had a fair idea that it would come to war, just as we did," Dualas observed.

"What I want to know is where in Benek's name is this damned Droken army coming from?" Berret asked.

"I've wondered that myself," Coryden said. "Morticai didn't know. He said that there was a mark on the map that seemed to plot the army's origin, but it was marked in lands that none have ever been to—at least, not that we're aware of."

CHAPTER NINETEEN

Rylan uttered a silent prayer of thanks as Mother Edana unwrapped Morticai's head; he doubted the corryn would have survived had it not been for her ministrations. While there were a few healers scattered across the world who rivaled her abilities, sadly, there were never enough. Even in his home kingdom of Abbadyr, known for its healing herbs, such healers were rare. Mother Edana motioned for him to come to her side.

"Brother Glaedwin," she said, "please come and hold this bandage for me."

She had carefully rolled the bandage as she removed it, and though it still wound a few times about Morticai's head, she held up the roll up for Rylan. He held it as she began to gently work the remainder of the bandage loose.

Rylan watched curiously; he could tell that some sort of cream lay on the wounds under the bandages.

"Mother Edana?" Morticai asked.

"Yes, child?"

"When will the itching stop? It's about to drive me mad."

"I am sorry you are finding it so troublesome, but I do not think the itching will stop until your eyes are completely healed."

"Well, I guess that's what I'm asking—how long will it take?"

"That is a question I cannot answer, little one. Each Levani works in its own time—who can say how long Glawres shall take? If I were to guess, I would say that it should not take as long with Glawres as with some of the Levani; impatience is as true of Glawres as it is of you, my child. You share many traits with your patron—I think it is why he favors you so."

Morticai sighed but did not reply.

Mother Edana carefully peeled off the last layer of the bandage and then directed Rylan, "Please, brother, check that cabinet by the door for a bottle of springwater. I have brought another bottle, but I do not wish to open it yet."

Rylan checked the cabinet and found a bottle of liquid. " 'Water from the spring of Levani Gwendiva,' " he read from the label.

"Yes, that's it."

"Doesn't Gwendiva's spring lie in the mountains west of Dynolva?" he asked, handing it to her.

"Aye, and it is a good thing that I had put back a dozen bottles. Although the Dynolvans have not yet hindered our people's travel, I would not want to run out."

She gently rinsed away the cream and surprised Rylan by using the water freely—a prime ingredient for many healing tonics, the water was expensive, even to the Faith.

Rylan mentally prepared himself for what would lie beneath the cream—he had seen grievous wounds before. When she finished, Rylan swallowed and forced himself to look down.

He gasped. Where Morticai's eyes had been there appeared to be some sort of a filmy layer . . . of skin?

"Looks pretty bad, uh?" Morticai said softly.

"Ah, uh, no," Rylan said, blinking. "Not really." Rylan

looked at Mother Edana. She smiled and nodded slowly.

"You are the only person besides myself who has seen how his healing is progressing, brother," she informed him.

Rylan said nothing further, waiting until she had reapplied the cream and wrapped Morticai's head with clean bandages. His intention had been to speak with her and learn how Morticai was healing—but what he had seen . . .

At last, she finished. Rylan helped her gather things up. Nelerek, waiting anxiously outside, entered the room as soon as they left it.

"Mother," Rylan began.

"Not here, child," she replied. "Come with me."

She led him to the common ward, where she deposited the bandages and supplies, and then led him into a small prayer room. They both knelt and offered up a silent prayer before she turned to him.

"You have questions?" she asked.

Rylan took a deep breath. "Yes, Mother." He looked at the small stained-glass window thoughtfully. "I worked for some time in the ward of Daric's Sanctorium in Abbadyr. While there, I saw many severe wounds. Indeed, I saw wounds such as those Morticai now suffers from, for, as you know, the Droken are fond of taking the eyes of those who might identify them. But, never have I seen such a . . . a film form over the eyes."

"And do you know what it means, brother?"

Rylan sighed. "I suppose that is my question. Do you know what it means?"

Mother Edana smiled at Rylan. "Glawres has already shown favor for this child of his," she replied. "Morticai has already survived the wound from Ducledha—which no man or corryn has ever before survived. Did you know that I had dreams before you rescued Morticai?"

"No, I did not. I knew that Patriarch Phelim—"

"Yes." She nodded. "Patriarch Phelim brought you Menahen's relic. That was also a sign of favoritism from Glawres."

"But I did not know that you had also had dreams."

She nodded again. "In my dream I made a very large pot of

the ointment that you saw me use on Morticai's eyes. It is a special healing ointment that we use here, but it is expensive and difficult to make, and so we usually make very small amounts of it and use it sparingly. In my dream I was making the large pot because I knew that I would need it for someone terribly injured. Of course, when I awoke, I did not know who that someone would be—but I made the ointment."

"So," Rylan ventured, "Glawres has given two people dreams concerning Morticai's injuries."

"Yes. And I believe that underneath that layer of skin, Morticai's eyes are growing back," she said, matter-of-factly.

"A-a miracle," Rylan uttered.

"Indeed. But why are you so shocked?"

"Dear Mother," Rylan explained, "although I know that the almighty Levani still perform miracles, I have never actually seen one."

"Did you not hear about the girl from Mitharvor who lost her legs—only to regrow them?"

"Yes, but—"

"But why would Glawres choose to perform a miracle on someone such as Morticai?" she finished for him.

Rylan looked down, thoughtfully. "Perhaps that was what I was thinking." He shook his head. "But if that is so, I am ashamed. The Levani do not look at worldly station, or even faithfulness, when they choose whom they shall bless."

Mother Edana nodded, wisely. "Indeed. They may even choose the unfaithful as proof of their mercy. But there is much faithfulness in Morticai that lies deep in his soul. Too deep for many to see, I suspect—but it seems clear that Glawres sees it."

"Does anyone else know about this?"

"I have told the Grand Patriarch, Patriarch Phelim, and Morticai."

Rylan blinked. "You've told Morticai? What does he think?"

Mother Edana laughed. "He said very little when I told him. I am certain that he thinks me quite mad."

* * * * *

King Almgren sat atop his huge bay horse and surveyed the remains of the once magnificent Mid-Keep. He sadly shook his head.

"I was afraid they would do something like this," he remarked to the large man sitting ahorse beside him.

"Aye, Sire, you were correct," replied the knight. "I must admit that I hoped they would defend it rather than this."

"I wish it had been so—I might have parleyed with them. I cannot doubt the loyalty of Lord Seabrook, but he is an independent man, and it is clear that his loyalty lies more with the Northmarch than with either Watchaven or Dynolva."

"Perhaps that is well," the knight replied. "Though Seabrook did not remain to parley with you, he has not remained to parley with the Dynolvans, either."

"True."

The king's oldest son, Bertel, rode up to them.

"Father, because we cannot defend this keep, would you that I ordered the troops on?" he asked. "It is only now noon—we could make several more miles and perhaps find a better location to array ourselves."

"Nay," Almgren replied, "I would not move the troops farther. I know this territory much better than you, my son. This plain continues for another full day's march before turning to hills. By the time we reached those hills, we would find them filled with Dynolvans. It will be better for us to wait here and let our men rest. I would much prefer to battle the Dynolvans on the plains, where I can see them, than in their own hills, where I cannot."

"Aye, lord," Bertel replied despondently.

"Should we send an emissary to the Northmarch to attempt parley?" the knight asked.

"I suppose so, though after this"—the king gestured to the burned out fortress—"I doubt they will change their position."

* * * * *

"What is taking him so long?" Coryden complained.

"Perhaps it is extra caution," Dualas replied. "Had they caught Evadrel, we would have known by now."

Coryden paced to the large bush at the northern edge of the small clearing and peered over it. Nothing but scrub lay before him, and nothing moved within it. He sighed and spun around. His tired men sat quietly, waiting for him to decide their next move. Knowing their captain, they had conveniently left him a path on which to pace through the middle of the crowded clearing.

A finch chirped in the distance. Coryden stopped pacing and looked questioningly at Berret. Berret smiled.

"Yes, that's Ordson," Berret confirmed. "Evadrel is returning."

"I don't see how you can tell him from a real bird," Coryden remarked.

"Sometimes I can't," Berret replied, with a smirk.

"He has someone with him," Dualas said, looking over the bushes.

Evadrel soon entered the clearing with a human.

"You obviously found them," Dualas remarked to the scout.

"Yes," Evadrel replied. "Captain, have you ever met Thoris?"

"No," Coryden said, nodding to the stranger.

"Captain," Thoris replied respectfully.

"I met him on the perimeter of the Northmarch camp," Evadrel explained. "I thought it might be best if he escorted us in."

Coryden nodded approvingly. "Better than being arrowed," he remarked dryly. His men rose and with the jingle of mail moved to their horses.

* * * * *

The band walked slowly through the huge camp. To Coryden's knowledge, never before had the entire Northmarch been gathered in one place at the same time. He blinked, realizing how powerful a force they actually were. *No wonder there was so much talk about where we would side in this war,* he thought.

Their entrance had already been whispered through the camp. At every tent, heads turned to stare. Evadrel and Thoris walked ahead of the squad, while the rest remained mounted.

Coryden and his men were covered from head to toe with grime from the hard ride; it didn't seem to bother those who stared, though Coryden noted a few knowing nods from those who could tell from their clothes that they had ridden long to come here. Just before they reached the command pavilion, two corryn ran up to them.

"Captain!" one of them hailed.

Coryden smiled at them. It had not been easy to convince his other two squad sergeants to go with the Northmarch. "Greetings Luwaren, Nildan."

"Is Morticai . . . ?" Nildan asked.

"We rescued him—Morticai is alive," Coryden said. "He is—hurt, but they say he will live." The full story would have to wait.

"Thank the Levani!" Luwaren exclaimed.

They had reached the command pavilion. Berret pulled the two sergeants aside to fill them in on recent events as Coryden and Dualas entered the huge tent.

Kirwin sat to the left of Lord Seabrook at a large rectangular table. Coryden swallowed and tried to push back the nervousness that gripped him. He had rarely seen Lord Seabrook, let alone spoken to him. Without a word, he handed Seabrook the sealed letter from the Faith.

With only a brief glance at the seal, Seabrook opened the letter and read it silently. His brow furrowed and he handed the letter to Kirwin. Seabrook waited until the human commander had finished before speaking.

"Why were we not informed of this service with the Inquisition?" Seabrook asked.

"For a time, we were working with them only while off-duty, and I did not think it was going to interfere with our Northmarch duties. When we were informed by the Inquisitor that we needed to remain behind and that he was pressing us into service to complete what we had started, it was too late to send word to Commander Kirwin." *Well, it sounds good.*

"I see," Lord Seabrook replied. "And where is the proof that this Droken 'army' exists?"

"I am sorry to report that it has been taken from us, my lord. Maps were found that showed the movement of the army, but before we could secure them, they were stolen."

Seabrook's eyes narrowed. "And how could this army be north of us? I think it unlikely that they could have sneaked past us."

"The army has not come from the south, lord, but from the north, from someplace far northeast of our kingdoms. If you do not believe us, then I would suggest you send scouts north to search for the army. I was very concerned that they would come upon you, unprepared."

"What of Morticai?" Kirwin asked.

Coryden took a deep breath. "We rescued him, Commander."

"And destroyed the Droken temple in Watchaven," Dualas added.

Kirwin's eyebrows rose.

"I see," Seabrook replied. "Commander McFerrin, take this letter to Commander Jarviel for him to read, and give orders for a patrol to scout to the north."

"Yes, sir," Kirwin replied.

"Your commander is very unhappy with you, Captain," Seabrook continued once Kirwin had left.

"Yes sir, I know," Coryden replied softly.

"Do you have anything to say about it?"

Coryden shook his head. "I am afraid that I cannot blame him. If I were in his position, I would also be upset. We just didn't have time to apprise him of the situation. He knew that Morticai was working with the Inquisition and knew that we were spending a bit of our off-duty time with him. When Morticai disappeared he knew that we were searching the city for him. I am at fault for not keeping Commander McFerrin informed, but at the time he was very involved maintaining order at Northgate, and I was very worried for the fate of my man."

Lord Seabrook nodded, slowly. "What else can you tell me of this army?"

"Although we do not know beyond all doubt, we have very strong suspicions that it is being led by a Droken prince named Luthekar."

After a moment, Seabrook replied, "Indeed? And have you seen this Droken prince? I have always thought him to be a bardic fantasy."

Coryden glanced at Dualas. "Yes, sir, we have."

Another pause ensued. "Pardon?" Seabrook finally asked.

"Yes, sir, we have seen Prince Luthekar," Coryden clarified. "In fact, Sir Dualas, Morticai, and I fought against him in Watchaven, and he wounded Morticai. Commander McFerrin filed a complete report on the incident, I believe."

"I see," Lord Seabrook replied, obviously surprised.

Kirwin returned with Commander Jarviel. Jarviel, a full corryn, glanced briefly at Coryden and Dualas and then stopped, and looked again. Dualas nodded politely; Coryden tried not to smile. *I guess he wasn't expecting to find corryn standing here*, Coryden thought.

Jarviel addressed Seabrook. "Do you believe this, sir?" he asked incredulously.

"I do not yet know," Lord Seabrook replied. "If there is an army to the north, our scouts will find it. The Grand Patriarch of Watchaven would not sign such a document if he did not, himself, believe it to be true. Captain, Sir Dualas, would you please wait outside a moment?"

"Yes, sir," Coryden replied and they stepped out.

"Well?" Berret asked anxiously.

"We don't know yet," Coryden replied.

And so, they waited. The rest of the patrol had shown up and sat in small groups with members of Berret's squad, swapping news. Finally, Commander Jarviel emerged.

"Come back inside, please," Jarviel said before disappearing back into the tent. The thought that the three officers could act as a tribunal flashed through Coryden's mind as he stepped back inside.

"Captain," Seabrook said, "we have discussed what type of punishment you and your men should suffer for your desertion. That you deserted cannot be denied, although the Faith obviously was a factor. At the same time, the Faith should have sent word to Commander McFerrin that they were pressing you into service. The situation would have been greatly eased if the Grand Patriarch had sent a letter *before* Commander McFerrin left Watchaven.

"I do not fault you for being concerned for your man's safety," he continued, "but you have lost men before and should be aware that at times such a sacrifice must be made. From what Commander McFerrin tells me, this Morticai got himself into this mess while off-duty, and though good may come of it, it does not mean that disobedience of orders can be tolerated.

"The fact that you have voluntarily returned is in your favor. And if this Droken army truly exists, your return with this information is to be commended. Those factors do much to help your situation. We have decided to place your men on heavy duty until it is determined whether or not this army exists. Once that has been determined, we shall make a final judgment.

"You are dismissed," he finished.

"Thank you, sir," Coryden said, though he hardly felt thankful at the moment.

* * * * *

King Almgren reread the note. Before him, the corryn messenger waited nervously between his guards. The tent was crowded, with his advisors trying to read the message, guards surrounding the messenger to deter any thoughts of assassination, and his five sons there out of . . . curiosity, he supposed.

"I want everyone out," Almgren announced, "except for Lord Jendall and Lord Hildric." He passed the note to his two top advisors as the room cleared.

"So," Lord Jendall remarked, "the Dynolvans have marched all this way only to propose a parley?"

Almgren shrugged. "Perhaps. I have never fully understood King Riamel."

"It could be a trap," Lord Hildric noted.

Almgren snorted. "I do understand Riamel that much, Hildric—it's not his style."

"Do you want to talk with him?" Jendall asked.

Almgren sat back and gazed abstractedly at the closed tent flap.

"Hmm. I can see no damage in it. It is true that much of this has transpired through ambassadors and counsels—perhaps we should meet face-to-face. What do you think of our tactical position, Lord Jendall? If we should parley and the talks fail?"

Lord Jendall tilted his head, allowing his shoulder-length hair to fall forward.

"We have the advantage of higher ground here, although this can hardly be called a hill . . ." he began.

"It's the closest thing to a hill for miles," Hildric interjected.

"True. And it would give us a slight advantage. The Dynolvans have better cavalry than we—"

"How can you say such a thing!" Hildric exclaimed.

Jendall glanced at the king, who was, indeed, giving him a dark stare.

"I am sorry, Sire," Jendall explained, "but it would be unfair of me to say that it was not so. It is not that the Dynolvans are better warriors, but I fear they have better horses."

"Why?" the king asked flatly.

"They have better grass than we."

Hildric snickered. Jendall looked at the blond noble and raised an eyebrow.

"That makes sense," King Almgren said, nodding.

The smile faded from Hildric's face.

"Well, I suppose we shouldn't keep Riamel's messenger frightened all afternoon," Almgren said, shuffling through a pile of papers on a small table beside him. He finally produced a quill, turned the note from Riamel over, and began penning a reply. "How far away have the Dynolvans camped?" he asked abstractedly.

"About half a day's march," Hildric replied.

"Hmm. There will be quite a bit to work out before we can meet. Jendall, I want you to handle the pre-meeting negotiations. I do not agree with Riamel's proposal of meeting without guards, and I will not meet out on that godforsaken plain. Also, I will not be ready to meet with him tomorrow. I want to give our scouts plenty of time to estimate his force's strength. Besides, it might be best to let him sweat a little, say two or three days. You can start by telling them that we will meet inside Mid-Keep. At least there, I need not fear a cavalry charge."

* * * * *

"Well?" Edris hissed. "What did the old geezer decide?"

Hildric dropped the tent flap, sealing the narrow gap he had been peering through. "Begging your pardon, my prince," he said through clenched teeth, "but you should not have come here."

Edris lifted his chin, defiantly. "And how else am I supposed to find out anything? Certainly not through my father's generous sharing of knowledge!"

"I would have contacted you, to be sure, Prince Edris," Hildric replied. He paced to a campaign trunk and dug through it. The noble soon produced a bottle and two glasses and set about pouring them drinks.

Prince Edris drummed his fingers on top of another chest but said nothing. Hildric handed him the drink.

"We are in luck, my prince," Hildric said, "and I propose a toast."

Edris slowly raised his glass.

"I toast Prince Luthekar's imminent victory. And I toast your imminent coronation."

"Don't play games with me," Edris snapped.

Hildric lowered the glass. "Then I shan't. Your father is going to meet with King Riamel in about three days' time. It should be a perfect opportunity to complete our assignment. If we can manage it properly, I believe that not only can we kill your father and brothers, but we can also lay the blame on the

Dynolvans. And if I have guessed anything about my counterpart in the Dynolvan camp, I would not be surprised to find that he, too, is laying such a plan."

* * * * *

Shouting echoed through the torchlit camp, announcing the return of the patrol Lord Seabrook had sent north. The Northmarch High Commander looked up from his work—they should not have returned this quickly.

Captain Nishan entered the pavilion, covered from head to toe in mud. Seabrook raised his eyebrows.

"My lord," the captain began, "there is, indeed, an army to the north of us! It . . . it . . ." The captain faltered.

"*Yes?*" Seabrook demanded.

"My lord," the captain continued, "I-I have never seen anything like this army. Sir, it must be sixty thousand men strong!"

"Impossible!"

"Nay, lord! It is true, though I wish it were not so. It lies just under a day's march away!" The captain's voice held a hint of panic.

"Captain Nishan!" Seabrook snapped. "You will calm down and give an orderly report! Did they see you?"

"No, sir," Nishan replied, once again in control of himself. "We rode until dark yesterday. Early this morning, we came upon them. We skirted a small marsh to avoid being spotted by their scouts, but we are certain we were not seen."

Midway through Nishan's reply, Commanders McFerrin and Jarviel had entered the pavilion. Lord Seabrook hesitated only long enough to be certain they had heard enough to know what had been found.

"Give the order to break camp," he told them evenly. He grabbed his quill and sat down at the large table. It would take the scouts several days to reach the armies of Watchaven and Dynolva, but it was the only warning he could give them.

CHAPTER TWENTY

Rylan Glaedwin surveyed the dimly lit room. Mother Edana sat by the bed, holding Morticai's hand. The Matriarch had sent him a message requesting he come here. Rylan noted that she had not brought her salve with her.

The Lady Adrianas, whom Morticai called Heather, sat on the far side of the bed. She had taken down her long hair and, though still beautiful, appeared weary. Rylan still wasn't certain how this lady of court had come to be so close to Morticai. He wondered if she had been the one sending Morticai the pigeon when he had convalesced here before.

"So," Mother Edana was saying, "your itching has stopped?"

"At last!" Morticai replied. "I was beginning to think it would continue forever!"

Mother Edana smiled at the Inquisitor. "For one of deep faith, little one," she said, "you have so little trust. Did I not tell you it would stop?"

"Yes," Morticai admitted. "You did. And I believed you. Truly. But it's been days!"

"Oh, Dyluth," Heather interjected, "all that matters is that it has stopped."

Mother Edana glanced at Rylan. "Shall we see how Morticai has healed, Brother Glaedwin?"

Rylan inhaled deeply. "Dear Matriarch, do you think it time? It has been only nine days."

"Aye, that is true," she replied, as she began to unwind the bandages about Morticai's head. "But the discomfort has stopped—and that, I believe, means that the healing is complete. We shall see."

"Mother?" Heather asked cautiously.

"Yes, child."

"You are going to let me stay?"

"Yes, child. You have come here every day—for that, you deserve to be here now."

Heather seemed confused but said nothing.

Morticai began to fidget with the wrappings on his wrists.

"What is wrong?" Mother Edana asked him.

"I don't know. I guess I'm nervous," he replied. "Mother Edana?"

"Yes?"

"You said that the healing is complete?"

"Yes, I believe it is, but we will not know until I remove the rest of this bandage and rinse off the ointment."

Morticai swallowed but asked no further questions.

Heather had taken her hand up to her mouth and appeared close to tears. Rylan moved to her side and took her hand. Mother Edana was removing the last bit of bandage. This time the healer did not ask for Rylan's help, and he noted that she seemed not to need it.

All Rylan could see beneath the bandage was a thick layer of ointment; Heather looked away—Mother Edana might have thought her ready to be here, but Heather obviously did not share her conviction. The Matriarch rinsed the ointment away, but this time, she used a cloth as she rinsed.

Rylan suddenly realized that, as the progress of Morticai's healing was becoming apparent to him, he had been tightening his grip on Heather's hand. He consciously relaxed his grip before speaking.

"Look!" he whispered, unable to keep a tremor out of his voice.

She did, reluctantly, and then with an audible gasp tore her hand from his grip and clasped both hands over her mouth.

Beneath the ointment had been what appeared to be a spongy layer of skin. Mother Edana carefully cleaned it away; beneath the spongy layer lay eyelids. And although they were still very short, eyelashes had even begun to return. Rylan softly released his breath.

Mother Edana took both of Morticai's hands.

"Morticai," she said firmly, "I want you to try to open your eyes."

"Mother Edana," Morticai complained, "please don't say such things!"

The Matriarch took his left hand up to his eyes.

"Feel that, child?" she asked.

Morticai began to shake.

"Now," she said, "obey me and open your eyes!"

It appeared to take a good deal of effort, but open them he did; a universal gasp escaped the room's occupants. Morticai had opened them wide, and in the second that he had sat in stunned silence with them opened, shock had claimed them all.

Rylan tried to look at Heather but couldn't bring himself to look away from Morticai. Morticai's eyes *had* been blue—they were no longer. The color had been changed, and it was something that even Mother Edana had not appeared prepared for. His new eyes were . . . purple—not the pale lilac that was common to some corryn, but a deep, vibrant purple, such as that found on the robes of kings—and in sanctums dedicated to Glawres.

The light must have been too much for Morticai's new eyes, for he immediately squeezed his lids into a painful squint. Then, he began to shout.

"I-I, my eyes! My eyes are back!"

Mother Edana let go of his hands and moved her grip to Morticai's upper arms. Rylan could easily see why she did so; Morticai bounced up and down on the bed like a child, squinting and shouting and crying.

Rylan swallowed again, and this time managed to look at Heather. She appeared shocked, as he himself was, but appeared frightened as well. Rylan wrapped an arm around her shoulder.

"Calm thyself!" Mother Edana shouted at Morticai. "You must calm down!"

Eventually, he complied, though he still seemed giddy with excitement.

"Morticai," Mother Edana began evenly, "you must calm down and speak with me."

"Y-yes?"

"*Can* you see?"

He apparently tried to unsquint, but was unsuccessful. "Well"—his excitement seemed to die—"no . . . not really."

"That's all right," Mother Edana soothed. "Do you see anything? You apparently can see light. Can you see color? Tell me exactly what you can see."

Heather began to cry, softly.

"I . . . I do see light," he said slowly. "It's too bright."

"I am sorry, but that is as low as the lamp will go," she replied.

"I see shapes," he continued, "but they're fuzzy. I can't tell what anything is." He took his hand up and then slowly moved it toward his face, stopping it about two inches from his eyes. "I-I can see my hand!" he exclaimed, as his excitement began to return.

Suddenly, he dropped his hand, shut his new eyes, and turned his head, listening. "Heather? Heather, are you crying?"

"Yes," she sobbed. "I'm—I'm sorry. I can't help it."

She spun toward Rylan and buried her face against his shoulder.

"Shhh," Rylan whispered to her. "She'll be all right, Morticai," he said. "She was not prepared for a miracle. It will take a little time for her to get over the shock."

Morticai sighed. "Yeah. I wasn't really expecting a miracle, either. I guess I should have known Mother Edana wouldn't lie."

"You need not apologize, child," Mother Edana replied. She placed her hand under his chin and moved his head back toward her. "I want you to try again to open your eyes. Do it very slowly—try not to squint. That's it," she coaxed. "You do not need to open them all the way. I want to look at the color of your eyes."

"The color?"

"Yes," she said. "Ah, that is enough." She shook her head. "It is just like the Levani of the sea," she said. "Glawres, the unpredictable—and one who loves surprise. He surprised even me."

"Uh? What are you talking about?" Morticai asked, and squinted again, apparently trying to focus on Mother Edana's face.

"Child, your eyes have changed color."

Silence.

"They have?" he finally asked.

"Yes, child. Were they not blue, before?"

"Y-yes. What color are they now?"

"Violet."

Morticai smiled weakly. "I've always wanted violet eyes," he said sheepishly.

"You mean the light shade that some corryn have?" Rylan asked.

"Yes."

"They are not quite that shade," Mother Edana replied.

"Huh? What shade are they?"

"You will see, child," she replied. "For now, you should lie back and close your eyes to let them rest. It will probably take a little time for your muscles to regain their strength. We are not yet finished," she said. "We must unwrap the rest of your bandages."

* * * * *

Rylan gently led Heather, who still cried softly, from the room. They went into the Sanctorium itself, and he led her to a deserted bench near the back of one of the upper balconies. She did not seem to mind being led there.

"Dear lady," he began cautiously, "this should be a time for rejoicing, not mourning."

She dabbed at her eyes with her kerchief. "I-I know, I suppose."

"Then, what troubles you, lady?"

She brought her emerald eyes up to meet Rylan's, and he found himself thinking that many battles had doubtless been fought for their favor.

"I am not unhappy that Glawres has given Dyluth back his sight," she began.

Rylan was momentarily puzzled until he remembered that Dyluth was the name Morticai had told him he was known by on the streets.

"And I do not wish to be ungrateful," Heather continued, "but it will never be the same. Glawres has *claimed* him—isn't that so?"

"That certainly may be," Rylan agreed.

"Things will never be the way they were. I have sometimes dreamed of going away with him, of having a life away from court—but now those dreams are forever dashed! He can never belong to me now, for he belongs to Glawres."

"But, Lady Adrianas," Rylan cautioned, "there is no greater honor than to be so claimed. Can you not share your love with Glawres?"

"It would never be that simple!" she replied, shaking her silver tresses. "How easy will it be now for the Droken to find him?"

Rylan blinked, realizing the import of what she was saying. Morticai's new eyes would be impossible to disguise.

She continued, "You seem to know little of his love of freedom, nor his love of danger. He will not hide from the Droken, as he should—it is not his way. He will live openly. And what will come of it, if not his death? Do I not have a reason to grieve, Father?"

Rylan took her hands gently in his own.

"Dear lady," he replied, "I feel in the depths of my soul that Glawres would not give Dyluth such a blessing if it were to lead only to his death. Please, be patient and allow Glawres to fully unveil his works. It is too early to know what changes Glawres has wrought within Dyluth that we may not be able to see. Please, let this be something that strengthens your faith, not something that weakens it."

"I-I will try, father," she replied, taking a deep breath. "I will try."

* * * * *

The light knock was obviously meant to not waken Morticai, should he be asleep. Getting up from the bed, Morticai walked to the door, a broad smile already on his face—he had strong suspicions who might be visiting in the predawn hours.

"Hi!" Morticai greeted, opening the door.

Nelerek stood in the hallway and, for a moment, did nothing but stare. Then, a grin matching Morticai's lit his face, and he was in the room, grabbing Morticai by the shoulders and spinning him around.

"It's true!" he cried, and hugged Morticai to him.

Morticai laughed. "Yes!"

"Gods, Dyluth!" Nelerek exclaimed, holding him back at arm's length again. "Or, perhaps I should say *your* god." He shook his head. "I-I cannot tell you how I feel."

"You should try being on this side of it," Morticai replied.

"Gods, Dyluth," Nelerek repeated in a whisper, "who would have thought?"

"I know," Morticai said. "I still don't know how I should feel."

"Can we turn the lamp up a bit? If you can stand it, that is. Heather said—"

"About the color?"

"Uh, yes."

"She's not taking this very well, I am afraid," Morticai said, moving to the bedstand to turn up the lamp.

"Well, it's not every day that someone you know has a miracle performed on him," Nelerek replied.

Keeping his back to Nelerek, Morticai replied, "I think there's a bit more to it than that, Nelerek. Are-are you ready for this?"

"Of course," Nelerek replied, confused.

Morticai turned around and sat on the edge of the bed. Nelerek stared, taking in a deep breath.

"Not quite what you expected?" Morticai asked.

"Ah . . . I . . . I knew they were violet," Nelerek began and moved closer, pulling the chair beside the bed around and sitting down in it.

Morticai smiled dryly. "It's a bit extreme, isn't it?"

"Well, I, uh, well . . . yeah," he finally answered. "But, gods, Dyluth, if Glawres has grown them back, I suppose he has the right to make them whatever color he wishes."

"I know. And in truth, I don't mind. I'm so thankful just to be able to see again. But I'm a little worried about what people are going to think. I'm afraid they're gonna think I'm a freak."

Nelerek scowled. "I am not certain that will be a problem, Dyluth. I mean, yes, it is a very unusual color, but I do not believe that you can judge it by our reaction."

"Huh?"

"Heather and I have both known you for many years with blue eyes, Dyluth. I think that may be affecting our reactions. You may discover that when you meet people for the first time they will quickly accept this as just an unusual shade of violet."

"I hope you are right," Morticai replied, though he noted that Nelerek seemed unable to stop staring.

"After all, it's not any stranger than your hair," Nelerek added with a smirk.

"What's wrong with my hair?" Morticai complained.

"Well, Dyluth," Nelerek asked gently, "how many corryn do you know in Watchaven with black and silver hair?"

"Uh," Morticai began. "Well, they say it's not that uncommon in Lorredre."

"That may be, but here it is. My point is that I don't think people are going to stare at you any more for your eyes than they already do for your hair."

"There is something else I need to show you," Morticai said.

"Yes?"

Morticai unlaced the cuff of his nightshirt and showed Nelerek his wrists.

"No scars!" Nelerek exclaimed. "Almighty Aluntas—then, you are completely healed? Heather did not tell me this."

"Well, you're almost correct," Morticai replied. "I'm a little stiff, but it's not too bad, and I still get an occasional twinge here and there, but it could be a lot worse. There are no scars—except for these."

Morticai shoved back the sleeves of his shirt, revealing the brands he had received during the ritual. Nelerek blinked, and then gently took Morticai's wrists, turning his arms so they were more in the light. On the underside of each forearm, a dark, indented scar defined with frightening exactness the brands that had been used.

"If Glawres could grow back my eyes, and remove every other scar, including some I've had since I was a child, why did he leave these?" Morticai asked.

Nelerek's serious eyes met his. "I suppose he intended to leave them," he said slowly.

"I've thought that also. Mother Edana believes that he changed the color of my eyes to mark me as his and that he may have left the brand for the same reason. But she didn't know why he left the Arluthian symbol, and that scares me, Nelerek. Did he leave it because he doesn't mind me being an Arluthian—or did he leave it because he *doesn't like* me being an Arluthian?"

Nelerek sat thoughtfully a moment before replying, "You have been an Arluthian a long time, Dyluth. And, it was being an Arluthian—not a very bright one, I must admit, but nonetheless being an Arluthian—that got you into this mess. If Glawres did not approve of your belonging, I would not have thought he would have grown your eyes back."

"I hope you're right."

Nelerek nodded. "So do I. I must admit, that scar may cause a few problems." Nelerek shrugged, "I don't think they would send you to the gallows for it, howev—"

"What about the Arluthians?" Morticai interrupted. "We're supposed to keep this symbol secret."

"Well, by now you should realize that it is not a very well-kept secret—after all, the Droken certainly knew of it. And I am certain that the Faith, as well, knows of it." Nelerek grinned, wickedly, "You will just have to make certain the ladies leave your shirt on, my friend."

Morticai snorted. "Now, that'll be a challenge!"

Nelerek laughed. "It is so good to have you back."

"At least for tonight," Morticai amended.

"Hmm?"

"I leave with the Inquisitor a couple of hours after dawn."

"*What?*"

Morticai took a deep breath. "We have to catch up to King Almgren—"

"Nonsense!"

"We have to, Nelerek!"

"Good gods, Dyluth!" Nelerek exclaimed. "You've not even had your eyes back a day and you're talking about traveling?"

"Nelerek," Morticai said, lowering his voice, "you don't understand—the Inquisitor is going to try to forewarn King Almgren of the Droken army. If all has gone well with Coryden, proof of the army should have been given to Almgren—but we can't count on that. Now, Heather found out that the king's fourth son, uh, Edris, was the one who issued that order against me, and she broke into his chambers—"

"Heather?" Nelerek asked, incredulously.

"Yes, Heather. Remember? She is my Arluthian ward, after all. Well, she found out two interesting things about Prince Edris. First, he took some things that one wouldn't normally take off to war—like his prized ivory collection. But she found somethin' more important than that." Reaching to the table beside the bed, Morticai handed Nelerek a paper.

Nelerek studied it, his frown deepening the longer he stared at it. "This isn't one of the cities," he stated.

"You're correct," Morticai said softly. "At least, it's not one of our cities."

Nelerek looked up. "Cuthaun? You think it's Cuthaun?" Stories of the hidden Droken kingdom had been told since before either of them had been born.

Morticai nodded. "That I do. Heather took the map to a mapmaker, and he confirmed that it's not any place he'd ever seen. Heather had him make two copies of it. I'm keeping one copy, and I'm giving you the other copy to take to the Arluthians. Rylan will deliver this one to King Almgren."

Nelerek let out a long breath. "Dyluth, do you realize how long people have searched for this place?"

Morticai nodded. "But that map still doesn't tell us where to find it. I mean, yeah, it'll be nice to have a street map once we can find it, but till then, it's not much help. But because of this"—Morticai gestured to the map—"we're certain Edris is involved. I've mentioned it to Rylan, but he says we don't have enough proof. I've got from now until we reach Almgren to figure out how to prove Edris is involved."

Nelerek sighed and leaned his head back against the chair. "You just don't give up, do you?"

Morticai looked down. "Nelerek," he said in a whisper, "while I was strung up in that damned temple I did a lot of thinking. If there was anything that I wanted more than my sight, it was that these damned demons be stopped! Glawres has given me back that chance—I'm not going to disappoint him. I've got to see it out to the end."

Nelerek's hand fell softly on top of Morticai's.

"Look at me, Dyluth," he whispered in reply.

Morticai met his gaze, and was surprised to see the Arluthian close to tears.

"I understand," Nelerek began. "I still fear for you, but I understand. However, I will not let you go alone. Too much has happened, and you have suffered far too much for me to allow it. Let me go with you."

* * * * *

Coryden gave a final nod to his sergeants. Luwaren, Nildan, and Berret nodded in return and raised their right hands. Coryden looked away from them and raised his own right hand as he watched Kirwin, sitting at the far end of the column.

The half-corryn captain swallowed and took one last deep breath; it had been a long time since he had performed a cavalry charge at Kirwin's command. The Northmarch had the largest cavalry in the known world but, as far as Coryden knew, a cavalry charge of this magnitude had never been attempted—anywhere.

Watchaven's force was arrayed just below the crest of the hill, one thousand strong. Dynolva was similarly arrayed on the back side of the hill on the opposite side of the valley. Lord Seabrook and his own force of one thousand were also somewhere on the other side, well out of Coryden's sight, but within Kirwin's sight, he was certain.

On the other side of the hill, most of the huge Droken army had already passed through the valley that lay between the forces of the Northmarch. Lord Seabrook had waited until fully half of the huge force had passed through the valley to give the order for them to get into position—to be certain the Droken scouts had passed well beyond them.

The command was given. As Kirwin dropped his hand, so did every captain and sergeant down the column. Down the line, every fifth man lit a torch. Coryden spurred his horse forward, staying stirrup to stirrup with the man on either side of him.

By the time they reached the crest of the hill, he could hear nothing but the unnatural thunder caused by the hooves of a thousand charging horses. Coryden saw the Dynolvan force on the opposite side of the valley and was awed by the sight, even as his horse carried him along in a group that was just as large.

The surprise was complete—the Droken force beneath them looked up in horror at the charging Northmarchers and panicked. Some of the drivers whipped their teams into motion, running down their own soldiers as they tried to flee the coming destruction.

A few in the front would probably manage to escape, but Coryden lost sight of them as the Northmarch cavalry closed in on the remainder of the supply train. He braced himself against the high-backed saddle, as his lance struck a draft horse before him.

He abandoned the lance and drew his sword. He cut down

two men and was heading for a third when the sound of Northmarch horns echoed above the din of swords, horses, and screams. Coryden pulled back on his reins and wheeled his steed around.

He glanced over his shoulder to see if he could spot any of his men. He could see Luwaren, but the rest were lost in the smoke of burning wagons and the dust stirred by the huge mass of horses. Spurring his horse, he charged back up the hill they had descended. There would be time to count their losses later.

* * * * *

Prince Luthekar's horse made its way through the still-burning wreckage. At first, some had attempted to extinguish the blazing wagons, but Luthekar had stopped them. There was no sense in it. They had lost what they had lost. The wagons had been fully ablaze within moments.

A quarter of his supplies had been destroyed. As long as nothing else went wrong, they would have enough. He had cached emergency supplies behind them, should a retreat become necessary, but now it would be a long march without supplies to reach that stash—unless he ordered the army to turn around immediately.

He pushed the distasteful thought away. They were too close to victory. Never before had an army made the thousand-mile trek from Cuthaun. It had taken years to build up and train the army and store enough supplies to support the long journey. It would be a disgrace to turn back now, without a single battle fought.

Luthekar stopped and stared at a body that lay beneath an equally dead horse. General Wilfram, who rode a few feet away, expressed the thought that already raced through his own mind.

"Northmarch!" General Wilfram exclaimed.

The prince narrowed his eyes and surveyed the hills to either side.

"It should not be a surprise," Luthekar replied. "No one, besides ourselves, has that many cavalry."

"But how did they know we were here? If they did not know, why are they this far north?" Wilfram asked.

Indeed. This complicated matters greatly. They would need to send their scouts out in all directions. The marching order must be changed in order to guard the remaining precious supplies. It would slow them when they could least afford it.

"See if you can find a Northmarch survivor," Luthekar ordered. "Give orders to rearrange our order of march—we cannot be caught so, again. I shall go back to the vanguard."

* * * * *

Coryden leaned against the large rock and closed his eyes. He and his men had hardly recovered from their forced ride to the northern border when they had been given the order to break camp and prepare for the assault against the Droken army. His men had paid for that lack of rest.

Out of his thirty-man patrol, he had lost two men—both from Berret's squad. Six more had been wounded—and four of them were from Berret's squad. It was a gamble he had been forced to take, though he knew that the odds had not been in his favor. Weary men make mistakes and die for it.

At least he could thank the Levani that none of the others' wounds had been immediately fatal. With further luck, their wounds would heal cleanly.

"Captain?"

Coryden opened his eyes. Dualas stood before him, a plate of food in his hands. Coryden sighed.

"You need your strength as much as any of us," Dualas said quietly.

"I know," Coryden replied and sank into a sitting position. Dualas sat before him and handed him the plate. Coryden stared at the food.

"I am afraid that will not suffice," Dualas finally informed him.

Coryden snorted. "You've spent too much time around Mother Edana, Dualas." He started eating. "How are our wounded?"

"Doing very well, I am happy to report," Dualas replied.

Coryden nodded. "Well, that's good to hear, at least. Have you heard anything about how they think the attack went?" Coryden asked between mouthfuls.

"A little," the knight admitted. "The scouts estimate we destroyed a little over a fifth of their supplies."

"Is that all?" Coryden asked.

"That is a goodly amount, Coryden," Dualas informed him. "They estimate that we destroyed over a thousand of the six thousand wagons in their train. It will not stop them, but it will certainly not give them good fortune. They have rearranged their order and slowed their march considerably—that, you must admit, was the true objective."

"Yeah, I guess so," Coryden replied. He shook his head. "It seems a steep price," he muttered softly. "So, what now? Will we be hitting them again?"

Dualas tilted his head thoughtfully. "Lord Seabrook has not yet decided, but if I were to guess, I would not think that we would strike again with our entire force. It would be much more difficult, now that our element of surprise is gone."

"So we're just going to sit out here?"

Dualas shrugged. "Perhaps. They could always turn to face us and lose more time.

"And if they did turn to face us?"

"I believe we would retreat. We cannot afford to face their cavalry—the scouts say they outnumber us two to one."

"*What?*"

"That is what they say. It took the scouts several forays to count them all—apparently they had scattered their cavalry into small groups with each infantry unit. Now they are massing them together."

"That doesn't sound good, my friend."

"We shall see. I think it is merely a show of force, to keep us from attacking again."

"I hope you're right, Dualas," Coryden replied, shaking his head. "And to think, there was a time when I thought it a grand operation when we'd join with three other patrols to hit a band of highwaymen."

CHAPTER TWENTY-ONE

"They're gone!" Morticai exclaimed, reining his horse to a stop.

"What?" Geradon asked. "Have they already pressed into Dynolvan territory?"

"No, no," Morticai replied. "I'm not talking about Watchaven—Watchaven is camped on this side of Mid-Keep, and Dynolva is camped on the other side. But the *Northmarch* is gone!"

"Slow down, Morticai," Rylan said. "How can you tell? How far did you go?"

Rylan, Geradon, Richard, Nelerek, and a dozen knights of the Faith sat in a circle in the tall grass. Nelerek's hawk perched on a nearby tree, having just finished its morning catch of food. They had taken a southern approach to Mid-Keep to avoid traveling through the already-trampled terrain left behind by Watchaven's army.

Morticai dismounted and moved toward the small group. His horse followed him, nosing his shoulder.

"All right!" Morticai said in exasperation, turning toward the horse and digging through his saddlebag.

"Dyluth," Nelerek urged him to continue.

"There!" Morticai said, ignoring Nelerek and holding out a small apple. "Now, go away, Silvia!" The horse snorted and trotted off toward the other horses, chomping on the apple.

Morticai sat down. "As I was saying, the Northmarch is gone. Or else they've been killed to the last man, and I think that a little unlikely. Besides, I saw no sign of it. No mass graves or pyres, at least. It does appear that Mid-Keep has been burned, but I think it happened a while back—there is absolutely no smoke. Both Watchaven and Dynolva are camped a couple of miles from Mid-Keep, on opposite sides of it, of course. I guess I got within two miles of Mid-Keep—"

"Morticai," Rylan admonished, "you were not supposed to get that close."

Morticai shook his head. "I'm sorry, Rylan, but I had to get a better look at Mid-Keep to be certain there hadn't been a battle."

Rylan sighed. "Very well. I understand your concern. From what you say of the two camps, it does not sound as though Watchaven and Dynolva have yet joined battle."

Morticai nodded. "You're right. It looks as though the two armies are just staring at each other. Maybe they're having a spitting contest—who knows?"

"So, what do you think has happened to the Northmarch?" Rylan asked him.

Morticai shrugged. "I don't know. I suspect they went north, because we've seen no signs of passage on this side of things. The only reason for them to go north that I can fathom would be to try to meet the Droken army, assuming Coryden got the message through. I certainly hope he did. I saw no sign of him."

"But, why would Mid-Keep be burned?" Geradon asked.

"I don't know," Morticai replied, shaking his head. "I'm just tellin' ya what I saw. It makes no more sense to me than it does to you."

"Well," Rylan observed, "we apparently will learn no more sitting here. Shall we?" He gestured to the horses.

"Might as well," Nelerek replied, getting up.

The rest of the small group rose and walked slowly to the horses. Rylan stretched, dreading the thought of riding again so soon. It had been a hard journey for all of them, with the possible exception of Morticai and the knights, who seemed used to the grueling pace. Rylan had worried that the activity might be a bit much for Morticai so soon after healing, but if Morticai had been wearied by the ride, he had not shown it. Currently, he and his friend were donning the helmets that they had brought to wear when they rode into the Watchaven camp.

Rylan had been surprised when Morticai had informed him that his friend would be coming with them; he had almost forbidden it. There was just too much that he did not know about this strange corryn friend of Morticai's—besides suspecting that he was an Arluthian. But Morticai had seemed set on it.

Just before they were ready to leave, the friend had arrived at the Sanctorium with complete Watchaven uniforms for Morticai and himself. It was to cover the fact that they were corryn, he had said. It was a point, but Rylan could not help but wonder where he had found the uniforms on such short notice.

* * * * *

It was already noon. Rylan glanced at Geradon, sitting beside him. Geradon nodded, looking at the sky. It had taken their group much longer than expected to be passed through the perimeter of the Watchaven camp. Then, once inside, it had taken yet more time to get word to King Almgren that they had arrived and needed urgently to speak with him.

Now they sat waiting under a canopy outside the king's pavilion, and Rylan wondered if King Almgren truly intended to grant the audience. Throughout the camp they had heard that a meeting was to take place that afternoon between King Almgren and King Riamel. Rylan feared that the king was too busy preparing for the meeting to wonder why this Inquisitor had ridden here from Watchaven.

Geradon leaned toward him and whispered, "We could try to bully our way in."

Rylan shook his head. "No," he whispered back, "my proof is not strong enough for that. I wish that it were."

A guard stepped through the door of the pavilion.

"Inquisitor, His Majesty will see you, now."

"Pray for me," Rylan whispered to Geradon, before rising to follow the guard into the pavilion.

* * * * *

"*Are you crazy?*" Nelerek whispered. "Do you know what they'll do to us if they catch us?"

"Hang us," Morticai whispered, dryly. "Believe me, it can't be any worse than what I've already been through."

The two corryn walked slowly through the Watchaven camp, saddlebags slung over their shoulders and helmets on.

"Then for love of the Levani, Dyluth, let's wait until dark!"

"We can't. Prince Edris may go to his pavilion when it gets dark. Our best chance is now, while he's in the king's pavilion, listening to Rylan." Morticai stopped walking. "There it is," he whispered, nodding his head toward a large, yellow-and-tan pavilion.

Nelerek took a deep breath. "Aye. With a guard, too."

Morticai shrugged. "Hey, as long as there's not a guard at the back, we'll be fine."

Taking a winding route, they worked their way to the back of the prince's pavilion. Several other pavilions had been pitched nearby, leaving a narrow zigzagging path between them. Nelerek scanned the nearby area before nodding to Morticai.

Morticai dropped to his knees and leaned his saddlebags against the pavilion. Should a passerby casually glance in his direction, it would appear that he was merely rearranging their contents. He flicked his knife out and quickly set to work slicing the lacings that held the pavilion's floor to the sidewall.

Within moments, the corryn thief looked up at Nelerek; after one last glance around them, Nelerek nodded. Morticai dropped flat, opened the slit, and rolled into the pavilion.

Once inside, Morticai lay still as his eyes adjusted to the dim interior and his ears took in the subtle sounds without. The noise of the camp, like the sunlight, filtered softly through the tent's walls. He sat up and removed the troublesome helmet. The tent was warm, making him wish he could remove his chain armor and padding.

The tent was what he had expected. The interior was not divided, and yet it obviously bespoke the station of the tent's owner. A cot, covered with a thin down mattress and topped with furs, made a comfortable raised bed. A small table served as a desk, with a wooden-framed chair, covered with leather, sitting beside it. Carpets were layered on the floor, and trunks abounded.

Starting with the trunk closest to him, Morticai pulled out his tools and set quietly to work. As long as he moved slowly, he could keep the chain armor from jingling, but it would slow his search. He hoped the guard had not been given orders to look into the tent at set intervals—they'd not taken the time to check that. The first trunk contained clothes.

So did the second. The third held the prince's armor and weapons. The fourth held more clothes. Or did it? The clothes seemed too neat, too flat—that was it, they were too flat. Morticai glanced to the pavilion's door; he had heard no movement or sound from the guard since he'd entered the tent. On the opposite side of the tent, Nelerek's shadow slowly shifted its weight from foot to foot.

Morticai carefully unpacked the clothes. Beneath them lay wooden boards—that was why the clothes had been so even. Beneath the boards, wrapped in soft cloths, was the ivory collection of which Heather had spoken. Morticai smiled. Why would a prince take something as breakable as carved ivory on a campaign? Was he afraid he might not be able to return to Watchaven?

He unloaded the ivory, still wrapped, a piece at a time. Outside the tent, Nelerek's shadow now rocked nervously from foot to foot. Morticai took out the last of the ivory. He had hoped to find more boards underneath the ivory, but instead he found the bottom of the chest.

Frowning, he placed his right hand on the bottom and felt down the outside of the chest. There was a forefinger's breadth of space between the bottom of the chest and the casing. Morticai scrutinized the inside but could see no way to reach the hidden area. The bottom was solidly attached to the sides. He repacked the ivory, boards, and clothes, and then checked the outside of the trunk.

A light tap sounded against the tent's wall. Morticai smiled and walked to where Nelerek's shadow stood and lightly tapped back. Morticai was beginning to suspect where he'd learned the impatience that Mother Edana kept fussing about.

Returning to the suspicious trunk, Morticai continued working around it, looking for a latch, sliding panel, anything that would allow access to the area between the casing and the bottom of the trunk. The back foot did not seem secure. In fact, it was not quite as tall as the other three feet, and didn't quite reach the ground.

Morticai smiled again as he fidgeted with the loose foot. It swiveled. Once it had been swiveled out, he could feel a round plate of some sort.

"You ready to eat, Turgal?"

Morticai's head snapped up. The question had been asked at the front of the tent, apparently of the guard. Morticai glanced to the rear of the tent; Nelerek's shadow had vanished.

"Aye!" a voice replied. "It's been too hot t' be standin' withou' any water, too!" the guard grumbled.

"I'm surprised you didn't bring any," the first voice answered. "You know, Edris doesn't mind—as long as it's not brew."

"Aye, I'll bring some tomorrow! Well, enjoy yer duty."

He heard the old guard walk away, as the new one took his position. Morticai sighed with relief Either the prince had given them orders not to look inside the tent or they were just plain sloppy.

The corryn turned back to the chest. With the foot swiveled out, he pressed on the exposed plate. With a soft pop, a panel on the front of the trunk edged outward, revealing a shallow drawer. Morticai smiled. If there was anything in Edris's possession to implicate him with the Droken, it would probably be here.

He took in a ragged breath at the sight of Droka's token, wrought in gold and beset with gems. Morticai swallowed and glanced away from it. He hadn't expected the sight to affect him so deeply. The Arluthian noted that Nelerek's shadow had returned to the back of the tent. He turned his attention back to the drawer and, trying to avoid looking at the token, he concentrated on examining the remaining contents.

He found a map, marked with checkpoints and a dashed line leading north. Morticai swallowed again. Prince Edris knew of the Droken army. Unfortunately, the army itself was not marked on the map. Further search of the drawer found a ring—the symbol on it meant nothing to Morticai—and a pouch full of gems. He took the ring and left the gems. This was it.

* * * * *

"Fire! Fire!"

Rylan stopped in midsentence. Only the cry of attack could have raised more panic in the tent-crowded camp.

"Fire! Prince Edris's tent is afire!"

"*What?*" Prince Edris exclaimed, jumping to his feet.

The king, his sons, and Rylan rushed outside. Not far from the king's pavilion, flames shot skyward.

"My tent!"

Edris ran toward the flames, with the rest following. Two more tents had caught by the time they'd made the short distance; men rushed everywhere, as bucket brigades were formed. Geradon came to a stop beside Rylan. Luckily some soldiers, quick about their duties, were already carrying trunks from the prince's tent.

"Blessed Levani!" Rylan whispered, blinking.

"Indeed," Geradon huffed, "what a disaster."

"No!" Rylan exclaimed. "Look, Geradon! Look at those two soldiers, the two with the helmets!"

The two were carrying a small, but apparently heavy, trunk from the tent. The shorter soldier looked up, scanning the crowd. Rylan saw the deep purple eyes through the helmet's eye slits and swallowed.

"Almighty Aluntas," Geradon whispered, having also seen the eyes.

Suddenly, the shorter soldier stumbled, and with a crash the trunk fell to the ground. As it fell, the front part of the trunk seemed to fall outward; on impact the contents of the drawer spilled out as the corner of the trunk split apart.

Standing just a little in front of Rylan, King Almgren stiffened. Despite the flames and panic, gasps were heard from the crowd who witnessed the "accident." Rylan pushed his way to the front and scooped up the token of Droka. As he spun around to face King Almgren, he could see Morticai wink through the eye slits of his helm.

"A token of Droka!" Rylan proclaimed loudly.

Aghast, Prince Edris stood frozen.

"And this is your tent, Prince Edris?" Rylan asked.

"Y-yes, of course it is!" he stammered. "This is obviously some type of hoax!"

"Indeed?" Rylan asked suspiciously. "You are certain that this"—he held up the token for all to see—"was not why you argued against me before your father?"

King Almgren's eyes narrowed. Geradon handed Rylan the rest of the contents of the drawer; Rylan glanced first at the map.

He held the map out to King Almgren "And this is not a map that lends truth to what I was telling your father?"

"I know nothing about this!" Edris countered.

Geradon handed Rylan something wrapped in a cloth.

Rylan frowned and opened it; inside lay a broken ivory carving of a dancer. "What's this?" he muttered.

"The trunk is full of them," Geradon said.

"What!" King Almgren cried. "You brought your ivory?"

Prince Edris suddenly backed up a step, but said nothing.

"Halt!" Rylan ordered. Having already maneuvered around the prince, the knights of the Faith stepped up to Edris, surrounding him. The flames from the three tents had been extinguished, and except for the pop of still smoldering tent poles, a silence had settled on the crowd. Rylan leveled a steady gaze at King Almgren.

"Your Majesty," Rylan said quietly, "I fear I must request that your son be remanded to the custody of the Faith."

The king swept his gaze slowly over to his son.

"Father," Edris said quietly.

Narrowing his eyes, the king swept his gaze back to Rylan.

"So be it," the king said, solemnly. "Come back to my pavilion, Inquisitor."

Rylan bowed his head, respectfully.

* * * * *

Lord Hildric shifted his weight uneasily. Word of Prince Edris's arrest had spread like wildfire through the Watchaven camp. As far as he had heard, Edris wasn't talking yet. If things went well here, it wouldn't matter. If not, he might have to make certain that Edris would be unable to talk.

The room in which he stood had been Mid-Keep's great hall. Now, even though it had been cleaned for the kings' meeting, the walls were pitted and the floors an unnatural ashtinged gray. Despite the smell of burnt timbers and lack of a roof, the structure's walls had remained structurally sound. The meeting would soon be starting. Hildric glanced at Jendall, beside him. Jendall appeared calm and prepared.

Soon, we shall see if you are prepared to watch a king die, Jendall, Hildric thought, repressing a smile.

Hildric glanced at their counterparts on the opposite side of the room. He recognized Lord Danvek, but he did not know the corryn who stood beside him. From the last message he'd received from Danvek, however, he knew the corryn with Danvek was also one of their kind.

King Riamel entered the hall with one personal guard. The king was tall, even for a corryn, with a powerful build that many thought the result of sorcery. His deep red hair was woven into an elaborate braid, which hung down his back. The guard beside him carried a Dynolvan standard. He thumped it on the ground twice.

On cue, King Almgren and his personal guard entered the hall from the opposite side. Moving at the same, calculated speed, both kings approached the small table that had been moved in for the meeting. The small table looked out of place, sitting in the middle of the huge room where the great table had once stood.

The guards placed their respective standards in stands brought in for the occasion and moved into position behind their kings. Once the monarchs were seated, Danvek and his aide moved to stand a few feet from their king; Hildric and Jendall did likewise. All was proceeding as had been agreed. Riamel would start the negotiations.

Suddenly, Almgren broke with the plan and spoke first. "King Riamel, I know that we agreed that you would begin the negotiations, but something has been brought to my attention that is of the utmost importance to both of us."

King Riamel tilted his head, thoughtfully. "Continue, King Almgren," he replied.

"Thank you. Earlier today I held audience with a representative of the Faith—an Inquisitor, to be exact—who had been sent to me from Watchaven with an urgent message."

Hildric stiffened and noticed that Danvek had, as well. Hildric glanced at Jendall, but he seemed not to have noticed. King Almgren continued.

"At first, I will admit, I thought him mad, but things have come to light since then that prove his words true. With your permission, I would have him address us."

"Permission granted," King Riamel replied.

Hildric blinked and gazed intently at Danvek, but the doors behind them were already opening. With a very slight movement, Danvek shook his head; with someone already entering the room, they would have little chance of successfully completing the double assassination. They would have to wait.

The party that entered moved to stand where both kings could see them. Hildric inhaled deeply, wondering if he should try to flee. Fighting back the panic, he remained, standing motionless.

The party consisted of four. Hildric had seen the Inquisitor before—at the palace, in fact—but Hildric had heard nothing of his business. Beside the Inquisitor stood a sorcerer of the Faith, a rare thing indeed, considering the Faith's view of sorcery. The sorcerer wore the full vestments of the Inquisition, along with a sash denoting his rank in the Order of White Sorcery.

Beside the sorcerer stood a knight of the Faith. The man was human, but tall, with an incredible build. He had entered the hall with a huge sword strapped to his back—Hildric was shocked that neither king protested this, but neither ruler uttered a complaint. Beside the knight stood . . . a guard? Hildric was not certain. The man wore a Watchaven helm and chain armor and, by his height, must be human. His scabbard was empty, so the knight's sword must have been intentional.

"Most gracious kings," the Inquisitor began, bowing respectfully, "several months ago the Inquisition in Abbadyr was informed that a Droken plot was rumored to be forming in Watchaven. I was sent to investigate and, with the help of my associates"—he gestured to his party—"was able to uncover many things."

"The plot was first discovered by a Northmarcher, who has suffered greatly for his work, and who, I might add, has recently had a miracle performed upon him. I have brought him with me and would have him tell you what he discovered ere he was captured by the Droken. Had it not been for his capture, we might have been able to provide this information sooner."

The Inquisitor gestured to the man in the Watchaven uniform. Hildric furrowed his brow. He knew of only one person who had been captured, and when he had last seen that man, he had been half-dead, blind, and obviously quite insane.

The man removed the helmet. Beside him, Lord Jendall gasped. Hildric swallowed, and moved his hands behind his back to hide their trembling. It was, indeed, the man he had seen in the temple. With unnaturally deep violet eyes, the corryn nodded first to the kings and then to Lord Jendall.

Hildric looked at Jendall, wondering what the connection was between the two men. Jendall returned the corryn's nod. Even King Almgren had noticed, and glanced curiously at Jendall.

Approaching his liege, Jendall said softly, "Once upon a time, we were at odds over the same woman, Your Majesty."

The king smiled and nodded knowingly.

Hildric glanced at Danvek, hoping that the terror in his heart did not show in his eyes. Danvek's eyes were troubled and gave him no comfort.

The Inquisitor introduced the corryn, "Your majesties, this corryn of the Northmarch was named Moranekor at birth but is now known as Morticai."

"Your Majesties," the corryn began, a slight tremor in his voice, "before I was captured, I learned that several nobles on Watchaven's Trade Council were involved in this plot, but I did not know what they were trying to do. I suspected," he said, with a quick glance at Danvek, "that Dynolvans were also involved."

Danvek paled visibly.

"It became apparent," the corryn continued, "that the goal of the plot was to drive Watchaven and Dynolva to war, which is a terrible enough plot by itself. However, before my capture I found a map that detailed the movement of an army, a Droken army, which at this time lies somewhere to the north of us, probably facing the Northmarch. I believe their plan was to bring our two kingdoms to war and then to crush both kingdoms with their own army."

Riamel looked at King Almgren and raised his eyebrows.

"You believe this?" he asked, incredulously.

"I do," Almgren replied evenly. "I did not, at first, but that was before I discovered that my fourth son was also involved in this plot."

Riamel signed himself and bowed his head. "I offer my regrets," he said. "But where could such an army come from? There are no kingdoms beyond ours."

King Almgren looked at the Northmarcher.

"I am not certain where the army is coming from," the corryn admitted. "There was a place marked on the map that appeared to be the origin of the army, but it was far outside our boundaries. I have heard tales that a kingdom of Droken existed, but before this I had always discounted it."

The Inquisitor spoke up. "Your Majesties, at this time, where the army comes from does not matter. What is important now is that you make peace so this army does not come upon us unprepared."

The kings looked at each other suspiciously. A corryn guard stepped cautiously into the doorway far behind Danvek and tapped his spear against the stone floor. Furrowing his brow, Riamel turned and looked over his shoulder.

"Your Majesty," the corryn said, bowing deeply, "Northmarch scouts have arrived and say they must speak with the kings. They insist that it is crucial."

The corryn with the unnatural eyes smiled broadly.

King Riamel looked back at King Almgren. Almgren shrugged.

"Send them in," Riamel said.

Two dust-covered Northmarchers, a human and a corryn, entered the hall. The corryn scout stopped midway to the table and only moved forward again when the human returned to him and tugged on his sleeve. Solemn nods of recognition were exchanged between the corryn scout and the violet-eyed Northmarcher.

"Your Majesties," the human scout began, "we have come to report that a Droken army of approximately sixty thousand men lies three days to the north of us."

"By the Levani!" King Almgren exclaimed.

"Sixty thousand!" King Riamel echoed.

The corryn scout laid a letter in the middle of the table. "We have brought a letter from Lord Seabrook," he said.

The kings stood, and both moved toward the letter. With a nod from King Riamel, Almgren opened it. Leaning over the table together, they read it silently. King Riamel looked up at the Inquisitor.

"Forgive my doubt, Inquisitor," he said. "It seems that you were quite correct, and I can assume that if the army exists, then so does the plot of which you speak."

"We have much to do," King Almgren replied. "Lord Jendall, stay here with me. Lord Hildric, go tell Prince Bertel that we will be breaking camp."

"Aye," King Riamel agreed. "Lord Danvek, give the word to our own camp that we shall be moving."

"Y-your Majesty?" the violet-eyed corryn interrupted.

"Yes?"

Danvek was moving toward the door. The corryn scout moved quickly to stand in front of him. Danvek stopped.

"I am sorry to say," the violet eyed corryn continued, "that I followed Lord Danvek in Watchaven one night when he met with one of the Watchaven nobles whom I-I later learned was the high priest of Droka. You might wish to reconsider whether you wish him to give such an order to your troops."

The king straightened. "Indeed."

The knight moved beside Danvek.

"Well, Hildric," Almgren snapped, "get moving!"

"Yes, Sire," the noble answered and quickly headed toward the door. With a sigh of relief, he exited without being stopped. Apparently this corryn had not known of his involvement. He would give Almgren's order—and then he must go north.

CHAPTER TWENTY-TWO

"Sir, Lord Hildric is here to see you," the guard announced.

Luthekar's head snapped up. He laid down the list of remaining supplies and came around the small table he was using as a desk.

"Lord *Hildric?*" he asked the guard.

"Yes, sir."

"Bring him in," Luthekar said. Clasping his hands behind his back, the Droken prince waited as an annoying tightness built inside him.

It was indeed the blond-haired, blue-eyed spy they had planted in Watchaven's court several years ago. Luthekar's eyes narrowed, and he suspected they'd changed to the red color that seemed to bother people so. He did not speak; it was not necessary.

"Y-your lordship," the mortal stammered, dropping to his knees. "I have ridden two days to reach you, Sire. Our plans have been exposed. Prince Edris and Lord Danvek have been taken by the Faith. Almgren and Riamel have joined forces and march this way to meet you."

"*How?*" Luthekar demanded.

"Th-the Inquisition, Sire. And a Northmarcher—the one who had been captured—"

"*What?*"

"Th-the Arluthian," Hildric said weakly.

Luthekar reached him in two strides and picked him off the ground with one hand. The Droken prince held the human a few inches away; Hildric shut his eyes.

"Look at me!" Luthekar demanded.

Hildric's eyes snapped open.

"What was the name of this Northmarcher?"

Hildric's eyes darted frantically from side to side. "It w-was, uh, Morticai—that was it—Morticai . . . Sire."

"Impossible," Luthekar said curtly, dropping him. "Even if he still lived, he would be nothing more than a crippled imbecile."

"The Inquisitor said that a miracle had been performed. Sire, I was at the ceremony in our temple, and I saw his eyes burned out; but when he stood before us at Mid-Keep, he had his eyes. They are a different color now, a strange color, but he has them. Nor did he seem to lack his sanity. Except for the unholy color of his eyes, he did not look or act as though he had ever been in our hands."

Closing his eyes, Luthekar bowed his head. He forced back the anger that gripped him. It would do him no good to kill this mortal. It had not been his fault. He had been faithful and correct to ride to him with this news. Something had gone wrong at the temple. What had happened to Ellenwood? Taking a deep breath, he reopened his eyes. The human lay prostrate before him.

"Get up," Luthekar said calmly.

Trembling, the man slowly rose.

"Tell me everything."

* * * * *

Luthekar sat, much later, amid the wreckage of his tent. He sighed. He hadn't actually destroyed anything, but he had made quite a mess. He rose and slowly walked to the one area he had been careful not to touch—his altar.

He sat before it, cross-legged, and after a moment's pause looked up at the pure gold likeness of the form Droka had worn when the god had met Luthekar's mother.

"Why?" he whispered. "Why have you let me come all this way and do all these things, if it was to be met with defeat?"

A smoky haze began to fill the spacious tent. Luthekar bowed his head in respect—he had known that his father would answer. There were some questions a child asked that demanded answers.

When Luthekar raised his head, he was no longer in the tent. The bleak landscape that surrounded him was deep red. It was cold; Luthekar did not complain. Before him, sitting like himself, was his father, the Almighty Droka. He wore the corryn form that Luthekar had always associated with him.

"It was necessary," Droka replied simply.

"Why?" Luthekar asked.

"Before now," his father replied, "the Levani were uninvolved. They protected their pitiful followers but would not face me directly—they have never faced me directly."

"But—" Luthekar began. "All the books say that you fought the Levani."

Droka shook his head. "No, I have not fought them. It was Aluntas, their master, whom I faced and who banished me to this place." He gestured to the barren landscape around them.

"I have waited all this time," he continued, "for the Levani to face me. Only then, once they are defeated, can I leave here for my rightful place with you."

Luthekar was puzzled. "But how—"

"The Levani Glawres has challenged me," Droka replied once again to the unasked question. "Had it not been for Glawres's intervention, you would not now be facing defeat. Because he has now intervened, I may also intervene."

"Then—" Luthekar began.

"No," Droka replied, shaking his head. "I cannot intervene directly in this struggle. As Glawres has done, I must work through my faithful followers. It will take time."

Luthekar sighed. "Then I must turn back." He blinked, realizing his father had let him finish a sentence.

"Yes, you must. You are wise to realize that truth, and I know it is painful, but such must you do."

"Mortern," Luthekar moaned. His human counterpart would taunt him endlessly for this defeat.

"Mortern shall not mock you," Droka replied. "I will visit him this night as well. You have nothing to be ashamed of, Luthekar. You have followed every instruction. You will not be blamed for the weaknesses of those beneath you."

There was one last question Luthekar wished to ask. . . .

Droka nodded in response to the thought. "Yes, this is in the Books of Prophecy. But you could not have known when Glawres would choose his agent or who it would be."

"Couldn't you—"

"I could not have warned you," Droka replied. "It was hidden, even from me. Long have I looked for a warrior follower of Glawres who would fulfill the prophecies; but they did not foretell that he would choose a child of the gutters, and I had looked for him in the palaces of the world."

Luthekar bowed his head. Never had he heard Droka come so close to admitting that he had made a mistake. When he looked up again, the form of his father, as well as the landscape, was already beginning to fade. The image shimmered, faded, and was replaced once again by the outlines of his own cluttered tent.

* * * * *

It was nearly dawn. Prince Luthekar sat with his feet atop a small table, tapping the dry quill tip against the edge of the board that held his papers. Soon General Wilfram would arrive at his tent, and they would finalize the plans they had discussed once his father had left him.

Damn the Northmarch! The thought had haunted him many times through the long night.

There was no way around it; his father, as always, was correct. They had to retreat; and yet, Luthekar would need to cut his army's numbers before they did so. They did not have enough supplies to make it back to the first cache site. Mortern had scoffed at him for taking the time to stock supplies behind them. "Preparing for defeat?" Mortern had asked.

But their father had agreed with the plan. "I would not wish you to face defeat, but neither would I be so confident against the treacherous Levani," Droka had said.

His guard entered the tent. "General Wilfram, sir."

Luthekar nodded.

"We are ready?" Luthekar asked, as the general sat down opposite him.

"Yes, lord," he replied. "I have chosen the thousand infantrymen. They travel to the foothills even as we speak."

"Good. You sent them with extra quarrels?"

"Yes, lord."

Luthekar nodded. "That should give us a thousand fewer mouths to feed and enable us to reach that cache site."

"I think it is quite fitting," Wilfram observed. "The Northmarch destroyed our supplies, forcing us to lighten our force; it is only just that they suffer for that mistake."

"Agreed," Luthekar said coolly.

"Do you truly think the Northmarch will turn toward the mountains when they see us approaching?"

"Yes," Luthekar replied. "They have few wagons—they must not have known about our force when they came this way. They will go to the mountains, because only there can they find enough game to augment their supplies."

"It is a shame we must lose a thousand men to them," Wilfram lamented.

Luthekar shrugged. "If our plan works, it will more than offset the damage the Northmarch has served us."

* * * * *

Lord Seabrook scanned the horizon for the first sign of the approaching army. His primary fear was ambush. Without it, Luthekar could not hope to catch the Northmarch's three thousand cavalry. Commander Jarviel reined in beside him on his huge, dappled steed.

"My lord, we are ready," he announced.

"And Commander McFerrin?"

"Also ready."

"Good. None too soon, it would appear," Seabrook pointed to the brownish haze that was forming on the horizon—dust from the huge Droken army.

"Surely they do not think they can catch us so easily," Jarviel observed.

"I would agree with you, but they are forcing our hand. We cannot retreat farther north—we are far too low on supplies. For the same reason, we cannot go east—the plain is too arid. We have no choice but to go west, toward the mountains, where game abounds, but I fear that this is what their commander wishes us to do."

"But we can easily reach the mountains before him," Jarviel replied.

"So it would seem," Seabrook agreed. "Perhaps he simply wishes to ensure that we do not attack them again. Give the order—we move west."

* * * * *

Morticai's breath burned in his lungs as he ran through the streets. He turned down a side alley—old Williams never locked his back gate.

Sure enough, it was open. He slammed the gate behind him, dropping the latch into place. Now, up and over the fence to drop into the alley on the other side. As he dropped to the ground, he heard the gate smash in on the other side of the fence. He had to get away. . . .

He turned left, then right, onto Shipwright's Road. A wagon lumbered past, slowing even more to turn onto a side street. Morticai hopped onto the back of it as it made the turn. That should do it.

No—a glance behind showed someone mounted on a black charger, galloping recklessly down the crowded side street. Morticai looked about desperately for an avenue of escape.

He leapt toward the mouth of an alley as the wagon passed by. His breath was knocked from him, as he slammed into the side wall of the alley. He ignored the pain in his side and scrambled to his feet to sprint down the alley.

He made a turn and . . . suddenly, the old cobbled streets disappeared. He was in an open field; he could see trees in the distance. Fear clutching at his chest, he looked behind him. A group of horsemen, wearing black Droken robes, had gathered on the far side of the field. In the fore of the group was the black charger. The armored knight on its back carried a lance, lowered toward him. He could see that its tip was glowing red hot.

He ran. He could hear the sounds of the hooves behind him. There were the trees, not far distant; he should be able to make it. Then, abruptly, he was in the trees. He dived beneath a bush; he seemed to have escaped. After a few moments his breathing quieted, and the fire in his chest cooled. He had done it! He had gotten away!

He lay back with a sigh of relief. Thank Glawres! Suddenly, a human's face appeared above him. No! Not a human—a corryn. The face began to change until it became Luthekar. Then it altered again, until it was the hideous design that had been on Luthekar's mask. He tried to move but found that he could not. The bush had wrapped around his wrists and held him tight. Luthekar's mask smiled, as a hot brand came toward him.

He woke up screaming. . . .

* * * * *

Morticai fidgeted with the lacing on the pack, finally pulling it out.

"That's the third time you've pulled it out, Dyluth," Nel-erek said. "What's wrong with it?"

They sat with their backs against a tree, just outside their tent. The Watchaven camp, now two days north of Mid-Keep, lay in a sprawl about them. They'd not had tents when they came from Watchaven, but King Almgren had insisted their party be provided with tents and any additional gear they might need.

"I don't know why they use such poor quality leather in these things," Morticai muttered, once again starting to lace the thong through the pack. "I can't get it to lie flat, and if it doesn't lie flat, it won't make a tight seam, and if it rains my gear will get wet."

"Oh," Nelerek replied. The Arluthian went into their tent and returned a moment later with a long thong. He dropped it into Morticai's lap.

"Where'd this come from?" Morticai said, looking up at him.

"Supplies for my hawk. I brought it in case I needed an extra jess, but I don't think I will."

"Thanks."

"Shouldn't Evadrel be back by now?" Nelerek asked, glancing northward.

Morticai followed his gaze. "Yeah," he said quietly.

"Do you think something's happened?"

"I don't think so; at least, I hope not. I'm not certain he should have gone out scouting so soon after riding here with news of the army, but Evadrel's always been careful." He shrugged.

"So, if you're not worryin' about Evadrel, what's the matter?"

Morticai stared at the half-laced pack. "Just tired. Tired, and worried about the Northmarch," he said. "That's an awful big army up there."

"I noticed you didn't sleep much last night," Nelerek remarked.

"Yeah," Morticai admitted softly. "Sorry I woke you up."

"Me?" Nelerek shook his head. "I was already awake when you decided to wake the rest of the camp. You never went back to sleep, did you?"

"No."

"There's Evadrel." Nelerek waved.

Morticai straightened. "News?" he asked the approaching scout.

Evadrel smiled. "Well, we're within a day's march of them."

"The Northmarch?" Morticai asked.

"No—the Droken," the scout replied, shaking his head and sitting down.

Morticai sighed.

"I'm certain we'll meet with them soon, Morticai," Evadrel said. "They would have had to flee when the Droken turned around. It will take time for them to circle back to us."

"What of the Drolton?" Nelerek asked. "Are we going to catch them?"

Evadrel shook his head again. "I doubt it. They are large, but we move no faster than they do. We will not be able to catch them unless they turn and face us of their own will, which does not appear to be their plan."

"That's just fine, if you ask me," Nelerek said. "I'm no soldier, and I'd prefer not to become one."

"Evadrel," Morticai said, "should we head out on our own?"

Evadrel looked at him, blankly. "You mean, to meet with the Northmarch?"

"Yeah."

"Dyluth," Nelerek said, "we can't do that!"

"Why not?" Morticai asked.

"Why not?" Nelerek echoed. "Because it's dangerous out there!" He gestured northward.

Evadrel smiled. "I'm afraid I agree with him, Morticai. The Droken have too many scouts of their own. We may not catch the main Droken army, but we have crossed swords with their patrols. I think it would be very difficult to get past them. Do not worry, friend," he said, "we shall join with the Northmarch soon enough."

* * * * *

Lord Jendall marched into the command tent.

"We simply do not have sufficient numbers to face them," King Riamel was saying.

"I know, I know," King Almgren replied. "I hate just letting them go! I want to know where in the name of the Dark One they came from!"

"Indeed, it appears that only the Dark One holds that information," Jendall replied.

Almgren snorted. "I suppose that means that we still have not had any luck capturing one of their scouts?"

"I am afraid you are correct, Sire," Jendall answered. "We have come close on several occasions, but each time the scout killed himself ere he could be captured."

Riamel shook his head. "What type of men are we up against?" he asked.

"Indeed," Almgren agreed. "Well, Jendall, your advice has always been good. What do you think of our situation?"

Jendall paused a moment before answering. "I think we should thank the Levani that they run from us. Although they nearly match us in infantry, they outmatch us in cavalry by a considerable amount. Even if the Northmarch were close enough to join forces with us, it would be an ill battle to fight.

"Additionally," he continued, "they have the advantage that they move through territory they have already passed through and are familiar with. We must take care that they do not use this knowledge to lay an ambush for us—and, for that reason, we are even now having to slow our march, while they increase theirs."

King Riamel sighed. "It appears that much of the knowledge we wish to learn will have to wait for another day, another battle."

Almgren nodded. "Aye. Perhaps the Northmarch will have more that they can tell us."

* * * * *

The foothills were a welcome sight for the tired Northmarchers; they had pushed to reach the hills before nightfall. The sooner they reached the protection of the mountains, the better. Now they wound their way slowly into the hills, paralleling a small stream.

The stream had apparently been much larger in times past, as evidenced by the ground upon which they rode. The thirty-foot-wide, flat section of stone was smooth, with a forty-foot bluff rising to their right—the original boundary of the stream. The stream had shrunk in size and shifted south, leaving the smooth path that they found so convenient. Brush still abounded at the edge of the stream, while loose rocks were all that hindered their travel.

Lord Seabrook scanned the terrain in front of them. He had thought the scouts would have rejoined them by now. He anxiously awaited news of what lay ahead and their recommendation for a campsite. Another hour or two of sunlight was all they would have.

The Northmarch high commander raised his hand and, as the command was relayed, behind him nearly three thousand horses were reined to a halt. Commanders McFerrin and Jarviel, riding to his right and left, looked at him expectantly.

"Kirwin, what do you make of that ravine ahead of us?" he asked.

"Steep, but I believe we can make it without dismounting."

"Jarviel?"

"I agree, lord. We should make the top of the rise well before nightfall."

"The scouts should have returned."

Jarviel and Kirwin exchanged glances. "Aye," Kirwin agreed. "The terrain is not so rough as to hinder them this long."

Jarviel nodded and scanned the surrounding area.

"Follow me," the Dynolvan commander said suddenly in a soft but urgent tone, and reined his horse to the right.

Lord Seabrook and Kirwin McFerrin rode behind him. He led them to the edge of the bluff and turned toward their rearward ranks. When they had traveled a short distance down the long column, he spoke again.

"I fear there are Droken in the brush on the far bank," he whispered.

Seabrook inhaled deeply. "You spotted someone?"

Jarviel nodded slowly.

"We must back the men out," Seabrook said. "I shall stay here. Feign an inspection and pass the word. When you have finished, at the sound of my horn, we shall retreat. We shall have to leave the wagons, so have the drivers jump toward the bluff. That should save them from the initial attack."

"Surely you are not going to stay in the open, lord," Kirwin protested.

"I shall remain here until you have reached the halfway point. Then I shall move between yon supply wagon and the bluff." Jarviel motioned slightly toward the mentioned wagon.

Nodding, the two commanders began moving slowly down opposite sides of the ranks. Captains and sergeants straightened, and as the word was passed, slack reins were tightened in preparation for the retreat. Lord Seabrook hoped that none of the Droken were cavalry—any good cavalier would spot the slight hand movements and know what they were about.

The commanders reached the halfway point. Lord Seabrook casually moved toward the wagon, as though he were also checking the ranks. He could see Kirwin, ahead of him, still moving down the long line of horses. The men were riding eight across on this wide stretch of rock.

That should save the men closest to the bluff, Seabrook thought bitterly. He had been a fool to bring them this far without hearing from the scouts—now his men would pay for his mistake. He had reached the supply wagon. Once behind it, he unstrapped his horn, holding it loosely near his hip.

Kirwin had almost reached the bottom of the hill. Though he could not see Jarviel, he knew the relative position of the Dynolvan commander. The commanders could not sound the retreat to the Northmarchers who had not yet started up the hill—they would figure it out on their own.

He raised the horn and blew. Seabrook watched as the

horses wheeled in unison. The Droken waited no longer. Seabrook spurred his horse forward, as horror clutched him from within—it was not bows that the Droken leveled at his troops, but crossbows. The cry of horses and screams of men mixed with the echoing hooves that raced down the slope. He held out a hand and helped a drover onto the back of his horse. By the time they'd made it halfway, tears streamed down his face—their losses would be tremendous.

* * * * *

At the base of the hill, a cry of anger rose as though from one voice. Kirwin watched in dismay as the order for retreat was again sounded—several captains had dismounted and were leading their men up the narrow, brushy southern side of the stream. Quarrels rained from Northmarch crossbows into the brush farther up the hill. As Droken screams mingled with those of the Northmarch, more Northmarchers rushed to push an attack against the better-positioned enemy.

With a growl of anger, Kirwin dismounted. For better or ill, the men had chosen to fight. He viciously hacked his way up the hill. The fighting was fierce, and the ambushers were forced to pull their swords and abandon their slow-loading crossbows.

Ahead he could see more of his men—they'd crossed the rocky stream in an effort to reach their attackers. The lack of discipline bothered him; but he also knew that his men had not been trained to fight battles against armies. When ambushed, usually by bandits, they had been taught to relentlessly chase down the ambushers—and thus did they follow their training and emotions.

He grimly noted that few of the men were corryn; it had been the Dynolvans who had been closest to the ambushers and had felt the brunt of the attack. He allowed himself a quick glance at the opposite side of the ravine. Dead and dying Northmarchers and horses lay everywhere. Clenching his teeth, he redoubled his efforts.

* * * * *

"You had best rein in, Morticai," Evadrel said, as his horse trotted up beside him.

Morticai sighed and reined his horse back to a walk. He looked over his shoulder and blinked in surprise at the distance he'd pulled in front of the joined armies.

"They'll accuse you of stealing the kings' bright moment," the corryn scout teased.

"Huh?"

"Look," Evadrel said, pointing to where the two kings rode side by side. The kings had removed their helmets and now wore their crowns.

"They want to be properly attired when we join the North-march," Evadrel continued.

Morticai smiled. "I'm sorry, Evadrel. It's just that Cory-den . . . Coryden doesn't know . . ." He trailed off.

Evadrel nodded, knowingly. "I understand. Coryden was very upset; we all were."

Although they had dropped back behind the kings, the two Northmarchers were still in the fore of the huge force behind them.

"What are you doing out here?" Nelerek asked, his horse trotting up beside them.

"Morticai was trying to be the first to meet the Northmarch scouts," Evadrel said.

Nelerek handed Morticai his newly refilled waterskin.

"Can't leave you for a minute!" Nelerek teased.

"Hey!" Morticai complained. Evadrel and Nelerek laughed.

"Look!" Morticai pointed ahead of them. In the distance, a small group of horsemen were approaching.

"Our scouts!" Evadrel exclaimed. "Stay here, Morticai. I will bring you all the news you wish as soon as the scouts have fin-ished greeting the kings." Urging his horse forward, he rode toward the crowd of nobility.

Morticai sighed. "Why does there have to be all this cere-mony?" he muttered.

Everything came to a halt as the scouts met with the kings. Soon after, Evadrel emerged from the crowd with three of the Northmarch scouts in tow. As they approached, Morticai noted their grim countenances.

"Something's happened," he informed Nelerek and urged his horse forward. He could hear the hoofbeats of Nelerek's horse behind him.

"What's wrong?" Morticai asked as he reached the group of Northmarchers.

The three scouts, strangers to Morticai, stared at his eyes in amazement. Ignoring them, Morticai turned to Evadrel. "What has happened?" he repeated.

"The Northmarch was ambushed by the Droken," Evadrel explained. "They lost Commander Jarviel and almost a third—"

Morticai inhaled sharply. "Coryden?"

"They don't know."

One of the human scouts found his tongue. "I know of him," the scout told him, "and I think I saw him afterward, but I am not certain. I'm sorry." He looked down, the pain in his eyes obvious, "We're still not positive who did and did not die. I'm certain that Lord Seabrook knows; he has the list of names. There were some who rode in several hours afterward—men who had been separated from us. We did not spend much time in camp; we spent most of the night hunting down Droken filth."

"When did this happen?" Nelerek asked.

"Last night, just before nightfall."

"How far is the camp?" Morticai asked.

"Just a few miles—"

"Let's go," Morticai said.

"Are-aren't you the one the Droken captured?" one of the scouts ventured to ask Morticai.

Morticai smiled grimly. "Yes, I am he."

"But—"

"It's a long story, okay?" Morticai replied. "Look, what about Berret Heimrik? Do any of you know him?"

"Aye," another spoke up. "I know 'im, an' I saw 'im last

night—Berret's alive for certain."

"Thank Glawres," Morticai said.

"Are you going back?" Nelerek asked the scouts.

"Aye, we are."

"Then we'll come with you," Morticai stated.

"I'll inform the Inquisitor," Evadrel said, starting back toward the group of nobility, where the Inquisitor was riding.

* * * * *

The Northmarch camp was abuzz at the news that the Dynolvan and Watchaven armies had joined. Throughout the camp, anxious faces showed relief as the news spread. The haggard faces still bespoke the sorrow that the previous night's defeat had laid on them.

Evadrel threaded his way through the camp, leading Nelerek and the anxious Morticai to the spot assigned to Coryden's patrol. They entered the area assigned to Kirwin's men, and at every tent heads turned as Morticai passed.

"I can see this is going to be a problem," Morticai said under his breath to Nelerek.

"They've all heard you were tortured, Dyluth," Nelerek replied. "You'd stare too, if you'll think about it."

"Maybe you're right," Morticai admitted, "but it's giving me chills."

They came to the tent that bore Coryden's standard—only to find it empty. Fighting back the lump in his throat, Morticai sank down onto a stool that stood in the middle of the otherwise empty tent.

"I'll find someone," Evadrel said, leaving him with Nelerek.

Morticai closed his eyes to avoid Nelerek's concerned stare; a moment later he heard the tent's door flap fall against the pole. He reopened his eyes; Nelerek had stepped outside, and stood looking this way and that. Morticai stood, and stepped outside. Nelerek glanced at him briefly, and then looked away again.

He's trying to leave me alone, Morticai thought distantly.

"I'm going to check this way," Morticai said absently. "Why

don't we go a little ways and meet back here."

"If you wish," Nelerek said quietly.

Morticai moved away from him, wandering slowly down the path. He was about to turn back when he spotted someone familiar.

"Coryden!"

Coryden spun as though an arrow had pierced his back. A bandage wound across his forehead, and his right forearm bore a splint. His mouth opened wordlessly.

Morticai smiled. "I know they're different," he said, "but they work."

Coryden blinked and ran up to him. He reached out to grab Morticai by the shoulders, but immediately winced and lowered his right arm to the level of Morticai's elbow.

"How?"

"Well, they say it's a miracle," Morticai began.

"I'll say," Coryden whispered, and then hugged him.

"I feared you'd died," Morticai finally said.

Coryden's eyes clouded with tears. "We lost six," he said, "with even more wounded—but I think they'll make it."

"I'm sorry, Coryden. I know it's not right, but I almost feel like I've caused all of this."

"No," the half-corryn replied softly. "If you hadn't discovered what you did, and if we hadn't been able to warn them, the slaughter would have been much worse."

"There they are!"

It was Evadrel, with Nelerek and the rest of the patrol, approaching from the direction of the tent. Their excitement was quickly replaced with an awkward silence, despite having been forewarned about Morticai's new eyes. It was Berret who finally spoke.

"I've always known you were stubborn, Morticai," he said, shaking his head, "but this beats them all."

A crooked smile crept slowly onto Morticai's face. It slowly spread to the others, and then they all broke into the relieved laughter of those who had been through too much. It felt good to be back.

CHAPTER TWENTY-THREE

"Well, it looks like we made it here in time," Morticai said. The coach stopped, its driver hurrying to help Richard unload the Inquisitor's trunks from the top side of the coach. The Watchaven dock was crowded with passengers waiting to board the ship bound for Menelcar. Coryden and Dualas had come with Morticai to bid farewell to Rylan, Geradon, and Richard before they set sail.

Rylan clapped a hand on Morticai's shoulder. "Your work truly defeated the Droken, Morticai," he said, somberly. "I am sorry that the kings did not give you more credit for it—you deserved more acclaim."

Morticai blushed and glanced away. "I'm glad they didn't," he replied. "All I wanted was to be able to go back to the Northmarch, and they did give me that."

"Have you had any problems from Commander McFerrin?" Geradon asked.

"No," Morticai said with a lopsided smile.

"I think he's a little unsure of Morticai, now that a miracle has been worked on him," Coryden said, smiling.

"As well he should," Rylan said. "And has your arm fully healed, Captain?"

"Yes, it seems to have," Coryden replied, stretching out his right arm. "I know I am still favoring it a bit, but that is nothing more than habit, now."

"What have they decided about the Droken army?" Geradon asked. "I heard the kings talking about charging the Northmarch with searching out their homeland."

Dualas replied, "I do not know if they will go that far. I had heard, however, that the Faith was considering giving the Northmarch the authority to investigate Droken activities that might affect the security of the kingdoms."

Rylan smiled. "Ah, yes, I believe that is under discussion," he said with a twinkle in his eye. "I wish that I could remain to see what becomes of their new plans."

"Maybe they'll let you come back," Morticai suggested.

"Perhaps," Rylan agreed. "And have you grown accustomed to your new eyes, Morticai?"

"Yeah," he said. "At least, *I* have." He looked down, "I still get stared at a lot."

"Much of that will pass, Morticai," Rylan soothed. Then, in a more concerned tone, "You remember everything I told you?"

Morticai looked at him blankly.

"About the Droken, and how they do not forget?"

Morticai sighed, heavily. "I do."

Rylan nodded. "I spoke to you about that before you were captured. It is even more imperative now. You must remember everything that I told you. King Almgren may have already forgotten the role you played in saving his kingdom, but the Droken will not. With your new eye color, you will be an easy target if you are not very careful."

Morticai looked down. "I know," he muttered.

Rylan looked at Coryden and Dualas. "I say this before your friends, because it is they who can most help you in future days, Morticai. Be mindful," he told them, "that the Droken may well send another assassin after Morticai."

Coryden glanced at Dualas; the latter, apparently not surprised by Rylan's warning, was nodding.

"If ever Morticai needs help," Rylan continued, "the Faith is there for him. Should he ever need sanctuary, the Faith is there. He may need to hide occasionally, until danger has passed. And if I have learned anything while I have been here," he said as a smirk crept onto his face, "it is that it will probably take both of you to carry him bodily to such protection."

Morticai looked up, blinking. "Hey! I'm not lookin' for trouble, y'know," he defended himself.

"Oh, yes, you are," Coryden countered.

Rylan smiled. "I will miss you all. Indeed, I wish I could take Sir Dualas with us," he said.

"Thank you, Inquisitor," Dualas replied, "but my place is with the Northmarch."

"I understand. I thank you for the good service you gave me when I needed it," the Inquisitor said.

The rope at the bottom of the gangplank was lowered, signaling that they would soon be setting sail. Around them, the crowd was filing up the plank.

"You'd best board, before they leave without you," Coryden said.

"Indeed," Geradon replied, hauling up to his shoulder the bag that held his most precious books. Richard carried another such bag, slung easily over his shoulder.

"May all of the blessings of the Levani continue to fall upon you," Rylan said in farewell.

"And may Glawres guide your ship," Morticai replied.

Coryden raised his eyebrows in surprise. He'd never heard Morticai utter a formal blessing.

* * * * *

The crisp air of Fading swept through the sumptuous palace. Prince Luthekar stood at the open window, his hands clasped loosely behind his back as he watched the leaves swirl past in the courtyard below. His losses had been minimal and yet devastating. Like a beaten dog, he had been forced to return to Cuthaun.

His hands clenched. He had lost the years it had taken to lay in the supplies they had used traveling to and from the northern kingdom. He had lost three hundred men and almost two thousand good horses when the Northmarch had attacked his force. And that had forced him to send the thousand men to hinder the Northmarch and lessen his need for supplies.

But worse than any number of men lost, he had lost his chance for surprise. Now reports came from within the northern kingdoms that the Northmarch had been empowered to search out from whence his army had come. He smiled coldly. It would be a long time before the Northmarch could manage the grueling overland trek to his lands.

And still, the scum that had caused this terrible defeat lived. Luthekar strode to his desk and picked up his quill. He had given much thought to how the proclamation should read.

Be it known to all that on this day, the second day of Kenaf, of the year of Droka two thousand one hundred and seventy-three, I, Prince Luthekar, do hereby proclaim the following:

A full-blooded corryn, known last to be in the human kingdom of Watchaven, called Morticai of the Northmarch, also called Dyluth, is marked for utter destruction for the following crimes:

- *Purposely and wantonly searching us out to do us harm;*
- *Giving his soul to Glawres and allowing Glawres to possess him;*
- *Joining with the Inquisition, to fight against us;*
- *Joining the Arluthians, who are sworn to our utter destruction;*
- *Attacking one of Droka's own sons, with intent to kill;*
- *Causing a faithful Dyagon to be slain;*
- *Causing the murder of our high priest in Watchaven;*
- *Causing a faithful servant, Prince Edris of Watchaven, to be captured and hanged;*
- *Causing a faithful servant, Lord Danvek of Dynolva, to be captured and hanged;*

- *Causing the destruction of our temple in Watchaven;*
- *Giving word to the enemy, thereby alerting the Northmarch to our plans; and*
- *Giving word to the sovereigns of the northern kingdoms, thereby alerting them to our plans.*

Further, be it known that this corryn is the height of a human, with black hair streaked with silver, and with deep violet eyes of an unnatural color, given to him by the foul Glawres.

Should any deliver to me Morticai, alive or dead, a reward of 25,000 korun shall be given. So it has been sworn before Droka.

> *Sworn this day, by my hand:*
> *Luthekar, Prince of Droka*